THE PREQUEL TO
THE #1 PODCAST

LIMETOWN

||||| A Novel

CREATED BY ZACK AKERS
AND SKIP BRONKIE
WITH COTE SMITH

SIMON & SCHUSTER
New York London Toronto Sydney New Delhi

Simon & Schuster
1230 Avenue of the Americas
New York, NY 10020

First Simon & Schuster hardcover edition November 2018

SIMON & SCHUSTER and colophon are registered trademarks
of Simon & Schuster, Inc.

For information about special discounts for bulk purchases,
please contact Simon & Schuster Special Sales at 1-866-506-1949
or business@simonandschuster.com.

The Simon & Schuster Speakers Bureau can bring authors to your
live event. For more information or to book an event contact the
Simon & Schuster Speakers Bureau at 1-866-248-3049 or visit our
website at www.simonspeakers.com.

Interior design by Lewelin Polanco

Manufactured in the United States of America

10 9 8 7 6 5 4 3 2 1

Library of Congress Cataloging-in-Publication Data has been applied for.

ISBN 978-1-5011-5564-2
ISBN 978-1-5011-5566-6 (ebook)

For Connie Akers, who won't get to read this, but without whom none of this would exist

LIMETOWN

CHAPTER ONE
IIII Lia

Lia's mother disappeared one month before the Panic at Limetown. Unlike those three hundred plus, hers was a gradual vanishing. She had been pulling away for months, maybe longer. Retreating from Lia and her father, to a hidden space no one else was allowed.

In the beginning, the space was mental. Lia's dad would ask her mother a question at dinner and receive a delayed response. She would forget minor anniversaries, which most people wouldn't celebrate in the first place, but that were treated like national holidays in the Haddock household. Gone was the mom who gave the house a housewarming gift ten years to the date she and Lia's father closed. The mom who well into Lia's teens snuck into her bedroom and left two quarters under her pillow in honor of the day Lia lost her first tooth. In her place was a woman who asked no one about their day, who made everyone coffee but drank her mug in the study, alone.

Lia was a senior in high school and had tragedies of her own. A boy she told herself she should like died stupidly over winter break. His name was Brad. They had been neighbors early in Lia's childhood, friends even, or so she was told, in a time and a house Lia didn't remember. This, before her mother received tenure and her father started his own landscaping company, affording the family a larger home in a more sterile part of town.

At school, Lia had watched all the other girls pair off with all the boys, coupling together, splitting apart, before finding another partner and starting the process all over again. It was like observing some sort of live biological experiment, one that Lia had never felt the need to participate in. Though, she supposed Brad was as good a candidate as any for a crush. He was everything she was not: popular, athletic, carefree, quick to laugh. But when she imagined what it would be like to walk down the hall with him, holding his hand or hanging onto his arm, as she had seen other girls do with their boys, she felt nothing.

Brad wasn't exactly a bad boy, though he had owned a used motorcycle. One night in late December, while on break before what would have been the final semester he and Lia shared together, Brad did what teenagers do. He threw a party, drank, made a bad decision, and crashed his bike off the state road. It was after midnight. No one found him until the following afternoon.

Lia sometimes thought about Brad lying on the side of the road. He always wore his helmet, so he wouldn't have died right away. He would have had time to wonder. Why him. Why now. Maybe near the end Brad would call out to someone. His father. His mother. Maybe Brad would shout God's name. Or maybe he would whisper, *Lia*.

Old mom would have consoled her daughter. She would have asked what was wrong and offered advice Lia wouldn't truly appreciate for years. But when Lia broke the news to new mom, she simply lifted her head from her coffee mug and said, "That's awful."

Old mom was gone.

A week later, the first day of spring semester, new mom was gone too.

—

Which was worse? Losing someone in an instant, or watching them disappear over time?

Lia didn't know anything was wrong right away. Her dad did a good job covering for her mother. Partners until the end. It helped that Lia was a self-admitted moody teenager. The fall semester of junior year, she had to take a strengths assessment, this boring exam that asked a hundred questions designed to determine what kind of person you really were, so you could plan your looming career accordingly. At the end, it gave your top five strengths, and the bottom three. Your weaknesses. Lia's number-one strength was intellection, which meant she was an introspective person who liked to be mentally challenged, and who liked to be alone.

At the bottom was sympathy. This came as a shock. She'd always thought of herself as a nice person, someone who could sense how others were feeling, when they were happy or sad. And maybe that was true. But her number-two strength was empathy, which meant, yes, she was very perceptive about the emotions of others, but that didn't mean she cared. She simply understood and, in her case, moved on.

She thought about that test often, wondering if her lack of empathy was the reason she never paired off with anyone. Or if it explained why she did not have any friends at school. She had acquaintances in Newspaper, and smiled politely to the girls she sat with at lunch, but beyond that her classmates seemed to recognize she wanted little to do with them. Everyone gave her space, a fair distance from which she could safely watch the world around her, which for reasons she could never explain, she never felt a part of.

The first week her mother was gone, her dad claimed she was at a conference. "Didn't I tell you?"

"I think I would have remembered," Lia said. She had a good memory, and thanks to her Newspaper teacher, Miss Scott, one of the saints of public schools, she had become quite observant.

"Oh, well, nothing to worry about." He patted her on the shoulder and retreated upstairs.

A conference was conceivable. Her mother was a biology professor at the local community college, and although her department showed little interest in whether or not she published, she attended at least one conference per year to stay up to date on the latest findings, as she put it. But Lia's quick Internet search revealed no stateside conferences the week of her disappearance. When pressed, her dad said the conference was probably very small, but very affordable.

—

Lia's first newspaper assignment when she returned to school was a preview of the basketball team's upcoming season. Under normal circumstances she would have promptly completed the assignment, but she was having trouble getting started with this one. Old mom might have wondered if her reluctance was related to Brad, who had been a starter on the basketball team before he died. *What if*, old mom might ask, *the story isn't what you're really avoiding?*

That isn't the problem, Lia told herself.

Then what is?

Lia told Miss Scott she wanted to interview some of the players' family members, so that she might go beyond surface level facts. And although Miss Scott lifted her eyebrows, she let Lia leave campus to work on the assignment. Miss Scott was great like that, giving her students enough rope to hang themselves, but trusting that they wouldn't. There was a rumor that before she started teaching she worked for the local newspaper until she was fired for exposing the corrupt city manager, who happened to be the brother of the paper's editor in chief. She must've known what it would cost her, Lia thought, to publish the story. Lia always admired people like that, those who knew the rules but broke them anyway. She believed that although many rules were arbitrary, most existed for a good reason. Her mother said she must've got that way of thinking from her dad, the kind of man who always sorted his recycling.

Lia drove straight to Brad's house and parked across the street. She hadn't been there since the night of the party. She'd gone with a girl who by all accounts she should have been friends with, and the two of them snuck away from the crowd and into Brad's room. The room was small and ordinary. A poster of an athlete on one wall, a band Lia knew but thought were terrible on another. It was all so— expected. The girl dared Lia to smell Brad's sheets or steal his underwear, but Lia had no desire to touch any of Brad's possessions. She felt nothing standing there, minus the small buzz she got from trespassing with her classmate, standing in the dark room with her. She eyed the girl for a moment, until the girl caught her looking and backed out of the room.

Lia left the car running in front of Brad's house and what she was told was her childhood home. Both houses were small, though hers had an extra window just below the gabled roof that must've belonged to an attic. A few minutes passed before Brad's mother came out to grab the morning paper. She noticed Lia idling across the street, and stared in her direction for a moment, confused, before offering an unsure wave. Lia put the car in drive and sped away.

You're afraid, old mom said, in her head.

I'm not.

You are. You've never felt loss before and you don't know what to do with it.

It's more than that.

You liked him.

I didn't. I only wanted to.

Why?

I thought I was supposed to.

And now?

Lia thought of the girl in Brad's room, of the slight buzz she felt from staring at her. It was a feeling that was both new and old, and that she pretended she didn't understand.

I don't know what I want.

Lia turned onto her street. Without thinking she had driven to the home she remembered. The garage door opened. She slowed down and watched her dad, who should have been at work hours ago, back out and head in the opposite direction of his job.

You want to follow him.

Lia stayed a few cars behind, like in the movies she'd seen, but her dad didn't look back in any of his mirrors. He drove over the speed limit, odd for such a stickler for the rules. Lia still had no clue where he was going, other than that he was headed downtown. Her mind wandered to various possibilities, none of which made sense. Besides her mother's conferences, her parents were boring. They never went anywhere. They worked, came home and cooked, and one weekend out of the month they went to a movie Lia had no interest in seeing. Yet now her mother was gone. And her dad was going who knows where.

She almost missed him when he veered down an alley and into the back entrance of a parking garage. Lia let her imagination churn. She saw her dad meeting some mystery man. The two of them sharing a cigarette, though her dad never smoked. A manila envelope stamped shut with a secret symbol would be exchanged, tucked safely into a trench coat.

But if he were meeting a conspiracy theorist or whistle-blower, this was the worst place. The lot was chock-full of squad cars. This was parking for the police station, which must have resided above. As she considered the possibilities, her dad's car disappeared from view.

Lia circled around until she found her dad's car, on the lowest level. He wasn't in it. She checked her phone. No service, but Lia's hour was almost up. If she left now, she could make an excuse Miss Scott wouldn't buy, but might permit. She parked instead, across from her dad, and waited. Fifteen minutes. Half an hour. The entire time her mind listed all the rules she was breaking, the ways she would get into trouble.

Finally, her dad appeared. His hands were empty, his head hung low. He didn't get in his car immediately. He leaned against the trunk. Maybe he was waiting for someone. The mystery man. Or maybe he was waiting for Lia's mother.

He heard Lia get out of the car.

"Hello?" he said. He couldn't see fully, not in the dark of the parking garage. "Who's there?" There was a tremble in his voice Lia hadn't heard before. Had she ever seen her dad cry? A sappy children's movie, maybe. In a picture of him in the hospital, right after Lia was born. "I'm not playing any stupid games, if that's what you're thinking."

Lia stepped forward. "Dad, it's me."

"Lia? What in the world—"

He pulled her in for a hug and scratched Lia with his rough face. Before today, he hadn't gone a day without shaving for as long as she'd been alive.

"What are you doing here?"

"I was worried about you," Lia said.

"Why aren't you at school?"

"Why aren't you at work?"

He laughed, a small sob catching at the back of his throat.

"Why are you at the police station?" Lia asked. Her dad looked around, his car surrounded by a sea of cruisers. "Is something wrong with Mom?"

Her dad looked away. Growing up, he was the softer parent, the one she ran to when the other said no. "There's nothing wrong with your mother," he said. "She's at a conference."

"Dad."

"It has nothing to do with you, okay? It's just . . . your uncle."

"My uncle?"

"Emile. Now let's get you back to school. You shouldn't be here."

He walked Lia to her car and opened the door. Lia repeated her uncle's name to herself. "Emile." She tried to conjure a picture of her dad's brother, but she had no real memories of him, only a faded dream of the two of them lying in a field somewhere, staring at the blue sky and making shapes out of the clouds. He was the black sheep. She knew that much. At home, the only time his name was spoken was when Lia's parents badmouthed him in hushed voices, whispers that quickly dissipated when she entered the room.

Her dad shut the driver-side door. "Seat belt."

Lia buckled up, put the car in reverse, but lingered on the brake. "Is he okay?"

"No," her dad said. "But he never will be."

—

Lia returned to school in time for fifth period. It was peer review day in English, which meant she sat in the back and watched the two girls in front of her evaluate each other's poorly written essays for five minutes before they gossiped for the remainder of the class. They talked about their hair mostly, or the laundry list of things that annoyed them: Abby's skirt, the cafeteria lunch that day. They also talked about Brad.

"Did you hear there's a memorial this Friday?" one asked.

"Of course."

"Are you going?"

"Of course. You?"

"Of course. One time we were this close to hooking up."

At the end of class, the TV bolted to the corner turned on automatically to air *NewsNow*, a fifteen-minute news program in which young, theoretically cool journalists tried to relay some piece of national news to the most inattentive generation in history. The girls in front of Lia continued to gossip, but she tuned them out. The reporter, a twentysomething woman, was talking about a place called Limetown, a town that until a few months ago didn't exist. Lia was certain she had heard the name before, though she wasn't positive where. Perhaps it was over dinner with her parents. They often talked about the news of the world for Lia's benefit, doing their best to encourage what then was a mild interest in journalism. But what they said about this place she couldn't remember.

The reporter said that if you asked the people of Sparta, Tennessee, who at fifty miles away were Limetown's nearest neighbors, the whole place appeared overnight. Magic, one man said. Not magic, his wife said. The government. The reporter, however, had done some digging. She was from Sparta originally, which, she explained, was the only reason she'd heard about Limetown to begin with. She hadn't found much, but she did discover a name: R. B. Villard, a telecommunications giant who, in the eighties and nineties, made the kind of money people sell their soul for. Role tape A: Villard, predictably male, white, and old, testifying before Congress, swearing to God that his recent purchase of three rival telecom companies did not pose a threat to the sovereignty of the field's remaining competitors. Role tape B: a montage of reporters from major networks reporting on the settlement Villard's company, Realore, was forced to pay shortly after.

"So, do we bring candles to this thing or what?" one of the girls said.

"Yeah," the other girl said, "it's BYOC."

"And now, this," the reporter said, gesturing toward the chain link fence behind her, tall and wide as the camera's frame. The fence appeared to be guarding nothing other than the Tennessee woods, but according to the locals, the fence made a semicircle around the town, which lay some hundred yards or so past the fence. The fence ended when it ran into a ridge. The ridge led to a small range of mountains, beneath which, the reporter said, were a tangle of caves that extended for miles, like tree roots.

Lia felt a heaviness in her chest. This town had nothing to do with her, but its mystery reminded her of the others in life. Her missing mother, her father's strange behavior. The feeling she felt at school, observing all the couples. That something inside her was missing.

"Locals claim the caves are where the town gets its name," the reporter said. "They're made of this." She held a small chalky rock up to the camera. "Limestone."

There were no pictures of Limetown. No records or blueprints at the county courthouse. *NewsNow* did not have the money for a helicopter, the reporter explained, but even if they had they were told on multiple occasions that because of Limetown, White County, Tennessee, was now a no-fly zone. It was the only no-fly area in the country that wasn't a federal building or military base.

"So will his family be there?"

"No," the other girl said. "That's what I'm trying to tell you. It's a secret. For close friends. No one else is supposed to know about it."

"For the moment," the reporter said, "all we know is what Realore tells us."

A week before the news story was set to air, after a deluge of phone calls and requested interviews, Realore issued a statement. Not to the reporter specifically, but to all media. It was brief, vague, and intriguing. The press release read:

> The mind is a tool humans have yet to maximize. Limetown and its inhabitants aim to change that. And in the end the world will be better for it. *Far best is he who knows all things himself.*

At the end of the segment, the reporter approached the fence's sole gate but was quickly escorted away by a security guard who looked like he worked nights at the local mall.

"So no one else knows about it?" the girl said.

"No one but us," the other said. "Unless you count Brad."

The bell rang. The TV shut off.

"That's kind of creepy," the girl said.

The other girl took her hand. "I know."

—

No one was home after school. Lia's dad had returned to work; her mother was still at her purported conference. Out of curiosity Lia tried the cell phone her dad gave her mother for Christmas, but it was new to her and she'd always claimed to be a bit of a technophobe. Lia's call went straight to voice mail. She didn't leave a message.

That night she couldn't sleep. She lay in bed rehearsing tomorrow, her normal routine, which she liked because it gave her a sense of control. She told herself that tomorrow she would focus on the story she was assigned for Newspaper. Not her dead wannabe crush, not her missing mother—not any of the different mysteries that had become knotted in her mind. She would go to the memorial, get quotes from Brad's teammates, and finish her piece on the basketball team's upcoming season. Because it didn't feel good, these growing mysteries, not for someone who only liked a good riddle if she was confident she could solve it.

After she planned tomorrow, her mind involuntarily replayed today. She saw her dad crying in the parking garage, heard the pain in his voice when he said his brother's name. Emile. Lia still knew nothing about him, but as she drifted off into sleep, her imagination, longing for answers, filled the void. She dreamed of her mother and Emile running off together. She saw him taking her for a midnight ride outside of town, swerving to avoid a deer, and running Brad off the road. Her mother standing over his body, saying, *We have to do something*. Emile grabbing her by the arm, pulling her away, the two of them escaping to Limetown, where they would start a new life.

—

Miss Scott gave Lia detention for never reporting back the day before. She laughed. "I can't believe it," she said. "Lia Haddock, of all people." She had Lia clean each desktop in her classroom, and when Lia was finished, she took her rag and spray bottle down each hall looking for gum. Lia had twenty minutes to kill, so she wandered slowly. She wiped the fingerprints off the wall of trophy cases surrounding the main auditorium, making her way to the small cabinet housing the plaques for nonathletic accomplishments, tucked in the corner of one hall. There were no fingerprints on its glass, only dust.

Above the band room were portraits of every previous senior class, including the ones from way back when her dad had attended. Lia had glanced at these before, and once or twice she'd found him in his class photo, his dark and embarrassing feathered hair, his thick eyebrows that he'd passed on to Lia. But where was Emile? He would have gone here too. She scanned the years before and after her dad graduated. She went a decade in the past, flashed five years in the future. There was no Emile Haddock listed.

As she made her way back to Miss Scott's classroom, she wondered when Emile had turned bad, bad enough that her parents rarely spoke his name. Maybe, like Lia, he carried around the persistent feeling that he belonged elsewhere. Maybe he didn't fit in in high school either. Maybe if he came back, he could help Lia. Maybe he could—

"You have three minutes left of detention," Miss Scott said, after

Lia returned to her classroom. She didn't bother lifting her head from the student essay she was tattooing red.

"You knew my dad, right?" Lia said.

"Your mother too. Good people."

"No. I mean, he went here. He was a student of yours." Miss Scott had said something that first day of class. Called Lia a spitting image. The apple of his eye. "What about my uncle? Did you know him?"

Miss Scott looked up. She took off her reading glasses. "What's this about?"

"I was looking at the class portraits. I didn't see any Emiles listed."

"That's because Emile was never a senior," Miss Scott said. "He had a difficult time."

"So you did know him."

She stared at Lia for a while, studying her face, perhaps looking for a trace of her uncle, a landmark from the past. "Not as well as I would've liked," Miss Scott said, "but I know your dad cared about him. He was very protective."

"Protective?"

Miss Scott had taught Lia interview techniques the first week of the fall semester. She showed her different ways to elicit information from a subject who was less than forthcoming. First: Repeat their words. Make them feel insecure. Force them to elaborate.

"For whatever reason," Miss Scott said, "Emile got in fights. Quite a few, before he dropped out."

"Dropped out?"

"Stop it."

"Stop what?"

"I know what you're doing."

"Doing?"

Miss Scott laughed. She twirled her red pen around her thumb, until the pen's point stopped, landing on Lia.

"Why didn't my dad get in trouble?"

"He did. But after a while, he wised up."

"But Emile kept fighting."

Second: When repetition fails, finish their thoughts.

"Well, from what I heard, he didn't start many of the fights. He just had a way of finishing them."

The bell rang. Lia grabbed her book bag. Third: It's okay not to ask every question. Press pause, walk away. Give the subject time to feel guilty for all the things they kept secret.

Miss Scott walked Lia to the door. "You're getting good," she said. "But you need to be careful."

Careful? Lia thought. But she knew better than to push it.

—

The rest of the week passed without event, and without the return of Lia's mother. Monday would mark two weeks that she'd been gone, and Lia's dad had taken to avoiding Lia altogether. Notes in the kitchen said he was working late. Or he left messages on their archaic answering machine, having called when he knew Lia wouldn't be home.

He was gone Friday night too, the night of the vigil. The strangeness of her empty house pushed her out the door. The vigil was held at Lost 80, a remote park in the middle of the woods good for fighting, smoking, and sex. Lia had been there once, with a boy who was too nervous to make a move. She parked away from the gravel lot and picnic benches. The cops knew about Lost 80 too. Most of them had gone to Lia's high school and never escaped after graduation.

Everyone gathered on the far side of Potter Lake. It was really more of a large pond, but the town was short on scenery. The tallest hill was called a mountain. The two girls from English were there, huddled together, faces glowing above a shared candle. It was difficult to tell how many other people were present. Someone had built a small fire, the only light other than the candles and orange dots from joints and cigarettes. It would snow later that night, and the sky was overcast, the moon nowhere to be seen.

"We should get started," a girl said. Abby, one of Brad's longest flings. She was a tiny girl with long dark hair, a button nose. She stood by the fire holding a sheet of paper. A poem, maybe. This whole thing was probably her idea. "Does anyone want to speak first?"

The frosted grass crunched beneath shifting feet. They watched each other's breath. Abby unfolded her paper. She looked down at her words and shook her head.

"I wrote something," Abby said, "in English class. But it's not . . . I don't think . . ." She folded the paper, put it in her coat pocket. "Brad was good to me. Though really, I wasn't that good to him." Some awkward laughter. "We dated for eleven months but I never liked him the way I should've liked him. Like he liked me." Lia stepped closer to the fire. Abby frowned. "Anyway, what I wrote was stupid. It was a dumb poem about how no one is ever gone. Like, how I can hear his voice, even though my parents are atheists and I know better."

Lia shivered. She heard her mother's voice tell her a ghost was passing through.

Abby took out the paper and dropped it into the fire. A few people closed in around her. The English girls, one of Brad's best friends. They took her arms and formed a chain, and together they watched her words burn.

—

The fire died, was brought back to life, and threatened to die again. Girls passed around weed and wine coolers. Boys shotgunned beer. Lia was too afraid to drink or smoke, but she stayed because she knew nothing waited for her at home. She lingered by the fire and wondered how long it would go on like this. What would happen if her mom never returned home, if Lia had to watch her dad slowly disappear too?

Abby put her hand on Lia's shoulder. " 'No man is an island,' " she said. "What a joke." It took Lia a moment to realize what she was talking about—the words carved into the tree a few yards behind her. "It isn't fair," Abby said. Her eyes were red from crying, or maybe it was the smoke. "Everybody liked Brad."

Abby took a swig from a wine cooler she'd tucked beneath her arm.

"You liked him, didn't you? Is that it?"

"No," Lia said. "I mean, yes, but—"

"Yeah, you did. You little weirdo. Tell the truth." Abby ruffled Lia's hair like Lia was a small dog. Lia tried to step away but Abby pushed her, catching her off guard. Lia fell, feet away from the fire.

A few girls laughed, a dumb boy meowed. Lia rolled away from the fire and into the darkness, shutting her eyes to make everyone disappear. What could she say? She thought she cared about Brad, but didn't? That until the night of the party, the night that Brad died, she'd let herself believe that Brad was, if not *the* answer, then at least *an* answer to her loneliness?

When she finally opened her eyes, Abby was gone. Lia sat up. Everyone was running. Into the woods, in all directions.

A few seconds later police flashlights streamed through the trees. Lia stood and ran.

━

She hid in the woods for an hour, watching the cops' half-hearted attempts to make arrests. They caught a few kids who were too slow or too high. One kid insisted to the cops that he didn't do anything wrong. But the others, they cried. They begged for mercy. Don't tell our parents, they said.

While she waited for the cops to leave the woods, Lia practiced apologies to her dad. *Sorry, I lost track of time. No, I wasn't drinking. I would never smoke. No, I wasn't at a friend's. I was at a vigil. I lost someone.*

When she finally made it home, the kitchen light was on but dimmed. Lia started to apologize before she even saw who was sitting at the table, watching the news.

"Mom?"

Her mother didn't turn to face her. She kept her eyes on the TV. A plane had crashed somewhere in the Pacific. There were over two hundred passengers. No survivors.

"You're grounded," her mother said.

"I'm sorry," Lia said.

"No, you're not. That's the one thing I've learned. People do what they want. Good luck trying to stop them."

"So how was the conference?"

"Illuminating," her mother said. "And nonexistent."

"Then where were you?"

"Nowhere, as far as I can tell."

Lia sat opposite her mother, blocking the TV. *Eliminate distractions*, Miss Scott said. *Confine your subject to the story.*

"Mom, I was worried. What's going on?"

"It's nothing you need to worry about," she said, though she still wouldn't look at Lia.

Don't let them off easy. If you let them evade, you'll never get the truth.

"You disappeared for almost two weeks for a conference that you just told me didn't happen."

She continued looking down. "I shouldn't have said that. I'm sorry. You deserve a better excuse. So does your dad."

"He didn't know either?"

Behind Lia a reporter narrated the crashed plane's projected flight path. Where it took off from, where it should have landed. Lia turned and watched for a moment as the reporter drew a large circle on a map of the ocean, an estimate where the passengers likely died. But really, he said, they could be anywhere.

When Lia turned back around, her mother was in tears.

"Oh, Lia," she said. "Something bad is going to happen there. I tried to warn him. I told him not to go back."

The news went to commercial. Lia's mother fixed her dark eyes on Lia, as if willing her to understand.

"Mom, I don't know what you're talking about. What's going to happen? Where?"

Lia heard a creak on the stairs. Her mother looked around her, worried.

"Mom, tell me what you mean."

The commercial ended abruptly. There was breaking news. They found the black box. And with it, the reporter said, hope for answers.

"Limetown," her mother said. "It will not end well. He needs to get out."

"Limetown? Who?"

Her mother leaned in, just before Lia's dad entered the kitchen.

"Your uncle," her mother whispered. "Emile."

Her dad stood in the doorway, recycling bag in hand. "So," he said. "What are we talking about?"

Lia's mother glanced at her, then quickly looked away.

"Nothing," Lia said. "A plane crashed."

Her dad raised an eyebrow, but didn't question Lia's answer. He turned to the TV. "Oh, I saw that. All those people. What a tragedy."

—

Lia was in Miss Scott's room, working late on the piece about the basketball team when she heard the news about Limetown. Before that, Lia would later think, it could have been an ordinary day. If someone was reporting on her life, if they took a snapshot of her on her way to school, they wouldn't know that she had taken her mother's car—newer and nicer than her pre-owned—to school that morning because her mother canceled her classes that week, and would for the rest of the semester. If they interviewed her dad, they might shoot Lia a passing smile as she rushed through the kitchen, only pausing long enough to say she didn't have time for breakfast. Until Lia got out the door and took off the mask, until she sat safely in her mother's car, which she would rifle through later, looking for any clue as to where she had been, she could have been any other naive midwestern teen with no idea how good she had it.

Miss Scott read the headline off the Internet, as if it were any other trivial story. "*Entire Town Vanishes in White County, Tennessee*. Huh. Look at that. *Limetown*."

As she read, Lia grew very hot. She felt nauseous. Over three hundred men, women, and children. Vanished. Every home and building abandoned. An entire town—gone. The next day there would be a full report on *NewsNow* and every other major media outlet. No cameras were allowed inside. *NewsNow* set up outside the fence, behind which billowed an enormous tower of smoke seemingly erupted from the trees. The reporter stood in front of the fence, desperate to know what had happened. But she had no answers. No one did. All she could do was direct the camera to the smoke and wonder.

"Are you almost finished?" Miss Scott asked.

Lia had been staring blankly at the computer screen, imagining all the ways someone could disappear.

"Lia?"

She didn't answer. Her head buzzed with the possibilities, all the things she didn't know, everything her parents were hiding.

"Lia," Miss Scott said. "Are you all right?"

"My uncle was there. In Limetown."

Another teacher poked her head in. Miss Scott waved her away.

Lia wiped her eyes, but they were dry. "I didn't even know him."

Lia looked up at Miss Scott. She wanted to tell her about her mom. About her uncle, the way her dad sounded when he said his name at the police station. She wanted someone to help fill in the strange gaps that had crept into her life, to sort through the possibilities and tell her what was true.

"There are too many questions," she said, knowing what Miss Scott would say before she said it.

She said, "You're only as good as the questions you ask."

She stood Lia up for a hug. Lia squeezed her as hard as she could.

"Something is wrong," Lia said, trying to describe the growing heaviness in her chest.

"That's your intuition," Miss Scott said. "A good journalist never ignores it."

Her intuition. Maybe that was what led her to Brad's house, to the police station parking lot. Maybe that was what set off alarm bells when she saw the story about Limetown. But was any of it connected? If she closed her eyes again, and concentrated hard enough, could she weave the threads together?

Lia lifted her head from Miss Scott's shoulder. "I don't know where to start," she said.

"Not yet," Miss Scott said. "But someday you will."

CHAPTER TWO

III Emile

Twenty-five years before the Panic at Limetown, Emile sat down at his desk in the back of the American History classroom. His teacher, Mr. Church, was noticeably absent, late for the third time that week. Emile was not surprised. He knew Mr. Church hated teaching. Often, while his students took a quiz, Mr. Church made a mental list of all the ways his life had disappointed him: the dream jobs he'd never pursued (he'd wanted to be a travel writer, once upon a time); the women he found more interesting than his quiet wife. Was it too late, he wondered, to become someone else?

He never said these things out loud, but Emile heard them just the same.

Emile had dreams of his own. Lately, they revolved around finding his mother, a woman he hadn't seen since he was six and only vaguely remembered. He'd always been curious about her, intrigued by the few bits of information gleaned from his brother, Jacob. But recently, that curiosity had morphed into something more. A compulsion he couldn't explain, a riptide swirling in his head, ready at any moment to drag him out to sea.

"Where *is* he?" the girl in front of him said.

"He'll be here," Emile said, more to himself than the girl. But she turned around and glared.

"Was I talking to you?" In her head, she called him a name. They loved to call him names.

Five more minutes passed, but no one seemed to notice. His classmates were busy cramming for the reading quiz Mr. Church gave every Friday. Emile watched the door, still expecting Mr. Church to burst in late, sweaty, defeated. Instead, a young woman walked in. Tall for a girl, Emile thought. Short red hair. She strode in with confidence, and several of the boys' minds went to the places they always went and never really left. She dropped her belongings on Mr. Church's desk and walked to the front of the class. For a moment the woman didn't say anything. She stood there, surveying, sizing everyone up.

"Why, Mr. Church, you look different today," one boy said. Austin Beckett, the class asshole. The classhole. He sat in the front corner, in the desk closest to the door, and turned to make sure all his buddies snickered at his joke. Emile kept his words to himself. He'd been in too many fights this year with Austin's friends, a bunch of farm kids who made fun of Emile because he was thin and had long hair, and didn't play a sport or hang out with anyone other than his brother, Jacob. Once they learned that Emile liked poetry, it was over.

"Why can't you just let it go?" Jacob had said. Emile had shrugged. He was good at fighting. He liked it. He enjoyed seeing these kids' false bravado recede into fear. But his brother was right. After his last fight, a bloody beating Emile doled out on school grounds, he'd been suspended for a week. One more such incident, the principal threatened, and Emile would be expelled, charges pressed.

The woman smiled at the class. "Mr. Church is dead," she said. "I killed him."

Emile was the only one who laughed.

"My name is Ginny Scott. If you earn an A on today's quiz, you can call me Ginny. If you don't, you can call me not surprised. Now take out a sheet of paper and something to write with."

The quiz covered early colonial America. Middle school stuff, really. Name the oldest colony; which colony was founded by the British in 1607; label them both on a map. Which early colonies thrived? Which ones disappeared?

Emile finished the quiz in less than five minutes. He covered his mouth so no one could see him smile as he listened to the other students struggle. The girl to his right hummed a mnemonic device, while the boy on his left leaned over to his clueless friend and whispered Jonestown instead of Jamestown. It was an understandable mistake, actually. It was spring now, but the tragedy was all anyone talked about the previous semester. The largest loss of civilian life in American history, let alone 1978. An entire town, gone. At the time, Mr. Church tried to connect the tragedy to his curriculum—to Jamestown, to Roanoke—and had actually been quite successful. The class talked about it in hushed whispers like campfire ghost stories and peppered Mr. Church with question after question—*What did the carving on the tree mean? Did everyone drink the Kool-Aid? Who survived?*

"Pencils down," Miss Scott said. She collected the quizzes, laughing at some of the answers as she flipped through them.

"What's so funny?" Austin asked.

"The American education system, apparently." A few students groaned. "Oh, it's not your fault," Miss Scott said. "You're simply not engaged. All your lives you've been taught to memorize, which of course has its usefulness, but you're not even memorizing the good stuff."

A girl in the front row raised her hand. "We're just doing what they tell us."

"Exactly," Miss Scott said.

"Well," the girl said, "what should we be doing?"

"You should ask questions."

"About what?" someone said. Everyone turned and looked at Emile. It took a moment before he realized he was the one who had spoken. It was the first thing he'd said in class all year.

"Whatever you want. But make it interesting."

Emile and his classmates glanced at each other. No one knew what to say. Except Austin, the classhole, who raised his hand and said, "What do you know about Jonestown?"

Miss Scott leaned against the chalkboard. "Quite a bit, actually. I was there."

—

She was a reporter, she explained. She studied journalism at a prestigious school on the East Coast the class had never heard of, took a low-paying gig with a revered newspaper after she graduated. She was one of two groups allowed to visit Jonestown before the mass suicide.

She left right before the second group arrived, a delegation that included a congressman, two of his staffers, and nine journalists—most of whom were executed.

"What was it like there?" someone asked.

"It was hot."

"Did you see the Kool-Aid?"

She did not.

"Did you meet the guy? Jim Jones?"

"I did."

"What was he like?"

"He was the most charismatic person I've ever met. And the most terrifying."

It was the greatest class he'd ever attended, Emile later realized, as he sat in the nosebleed section of the bleachers, waiting for his brother to finish track practice. Below, his brother sprinted around the track, far in front of everyone else. Jacob was different too, but in a way society had agreed to appreciate. He was beloved by his peers, as well as his teachers, who, despite their own failings, still had the ability to recognize greatness in others. Jacob, a senior, approached a freshman runner, whom he could easily lap. Instead, he slowed his pace to match the kid, even offered him an encouraging pat on the shoulder as the two circled the loop for the final time. Perhaps that's what made today's class so remarkable. For the first time in his recent memory, Emile's mind raced alongside others, not far ahead.

He learned that although Jonestown ended in South America, it did not begin there. He learned that Jim Jones was from the Midwest, like Emile's mother was from the Midwest. Jones eventually made his way to a small town in Northern California, then to San Francisco, before departing for South America. Ginny did not know why he left California, or what he left behind. "Though," she said, "that certainly is a good question." She said she would have to look it up, and that that was the class's homework too. "Write down a question to which you don't know the answer. Something you're curious about."

In his mind Emile wrote down questions he had about his mother. Where was she? Why did she leave?

"Once you have your question," Ginny said, "search for the answer. On Monday, we'll discuss what you discover."

—

Jacob dropped Emile off at the library after practice. On the way, Emile closed his eyes and tried to picture her. Their mother. He remembered her state of mind more than her face. The way it rocked from one fear to another, like a rowboat in a rolling sea. Sometimes, late at night, Jacob would tell Emile stories about what she was like. How she never allowed visitors. How she never let the boys leave the house.

Why not?

She was afraid.

Of what?

That I was like you.

There was more to it than that, Jacob later confessed. Once their father ran out on them, their mother never left the house either. She stayed inside long enough for her mind to break. Jacob had only talked about that day once. How he waited until their mother fell asleep in front of the TV, her face frozen in its perpetual worry, before waking Emile and sneaking out the window of the bedroom they shared. It would have been dark then. The deep black of winter. Their nearest relatives, whom their mother had estranged herself from, lived a mile away. It was either run through the snow, barefoot—their mother slept on their coats and boots in case the boys got any ideas—or give up and sleep on the side of the road.

After Jacob and Emile left, after their mother learned that her brother and his wife had taken them in, she disappeared. No one knew where she went, or why she didn't try to take her boys back.

Emile didn't remember any of this, but sometimes, if he closed his eyes and thought hard enough, he thought he could feel the cold of the snow stinging his feet.

—

Emile did not like the library as much as he thought he would have liked the library. It was quiet, yes, but often busy. And when people's mouths were shut, their minds simmered. Still, there were spots he could go, pockets of isolation deep in the stacks. Over the years, he became something of an expert at finding these pockets, no matter where he went. At school, there was the nosebleed section of the bleachers, of course, or the Newspaper room, a new concept for public schools and thus unused so far, or the northwest stairwell, which for some reason always smelled of urine. But mostly Emile enjoyed roaming the halls while classes were in session. At least once a day he'd fake having to go to the restroom so that he could wander in near-perfect silence, the buzzing of a seemingly empty building. This buzzing was his favorite sound.

Emile sat down in the Bulgarian Lit section, took out his pencil and paper, and at the top he wrote "Questions." He scribbled a question about his mother, then scratched it out. He knew he couldn't share anything like that with the class, so he came up with a few questions about Roanoke and Jonestown instead. Does anyone live in Roanoke now, or do locals stay away out of fear? The news said thirty-three people escaped Jonestown. Where are they now? Do they still believe in whatever led them to South America? He thought of the questions as practice, before he tackled the real mysteries of his life.

Emile put his pencil down. Then he remembered what Ginny had said: *The best questions are the questions your first questions ask.* Emile sat back in his chair. He wasn't entirely sure what that meant. He stared at what he'd written. What did his questions have in common? He tried to connect the tragedies. He couldn't. He didn't know enough. Instead, he searched for words his questions shared. The only meaningful one was "now." What happened to the survivors, and those who came after? What was left of all that was destroyed?

The very best questions, Ginny had explained, are the ones that teach you as much about the mysteries of yourself as the mysteries of the world. Austin laughed when she said this, and admittedly, Emile found it a little corny, something out of the latest kung fu movie. But there, alone in the stacks, it was easy to imagine that Ginny was right. He thought about his mother again. He picked up his pencil and wrote the word *now*, over and over, in sprawling columns that covered the page, until there were no more blank spaces.

———

His guardians would be asleep by the time Emile made it home. They were his uncle on his mother's side, and his aunt. But they did not like it when Jacob and Emile called them that. Nor were they to be considered parents, a title, they believed, that should only be reserved for the brothers' true mother and father. At home, meals were prompt, the food perfunctory—meat, side, vegetable—and the conversation limited. Every act was measured, not necessarily in a cruel way. They were dutiful, austere people, and Jacob explained that it was because of their religious background. They weren't fanatics or anything, just big fans of the modest life. Their uncle worked at the co-op, their aunt stayed home, and both volunteered at the church. They slept in the same room, in twin beds pushed comfortably apart. They had no kids of their own, having lost their only child in infancy.

Emile sat down with Jacob for a glass of milk at the kitchen table, the questions from his homework still swirling in his head. "Do you ever think about Mom?"

"Of course," Jacob said. "You know I do."

Emile was aware of this, but he also knew Jacob wanted to talk about her less and less. He'd been this way the last year or so, wanting to focus less on the past, more on his future, which everyone described as bright.

From the living room, the guardians' cuckoo clock sounded. Jacob told himself it was getting late. "I'm going to bed."

Emile finished his milk and followed him to the room they shared, where Jacob lay in the dark. He wanted to be left alone. Emile changed, got into his bed, and whispered questions into the night.

"Where is she now?"

"What does she do now?"

"Does she have another family?"

And, "Will she ever come back for us?"

Jacob didn't speak, but Emile felt a familiar longing in his brother, not that different from the pull that had tugged at Emile. It was like this sometimes with his brother's thoughts. Everyone's really. He didn't always catch fully formed words or sentences. Sometimes he recognized a mood or an emotion; other times, a memory. Tonight, Jacob's pull dragged up an image of a boy on a porch, watching a car drive away.

Emile's imagination took over from there. The car belonged to their mother. She had come to retrieve the boys after they escaped, but the guardians had turned her away. Fine, she might've said. But when they're ready, they'll come for me. She got in her car and drove west, rolling the top down once she hit Arizona. Maybe she reached the coast of California, working jobs at various motels (she had been a housekeeper here in Lawrence, Emile was told, before her breakdown) until she found the perfect spot, her own pocket of isolation. It would be scenic, unlike Kansas. Or maybe she drove north, settled down in

Minnesota or Wisconsin. Maybe she would meet a nice man—a minister maybe—who was charming and beloved by his fiercely loyal flock.
Their mother would resist his advances at first, until he showed her
that there was a normal life out there if she wanted to live it. His flock
could become their family, and she would never have to worry how any
of them would turn out. She would never have to be afraid if any of
them were special and what it would cost her.

But all he knew for certain was that no one in town had seen her
since the night they left.

"What if we found her?" Emile wondered out loud.

"Why would we do that?"

Because we have nothing else. Meaning, Emile had nothing else. No
friends, no tethers to this place. Because their last semester together
was nearly over, and when Jacob left in a few months, Emile would
truly be alone, the only thing keeping him company the feeling that he
belonged elsewhere. *Because of the pull.*

"You don't remember what she was like," Jacob said.

Emile tried to peer into his brother's mind again, but all he saw was
a ghost of a woman rocking in a chair, wagging her finger when Jacob
pleaded to leave the house to get some fresh air. He saw a door, not on
the wall, but on the ceiling, closing his brother into perfect darkness.

———

Emile spent the weekend at the library. Jacob traveled for a track meet
and returned draped in medals. When Emile showed up to American
History on Monday, Ginny sat in Mr. Church's chair. She informed the
class that Mr. Church would not be returning and, no, she didn't know
why. She then told the story of her childhood dentist, a man beloved by
the entire town, who had a wife, two daughters—the whole bit. One
morning the dentist got dressed, ate breakfast, kissed his wife and kids
and went out to the garage, where he started the car with the door shut
and waited for his death to arrive.

"The point is," Ginny said, "we may think we know each other,
but what do we really know? Everyone has their secrets."

"You think that's what happened to Mr. Church?" one boy said.
Art, one of Austin's cronies.

"God no. Are you listening to me?" Several students shifted in
their seats. "Take out your homework. Let's see what you discovered
over the weekend."

A few classmates had completely forgotten about the assignment; one girl claimed she completed it but left it at home and, no, she couldn't remember any of the questions she asked.

"You know what the Australians would say about that, don't you?" Ginny said. "Sounds sus. As in suspect. Yes, very sus indeed. Have any of you been to Australia?"

No one raised their hand.

It was Emile who finally broke the silence. He began by admitting that, like the rest of his classmates, he was very interested in Roanoke.

"This got me wondering what Roanoke was like now, so I went to the library. Spent the whole weekend there."

A few students giggled, but Ginny nodded—Emile's cue to continue. He told the class that today Roanoke was a place called Manteo, North Carolina, a small town in Dare County with a population of 547 people. Manteo was named after a Croatan Indian who helped the English settlers survive when they first landed and started their settlement. He told them that the town's population saw steady growth in recent years, thanks in part to the current mayor embracing the area's dark history, turning well-known tragedy into tourism. A play about the colony's vanishing was performed, ghost tours were given. All this, and still no one knew what really happened to the settlers.

So what, one student thought. And: *freak*.

"The problem," Emile said, "I think"—*doofus, loser*—"what I discovered is that the English waited too long. I mean, three years passed before White returned. That's a really long time, isn't it? By then the entire colony had been erased."

So, the class thought.

"So?" Austin said.

"Yes," Ginny said, "what exactly is your point?"

Emile thought of his brother. He saw him running away from their childhood home, away from their mother, yes, but also away from the answers Emile now felt he needed.

"I was just thinking," he said, "what if that's what happens with Jonestown? You don't see it on the news anymore. We're expected to move on?"

"So what do you want to do?" Austin said. "Fly to South America? You wanna drink the Kool-Aid? Be our guest."

The class laughed.

"Quiet," Ginny said. She turned to Emile. "Is that all? You want to know what the dead are up to?"

Not only the dead. There were survivors, but no one ever talked about them.

"The dead don't talk," Austin said. "Maybe you should try it." The class laughed again. Emile heard the waves of agreement—*give it a rest, freak*—from his classmates. *Take a deep breath*, Jacob would say. *They're just words, nothing worth getting riled up over.* Emile clenched his fist, but didn't say anything. "There you go," Austin said. "Now you're getting it."

The bell rang. The students gathered their things, but Emile lagged behind. He would wait until Austin was long gone before he made his way to his locker.

"Hey, Jonestown," Ginny said, "can I talk to you for a second?" When it was just the two of them, she shut the door.

"Everything's fine," Emile said. "I'm just weird. That's all."

Ginny sat down in one of the student desks. She looked very much out of place. "You are weird, but that's not what this is about." She gestured for Emile to have a seat. "Or, I guess it is . . ."

"Emile."

"Emile. You did an excellent job with today's assignment. At first I wasn't sure where you were going with it, but it's pretty cool where your questions led you." She folded her arms. "Hey, I wanted to ask you something. Why did you go quiet when that boy made fun of you? That Allen."

"Austin."

"Why didn't you say anything?"

Emile shrugged. "They're all thinking it."

Ginny sighed, as if she were disappointed.

"Do you know what I did before I came here? After my stint at the *Times*? You know the *Journal-World*, the local paper? I worked for it. I did more than work for it, actually. I was a senior editor. Can you believe that? I was the only woman there, and the youngest editor by far. You understand what I'm trying to tell you?" Emile did not. Her thoughts were clear but their meaning was hard to read. "Every day some asshole like Austin told me I didn't belong there. Do you think I stayed quiet?"

"I can't get in any more fights," Emile said. "They'll expel me."

"Yeah," Ginny said, almost with a laugh. "They expelled me too." She slumped back in the desk, and for a moment her thoughts drifted away from the classroom. She focused on an office. It was her former boss's maybe, some guy with a bad tie and even worse haircut. He was yelling at her, while Ginny stood there, staring at her reflection in the framed degree that hung above her boss's head. She was not crying or worried, as Emile thought he would have been. She was grinning, as if to say, *so what?*

"You got fired?"

"And I'll tell you what," Ginny said. "It was worth it."

She didn't say anything more, and the two of them sat until another bell rang. It was Ginny's free period, but Emile was late for Algebra.

"You weren't scared," Emile said, "were you."

"Of losing my job?"

"No," Emile said. "At Jonestown. I can tell. When you talk about it, your mind is calm."

Ginny's face changed. She looked at Emile the way they always looked, when they suspected he was more than a little strange.

"I wasn't afraid," she said. "But I should have been."

—

Emile ditched his last two classes. He walked home, which, at nearly ten miles away, really wasn't a walkable distance. But it gave him time to think. The more Ginny talked, the more he felt that the two of them had a lot in common. "Do you ever feel like you belong somewhere else?" he asked her, just before he left. "Of course," she said. "I'm a reporter. I'm always looking for the next big thing."

He was on the outskirts of the city, still a mile away, when he heard the engine. A black truck roared by. It swerved to a stop half a football field ahead, reversed until it was even with Emile. It was an enormous vehicle, and older than Emile, who backed away from the road, into a small ditch. He knew who the truck belonged to.

"Hey," Austin said. "Where you going? The asylum's thataway."

Emile stayed where he was. He always imagined there'd be a crowd present when he finally fought Austin, cronies who'd descend on Emile if the fight began to go his way. But no crowd meant no witnesses, which meant maybe he wouldn't be expelled.

"Well," Austin said, "what's it gonna be? We're wasting gas here."

He reached across the cab and threw open the passenger door. It took a moment for Emile to understand.

"Are you serious?" He searched Austin's mind, saw a small lake, an unfamiliar shore. A private place where two guys could go and beat the shit out of each other and not be bothered by a principal or the police.

"C'mon," Austin said. "I ain't got all day."

Emile climbed into the truck. As he shut the door and put on his seat belt, he thought about what Ginny said about Jonestown. How she should've known better than to not be afraid.

—

Austin blasted rock on his radio the first few minutes, and Emile looked out the window as they flew past the road that led to his aunt and uncle's house. A few miles later they climbed a back road and when they reached the top the lake appeared, seemingly out of nowhere. Austin drove down to the shore, where an old rowboat waited, tied to a makeshift dock. He got out without saying a word and grabbed two fishing poles out of the back, along with a small tackle box. Emile understood that he should get out, and when he did, Austin handed him one of the poles. They climbed awkwardly into the boat. Neither spoke as Austin rowed them away from the shoreline. When the truck was a dot behind them, Austin stopped rowing and cast his line. He asked Emile if he'd ever fished before. Emile hadn't. His guardians never took him anywhere.

"That's too bad," Austin said. "You should probably cry about it." He laughed to himself and Emile thought about punching him right then, ending whatever this was. But when he looked inside Austin's mind, he felt no waves of anger.

"So that new teacher is a real bitch, huh?" Austin said.

Something tugged on his line. Once, now twice. He reeled in slowly, but when the hook came out of the water, there was nothing attached, not even the bait.

"Why am I here?" Emile said.

Austin dug a worm out of his tackle. "Isn't it obvious?" he said. "I needed a fishing buddy. Not safe to be out here alone."

"But you're an asshole."

"Yeah."

"And you already have friends. I've fought every one of them."

"I know," Austin said. "That was hilarious." He swung his pole back and recast. Emile watched the line fly in what seemed an infinite loop before it settled gently on the water. "Besides, those guys aren't my friends. Any friend of mine would know how to throw a punch."

He kept his eyes on the water, reeling in aimlessly.

"I can't stay out here forever," Emile said.

"Why not? You got a study date with the history teacher?"

"I have to meet my brother."

"Your brother," Austin said. He set his pole down. "He's like your only friend, huh?" Emile didn't say anything. "What are you going to do when he graduates? Hang out with the teacher?"

Emile set his pole next to Austin's. He'd done his best to not think about the end of summer, when Jacob left to run track out of state on a partial scholarship in Utah, which, even though it wasn't on the coast or anything, felt impossibly far away.

Austin laughed. "Nah, man. You can't be friends with the teacher. The teacher?" He laughed some more. "You need someone your own age."

"Who? Like you?"

"Why not? I can be weird." Austin smiled now, and stared at Emile, almost daring him to smile back. "You wanna be weird together?"

He stuck out his hand. He wasn't thinking about fishing. He was sitting on a bale of hay, on top of a hill, somewhere on his family's farm, Emile assumed. The sun was setting over the land he worked, coloring a field of corn purple and blue.

"C'mon," Austin said, "who else is gonna stop you from doing something stupid like running off to Jonestown?"

—

It was dark by the time Austin dropped Emile off at home. The guardians had already eaten. A plate of leftovers waited tin-foiled in the fridge. Jacob was in their room, still in his tracksuit, lying on his bed with his trigonometry book covering his face. He asked Emile where he'd been.

"Austin Beckett? Isn't that guy kind of a jerk?"

"Yeah," Emile said. "I don't get it."

Jacob sat up. The book fell off his face. "Well, *you know who* are mad at you. They got a call during dinner, which made them mad enough. It was someone from the school. I didn't hear the whole thing, but it sounded like you've been skipping. You know anything about that?"

"Maybe," Emile said. He sat down on his bed, opposite Jacob.

"Hey," Jacob said, "forget those kids. Things will get better. I promise." He reached over and patted Emile's knee, as if that settled everything. And Emile could tell his brother truly believed what he said. In his vision of the future, he excelled at college, on and off the track, in ways that would ensure a long and happy life after he graduated. He met a girl his last fall semester, they got married in the spring. He got a job and they lived in a bigger, nicer house than the guardians would ever be able to afford. This plan floated on the surface of his thoughts.

"For you, you mean. Things will get better for you. I'll be stuck here."

"You'll come with me," Jacob said.

"Yeah. In two years."

Jacob said he would visit, but they both knew he wouldn't have the time. He would have meets over spring break, summer vacation too, if he ran well. Maybe he could return for Christmas, but how would he pay for the flight home? Neither saw the guardians helping. And even if Emile survived the next two years, what would he do while Jacob finished college? He didn't play any sports. He was good, but not great at school. He wouldn't have any scholarships waiting.

"Well, I don't know what else I can do," Jacob said. He was getting angry, upset in the way Emile imagined all older siblings got upset. Mad at the world for assigning them a little brother or sister to watch over, to hold them back when all they wanted to do was march forward. But was it any better to be the younger sibling? To be compared to, reliant upon, and ultimately abandoned by an older, better version of yourself?

—

When Emile arrived to American History the following afternoon, the desks were arranged in a circle. "We're going to try something different today," Ginny said. "Sit anywhere you'd like." Austin saved Emile a seat. A few students stared at this new arrangement—*Why is the freak sitting next to him?*—then settled into their own seats. The bell rang.

"I reviewed all of your questions last night," Ginny said. "It took me an entire bottle of wine, but I did it. To no one's surprise, they weren't great. You asked simple questions. All yes or no." A few snickers. "Obviously you don't get it. You're still thinking small."

Austin, pretending to take notes, wrote a message for Emile, and slid it to the edge of his desk. *What crawled up your new friend?*

Ginny continued. "You're sitting in a circle as a reminder that everything you do or say can be seen by another person, *affects* another person. You say you want to know about places like Roanoke and Jonestown, but you ask questions as if those places aren't real, as if the people who died or disappeared didn't really exist. 'What kind of tree was "Croatoan" carved on? Who mixed the Kool-Aid?' You need to realize that we're all interconnected. Write this down. 'Any man's death diminishes me.' "

The class looked around before reluctantly doing as they were told. Austin kicked Emile under his desk, passed Emile another note: *Let's get out of here. Lost 80. Do you know it?* When Emile ignored him, Austin raised his hand and asked if he could be excused to the bathroom.

"Sure," Ginny said. "But were you ever really here?" Austin left. "Now where was I? Ah yes. I was just about to tell you what happened to Mr. Church."

—

Ginny began by confessing that she should not be telling them this. But she had taught them the importance of asking questions, of sharing the answers, no matter what. That is our responsibility to one another. After all, a question is a connection. A promise, really. It's a way of saying that if something happens to you, I'll ask why. I'll ask how. If, like Mr. Church, you go missing, I'll seek you out, find out what happened.

To prove her point, she'd interviewed a few colleagues in the teachers' lounge. They told her Dale Church was an amazing teacher, once upon a time. He loved his job. He had a way with his students, more than one interviewee said. He saw the future in them. The students tilted their heads, trying to reconcile the man Ginny described with the one they knew, the teacher who assigned in-class word searches and coloring sheets, who on more than one occasion nearly nodded off during his own lecture. That was their Mr. Church. So what happened?

What happened, Ginny explained, was time. Time erodes hope.

It washes away our very will, if we let it. Rarely is it a single event, a giant wave that crushes us. More common are the smaller waves that take us away, slowly, inch by inch, until, like this sentimental speech, we get carried away. But wasn't he married? Didn't he have kids? A few students flinched, their minds settling on memories of their own fathers leaving. Emile thought of his mother. He was married, Ginny said. But time had its way with family too, severing the connections he once forged with his wife and children, until there was nothing tying your poor Mr. Church to this town.

Emile continued to think about what Ginny had revealed as he made his way to Lost 80 after school. Austin's truck was parked away from the picnic benches, under a large oak tree. Emile found the trailhead and wandered into the woods, down toward the pond. He came upon Austin sleeping near the water, using his book bag as a pillow. Austin had his shirt off, his belt buckle undone. His chest and stomach were ghost-white from the winter. It was a strange thing for Emile to realize, but he was happy to see him.

"What'd she say?" Austin asked. His eyes were still closed. Emile lay down next to him.

"She didn't care," Emile said. "I probably could've ditched too."

"No. About Mr. Church. What happened to him?"

Nothing. Something. No one knows. A teacher close to his wife said that he left for school last Friday and never came home. His kids are grown, live out of town, but not far away. They haven't heard from him either.

"So what was the point of the story?" Austin said. "Life sucks?"

"She never said. She passed out a poem. We talked about it until the bell rang."

A gust of wind rippled the water. A large willow tree hung above them, waving. Austin sat up. "Hey, I got you something." He reached behind him and pulled a stick from his book bag.

"It's a stick."

"You don't like it? I thought you could use it to roast marshmallows with all the Jonestown survivors, when you find them."

"Great."

Austin smiled. "Hey. I have another idea." He dug in his bag again and pulled out a small blade. "Borrowed this from my dad. It's his whittling knife. I thought we could carve something into a tree."

"What, like at Roanoke?"

"Yeah, weirdo. Like at Roanoke. Here." He handed Emile the knife, which looked pristine, like it had never been used before. "Don't worry. My dad's out of town. A farm show in Hays. I'll clean it up before he gets back."

Emile glanced inside Austin's mind, but he didn't see his father. Only a woman, Austin's mother, he supposed. She was sweeping the front porch. No, she was sitting in the kitchen, reading something. A Bible. The guardians had the same edition in their living room.

Austin stood up and started surveying nearby trees, running his hands over brittle bark. He found a good candidate in a nearby maple. "Over here. You go first."

"What should it say?"

"I don't know. Something cool."

Emile stood in front of the tree, considering what to carve. A thousand ideas swirled inside his head before he decided. He stabbed the maple deep, the dark bark oozing with every letter.

—

It took much longer than expected. Track practice was over by now and Jacob would be wondering where the hell Emile was. Emile pushed those thoughts aside as he turned and revealed his work to Austin.

"No man is an island," Austin read. "What the hell does that mean?"

"It's from the poem we read in class. She kept trying to make this point, about all of us being interconnected or something."

Austin tilted his head at the carving. "Huh. That's not bad, I guess. But I get to do the next one."

"Actually, I need to go. My brother's waiting."

"Already? Fine. Whatever. I'm gonna stay. Maybe camp out. Come tomorrow I'll have a whole book carved in these trees."

"You're going to stay out here?" Emile said. "All night?"

Austin looked at the knife, though he didn't think of his father. He thought of his mother. "Yeah," he said. "It's cool. I can do whatever I want."

—

Emile agreed to meet Austin at Lost 80 the following day after school, so Austin could show him what he'd etched into the tree. He ditched after Ginny's class, but when he arrived at the park, Austin was no-where to be seen. He looked everywhere, even searching the trees for a hand-carved apology. He waited beneath the willow tree as the sun ran through its colors, and when the moon showed up instead of Austin, Emile started home.

Jacob was washing the dishes. It was a Tuesday night, which meant the guardians were at church.

"You're lucky they're gone," Jacob said. "The school called again."

Emile took the towel off his brother's shoulder to help dry. "What'd you say?"

"I pretended I was them. It was easy. I just used as few words as possible." He passed Emile a spotless pan. "I don't understand. Do you want to get kicked out?" Emile didn't say anything. "You were with Austin again?"

"Yeah."

"Well, I'm glad you have a friend, even if he is a jerk." Jacob took his hands out of the sink, told Emile to finish up. "Just be careful, there's knives in the water."

The next morning Austin was waiting for Emile in the school park-ing lot. Jacob parked next to Austin. Emile got out with his brother. Austin was still wearing his work overalls, which were soiled at the knees and looked damp everywhere. His face was grimy with dirt. He left the truck running.

Jacob looked Austin over. He did not approve. "You all right?" he asked Emile.

"We're fine," Austin said. "Buzz off, track star."

Jacob walked away, shaking his head.

"What's going on?" Emile said.

Austin looked around nervously. "I'm sorry I couldn't make it yes-terday. Do you forgive me?"

"It's fine. Are you okay?"

"I told her," Austin said. "You know, that I was weird too. I thought she would understand. More than him."

A car full of students pulled up next to them. All Austin's friends, all Emile's foes. They stared.

"I gotta go, all right? She's probably looking for me. But I'll meet you at the tree tonight. Bring a bag."

"What?"

"Here," Austin said, and handed Emile a folded note. "This is all you need to know."

He hopped in his truck and drove off before Emile could say yes or no, before he could even think to look inside Austin's mind. Emile decided not to read the note right away. He would save it until after school. Otherwise, he would be distracted the entire day, tempted to ditch, assuming that's what Austin wanted. And maybe Jacob was right: there were only so many times Emile could screw things up before he felt the consequences. What would he do if he got kicked out of school?

He tucked Austin's note into his American History textbook. That afternoon in Ginny's class, they sat in a circle again, the seat next to Emile noticeably empty. Two of the boys from the parking lot grinned in his direction. They whispered to each other and laughed. Terrible names popped up in their thoughts, worse than usual. Emile tried to filter the noise out, but the hate behind their words was stronger too. He felt his own anger rising in response. He stared straight ahead, told himself to focus on Ginny's lecture. Something about a final project. She used the word *capstone*, something they would present at the end of the semester, a little over a month away.

"The subject is your choice. This is your education. But it should reflect a mind driven by inquiry and interconnection. Ask a question that isn't being asked. Show us why your answer matters. How we're all a part of it, whether we realize it or not."

Emile glanced at the empty seat next to him. He could almost hear Austin say, *Give me a break*. He couldn't wait to tell him about class tonight, about what strange things Ginny said. He would make his new friend laugh, there in the dark, by the tree, and take away the pain that plagued him. Then, when Austin was ready, Emile could ask him what was wrong. They could talk about Austin's family, his mother or father, if they were the problem. He could become someone Austin could talk to, if, like Emile, he didn't have anyone else. And maybe someday, in return, Emile could share his own stories. About Jacob, the guardians. About his mother. He could even tell him about himself, what made him different. Austin could be the first person Emile shared his secret with.

Ginny passed out the assignment sheet. Emile folded it in half and opened his textbook to place it next to Austin's note, but the note wasn't there. Immediately he felt his face flush. He checked his pockets, beneath his seat. His heart drummed in his ears. Ginny carried on. "Part of your assessment will be based on how well you demonstrate an open mind. Will you put aside your preconceived notions? Will you let the research take you where the research wants to go?"

Emile slumped in his seat, retracing his steps that day. If he was lucky, the note was at the bottom of his locker. But he could have lost it at any time. He could have dropped it anywhere. Anyone could have picked it up.

Something inside Emile made him want to skip the rest of school and run directly to Lost 80, even though Austin wanted to meet him at night, for reasons he didn't explain. Maybe it was safer then, to meet where and when no one could see them.

Ginny finished going over the assignment.

"Do you have any questions?" she said.

No one raised their hand.

She shook her head. "That's not a good start."

—

Emile lied to Jacob that evening. He had his brother drop him off at the library after dinner, claiming he wanted to get a head start on his capstone project, then snuck out the back and made his way to Lost 80. It was a cold, long walk. The sun had fallen quickly and took with it any memory of warmth. By the time Emile arrived at the park, his hands were numb inside his coat pockets, where they sat balled up into fists.

He did not see Austin's truck. Perhaps he was early. Maybe the note specified a time, or a specific part of the park where they would meet. Emile assumed Austin would wait by their tree. He walked there. No one. He ran his hand over the carved verse. Frost had settled on the tree, giving each letter a velvet touch. Emile whispered the words he'd carved, as if they were a magical spell that would make his friend appear.

It didn't work. He waited. He sat down and leaned against the tree. He dared himself to close his eyes, just to see what would happen. When he did, he heard something. A voice. No, voices. Fevered, roaring. Violent. He sprung up and ran in their direction. The closer he got, the more the voices grew. Or, not grew exactly. Changed. They weren't louder. They were more forceful.

Emile stumbled into a clearing, where he found three men, huddled together, hurling names and slurs at someone unseen. Worse than anything Emile had ever been called.

One of the men turned and saw Emile. Though it wasn't a man at all. It was a boy, one of Austin's supposed friends.

"Hey, look," the boy said, "it's the boyfriend."

The others turned. The moon was bright enough that Emile could see all of their faces. Art, one of the snickering boys from Ginny's class, stood between two other boys from the school parking lot. Emile had fought them all before, bloodied all their noses, and they his.

The biggest one, Bill, stepped forward. "That what you're doing here, huh? Looking for your date?" Another muttered the same slurs Emile had already heard, threw in a few curses for good measure. "The thing is, I don't think he's up for it. Doesn't look so hot to me."

Emile didn't understand. Not until Art, less resolved than the others, let his guilt in. Emile saw Art wanting the others to stop as they punched and kicked. He saw Art's hand reach out to pull them away, but he wasn't strong enough.

"Move," Emile said, and he walked into Bill, who blocked the way for a second before stepping aside. Emile saw what he knew he would see. Austin, lying on the ground. His head was turned to the side. His arms clutched his chest, shielding himself, maybe, or trying to hold what was left of his beaten body together. Emile stepped to the other side of him. He saw Austin's face, dark and bloodied, almost beyond recognition. One eye was swollen shut. The other hung open, white and lifeless.

"We found your note," Bill said. "Guess you dropped it. Real romantic."

Austin was unconscious. Emile heard nothing from him. He kneeled down and put his hand to his friend's chest to check his breath. His shirt was damp and reeked of urine.

"Let me read a snippet: *You're the only one who gets me. How is that?*" Bill crumpled the note into a ball, threw it at Austin's motionless body. "Makes me fucking sick."

Emile lowered his head. How did he not hear it? How could he have not realized it before?

Art spoke up. "We were just going to mess with him. But he got so mad."

"He was gonna run away with you," Bill said. "To San Francisco or some shit? Or was it Jonestown?"

Emile stood up. He turned to the boys, his classmates, his peers.

"Ask me, his mom did the right thing, kicking his faggot ass out of the house."

Emile stepped toward Bill, who boasted a bloody lip from where Austin must've fought back. Bill straightened his back. "Go ahead," Bill said. "Austin was ten times tougher than you. Now look at him." He puffed out his chest and clenched his fists, but Emile felt the hesitation, even as two of the other boys egged Bill on.

"Are you sure?" Emile said. "You don't seem sure. You seem afraid."

"Screw you," Bill said, but the wave of fear rose higher. He tried to ignore it, to manufacture the hate he'd relied on earlier. He called on what he'd been told all his life, about sissies like Austin. Emile tilted his head and listened carefully. He heard Bill's hate-filled stepfather, his gravelly voice. He looked at the other boys. He cracked his knuckles, knowing that if he listened closely, if he asked the right question, he might understand why each of them was here, how they were all interconnected, despite what they had done tonight—or because of it.

"Shh," Emile said. "Do you hear that?" The boys looked at one another, confused.

"I don't hear nothing."

"It's your father. No, wait, he left you. Couldn't stand you or your mother. No, it's your stepfather. You're watching a game. Baseball, I think. Yes. The crack of the bat. You're in the kitchen. Your team just signed a new player. He's from Cuba, and he's amazing. But your stepdad doesn't approve. He lets you know it. Calls the Cuban inferior. You're just a kid. Still, you know what he's saying isn't right. You want to say something, but you don't. You never do." Emile stepped closer. "Is that where it started? It's all you can think about."

Emile heard the swing in Bill's head before he saw it. He ducked and caught him in the stomach, dropping him to the ground. Art ran. The other stood and watched. What Emile liked most about fighting is that while he was in the middle of it, while he was smashing Bill's face in, over and over, he couldn't hear anything. Not even his own wild thoughts.

"Stop! You're killing him!" the other boy said.

Not yet. Emile would be done when the face beneath him looked like Austin's. He clenched his fist tighter. His knuckles were numb, so he punched harder. He wanted to feel it, feel what his power could do.

"Stop," the boy said. "Please stop."

—

Emile wandered away from Lost 80 in a daze. He left behind two battered bodies and a crying boy who didn't know whether he should stay or run for help.

As he walked down the gravel road to the guardians' house, he felt strangely calm. Odd, considering what he'd done. His hands still rang from the impact, as if calling out to Bill, echoing his pain.

It wasn't until he stepped through the front door that it all set in. Luckily only Jacob waited up. But the look on his brother's face when he saw Emile's knuckles, his shirt, both stained with someone else's blood—why did it take seeing another's grief for Emile to understand the significance of his actions?

Jacob asked him questions, and Emile answered, and Jacob asked more questions through tears. "They're going to come for you," he said.

"I know."

"You'll be arrested. You can't. You can't just—"

Yes. He knew. He would be expelled. He might go to jail, prison maybe. The guardians would disown him. You couldn't do what he did without consequence. That too was what it meant to be connected.

Jacob put his head in his hands. He wasn't thinking about Emile's future. He was thinking about his own—college, track, his dream girl—the future that once beamed so bright in his mind, now dimmed to a dull flicker.

He wiped his face with the back of his hand. "We have to leave. We can't stay here."

"And go where?"

"I don't know. Someplace far away."

Emile thought of Jonestown. "No. It's my fault. I should go."

"Are you serious?" Jacob said. "You can't even drive."

Emile sat down on the couch next to his brother. His hands had stopped ringing, and now throbbed with a dull ache. He stretched them to relieve the pain, rested them on his jeans. In his front pocket he could feel the note from Austin. He'd picked it up when the fight was over, though he still hadn't read it. He didn't know if he ever would.

"You didn't see what they did to him."

"I know."

"No," Emile said. "You don't. What they said, what they were thinking—that's what they say and think about me. All the time. And they don't even know me. They don't know what I can do."

Emile sunk into the couch. Finally, his brother spoke. "We need help. I don't know how or where, but we have to do something."

"There's nothing you can do," Emile said. "It's who I am."

"Hey," Jacob said. "Stop acting like you're alone in this."

"Sure."

"I mean it. I'm going to help you, okay? We're going to figure this out. I promise."

Jacob patted Emile's hand where it hurt. "Let's start by getting you some ice."

"Thanks." He disappeared into the kitchen, leaving Emile on the couch rubbing his knuckles. Jacob was right. He needed help. And no one here could help him. No one could understand.

Emile leaned back and closed his eyes. But in the dark he saw Bill's face, grinning, then disfigured. He saw Austin, happy then broken. Jacob returned with an ice pack. Emile kept his eyes shut. Did he fall asleep? He heard Jacob's voice. *Wake up. We have to leave.* He pushed the voice aside. Another floated in. His mother's, perhaps. No, it was Ginny. It was earlier in the day. She was talking about the capstone project, telling the class that no one was allowed to research Jonestown. That was her thing. They had to find their own. Besides, she explained, it ended terribly. "You don't want the same for you," she said.

"So what do we do?" a boy said. It was Art, the guilty one. "Where do we start?"

Ginny threw up her hands. "Haven't you been listening?" (*Wake up*, Jacob said. *Come on, it's not safe.*) "When I say 'we're all connected,' do the words even register? Or do they pass through you like a ghost?"

And when she said "ghost," she smiled at Emile. And her face flickered. It transformed. To Austin, to Jacob. Then to the blurred image of his mother.

Come on. I think I hear sirens.

Emile opened his eyes. The noise grew louder.

CHAPTER THREE

███████████ III Lia

In the beginning, Lia searched for answers. She asked what she thought were the right questions. *What happened at Limetown? What were they doing there? Where was her uncle, Emile?* The government appointed a Limetown Commission, which issued a brief summary of what they knew so far. They didn't reveal much, only a description of the town—how many houses, how many shops, how many people, and their names. The summary did not say what everyone wanted to know, which was what they were doing in Limetown, nor did it speculate as to what happened to its three hundred plus inhabitants. There was a large facility at the edge of the town, the commission could tell you that, but what was going on inside they had no idea. They promised a comprehensive report after a thorough investigation.

Perhaps it was her intuition, as Miss Scott had called it, but Lia was convinced that while the rest of the world waited for the Limetown report, she could find the answer. She waded through the Internet, rereading a hundred different news stories, all of which reported the same facts with different words. One writer's *disappearance* was another's *vanishing*, a *fading into thin air*. One reporter wrote that everyone *evaporated*, as if what happened was as natural as the weather.

From there she sifted through Limetown conspiracy sites, with theories as poorly constructed as the virus-plagued web pages where they resided. Alien abductions. Interdimensional travel. Secret organization of the world's richest and most powerful. None of it made sense, and as time went by, the articles appeared with less frequency and the posts on the conspiracy sites went cold. People moved on. Except for Lia and her parents. For months afterward, they continued to search.

Lia graduated that spring, near but not at the top of her class. Miss Scott said she could have been valedictorian, if only she applied herself, but it became increasingly difficult to care about anything other than her family, and, by extension, Limetown. She told Miss Scott this when she missed multiple article deadlines. She told her sometimes her mom left and was gone for days, and when she returned she acted like nothing happened. Lia asked her parents questions. She tried the tricks Miss Scott taught. Her parents didn't break. They said, "Worry about your own work."

Miss Scott said, Lia, you're not the only one living with loss. We're all working with ghosts looking over our shoulder.

Lia graduated. Miss Scott left on vacation, and every student pretended it was normal to go from seeing each other every day to hardly at all, or never again. When the summer was over, Lia would move to New Hampshire to attend the same small and expensive college where Miss Scott had done her undergrad, though she wouldn't be in New Hampshire for long. Her mother had convinced her to spend the first semester studying abroad. The suggestion had come in between one of her mother's disappearing acts. One of her students, whom her mother had written a letter of recommendation for, had emailed her saying he had to drop out of the program he planned on attending in the fall. He was supposed to spend the semester at Deakin, a public university in Melbourne, but couldn't come up with the funds. "It actually sounds pretty great," Lia's mother said. "You take a couple of classes in the morning and intern in the afternoon or the evening." She explained that it was a little late in the game to apply, but you never know. There might still be an open spot.

"Anyway, I thought it might be good for you," her mother said. "Could be a nice reset button. Plus," she said, "you've never been overseas. Who knows what you're missing?"

At the time the thought of leaving Lawrence, of not just escaping the Midwest but the country entirely, had been very appealing, but with the recent mysteries and her mother's strange behavior, Lia had gradually grown unsure. People went abroad to find themselves. But Lia found it hard to imagine her future when she didn't even understand what was going on in the present. Her mother continued to disappear, but Lia didn't know why. She had an uncle whose connection to her family was a tightly held secret, and who had lived in a town whose population had vanished entirely. How could she think about the next four years when every day threatened to erase what she thought she knew about the previous eighteen?

Before summer vacation started, Miss Scott set Lia up with a job at a small newspaper just outside Lawrence, in a town called Perry. It'll be good for you, Miss Scott said. Something to keep that brain of yours busy. Perry used to be part of Lawrence, Lia learned from Art, her new boss, before the state split the towns into two during redistricting, around the time Lia was born.

"In fact," Art said, "I believe it was the same year. Well, that's something you can check on. That's your job. Check the facts."

Lia was paid little, and the work was tedious, but the tasks were manageable, and there was satisfaction in asking someone a question and getting a definitive answer. Most days she sat at her corner desk playing solitaire, waiting for Art to hand her an article with a bunch of numbers and quotes circled. She could check most of them over the phone, though she preferred to do so in person. Miss Scott had taught her that people talked more face-to-face, when there was less room to hide what they really thought.

In her second week on the job, Art sent her to an old couple's house that was "out in the boonies," as he described it. The article was a boring piece about city expansion. Perry wanted to buy a plot of land, but the couple wouldn't sell. Didn't see the point, they said. They'd lived there their entire lives. Plus, their kids were gone and they didn't need the money.

"They won't answer my calls," Art said. "Go poke around a bit. Check these offer prices the city gave me. You can take a picture if you want, though I doubt we'll run it." Lia asked him for the name of the couple, but he said he couldn't remember. It was Sanders or something. Anyway, she could check that too.

The house was on an old, loose gravel road off of Highway 40. Lia drove slowly up the long driveway, giving the couple plenty of time to hear her approach. No one came out. She climbed the porch, knocked, and waited. She circled around back, found an empty clothesline and nothing more. She was ready to leave when a car pulled up. An old woman stepped out. She was in her seventies, maybe, wore a print dress that was last in style before Lia was born.

"We don't want any," the woman said, and walked past her. Lia told her she wasn't selling anything. She was from the paper. "We don't want that either."

The woman searched in her ancient purse, rattling around pill bottles and a coin purse before digging out a house key.

"I'm just here to check some facts," Lia said. "About the city's offer. Then I'll be out of your hair. My name's Lia. Lia Haddock."

"Haddock?" the woman said. She turned and looked at Lia, her initial suspicion fading. "And you work for the paper?"

Lia nodded. The woman's gray eyes shifted, performing some secret calculation.

"Well then," the woman finally said, "I suppose you better come in."

—

The house was small. Two bedrooms, one bath, one floor. It was the kind of house people were perfectly happy with, until they realized they could have more. So said the woman.

"Is your husband here?"

The house felt and looked empty. In the living room sat a single chair in front of the TV, an ancient box with rabbit ears. There was no couch, no end or coffee tables. In the kitchen there were no magnets on the fridge, no dishes in the sink.

"He's at church." She grabbed a rag from a kitchen drawer and started wiping the TV. A thin layer of dust filmed the screen. "But he doesn't take care of the financials."

"So is it true? You're not going to sell."

"He wants to. Give the money to the church. I imagine he thinks they'll build a new one and name it after him. But it's not our house. Not really. We just look after it."

"You don't live here."

"We live up the street. The city's offered on both. I'm sure the numbers you have are correct, but I'm keeping this house until I die. In case the old residents come back. That's the Christian thing to do."

"When did they leave?"

The woman stopped her dusting. "Many years ago," she said. "Before you were born." For a moment her face softened, perhaps drifting into the past. Finally, she shrugged. "You can look around, if you want. Doesn't bother me. Just don't go in the attic. It's not safe."

Lia left the woman in the living room, though she could feel the woman's eyes on her as she made her way down the hall. Everything creaked, the wooden floors, the doors to the bedrooms. The first room was the master, dark and unadorned. Lia removed the lens cap from the camera that Art had lent her, but there was nothing to capture. No pictures on the wall, only the dark curtains, shielding the room from the harsh light of summer.

The second room was down the hall, opposite the bathroom. It was smaller, a child's room. There were two beds, pushed together awkwardly with no space in between. Lia ran her hand over the walls, found faint lines where crayon had colored torn wallpaper. She opened the closet, empty. When she turned around, she gasped. The woman was standing in the doorway, staring.

"Find everything you need?" she said.

"I didn't find anything."

"That's a shame."

Lia took a picture of the house before she left, from the front yard. The woman stood watching behind the screen door.

"Oh, I need to double-check your name," Lia said.

The woman mouthed her name behind the screen. Lia couldn't hear her clearly, but it sounded like she said "Sinner."

—

After work, Lia went home and was surprised to find both of her parents' cars in the driveway. Inside, they prepared dinner. A special meal, her mother said, in honor of Lia completing her first week of work. (It was only her fifth actual day, but she didn't argue.) Her father chopped vegetables while her mother monitored a sizzling pan of meat. They talked about the weather, a possible thunderstorm. If Lia didn't know better, they could have been any normal family.

But she did know better. That evening, as a distraction from the weird normalcy that had taken over her house, Lia opened a book she found lying on the coffee table. But she couldn't concentrate. She read the same sentence over and over, inadvertently turning the words into a chant. The chant was interrupted by her parents' voices, a murmur until Lia opened the door and their words traveled upstairs. She stepped into the hallway.

"I know, I know," her mother said. "But a woman I met at a conference, she knew someone who worked at this lab. If I could find—"

"And then you'll be done? God, Allie, you just can't help yourself."

"Don't tell me what I can't do."

There was a brief silence, filled by the whistle of a heavy wind.

"Just say what you mean," her mother said. "You don't want him here."

"We tried that."

"That wasn't his fault."

"Of course it was."

"We have to find him."

Her father sighed, as loud as the wind whirring outside. "We can't keep pretending," he said.

"Pretending what?"

"Maybe there isn't anything to find."

The downstairs went quiet. Then the door slammed. A moment later something slammed in the kitchen too, her dad's fist on the table, perhaps. Again and again. A wolf at the door. No, each pound was a question, bouncing in Lia's head. They kept adding up, these questions— about her mother, her uncle, Limetown, about her past and her future.

Lia retreated to her bedroom. She needed to get away from the pounding below. She tried different corners of her room, of the house. The pounding downstairs quieted, but the questions did not. She needed higher ground. She found herself below the attic door. It was late by then, and the day had already begun to replay itself in her mind. The house. The woman, whispering "sinner" behind the door.

Don't go in the attic, she said. *It's not safe.*

Their attic was much smaller than Lia remembered. But it was not unsafe. Years ago, when she was still a kid, her mother strung Christmas lights throughout so nothing could hide in the dark. She'd done the same thing at their old house, or so she said, though Lia didn't remember.

She found the light switch and smiled when the room lit up green and red, yellow and blue. Bright moonlight poured through the attic's circle window, casting a spotlight on a stack of boxes. Lia sat down next to the boxes and opened one. She found old family albums that she'd combed through before with her mother, on a snow day when both their schools were closed. The photos starred a littler Lia, dressed up in a variety of embarrassing outfits, including more than one polka dot dress complete with frilly shoulders, ill-placed hairpins in her short hair. Her parents smiled down at her. Not pictured anywhere was Emile. Or any other family member. No aunts or grandparents, which made sense, she guessed. Her mom and dad had told her so little about their respective families. They were all either dead or disappointing, she was told, and in many cases, both.

In another box she found an old typewriter, preserved in its shell. She clacked it open and found no notes inside, no letters or forgotten messages. Next to the typewriter was an old Polaroid camera and a plastic bag filled with what she initially thought were photos, but upon closer inspection turned out to be postcards from different years and places—Colorado and Utah, Idaho and Oregon. Beneath the postcards were a few books, stuffy poetry and science fiction. Lia thumbed through a few, found a John Donne collection at the bottom, bookmarked at a poem called "The Dream." "Dear love, for nothing less than thee / Would I have broke this happy dream . . ." Lia rolled her eyes, and was about to return the book to the box when she noticed a lump in the book jacket. She fished it out. It was a note, folded into fourths, and on the front was a drawing of a bird, etched deeply into the paper like a carving on a tree. It reminded Lia of a hairpin she used to have as a child, one she lost she couldn't even remember when. On the back of the square was an old piece of tape, which peeled off easily when Lia slipped a fingernail beneath it. The square unfolded, blooming like a flower, revealing neatly written words, addressed to no one.

I watched you for a long time before all of this. You always had that far-off look on your face, like you were tuned into some station only you could hear. You're the only one who gets me. How is that? How do you know who I really am?

Meet me where we meet.

A dark stain rendered the signature illegible.

"Lia?" Someone was calling up to her. The voice was a ghost in the attic. "Honey, are you up here?"

Her eyes adjusted and she could see her dad's head poking up through the attic door. "What are you doing?"

Lia put the book back in its box, but palmed the note like a magician hiding a playing card. "Just bored," she said. "Thought I might build a fort. You know, like old times."

Her dad climbed a few rungs, so Lia wasn't talking to his disembodied head. "Is that Emile's old stuff?"

"I don't know. It's mostly books."

"Your uncle was a big reader. A lot of poetry. He tried to get me into it, but I never understood."

"Does this typewriter still work?"

"I have no idea. Honestly, I thought your mom pitched this stuff a long time ago."

Her dad sighed. The mention of Lia's mother seemed to deflate him.

"Is she back yet?"

He shook his head. "I'm assuming you heard us."

"Hard not to," Lia said. "Was it about Emile?"

"It was."

"You guys never talked about him before."

"He's still family," her dad said. "We're all he's got."

Yes, but wasn't he always family? Hadn't he been family for the last ten years, or however long it'd been since she last saw him? What had changed other than the fact that now he was missing?

"Don't worry about any of this," her dad said. "Worry about having a weird roommate this fall."

"Dad. Come on."

"Look, you know how long it took me to finish school. I took the road less traveled and it got me everywhere except where I wanted to go. You understand?"

Before she could answer, however, before she could tell him he missed Frost's point, or ask him how anyone could know what path was best, the garage door rumbled to life, shaking the attic walls and announcing the return of Lia's mother.

Her dad descended a few rungs, then stopped, his head and neck still visible above the floor. "Hey, Lia. That 'road less traveled' stuff. That's poetry, right?"

"Yes, Dad."

He smiled and climbed down into the hallway. A moment later Lia thought she heard her mother's voice, calling for her dad, apologizing. Or maybe it was the other way around.

—

Art was angry when Lia arrived at work the next morning. The Sinners had had a change of heart. They were going to sell their homes after all, which meant Art had to rewrite the whole damn article.

"But I just talked to them," Lia said. "Mrs. Sinner said she didn't care about money."

"Sinn*ard*," Art said. "And that's just something people say. No one cares about money until they do." He instructed Lia to run by the house again, check the new number. "And grab a pull quote, would you? I'm tired of talking to these people."

Lia drove to the house where she'd met Mrs. Sinnard the day before, but no one was home. She tried their primary residence. It was a mile down the road and identical to the one she'd visited previously, except for a coat of bright sunflower-yellow paint. She peered through the screen door. Mr. Sinnard, Lia guessed, old and overalled, sat in a rocking chair, watching what sounded like the news. He waved Lia in, but didn't speak. On the news, a man recapped the previous day's tragedies. The plane crash was long forgotten; he promised instead to update viewers on Limetown. Lia stood and watched over Mr. Sinnard's shoulder. The update, however, was that there was no update. No one had been found. The government continued to claim the Limetown Commission's investigation was ongoing, but they spoke to the public with the same tone a weary parent tells a pestering child: "We'll see."

Mrs. Sinnard appeared from a back room, her white hair covered with a lavender headscarf, a fanny pack wrapped around her waist. From somewhere Lia couldn't see, a cuckoo clock chirped birdsong. "You've returned."

"You changed your mind," Lia said.

"And the world wants to know why."

"Just Art, my editor."

"Art," she said. "Of course he became a reporter." She looked at Mr. Sinnard, as if for affirmation. But he kept his eyes on the TV.

"You know him."

"We knew everyone, once upon a time. Mostly through church. Back when things like that mattered."

"Is that why you're selling?"

She glanced again at Mr. Sinnard. "You look like him, you know. Those dark eyebrows, thick as caterpillars."

"Who?"

"Your father, of course." Mrs. Sinnard paused. "You didn't talk to him about your visit?"

Lia shook her head. She felt the pounding in her head returning. "Why would I?"

"I guess they never told you about us."

Mrs. Sinnard floated to the dining room window, which faced west toward the other house. "Did you bring your camera?"

"Yes," Lia said. Miss Scott had always said you never know when your word won't be enough.

"Good. There are some things I want to show you in that old house, before it's gone."

—

Mrs. Sinnard drove Lia the short distance to the old house. It was approaching the middle of the day. The sun shone unfiltered, and the air was menacing with humidity. Inside the house was no relief. The Sinnards kept the air off to save money, Mrs. Sinnard explained. She had Lia open the front and back windows, praying for a cross breeze.

"You saw the rooms, yes? But you didn't see the attic." They walked back to the kitchen. The attic door was already open, the ladder down. Mrs. Sinnard pointed up.

"You told me it wasn't safe," Lia said.

"Don't worry: You're a Haddock. You'll be fine."

Lia took a step, hesitated. "What's up there?" she said, but Mrs. Sinnard wouldn't say. Only, "Don't you want the whole story?" Lia looked up. She ran through the different ways an attic could be unsafe. An unstable floor or ceiling. Outdated insulation that irritated the eyes and burned the skin. But what if there was more? She thought of her family's house. What if this attic, like theirs, had its own secrets, boxed away? She had the impulse to find out.

The ladder shook under Lia's weight. She reached for the floor to pull herself up. Her hands came away covered in dust. The air was stuffier up here, the room much darker than her parents' attic. There was no window, no Christmas lights. Lia stepped carefully, scanning the attic, corner to corner, board by board.

She called down to Mrs. Sinnard. "What am I looking for?"

No one answered. The floor groaned beneath her. She made her way to the back, where she found a cloud of cobwebs.

"There's nothing up here," Lia said. "I'm coming down."

Silence.

"Mrs. Sinnard?"

This time came a reply. But it wasn't a voice; it was a slam, a click, and then, darkness. It took Lia a moment to realize what had happened. Mrs. Sinnard had closed the attic door, locked it shut.

Lia's heart jumped in her chest. "Hey! What are you doing?"

Lia crawled back to the door, grasped for a handle that wasn't there. She yelled for Mrs. Sinnard to let her out.

More silence. She yelled again. She counted her breaths like sheep. One, two, three. Four, five, six. "Are you there? Please let me out."

Finally, a voice.

"Not yet. Close your eyes. Are they closed?"

"Yes," Lia lied.

"Now imagine I am gone. There is no one coming to get you. It's you and God. That's it. That's what I saved them from. They prayed and prayed, and God sent me. I saved them, and still they ran away." She started to cry.

Lia's breaths quickened, seven, eight, nine. Ten. "Who? I don't know what you're talking about."

"Your father. And your uncle."

Lia tried to process what Mrs. Sinnard was saying. She closed her eyes, stopped counting her breaths. Her father never talked about the people who raised him. Lia only knew that his guardians had taken him in after his mother was no longer able to care for him and Emile. She'd never thought that his guardians would still be alive. Or that they would live so close by.

"You . . . were their guardians."

"We knew what my husband's sister was."

Not just guardians—family. Lia imagined her dad as a child, holding Emile's hand where she now stood, their troubled mother below. Her dad must've thought of his mother whenever Lia asked to play in the attic. "He never talks about it," Lia said. "He never even told me your name."

A last sob caught on a laugh. "Yes, well, I don't blame him. It wasn't easy for us either."

Lia's breaths slowed.

"All right," Mrs. Sinnard said. "I'm going to let you out now, but you need to promise me that you'll come see me again. Say it's for work. There's a history here. And you're a part of it."

Lia opened her eyes. There was a message on her phone. It was from her dad. *Call me when u can. Something to tell you.*

"Lia? Are you listening?"

She clicked her phone off.

"Yes," she said. "I promise."

—

Lia called her dad on the way back to the newspaper office, half listening the entire time he talked. Her brain was filling up with all the questions she had for him. Why did he never tell her about the Sinnards? Why did he return here, to his hometown, if his childhood was so unhappy? Why would he want them close?

"Apple, are you there?"

He never called her that anymore.

"Family meeting. As soon as you get home."

When Lia didn't respond, he hung up.

—

Family meetings were rarely good news. Normally, the meetings began with a sad attempt at humor by Lia's dad, before getting to the business at hand, which usually involved the ways in which the family was disappointing one another. When Lia entered the living room, her mother and father were sitting on the couch. This family meeting was different. Her father did not joke.

"We've made a decision, your mother and me. Something we think is the best for the family," he said. Lia's mother sat tucked into the corner of the couch, her face pale. Lia stared at the space between her mom and dad and tried not to see it as the most obvious of metaphors. "Lia," her dad said. "Did you hear what I said? We're moving."

"What? Moving? Where?"

"Washington. State. We think. Or Oregon. Your mother likes Oregon. Anyway, somewhere remote and beautiful."

Lia pulled up a map in her head. Even after Australia, her parents would be on one coast, she on the other. "Why?"

Her dad glanced at her mother. He bridged the gulf between them and rested his hand on her knee.

"We could use a fresh start too. And you'll be leaving soon for college, so. We no longer have a reason to stay."

Lia never understood how adults could say something absurd and act like it was perfectly reasonable. "But this is our home."

"I know," her dad said. "But it's just a house. All the things you want to keep but can't take, we can hold on to." He talked a little more, filling in the ancillary details, while her mother turned and stared out the living room window, saying nothing. They wouldn't put the house on the market until the summer was over. They would quit their jobs and find new ones. People do this kind of thing all the time, he said.

Lia looked at her mother for support.

"I don't get why you guys chose to live here in the first place. It doesn't make sense." She thought of the Sinnards, who were also selling a house suddenly. "Nothing makes sense."

"That was your dad's idea," her mother said, finally chiming in.

"Alison."

"Why can't I tell her?"

She took his hand off her knee.

"We came back for Emile," her mother said. "So he would know where to find us."

"Why would he need to find you?" Lia asked. This time her mother glanced at her father before she continued.

"Because he's done this before," her dad said. "Disappeared, then—"

"Not like this," Lia's mother said.

"Well . . ."

"Like when he and dad dropped out of high school," Lia said.

Her parents looked at each other. "How do you know about that?" her dad said.

Lia could have told him the truth then, about how she had come to meet Mrs. Sinnard, and the things Mrs. Sinnard revealed to her after she came down from the attic. Instead, she chose to protect her source.

"I found some postcards in Emile's things. They were all blank, but one had a date. It was from Colorado, I think. Nineteen seventy-nine. I did the math."

"Let's stick to the meeting's agenda," her dad said.

"What else is there to say?" Lia said. "You're moving. I'm moving. That's it."

Her dad's eyebrows—her eyebrows—fell.

He stood up and went out to the backyard, which, he explained, would need a lot of work before the house went on the market.

"He thinks he's doing what's best for us," her mother said, after Lia's dad left. "That's all he wants."

"What about you? What do you want?"

"I want you to go to college."

"Duh."

"Lia," her mother said. "Would you believe me if I told you it wasn't worth it? Finding the answers to all these questions you have. All this trouble." Lia didn't say anything. Her mother smirked. "Yeah, me neither."

Lia curled up in her chair. "I want to," she said. "I just— it's like there's this part of my brain that won't turn off."

She stopped there. She didn't tell her mother about her trouble sleeping, how lately she'd lie in bed, different scenarios running in her head—her mother leaving, not returning, Emile returning, Emile not returning, her parents learning that he was dead or, worse yet, never learning anything at all—how she analyzed everything she'd seen or heard that day, seeing a mystery in every little thing, pulling every thread, so that when morning came, she woke up feeling unraveled.

"It takes practice," her mother said.

"Or distance."

Her mother looked at Lia, annoyed. Her eyebrows were different from Lia's and her father's. Lighter, livelier.

"I got you something," she said, and went to the kitchen. She returned with a small box. "It's a GPS," her mother said, before Lia had a chance to open it.

"I see that. What for?"

"For the one-month anniversary of your graduation."

Lia didn't tell her that wasn't for two weeks still. She turned the box over in her hands. "Sure you don't want to keep it? You know, for your big move."

"Lia, this is what's best. For the family."

"Yes," Lia said. "You seem real excited."

Her mother sat back down. She shook her head and laughed. "Okay, Lia. You're an adult, right? You tell me what I should do. Should I look for Emile? And how do I do that and keep this family together?"

"Mom."

She leaned forward. "No, let's hear it. Should I drive all night to Limetown? Because I've done that. Should I show up on that asshole Villard's doorstep and promise not to move until I got answers? Did that too. And guess what? I got nothing."

She leaned back against the couch, her arms crossed.

"You know your dad went to the police, looking for me? I can't leave him again like that. He doesn't deserve it."

Lia didn't have the answers either.

It would be days before they would look at or speak to each other again. Lia accepted the spot at Deakin as an apology to her mother.

—

A couple of weeks passed. When Lia wasn't at work, she hid in the attic. Her parents had gone from never around to home all the time, and the attic was the only place she could be alone. She knew she should have been packing. But for every box she packed downstairs, she allowed herself to open one above. Few were labeled, which allowed Lia to make up her own stories about whom they belonged to. A pair of hiking boots, her dad's size. She remembered her dad telling her that before Lia was born he backpacked through national parks in Colorado and Utah. But why couldn't the boots belong to Emile? Maybe he liked to hike too. Maybe before he left he gave them to her dad and said, *Here, hold on to these for me. Until I come back*.

What Lia liked she kept for herself. A yellow scarf, for example, soft and warm. A Moleskine notebook, its pages blank. An old pin from the World's Fair. All these she hid in her room, safe from the emptying of the house, in a box she labeled COLLEGE.

On the weekend, she lied to her parents (as, she believed, they had lied to her), and drove to Mrs. Sinnard's house. Mrs. Sinnard liked Lia to come on Sundays, while her husband was at church. When Lia asked her why she didn't go anymore, she explained that she had an entire life to say her piece to God. If He hadn't gotten the message by now, she doubted He ever would.

They drove the mile to the vacant house together. A few city workers were planting poles for construction fencing, outlining the property borders, preparing the house's demolition.

"It comes down on Wednesday," Mrs. Sinnard said. "Middle of the week, just like that."

It was another humid day. Scattered thunderstorms teased relief.

"How often did you visit the house? When my dad and uncle lived here."

"We were never invited." She took Lia's hand, and they walked around to the back of the house. One of the workers had spray-painted a big X on the side, so there wouldn't be any confusion as to what should be destroyed. "After their father left, I never saw those boys. Not once. When she went to the store, she locked them in the attic."

"How do you know what it was like, if you were never allowed inside?"

"Your father told me. The night they ran away. They walked all the way to our house. I'm not sure how they found it. I know it doesn't seem far by car, but that night there was a major snowstorm. When they made it to our doorstep, only your father's feet were cold. He must've carried your uncle the entire way."

She let go of Lia's hand and drifted inside, through the back door. Inside, the house was gutted. The drywall and plaster had been torn down, the copper wire and piping ripped out. Lia followed Mrs. Sinnard as she floated from room to room, her arms folded across her chest, as if a chill followed her wherever she went.

"Why hasn't he ever mentioned you?"

Mrs. Sinnard ran her hand over the windowsill, which was painted shut. "We should have been better to them, but we were afraid, like everyone else."

"Afraid?"

In the window, Mrs. Sinnard lowered her eyes. "We'd been parents once before. It didn't work out."

Lia stepped closer. "And that's why you were afraid? You're not telling me everything."

"No, I am not."

"Why?"

She stood by the window; sprinkles beat the pane.

"Because I'm still afraid. And you should be too."

"Of what?"

"Of what happens," Mrs. Sinnard said, "when your uncle is around."

The rain started to come down in full, the drops turning into fat punches. Lia looked out the window. She was from Kansas. A storm like this was nothing. Still, she felt a tingle of fear, picturing a grown woman afraid of a boy. Still afraid after all this time.

"Tell me," Lia said. And when she refused, Lia tried using every technique she'd learned from Miss Scott, but all Mrs. Sinnard said was:

"Let's get out of here before the whole thing comes crashing down."

—

Mrs. Sinnard asked Lia to return on Wednesday, the next time her husband attended service, which was also the day of the demolition. Lia agreed, but explained that she wouldn't be around much longer after that. She told her about Australia and how her house was filling up with boxes.

"Once I'm gone, I doubt I'll come back," Lia said, hoping to speed up whatever revelations remained.

"I see," Mrs. Sinnard said. But she would not share the secrets Lia most wanted to hear.

Work was uneventful Monday, though on Tuesday the article about the Sinnards' properties finally ran. Art ended up placing one of Lia's photos along with it, the first of anything significant she created for the paper that made it to print. She worked late that evening, helping Art fact-check a back-to-school weekend insert. The sun had long set by the time they were finished, and when she got home, the house was dark. Lia magnetized the article with her photo to the fridge and called for her parents as she weaved through towers of boxes in the living room. Through the sliding glass door that led to the yard, Lia saw her father, standing in front of a sizable bonfire.

Out back the air was thick with smoke. Lia thought of the bonfire at Lost 80, Brad's vigil, which somehow felt like a lifetime ago, though the memory of returning home and finding her mother, pale and panicked, still raised her skin. She touched her father's elbow.

"Where's Mom?"

Her dad shrugged. He had a beer in his hand, and several empties littered the grass around him. "Gone," he said. "Always chasing, never realizing."

He was practically singing. Lia asked him where she went.

"Who? What, when, where, and why. These are the questions, honey." He finished his beer and dug another from a cooler. "Who, your mother. What? I don't know. When and where, I don't know that either. But why!" He toasted the star-speckled sky. "For Emile. Always Emile."

He sat down in a lawn chair.

"Do you know when she's coming back?"

"I do not."

He lowered his head to his chest, in shame or sorrow, it was difficult to tell. Lia hadn't seen him like this before. She turned away and stared at the fire. It was then that she saw what sat atop the flames. The burnt clothes, the curling boxes. Books of poetry, their words on fire. Lia circled around to find the other items, some of which refused to burn. The typewriter was blackened but otherwise unimpressed by the heat. Her hand went to her neck, and she thought of the yellow scarf, safe in her room, hidden at the bottom of her box for college.

"What if he comes back?" Lia asked.

"He won't. He left that stuff the last time he was here. You were little. You don't remember."

Lia shook her head. She didn't tell him that she tried to, that she wore his scarf and rubbed his pin, hoping for a memory, a piece that would solve the puzzle.

"Why did he leave?"

"Why did your mother leave? Why does anyone leave? Either because they're cowards or martyrs. Maybe both."

"Mom's not a coward."

"No," her dad said, "she certainly is not." He picked up a branch and poked at the fire, stirring the embers. Lia left him out there to watch what remained burn.

She went inside and up to her room. The walls were blank. There were boxes where there weren't boxes before, labeled in her mother's handwriting. She must've grown tired of Lia dragging her feet. Lia found the college box in the back of her closet, where she'd left it. She dug for Emile's book of John Donne's poetry, which she'd stashed with the yellow scarf. She opened the book to the note, thinking that if she reread it, she might discover something hidden between its lines. But there was another note paper-clipped to the original that she hadn't seen before. She did not recognize the handwriting, though as she read it, the voice sounded familiar.

> *Here is what I will not do. I will not tell you how sorry I am. You are right not to want me here. I will not tell you where I'm going. You are right not to follow. And I will not tell you what you mean to me, what you have always meant. You are right not to care.*
>
> *But I will tell you this. You are the only one who understands me. This house, everyone inside, is the closest I've ever come to a home. Should anything happen to me, know that my last thought resides here.*
>
> *And now good-morrow to our waking souls.*
>
> *E*
>
> *P.S. Tell the Apple I love her.*

E was Emile. Lia was the Apple. That she understood. It was what her parents liked to call her, though she didn't remember why. The rest confirmed what she'd gleaned. Emile had stayed with them when she was little. He was happy. Then something bad happened. Something he had done? He left. Where did he go?

Mrs. Sinnard had said she was afraid of what happens when Emile was around. Lia suddenly felt that she could not wait until tomorrow to find out why. She wanted to go to the Sinnards' house tonight. Mr. Sinnard would be angry, Mrs. Sinnard would be startled, but before she knew it, summer would be over. They were running out of time. Lia could be direct and forceful, as Miss Scott had taught her, and in doing so, she would finally get the answers she needed.

—

The streets were empty. The sky was the same. It was past ten when Lia drove up the long dirt road to the Sinnards' house. The living room light was a beacon.

No one answered when she knocked, though she could hear the

TV inside. She kicked a begonia pot by the front door, frustrated. She knocked louder, until finally the locks clacked and the door opened, revealing a sliver of Mr. Sinnard's face.

"It's you," he said.

"I need to see her."

He opened the door slightly, but stood in her way. "It's late."

Lia ducked under his arm. She scanned the living room and kitchen, before starting down the hall.

"Excuse me. What do you think you're doing?"

"I can't wait," Lia said. Her head and her heart throbbed. Both of the bedroom doors were shut. She opened the first door, an unused guest bedroom.

"Have you lost your mind?"

She opened the other.

Mrs. Sinnard was asleep. A Bible lay folded across her chest. A small lamp cast the room in low light. Next to the lamp were a glass of water, her fanny pack, and several bottles of pills.

Lia sat next to her on the edge of the bed.

Behind her Mr. Sinnard said, "I told you."

"Mrs. Sinnard," Lia whispered. "It's me." She took Mrs. Sinnard's hand, cold and clammy.

"That's enough," Mr. Sinnard said.

Mrs. Sinnard's eyes shot open, as if she'd woken from a terrible dream. She coughed. Lia handed her the glass of water.

"My mother is gone. I think she went looking for my uncle."

Mrs. Sinnard took a slow sip of water.

Lia took the glass back, held it hostage. "Why are you afraid of Emile? What happens when he's around?"

Her face fell at the mention of his name. "People get hurt," Mrs. Sinnard said. "It was the same way with their mother. I can't explain it. Trouble follows that family."

"You mean my family."

Mrs. Sinnard stared at the water, her mouth shut. Lia handed her the glass. She sat up and drank what was left in one long gulp. When she was finished, she lay back down and closed her eyes.

"She won't find him, you know. She's too far behind."

"Behind?"

"The people who were here before."

"Before? What people?"

"Before you and I ever met." She pulled the blanket up to her chin. "They were in suits. They said it was about the house; they were assessing its value or something. They asked a lot of questions, about the house, its history, about the people who lived there before. They were a lot like you."

"What did you tell them?"

"I told them they were wasting their time because I wasn't selling. But they didn't really seem to mind. They asked if your dad ever came out here. I said no. What about his brother? they asked, and again I told them no. After those boys left, they never came back."

"What do you think they wanted?" Lia said.

"I don't know. The whole thing was odd. Anyway, a few weeks later you showed up. A sign from above that I should sell."

"Me? Why did that matter?"

"Well, when it was clear your father never even told you about me, I realized I was too old to be caring about a past that didn't care about me."

Mrs. Sinnard's eyes stayed shut, as Lia considered what she meant. Mrs. Sinnard had been holding onto the house down the road all these years, hoping Lia's father and uncle might return. But her father had lived one town over Lia's entire life, and he'd never even mentioned her existence.

"Those men," Lia said. "Did they say they were from the city?"

"That's what I'm trying to tell you," Mrs. Sinnard said. "I don't think they were."

—

Lia drove to Lost 80. It was late; her dad would be worried, but she needed time to think. She sat under the island tree. If this were a news story, there was not much she could report. Few facts, a lot of speculation, an elderly source a reader would have no problem dismissing. But a part of her also knew that she was heading in the right direction, even if she had no idea what that direction was or where it would take her.

She woke to a hand holding her own, the same way she had jolted Mrs. Sinnard from a bad dream.

"I thought you might be here," her dad said. He clicked his flashlight off and sat next to her.

"How'd you know?"

"This was one of your uncle's favorite spots. Back then it was more of a secret."

Lia flipped her phone open to check the time. It was dead.

"It's after two," her dad said, "well beyond the time for me to freak out." Lia apologized. Her dad squeezed her hand. "It's funny, when you're a parent, a part of your brain never stops worrying."

"I know, Dad."

"No, you don't. You can't, and you shouldn't. When I was your age—" He let go of her hand, rubbed his eyes. She could still smell the fire on him. "I don't know what I'm trying to say."

Lia patted his knee. Crickets and frogs were out in full force, greeting one another, or sounding the alarm.

"I saw your article," her dad said. "On the fridge. That was our house, you know. I lived there."

"I know," Lia said. She didn't tell him about Mrs. Sinnard. She wasn't sure if he would want to know. "Why did you leave them? The Sinnards."

"We went looking for our mother."

There was an awkward silence as they both thought about Lia's mother, also missing.

"Lia, I mean it, I was worried sick."

"I'm sorry."

"You can't just disappear on me too."

Even with the chirping, Lia could hear the concern in his voice. She tried to put herself in his shoes.

Lia stood up. She found her dad's shadow and laced her arm in his. He could be the credible source. He was close to it all. But for now, she just put her head on her father's shoulder and pretended that his feelings were more important than the answers she sought.

She squeezed his hand like he had hers. She was leaving—she had to—but she knew deep down that the questions about her mother, her uncle, and Limetown would always follow her.

"Dad," she said. "I'll be fine. I'm going to Australia, not the moon."

CHAPTER FOUR

▐▌▌▌ Emile

Jacob drove the long gravel road away from the guardians' house. Neither brother talked about what just happened, what Emile did to those boys at Lost 80, or what it meant for them to leave like they did. Without warning, without telling anyone, and without Jacob finishing school.

They drove west. Once they were on the highway, Jacob turned the radio loud to stay awake, he said, but also to keep Emile out of his head. He listened to country music, sad songs about whiskey and betrayal. Emile decided to respect Jacob's privacy, considering what his brother had just sacrificed for him—graduation, and the dream that went with it. But this meant that he had no idea where they were going, only that they were looking for their mother, who, despite what she had done, was the only person they could think of who could help them understand why Emile was the way he was.

Emile drifted in and out of sleep. There were no lights, few towns, and little elevation once they made it past the Flint Hills. Outside the world looked as if it were underwater, so far beneath the surface the sun and moon were just memories. Each time Emile woke he waited for a road sign to give him another clue. In between dreams he wondered about the people they left behind, for better or worse. What would happen to Austin? What would happen to the guardians? Would either of them come looking for them or, with a sigh of relief, would they wipe their hands and say good riddance?

"I have an idea," Jacob said as they cruised Kanorado, a town that was more of a border marker than an actual destination. He turned the radio down between songs and let Emile in. Emile saw two hands wrapped around a book. His mother's hands. She turned the page and pointed at a picture. It was a beautiful landscape, mountains all around. Jacob recognized the beauty of the scenery, even though it felt a universe away.

"Where is that?" Emile said.

"Archer Park," Jacob said. "A small town north of Estes. She used to talk about it all the time."

"You think she went there? When she disappeared?"

"I think it's a start," Jacob said, and he tried to turn the radio up before Emile could peer any deeper. But Emile caught his hand.

"Wait," he said, "how long have you had this idea?"

"I don't know," Jacob said. "A long time, I guess."

"Why didn't you ever tell me?"

"Because she left us, Emile. We might have been the ones who ran away that night, but she's the one who disappeared for good."

Emile looked at his brother. His face showed no emotion as he stared at the road. But inside there was a cresting wave. Sadness, bitterness, and anger. Emile watched him for a moment, before Jacob finally turned the radio back up, ending the conversation. They drove across the Kansas-Colorado border, through Denver and Boulder, under the cover of night. Emile stared out the window, and every once in a while he caught a glimpse of a mountain silhouetted by the moon, hovering.

He woke at a truck stop just outside Archer Park, a little after dawn. Jacob was outside the car, gazing down at the town blanketed in fog. "It's strange, isn't it?" he said. Emile followed his brother's eyes, which landed on a large white house hanging above the fog. "That's the Eldridge. Looks like something out of a painting."

Jacob got back in the car and they descended into town. The Eldridge was a hotel, Jacob had explained. Supposedly haunted. Famously so. He pointed and narrated their entire first lap around Archer Park, as images from their mother's book came to life. This little park, this quaint pizza place. If there was a plan beyond this for finding their mother, Emile didn't know it. Jacob seemed content following the landmarks of his memory.

Eventually the sun rose, watery behind the gray sky, and out came the dead, workers stumbling around downtown until the coffee kicked in. Jacob parked at the hotel, tapped the dashboard clock. "We should be in school now," he said. As if on cue, a yellow bus rumbled by. Emile thought of Ginny's class. He saw her taking attendance, calling Emile's name, calling Austin's, and no one responding. The students would look at one another. Already, the rumors about what happened at Lost 80 would have started to fly. Miss Scott, with her self-proclaimed investigative prowess, would learn the truth. She had not asked the right questions the day she and Emile met.

"I'm going inside," Emile said, and kicked open the car door. Jacob followed Emile through the visitors' lot and up the stairs to the front entrance. The main lobby of the Eldridge was a wide-open space covered in wood. The floor, the walls, the beams that held the ceiling in place—every part looked tailor-made to creak in the night.

They were too early for check-in, not that they could afford to stay. The lobby was mostly empty. An old couple sat by an enormous fireplace, its hearth still glowing with last night's embers. The woman spoke loudly to her nearly deaf husband. She was awake all night, she said, bored out of her mind, while her husband snored by her side. She said she wished a ghost would visit her. At least then she would have someone to talk to.

"What would ghosts want with someone our age?" the old man said with a laugh. "We're practically their peers."

Emile found Jacob at the opposite side of the lobby, staring at a framed American flag hung above a large bookcase. With no one to stop them, they wandered the hotel. They took the grand staircase to the second floor, walked its narrow halls, and Emile tried to take in every detail. The yellow carpet, the heavy doors, the doorknobs engraved with the initials *SE*. They paused at the odd-numbered rooms. A hotel pamphlet Jacob took from the front desk said that out of all the rooms rumored to be haunted, none were even. Emile put his ear to several doors and listened, but most guests were asleep, their rooms quiet. It was the same on the third and fourth floors. At the south end of the fifth, through a small service door, they discovered a large stair-well. If you peered down the well, the pamphlet read, you could see all the way down to the basement.

"A maid threw herself down this stairwell," Jacob said, "suppos-edly."

He quoted the pamphlet: " 'Several workers and the occasional straying guest have reported strange sounds coming from the bottom of the well. Some say a low moan, others a sharp cry.' "

Emile listened for a moment. "I don't hear anything."

"Of course not," Jacob said. "It's just a story."

They continued to stare into the black well. "You think she worked here?" Emile said.

"She didn't have any other skills. Didn't finish high school—"

The realization cut him off. Emile wanted to reassure him. He would return to Lawrence whether or not they found their mother here, and finish school. But Jacob's mind was full of doubt, something that Emile had rarely felt in his brother. "Let's get out of here," Jacob said.

Downstairs the lobby had become busy, as guests descended from their rooms. Jacob waited off to the side, by the fireplace, while Emile asked the receptionist if an Elizabeth Haddock worked there, had ever worked there. The front desk apologized, saying that that sort of information was private, and that if Emile wasn't a registered guest, he should probably come back when the official tours started, around noon.

Outside, the gray parted, revealing a warm sun that accompanied Jacob and Emile as they continued their self-guided tour of the hotel grounds. There was a small barn off to one side of the hotel, where residents could rent an old horse for a scenic trail ride. On the other side sat a large A-frame that once served as a guesthouse for Eldridge's friends and family, and had been converted into a chapel for guest weddings.

Emile sat down on the chapel steps. He had begun to feel the el-evation. His head ached, his body buzzed, and he suddenly felt both exhausted and discouraged.

Jacob stood above him, consulting the pamphlet. "We should check one more thing, then we can go."

He left Emile sitting there and headed up the hill behind the hotel. Emile followed him toward a fence guarded by trees, enormous pines standing sentry. The path ended at an open gate with a sign that read EMPLOYEES ONLY. Behind the fence were two smaller hotels, or so it seemed. Long buildings with three floors, curtained windows, blinds drawn. A kid around their age exited one of the buildings, carrying a duffel bag.

"This is where they live," Jacob said.

"Who?"

"The workers." He pointed to the left, to the right. "Guys, girls."

Two girls in uniforms, about the same age as the other kid, emerged from the other dorm. Jacob watched them until they disappeared through the gate. Emile heard him think about college, wonder if this was what it would have been like.

"She wouldn't have worked here," Jacob said.

"Why not?"

"Look. They're all teenagers." He was right. Every worker they'd seen here, even the person they'd spoken to at the front desk, was young.

"But this place must have been important to her," Emile said. "Why else would she have shown you the book?"

"She could have visited once," Jacob said. "Or maybe she worked here before we were born. But she wouldn't have come back here." The brothers didn't know the exact age their mother was when she disappeared, but Jacob guessed she probably would have been well into her twenties. His mind turned into a street sign that read DEAD END.

They decided to take a lap around, since they were there. But the dorms were locked, and there was nothing behind them except a solitary bench, where a long-haired teen was smoking brazenly near the forest. He was dressed differently from the others, in slacks, a button-down shirt, and a tie that was too big for his narrow frame. When he saw Jacob and Emile, he stood.

"New recruits?" he said. His name was Max. It said so plainly on his name tag.

A light breeze carried Max's smoke to Jacob, who shook his head. Jacob disliked cigarettes and anyone who smoked them.

"Then you probably shouldn't be here."

"We're looking for someone," Emile said. "We think she might've worked here once."

"Never mind," Jacob said, "it doesn't matter."

"What's her name?"

"Elizabeth," Emile said, before his brother could stop him. "Elizabeth Haddock."

"Haddock," Max said. "Haddock. Nope. Can't say I've had the pleasure." He took a long drag. "But a lot of people don't last very long. Can't cut it, you know. Others are just weirdos. Obsessed with the mystery of the place. Ghosts and what have you."

The word *crazy* drifted across Max's mind.

"She wasn't crazy," Emile said. He felt his name-calling defenses, honed during high school, go up.

"Who said she was, chief?" Max eyed Emile suspiciously as he puffed the last of his cigarette. He patted his pockets for the pack, but came up empty. "I'm guessing neither of you fine citizens smoke? No bother. I've got to get to work anyway. These grounds won't tour themselves."

He pulled his hair back into a ponytail, straightened his tie, and started to walk away. He paused at the gate. "Hey, you guys like mountain hiking?"

Emile and Jacob looked at each other. "We're from Kansas," Jacob said.

"Ah." Max thought for a moment. "Well, a few of us are getting together after work, meeting here around midnight. There might be somebody who can help you find what you're looking for. He's worked here even longer than I have. Kind of sad, really. Anyway, your call."

"Thanks," Emile said.

Max bowed. "You're most welcome. Now get the hell out of here. This is private property."

—

They had the rest of the day to kill. Emile could tell Jacob didn't like Max, but since they had no other leads, not to mention nowhere else to go, he had tacitly agreed to meet him that night. They would need hiking boots, so they drove downtown. Tourist season had yet to begin. The streets lay dormant, the kitschy shops empty of everyone but employees and lonely regulars. They bought the cheapest boots they could find, which weren't that cheap and caused Jacob's mind to churn with worry. Emile worried in turn. What if she wasn't here? What if they were wasting their time? What hope to find any answers would Emile have then?

Emile found comfort walking around the carefully cultivated downtown. He couldn't explain it exactly, why he found solace in such an artificial setting. The old-time barbershop, the tiny movie theater, the soda shop. All had the makings of a Hollywood set, some corny show where everything went right, where the conflicts were simple and easy to resolve, and in the end, things would always return to the way they should be.

Later that afternoon, they slept in their car, and after they slept, they ate cheaply at the pizza place. Emile didn't finish his meal.

"You going to eat that?" Jacob asked.

"I'm not that hungry. I think it's the elevation." Emile pushed his half-eaten slice across the table, but Jacob shoved it right back.

"Well, you might want to save it for later. Cuz we're about broke."

"We are?"

"Yes, Emile. Things cost money. Gas, pizza. We're going to need someplace to stay too."

"I know that."

Jacob got up to pay the cashier with the last of their money. Emile followed him out to the car, where Jacob sat with the keys in the ignition, but the engine off.

"Okay, I know that you're mad. You don't like Max. You're worried this isn't going to work. You won't make it back in time to finish school. You'll never go to coll—"

"Don't do that," Jacob said. "Don't tell me what I'm thinking." He stared out the windshield for a long moment, and Emile felt his brother's mind swirl, thoughts flowing to meet opposing currents. There was hope and skepticism, bitterness and worry, desire and duty. "I'm going to help you," Jacob finally said. "I said I would help you. But have you considered what will happen if we don't find her? Or, if we do and something really is wrong with her?"

Emile didn't say anything. He had asked himself those questions but hadn't worried about the answers. It was one of the perks of growing up a younger brother, he supposed. He could let Jacob do most of the worrying.

Jacob started the car and turned the radio up. "Never mind," he said. "Let's just forget it."

They drove to the Eldridge. It was dark by then, but they put on their hiking boots anyway and snuck behind the hotel to the employee dorms. The gate was left open. Max and several other workers were gathered around the bench. They were all around Max's age, maybe a little younger, and were dressed in street clothes and sneakers.

Jacob didn't say hello. "I thought we were going hiking."

"I never said that," Max said. "I asked you if you like hiking. You need to work on your deductive reasoning, my man." A few of the workers laughed. "Cool boots, though."

"Are you kidding me?" Jacob said.

"No," Max said, "I really like your boots."

Jacob walked away. Emile let him. "So what are we doing?"

"We're going drinking."

"And then you'll help us?"

"Of course. I believe it was Brother Epp of the Capuchin order who once said, 'Because without beer, things do not seem to go as well.' "

Emile grew impatient. Maybe it was Jacob rubbing off on him. He looked inside Max and felt an excitement, a whirring. But he could get no further.

Max stood on top of the bench and raised his hand. "My fellow Mensa, we are gathered here to celebrate the sacrament of holy matrimony between mankind and alcohol. As the Good Book says, what bottle of booze God places in our hand and joins with our stomachs, let no man put asunder. Also, we have some special guests tonight, so let's show them what it looks like when brilliant minds drink too much and make questionable decisions. To the hooch!" And with that he jumped down and began marching the workers toward the gate. "Come, my brothers!" he shouted behind him. "All will be revealed!"

He led them to the chapel. Emile followed, trying to regain hope, though he could feel Jacob's doubt and annoyance dragging slowly behind. They entered through a hidden door on the side. The lights were off, but the pews and altar glowed with a rainbow moonlight that snuck in through stained glass windows.

Max led everyone down the aisle. "Now, if you pay close attention, you'll notice an equal amount of windows, pews, and doors on each side of the chapel." He spoke loudly, not worried at all about sneaking around after hours. "That's because Shalor Eldridge, the founder of this here hotel, was obsessed with Georgian architecture, the defining characteristic of which, as we all know, is symmetry. In fact, Eldridge applied this idea of symmetry to everything he could think of. Perhaps you noticed that in the hotel, the Eldridge library is opposite the Eldridge gymnasium. This is no accident. 'He who balances his life properly will never have his life hang in the balance,' Mr. Eldridge famously said." Max grinned widely. "This, of course, was right before he hung himself."

Emile glanced at Jacob, to see what he was thinking. He looked more annoyed than anything. Emile was unsure how much more Jacob would put up with, how much either of them could endure before admitting they were wasting their time here. The workers splintered into small groups, drinking and laughing in different corners of the church. Max stayed near Jacob and Emile, who felt tired already and wanted nothing more than to lie down in a pew and sleep forever.

"What exactly are we accomplishing here?" Jacob said.

"We're not accomplishing anything, Haddocks. We're waiting."

"For what?"

"For the Minister. This is a church, isn't it?"

He walked away, joining some of his coworkers, who toasted Max.

"She's not here," Jacob said. "This is stupid."

Emile felt nauseous. "I need to lie down."

"We should leave."

"Wait," Emile said. "Let me sit for a bit."

Just for a moment, he thought. *I only need a moment.* He reclined in the pew and shut his eyes. But when he opened them he could tell that more than a moment had passed. The light had changed. Or, it had left completely.

"There he is," Max said. He offered his hand and helped Emile sit up. "See, he just needed a change of scenery."

The scenery had indeed changed. They had removed him from the church. Gone were the pews, the stained glass windows, and the altar. In their place was the cold slab he currently sat on, yellow work lights, and walls made of stone. A few faces came into focus. Max's. Jacob's. But there was a new face as well, older, someone Emile didn't recognize.

Max patted Emile on the shoulder. "Emile, the Minister. Minister, Emile."

The Minister stuck out his hand. "Please, my name is Vince," he said. He was in his early thirties maybe, though sprigs of white had already begun to sprout in his black hair.

It took Emile a moment to get his bearings. He had passed out, Max said, keeled over just like that. "Your brother wanted to take you to the hospital, but I knew better. Same thing happened to me when I first came here. The other workers too. My theory is that because we're all geniuses, because we use a larger percentage of our brains, we need more oxygen. So while the elevation is bad for everyone, it's particularly problematic for people like me and you. Your brother, well, not so much." Jacob didn't laugh, nor Vince. "Anyway, all we needed was to get you somewhere a little lower. This is where we work best."

Emile wondered where exactly they were.

"We are beneath the hotel," Vince said.

They were more than one hundred feet below the earth's surface, Max explained. Fifty feet above them was a series of tunnels, and above that was the basement. On the basic tour, you could visit the basement, where Eldridge made and stored his moonshine, a watered-down version of which was now available in the gift shop. But if you went on the premium tour, twice the price of the basic, Max would take you even farther down, into the treacherous tunnels, which, if the rumors are to be believed, once served as the western leg of the Underground Railroad. It was in this spirit of freedom that Eldridge chose the location for his family home and hotel, a place where people of all creeds and colors were welcome to stay and breathe in the mountain air.

Here, Max winked at Emile. "But that's not the whole story." For while Eldridge was indeed a fan of history, he was more interested in what lay below the tunnels.

"What was that?"

"Limestone."

"Limestone," Emile repeated.

"That's right," Max said. He explained that Eldridge, like himself, was from the West Coast. He only came to Colorado after a falling out with his father, a gold miner in California who struck it rich. Anyway, the story goes that on his way east to these here mountains, Eldridge fell ill. Probably dysentery, typhoid, or some other disease he picked up on the Oregon Trail. The point is he was in bad shape. Ready to call it, when his second wife brought in some Eastern medicine witch doctor claiming he could cure any ill through the magic of crystals. What did Eldridge have to lose? So the doctor worked his voodoo and voilà, a week later he'd gone from waiting outside death's door to ding-dong ditching the Grim Reaper himself.

The only catch, the doctor told him, was that if he wanted to stay among the living, he needed to find a place where the air and water were as clear as crystals, and where minerals flowed in abundance, untouched by the impure hands of man.

"And here we are," Max said.

"And you believe that," Jacob said, speaking up for the first time since Emile's revival.

"Of course not. It's complete bullshit. Limestones aren't crystals. Eldridge probably just had a bad fever that finally broke. But that doesn't mean this underground is completely devoid of scientific value. Plus, it's a great place to bring a girl."

Emile wanted to laugh. In some ways, Max reminded him of Austin, but that made him remember how he had left Austin, unconscious and covered in his own blood. Even though Emile had defended his friend that night, he still felt guilty for leaving him there alone.

"You're not drinking," Max said. He was already on his third beer. "You need to drink. It'll make what I have to say easier to swallow."

"You haven't told them?" Vince asked.

"He hasn't told us anything," Jacob said.

"I thought they should imbibe some of the sacrament first. Easier to get them out of the fold and into the flock, if you know what I mean."

Vince asked Jacob to sit down next to his brother. "Max should have told you before inviting you here. I apologize."

Jacob ignored Max and spoke to Vince. "We're looking for our mother. Her name is Elizabeth Haddock. She might've worked here. We wondered if she came back here around ten years ago."

Vince rubbed his clean-shaven face, combing his memory. "Haddock," he said, his mind pulling up fleeting images of various women he'd worked with. In one image, he walked a woman down a long, dark hall, his hand on her shoulder. In another, he sat with a different woman on a small bed, his hand trying to steady her trembling knee. "I'm sorry. That was before my time. Why is it you think she came here?"

Jacob thought of the book, his mother pointing and reading to him. It had seemed so important. "Just a hunch."

"I see," Vince said. "Well, the Eldridge has been home to some very gifted young women in its time. From all over."

"She wasn't gifted," Jacob said. "At least, I don't think so."

"Oh. Well, in that case there's no reason she would have stayed here," Vince said, matter-of-factly. "Unless . . . perhaps it wasn't about her." Vince smiled for the first time, revealing off-white teeth. "There must be something about you two, otherwise Max wouldn't have brought you here."

Emile glanced at Max. "What can I say?" Max said. "I have an eye for talent."

"Indeed you do," Vince said. "Max here is the best recruiter we have. Aren't you, Max?"

"Well."

"Go on, Mr. Tour Guide. Tell them what you do. What *we* do. Perhaps it is something they're interested in."

"This isn't why we came here," Jacob said.

"Then perhaps this doesn't pertain to you," Vince said.

Jacob went quiet. Emile could tell his brother wanted to leave, but that he would stay out of pride. And for Emile, whose interest had been piqued slightly. No one before had suggested that he was talented— just different.

"I don't want another history lesson," Jacob said.

Max pretended to brush his hair, straighten an imaginary tie. He stood up straighter, and looked more like a magician than a tour guide, ready to dazzle his audience with a trick they'd never seen before.

"This isn't about the past," he said. "It's about the future."

———

"The Eldridge is not a hotel," Max began. "I am not a tour guide, Vince is not a minister, and if you stayed here, you might look like a bellhop, but you would become so much more." He continued with a caveat. "There is only so much I can tell," he explained. "The rest has to be shown. But only if you say yes. We don't want hotel secrets getting out, should you pass up the opportunity of a lifetime."

"What opportunity?" Emile asked.

Max held up his hand. There would be time for questions at the end. But first, "The human mind is a mystery," he said. "Take my own. I am a genius, self- and board-certified, but I have no idea why. My parents didn't know either. They never understood me, had no idea what to do with me. Used to fight about it all the time, until—"

As he spoke, Emile saw a living room, a fight, a falling glass.

Vince cleared his throat.

"Right," Max said. "Let me put it another way. We've all heard stories about the extraordinary things the mind can do. Whispers about people with 'special powers.' A friend had a cousin who could talk to the dead. So and so's late great grandma could zing a spoon at your head just by looking at it. But no one takes them seriously." Emile felt his face flush, and was glad that no one noticed him redden. "But not here. Not us. The Eldridge welcomes those who claim to be gifted. We don't judge or mock. We listen to what they have to say."

Emile and Jacob exchanged glances.

"You listen," Jacob said. "That's it."

"To create the future, listen to the present. That's our motto," Max said. "I know, it's kind of derivative—we're still workshopping it. Anyway, we, the interviewers, put each subject through a series of tests. All us baby faces might look like we just popped out of a test tube, but we're actually some of the finest scientific minds in the world today. Or, we will be."

Jacob stared blankly. Emile felt the mistiness of his brother's brain as he tried to work out what Max had revealed, simultaneously wanting to know more and to find a reason to dismiss what Max was saying. "Don't tell me you don't understand," Max said. He ran his hands over his face. "Okay. Listen. We are trying to figure out what the mind can do. If we hear about someone special, we find them, invite them here, and study them. That's it. For now, anyway."

"Do you mean . . ." Emile paused before he said the word. He had never used it before, ". . . you study people who are psychic?"

"Sure, I guess you could call them that. "

"You listen to them," Jacob said. "What does that mean?"

"We verify," Max said. "At this stage we're most interested in separating the fact from the fiction."

"Why you? Why are all the workers so young?" Emile asked.

"I told you, Haddocks. We're geniuses. We might not have any psychic powers like our subjects, but we're very good at thinking outside of the box, pushing the envelope of scientific study, or whatever cliché floats your boat. The age thing's just some dumb rule."

"Max," Vince said.

"Well it is. One of the bigwigs read an article that said the human brain peaks at twenty. To tell you the truth, I think they like that we're very impressionable at this age. It means we'll do whatever they want, without asking too many questions."

Vince stepped forward from the shadow, where he had been quietly listening.

"We just came here to find our mother," Emile said, even as he wondered about what exactly they were proposing.

"Is that right?" Vince said. "In that case, you should have little trouble saying no to what I'm about to offer."

—

Emile could hear his brother's mind turning along with his body, which rustled at the over-starched sheets. Max put them up on the Eldridge's top floor, in one of the haunted rooms. They had yet to discuss what Max and Vince proposed. A job, working at the Eldridge, as one of the listeners/scientists. Even though Emile had been adamant that he wasn't a genius. In high school he was an above average student at best. But Vince disagreed. He said that Max wouldn't have brought Emile here if he weren't special.

"You can't seriously be considering it," Jacob said. Emile didn't answer. He folded his arms behind him and gazed at the ceiling, Max's words echoing in his head. "I'm not sure I believe a thing he said," Jacob continued. But of course he did. That was what was so exciting, what was keeping Jacob awake.

Emile sat up. On the wall opposite his bed there was a wide mirror hanging above an empty dresser.

"I mean, you just met these guys," Jacob said. "They're taking advantage of you."

"But we could live here. We would have a place to stay." Emile wouldn't admit it, but already he'd let himself imagine a life at the Eldridge. Working mornings in the hotel, smiling warmly as he completed menial tasks like cleaning rooms or washing dishes in the kitchen. Then, at night, he would join the others. He could help them in their work, listening. He still wasn't sure what that meant exactly, what it looked like, but if there was one thing he was good at, it was listening.

And what if what Max said were true? What if there were people who were like Emile? Who possessed gifts like him. Felt alone like him. What if these were people he could talk to, listen to, learn from? Or, better still, none of the above. What if these were people he would never have to explain himself to, because they were naturally more like him than Jacob or Austin could ever hope to be.

"We came for Mom," Jacob said.

"I know."

"No, you don't get it. Or maybe you do and you're just trying to be nice. They don't want me."

Emile slid down the starched sheets. He didn't bother lying to his brother, pretending what he said wasn't true. Instead, he tried to imagine that same life, staying here, working at the Eldridge, without Jacob. The two of them giving up, it seemed, on ever finding their mother. Suddenly, he felt very alone. He sat back up, and was startled when he caught himself in the mirror. How afraid he looked.

—

Jacob was gone when Emile woke. His bed was made and there were no signs of his belongings.

Emile got dressed and went downstairs. A few guests had descended to the dining room for the complimentary breakfast, staring through bleary eyes at plates of bacon and eggs. Emile recognized the servers from last night, flying from table to table, bright as the new sun. A waitress waved at him, and a busboy threw him a nod, but when asked, neither had seen Jacob. Both said Emile shouldn't worry. Eat, they told him. Free of charge, of course.

Emile pushed through the dining room and into another lobby, with another fireplace, in front of which sat another old couple. The déjà vu dizzied him. Or perhaps it was the elevation. He ran through the second lobby, through another set of double doors, dreading another fireplace. Instead, he found a single door, and through that door a long hallway that reeked of chlorine. No one had mentioned a pool. He looked for a sign, but there weren't any. The hallway stopped abruptly, as if the architect had made a mistake. There was a window at the end, and a door on the side that was locked. When Emile looked out the window, he didn't recognize any of the landscape. There were steep green hills lush with trees, more scenic and beautiful than anything in Kansas, but nothing he could attach any meaning to. He looked out the window for a while, not knowing where his brother was, and for the first time since they drove away from what had been their home, he felt lost.

He managed to find his way back to the second lobby. The old couple had vanished. In their place was a young man kicking his sneakers in front of the fire. Max.

"You look bewildered, Haddocks. Like you've come to a fork in the road, picked it up, and jabbed yourself in the eye."

"I was looking for my brother."

"Did you check the lobby?"

"This is a lobby."

"This is the east lobby. You want the west. Or maybe it was the north?" Max grinned to himself. "Your brother doesn't want you to stay, Haddock. He's speaking to the big man right now."

"Vince?"

"No, not Vince. The big man. You got corn growing out your ears?" Emile didn't understand. He opened his mouth, but was shushed. "Not here," Max said. "Follow me."

They went down to the tunnels, to the limestone. "The wonderful thing about being so far below the earth," Max said, "is that no sound can make its way in or out. Eldridge, for all his genius, was quite paranoid. He conducted all his meetings underground, even though it's damn near impossible to heat."

They wound their way through the tunnels, and the deeper they went the more Emile felt he was going the wrong direction. They emerged into a different space from the night before. The lighting was better and there was more room. There were a few picnic tables, some stools, and what looked to be a full bar.

"Coffee?" Max asked. He stepped behind the bar and poured himself a cup. Emile was too anxious to sit. "Your brother found me this morning," Max said. "He told me what was plaguing him. And he's not wrong. Not completely, anyway. They don't want him. They want you." Max leaned on the bar. "And his concerns aren't without merit.

There's a lot going on here, Haddock. And from what I can tell, it's not all paradise."

"You're here."

"For now," Max said. "But I'm about to age out."

Max took his mug in both hands, blew away the steam. Emile looked down at his own hands, which held nothing.

"Ah, don't go all mopey on me. I'm off to college! The best years of my life, isn't that what they say? I'm going to meet a beautiful girl, fall in love, make some babies. Everything goes right, I'll be changing the world and diapers by the time I'm thirty."

Emile paced the bar. Max's plan reminded him of his brother's, which reminded him that if he chose to stay here, he would be starting over, alone.

"What would I do?" Emile said. "If I stayed."

"Depends on your talent. Right now I'm into parapsychology. You know, paranormal phenomena. But as you can tell, I'm really good at talking to people. Helps a ton when I'm interviewing. A lot of these people, they've been laughed at their entire lives. They need to believe I'm someone they can trust."

"Are you?" Emile asked.

"Most of the time."

Emile didn't know what to do. "I want to talk to my brother."

"Of course you do. The thing is, he's with the big man now, and the big man has the gift of gab. Or at least, he can when he wants to." He drummed his fingers on the bar. "Why don't we go see a movie? There's a small theater in town that shows old movies sometimes. Maybe they'll play *The Wizard of Oz* for you."

"I've never seen it," Emile said.

"Really?" Max laughed. "And yet you walk around here like a twirling tornado dropped you out of the sky."

"I don't want to see any movies," Emile said. "Either take me to my brother, or show me your work so I can make up my mind."

"I can't," Max said. "There are rules, Haddock. Consequences." His mind flashed to a young woman in tears, dragging her packed bag down the dorm hill and through the open gate, Vince locking it behind her. Max leaned over the bar. Emile could feel Max's mask slipping. "Remember, there's nothing you have that can't be taken away. You might think you don't have anything. You might say to yourself, how can they take away something that isn't there? But they'll find it. Whatever it is you have. And they'll make it disappear."

He held Emile's stare. Finally, Max leaned back from the bar and took a casual sip from his cup, readjusting his mask.

"Show me," Emile said.

Max shook his head. "All right, fine. You want us both kicked out, that's up to you." He dumped the mug into the sink. "You know, for someone who doesn't know anything about Oz, you sure are interested in what's behind the curtain."

———

Max made Emile change into his hiking boots. Emile didn't understand why until they got in Max's jeep and started driving into the mountains. In a matter of minutes Archer Park was fully behind them. It was a clear, chilly April day, too cold to be riding around in an uncovered vehicle. The air roared around them, making it impossible for Emile to ask any questions, which, he supposed, was probably the point.

Twenty minutes later Max pulled off onto an unassuming dirt road, which stopped at an unmarked trailhead. Max cut the engine. "All right," he said, "let's hoof it."

"There's nothing out here."

Max got out. "That's kind of the idea." Emile stayed in the jeep. "What's wrong? You afraid, Haddock? Big brother's not around?"

Max slapped the hood and set off down the trail. Emile kicked the door open and ran after him.

Max laughed at each question Emile asked along the way. No, they didn't conduct any experiments at the hotel. Would be a bit risky, don't you think? A guest wanders through the wrong door and, whoops, there's a secret lab.

They came to a shack, what looked like a rest stop for weary hikers. Max detached a nest of keys carabinered to his hip. "Pretty high-tech, huh?" He opened the door to the shack and disappeared inside. "Come on, Dorothy," Max called. "Toto is waiting."

Emile peered in vain into the darkness. He told himself he wasn't afraid, that he didn't wish his brother were there.

They spiraled down a surprisingly noisy metal staircase. At the bottom there was a desk, and at the desk sat the young woman who waved at Emile back in the dining room. She eyed him suspiciously. "Relax," Max said. "He's with me." Max led Emile down a long, poorly lit hallway. Emile didn't notice the doors at first, or their windows. He passed room after room, keeping his head down, until he remembered that he was here to look.

Max stopped at a door. He slid open a window. A woman approached. She looked old enough to be Emile's mother.

"Don't worry," Max said. "It's not as bad as it looks."

Emile resisted the urge to put his hand to the window, afraid of the level of despair he would feel if he got too close. "Who are they?"

"These are my percipients."

"These are the people you listen to?"

"Of course. This here's Brenda. She's from Florida. Big fan of musicals. Once she's done here, we're going to fly her to New York so she can see a real show on Broadway. Isn't that right, Brenda?"

The woman didn't answer. Emile was reminded of an animal shelter, the desperate creatures locked away, waiting to be rescued, for a stranger to walk by, point, and bring their salvation. He felt an instinctive responsibility to help, despite having just seen Brenda for the first time.

"You keep them here? Locked up like this?"

"Don't worry," Max said again. "They knew what they were getting into. It's all in the paperwork." Max eclipsed the window, blocking Brenda from Emile's view. "C'mon. Let me show you where the real magic happens."

Another door. Another young person, this time a boy, at another desk. When they were buzzed through, Emile could taste the worry in his throat. Max ushered him into a small room with mirrored glass on three sides. In the center of the room were two tables facing each other. Max invited Emile to sit.

"What is this?" Emile asked.

"Ah ah, I ask the questions here. Remember?" He winked at Emile. "Now, percipient, tell me about your dreams."

"My dreams?"

"Yes. You said that the visions only come to you in your sleep, correct? These 'warnings'?"

Emile thought of his dreams. There weren't many as of late,

perhaps because he did most of his dreaming during the day, imagining what it would be like to find his mother.

"I don't have any dreams," he said.

"Oh, c'mon. Don't be shy, Brenda. If you didn't dream you wouldn't be here. We wouldn't be taking care of your family's staggering amount of debt thanks to your husband's gambling problem in exchange for your participation. And you'd never get to see *Phantom* on Broadway!"

Emile didn't answer. He looked around him, at the mirrored glass. There was no one on the other side. He would've felt them. But that didn't mean they weren't present during a regular session. Jotting down notes in lab coats, laughing to themselves when a subject, a percipient, said something out of the ordinary.

"Stop messing around, Max."

Max didn't break character. "Who's messing around?" He looked down at his pretend folder, Brenda's case study. "One dream," he said, "and then you can go."

Emile swallowed the burning in his throat. He pictured the real Brenda here, wanting to be heard and not judged. But that wasn't what was going on. Max's tone was all wrong. It wasn't the open mocking Emile had suffered before, in high school, but it was similar somehow, in the way it made Emile feel. Trivial, dismissible.

Emile dug his fingers into his palms. If Max didn't understand the importance of listening, the power of it, then perhaps Emile could show him.

He recalled the images that flashed through Max's mind when Max brought up his parents the day before, when he was explaining the Eldridge's mission. A living room, a fight, a falling glass. Emile could piece the rest together since then. First, when he found Max sitting in front of one of the hotel fireplaces. Then again, when Max described the life he hoped to lead after college. They were always floating on the surface of his mind, the family he'd left behind, the family he feared he'd never be able to re-create.

"Okay," Emile said. "I'll tell you." He leaned forward. "There is this one dream. This dream I've had since I was a child. You want to call it a vision? I don't know. To me, it's a record on repeat."

"Good. Tell me everything you remember."

"I'm a child, playing in the backyard. Through the back window

I see my parents fighting. I can't hear what they're saying, but their mouths are opened big like alligators', wide enough to swallow each other. I know they're fighting about me. They're always fighting about me. What to do with me. I'm a handful. I get into trouble. I disappear and the police bring me back. Send him away, one of my parents says. We don't have the money, says the other. One of them storms out. Sometimes it's my mother, other times my father."

"That's horrible," Max said. Emile felt the rush of thoughts behind Max's calm face. Max's parents. His past.

"That's not all."

"No?"

Max cleared his throat. He'd started to sweat.

"There's more," Emile said. "Would you like to hear it?"

"No," Max said. "I mean—shit." He stood up, pushed his chair in. He walked up to the mirrored glass. "Didn't think you had it in you, Haddock. No wonder they want you so badly."

—

They were silent on the drive back. Emile needed to find his brother. He needed to tell Jacob he was right. There was something off about this place, what they were doing. They needed to leave.

He checked the haunted hall, both lobbies, their room. Nothing. He asked bellboys, receptionists, concierges. No one had seen Jacob. They had seen guests. The guests had seen ghosts. But no one had seen his brother.

Emile walked out the front entrance. A valet stood at the bottom, surveying the long hill for cars. Emile thought nothing of her, until she turned around. It was the young woman from the facility's first desk, the dining room server who'd eyed him suspiciously.

"Check the chapel," she said. "People always run there when they don't know what to do."

Emile glanced at her, her dark eyes. "You have a lot of jobs."

"I go where I'm told." She nodded at the chapel. "You might try the same."

A car wound up the long driveway. A middle-aged couple exited. The husband handed the keys to the valet, who waited until they were in the hotel before rolling her eyes.

"Hey," Emile said. "You're not wearing a name tag."

The young woman turned. It was an attractive face, Emile thought, the kind of face that would have looked straight through him in high school.

"What does it matter?" she said. "You're leaving, right?"

—

He didn't go to the chapel. Jacob wasn't religious. Instead Emile went to his room. He would wait there. He was tired from the day, from the trip up and down the mountain, from the drastic changes in elevation. He shut the curtains and lay down. He didn't sleep but he wasn't fully awake either. He stared at the ceiling fan and imagined its blades as different paths his life might take. On one blade he left here with Jacob, and after a few weeks more of searching, they found their mother. She was better now. She apologized and took them in. On another blade they went home and told the guardians everything that had happened. The guardians, feeling guilty for never welcoming their nephews into their hearts, made a few phone calls to find Jacob a scholarship at a small Christian university with a strong track program, and in the end, all was forgiven or forgotten.

These futures hovered above him, until a switch was flicked and the fan began to whir, turning the different paths into one indistinguishable blur. A sharp chill struck Emile's chest. He sat up, expecting to see the ghost in the mirror. Instead, he saw his brother.

Jacob sat at the foot of the bed, his back to Emile.

"I've been looking for you," Emile said.

"Sorry," Jacob said. "I went to find Vince, to tell him we weren't staying."

"Good. I mean, I agree. There is something strange about this place."

Jacob lifted his head. "Someone else found me. Someone higher up."

Emile remembered what Max said earlier about the big man.

"They know things," Jacob said, his voice forlorn. "About us. I don't know how, but . . ." He lowered his head again.

Emile leaned into his brother for warmth, but Jacob felt just as cold.

"Mom came here, a long time ago. I wasn't even born yet. But she was pregnant." Jacob rubbed his legs, trying to steel himself. "She was worried. I guess her own mom had been taken away from her when she was little."

"Taken away," Emile said. "Why?"

"They think maybe she was like you. And that her family thought she was crazy. I don't know. But Mom was worried the same thing would happen to me, if I was gifted. She had heard about this place, somehow. The people here wanted to help, but there was nothing to do. Not then anyway. She was supposed to come back after I was born, if I turned out to be, you know, like you. But she never did."

Emile let Jacob sit in silence for a moment, trying to follow his brother's thoughts. They moved too quickly. It was like trying to catch raindrops in your hands.

"Even though I was—why didn't she come back? Did they say where she is now?"

"Something happened."

"What do you mean?"

"Emile," Jacob said, and Emile heard his words before his brother said them. "Emile, she's dead."

Emile shook his head. "What? She can't be." Someone would have heard. Someone would have told them. He felt the pull in his chest being replaced by panic. "How? When?" His eyes started to burn before he even realized why.

"They found a death certificate in Kansas's Department of Health records. She didn't die too far from home, or too long after we left . . ." Jacob trailed off, unwilling to voice the question rattling in his head. If they had stayed in that house, if they had been there—

"So there's nothing—there's no one—" The rest of his words got stuck in his throat. He tried to swallow them, to push them down into the well of his stomach.

"We should leave," Emile said, wiping his face. "Right now. There's nothing for us here."

Jacob sighed. "I know," he said. "I know you want to."

"So let's go."

"We can't."

Of course we can, Emile wanted to say. But before he could get the words out, Emile saw his brother sitting in an office somewhere that morning. The scene brightened. A curtain was pulled back, letting in daylight. A voice was saying things Jacob didn't want to hear. "It is the best thing to do for him," the voice said. "For both of you."

"They want to help us," Jacob said. "To make up for not helping

Mom. They said they'll pay for my school, all of it. Yours when you're ready."

Emile pressed his palms into his wet eyes, until the blackness burst with stars. He didn't want to hear the bargain his brother had made. He thought about the dream he could have confessed to Max, in which he hid in the attic with Jacob. Why he was hiding he never understood. Was it from his mother or someone else? He took his hands away from his eyes and opened them, watched as the stars drifted across his vision and faded into nothing.

"You're just going to leave," Emile said.

Jacob winced. "I would come back. I promise."

The voice returned. "He will be fine. More importantly, he will be safe. But should you both leave, we can no longer guarantee his protection."

"From who?" Emile said, in the room. Jacob said, in the office.

"From anyone," the voice said. "Your brother is gifted. That's why you came. You know what the world does to those who are gifted. As did your mother."

"Did they find our mother? Is that what happened?"

"We can't be sure," the voice said. "But she loved you. More importantly, she trusted us, son. So much that she read to you from that gift shop book every night, just in case, so you would know where to go, when you were ready."

The curtain to the office window closed, shutting Emile out.

Jacob said, "If there really are people after us, after you . . ."

Emile shut his brother's voice out. He didn't want to hear any more. He tried instead to imagine his life here, once again. Working in the kitchen, as a cook or a busboy, someplace he could keep his head down and be left alone. He tried to imagine walking down the long hall, nodding at his subjects through locked doors.

"I think this is the best we've got," Jacob said. He wouldn't look at Emile as he spoke though, and Emile realized that, this time, maybe what was best was best for Jacob, and not for him. But try as he might to feel angry, or betrayed, Emile could not begrudge his brother, who had watched over and defended him since he was a child. Who the night of the snowstorm had carried Emile barefoot through the snow, to what he thought was a better life.

The two of them stood up. Emile let his brother hug him. He let Jacob promise again that he would come back.

"I am always here for you," he let Jacob say. "No matter what."

Then he let Jacob leave, and when he was gone, Emile turned the fan off. He was alone. He put his jacket on. He got back under the covers, trying to warm his entire body, but nothing he did would erase the bumps on his flesh.

CHAPTER FIVE

III Lia

Lia arrived in Australia on a Friday, and she was not alone. She met all ten of her classmates in Melbourne's crowded airport, including a tall and loud girl named Julie who had sat next to Lia on her connecting flight out of Los Angeles. Despite Lia's clear signals that she wanted to be left alone—headphones over her ears, book in front of her face—it was a long trip and Julie was persistent. They ended up talking for nearly half the time they spent over the ocean. Or, Julie did most of the talking, and Lia found herself happy to sit there and listen. She was happy too when, after the two departed the plane, Julie touched the crook of Lia's elbow, guiding her the right direction into Customs, then, later, the small of Lia's back, as they approached baggage claim, where they picked up their luggage and received welcome packets from the study abroad counselor. Long after her classmates squeezed into a taxi to campus, Lia's skin felt a familiar buzz where Julie's hand had been.

On the drive to Deakin, Lia tried to take in what would be her home for the next four months. The immediate landscape was fairly stark and flat, but soon they arrived in outer Melbourne, a wide sprawl of suburbia. Lia was struck by how much it reminded her of Kansas, of the place whose mysteries and drama she'd flown across the world to escape. She tried to not think of the similarities as a sign.

Once in her dorm Lia opened her welcome packet to discover two pieces of unexpected news: she would room with Julie, and intern at a public radio station. The first, surprisingly, thrilled her; the second, not so much. Lia assumed her internship would be working with a local paper, and pictured herself in the same sort of office where she'd spent the previous summer, fact-checking for Art. And this was true, for everyone except her. While her classmates were assigned desks at various papers with words like "Sun," "Observer," and "Herald" on their front pages, Lia was sent to DJHK, a public radio station. She protested to her study abroad chaperone, a well-meaning but privileged master's student who was studying communications and whose parents owned a vacation house in Perth. Lia didn't know anything about radio and had never been fond of her own voice, which she had always considered too sweet-sounding for how she normally felt. The girl told Lia she was really sorry, but media was media.

That night, Julie and Lia skipped orientation and went out to drink watery beer. Lia thought about how nice it was to spend time with someone who wasn't weighted down by any drama. Nicer still when, as they walked back to their dorm, Julie took Lia's hand and rested her head on Lia's shoulder.

They spent the weekend touring the campus—a small suburban bubble on the eastern outskirts of Melbourne—and suffering through even more orientation. Lia's first day at the station was on Monday. Her supervisor was Wiley, a large fortysomething male with no distinguishable marks other than his receding hairline and faded comic book T-shirt. On Lia's first day he told her he didn't know what to do with her. They were sitting in the production booth. Lia liked the room more than she expected she would, its strange quiet. It was as if the air had been vacuumed free of any noise or worry. It reminded her of an attic.

"What if I helped out in here?"

"And do what?" Wiley said. "There's barely enough work for me. Don't tell anyone I said that."

"So why did you hire me?"

"Your chaperone was pretty. I work in public radio. I didn't know how to handle it."

Eventually he did find a job for Lia, something he said should easily last the semester. Early that evening he showed her a long but narrow closet stacked with old tapes and reams of dot matrix computer paper.

"I want us to go digital," he said. "See all this? These are transcripts of all the shows we've done the past few decades. I want you to type them up and put them online. Oh, you're gonna need to make a website first. You know how to do that?"

Lia lied and said she did, though it depressed her to think of spending the entire fall in this closet, while Julie and her classmates were out there, covering real news stories.

"Great. We'll get you a desk. You have a laptop, right?"

"Are these organized by year or anything?"

"Let's say yes," Wiley said, and after retrieving a wobbly desk, shut her in.

Lia took out her laptop and worked hard those first few hours. But once Wiley left, and she realized his replacement probably didn't know that this room or Lia existed, she took her time reading deks and headlines. She had fallen into a bit of a rabbit hole, she thought, if when Alice fell she tumbled into a world of perpetual boredom. Most of the transcripts were unbelievably uninteresting. Or, if they were interesting, they were dated. Stale reports of crimes committed and personal tragedies whose endings were written years ago. There were, as Miss Scott would say, no more questions worth asking.

It was after midnight by the time Lia returned to the dorm. Everyone else was asleep, no doubt exhausted from their first days, which, Lia was sure, were much more compelling than her own. She snuck into her room without turning the light on. Julie slept in the bottom bunk, and Lia climbed to the top as quietly as she could.

"Everyone hears you," Julie said.

"Sorry."

Julie rustled below. "You got mail."

"Really?"

Julie's hand reached up holding a large postcard. Lia slid to the back of the bed and read under the dim light of her phone.

Apple,

I know you are upset with me. You must be. But you should know that I'm done disappearing. The answers I've sought have only led to more questions. When would it end? It would never end.

I know what I want. I want to be happy. I want to hear your voice, the excitement in it when you talk about your life, about school and work, and someday, when you're ready, your own family. Most of all, I want to be here for you. No matter what. God, I sound so sentimental. But if I've learned anything from this whole mess, it's the importance of telling the ones you love how you feel, before it's too late.

I hope this was waiting for you when you arrived. Tell me about Australia. Tell me what you discover on the other side of the world.

Lia reread her mom's words several times, before flipping the postcard back over, expecting a picture of rain and tall green trees, a microcosm of their new home in Oregon. Instead, an elk lorded over a crystal lake that reflected purple mountains.

"Who's it from?" Julie said.

"It doesn't matter."

She hid the postcard in one of her pillowcases. She had two pillows, because Julie liked to sleep with her head against the mattress or, if Lia was willing, Lia's chest.

"Do you want company?" Julie asked. She reached up to touch the bottom of Lia's feet.

"No. I think I want to be left alone."

—

In the morning Lia acted like nothing happened. So did Julie. Lia got ready, and on the way to a visual media class, Julie told her about her first day interning with a beat writer for some nationally famous rugby team. She might even get to go on the road and help cover an away match.

"So how was life at the station?" Julie asked.

Lia was embarrassed to tell her about her experience, the small, dark closet, the towers of transcripts. "I don't want to talk about it."

Julie stopped. She zipped up her gray hoodie quickly, in a way that said she was annoyed. "God. Are there any subjects that aren't off-limits?"

Lia apologized. She said she was homesick, which was true. But she was also sick of home. The postcard she'd received was an unwanted reminder of all the problems she'd left behind, and the questions that lingered. Limetown. Her uncle. Her mother.

Julie wrapped her arm around Lia's waist. She pulled Lia close. She said, "Look at this, my first hostile interview." Julie smiled. If old mom had asked, Lia might have been embarrassed to admit what she was feeling.

—

The next two days the internship was a monotonous slog. But when Lia showed up at the station on Thursday evening, Wiley was buzzing around the station with excitement. Apparently, the star of a locally syndicated sci-fi show Lia had never heard of had agreed to an interview. "By yours truly," Wiley said.

Wiley's excitement did not carry over to Lia's closet. The work was the work, unremarkable and outdated. Lia couldn't imagine anyone anywhere wondering about articles like "Indigenous Spores of the Temperate Coast" or "Personal Computers: Future or Fad?"

After eight, she took a much-needed break, drinking the break room's questionable coffee and contemplating the poor decisions that had led her to this sad station of radio and of her life.

When she returned to the closet, the stack of scripts she'd left on her desk was gone. In its place was a single transcript from a different decade. Lia looked around, as if there was anywhere someone could hide in such a small space. She said hello to the empty closet. When no one answered, she sat down at her desk and read.

A schizophrenic man in his thirties, named James, had made a miraculous recovery thanks to an unorthodox treatment. James's brother knew someone who worked at DJHK, and the station invited James on to discuss his recovery.

HOST: Tell the viewers what it was like for you before the treatment.
JAMES: I don't entirely remember. But I know I had a tough time sorting things.
HOST: What sort of things?
JAMES: Reality. Real from fake. Fact from fiction. I remember waking up with these wonderful ideas about the secret ways the world works. But when I rushed to tell someone—my

brother, for example, or my sister—they would just stare at me. Like they couldn't understand. Like something inside of me was broken.

(*James cries*)

HOST: Take your time.

JAMES: And then I was sitting there. In that facility. There were two of them.

HOST: Who were they? Doctors?

JAMES: I don't know.

HOST: Psychologists?

JAMES: No. No. They made that very clear.

HOST: What were their names?

JAMES: I never found out. I wish I did. I wish I could thank them.

HOST: What would you say? If they were here with us, or somewhere out there, listening today.

JAMES: I would say . . . I would tell them . . . I need their help again. But not me. I have a daughter. That's why I'm here. Why I agreed to this. I'm worried she's like me. Worried that—

"Lia."

Lia jumped. "Wiley! Goddammit." She touched her chest, calming her pounding heart. "Were you there the whole time? Did you do this?"

"Do what?"

Wiley blinked through his unfashionable glasses, his eyes two goldfish trapped in fishbowls.

Lia took a breath. "How'd the interview go?"

"Terrible. I should've never allowed myself on-air. What do you got there?"

Lia didn't realize she was still holding the transcript. "I don't know. It's about these miracle workers or something."

Wiley took the transcript from her hands and skimmed through it. "You know, this will go faster if you don't think too hard." He rolled up the transcript and itched his beard with it.

"I'm not thinking too hard," Lia said. "This internship—I'm not thinking at all. That's the problem."

"I'll try not to be offended by that," Wiley said, and ducked into the hall. Lia followed him.

"Wiley, I'm dying here. There has to be something else for me to do."

"Like what?"

Lia searched her brain. "I don't know," she said. "What about . . ." She searched the hallway for an answer, but all she saw was the miracle-worker transcript crumpled in Wiley's paw. "What about a follow-up?"

"A follow-up? You mean reporting the same thing twice? We barely have the money the first time."

"Not the same story," Lia said. "Or, yes, the same, but a differ-ent chapter." She took the transcript out of his hands and unrolled it, smoothing the pages and looking at the names. "Like, whatever hap-pened to James, for example? Don't you want to know? Or his daugh-ter maybe? What about her? Is she okay?"

Lia could feel her mind start to turn; even if she was making the questions up as she went, it felt good to let that part of her brain work again, to turn it on and set it in motion, and for a second there she saw herself tracking down James, his daughter. Investigating, solving a mystery, even if it was of her own invention.

"Lia," Wiley said. "Did you hear what I said?"

Wiley was staring at her, a mix of annoyance and pity on his face. "I'm sure everyone is fine. Now if you'll excuse me, I have a crisis of confidence I need to attend to in the men's room."

—

Lia returned to her dorm on an old bike Wiley had lent her for errands, winding through Melbourne's alleyways and past the bars, cafés, and music venues she had yet to frequent. She'd read in her orientation packet that Melbourne was an artist's city, filled with murals, muse-ums, and pop-up galleries down random laneways. Even her boring dorm building had a sizable sculpture out front, a large bronze, blocky figure that looked like it was doing Tai Chi.

When Lia got to her room, there was a boomerang on the door. Julie's idea of a joke.

"I thought you had company," Lia said. This, after she put her ear to their door, listening for an unfamiliar laugh.

"Would that have bothered you?"

"Maybe," Lia said, and she was surprised at how true the statement was.

Julie popped up from her bed. She told Lia she was going on a late-night run, and to please leave the door unlocked. She wasn't taking her key.

"I might stop at a pub after," she said, "see what's shaking with the sheilas."

"Do they actually call them that?"

"Doubt it. But there's only one way to find out." She squeezed Lia's hip. "We could meet up."

"Sure," Lia said, knowing she wouldn't. "Text me later."

But once Julie was out the door, Lia felt relieved. She'd ignored what Wiley said, and decided that the only way out of that depressing closet was to show Wiley that she deserved to do more than transfer someone else's stories from one medium to another. It's what Miss Scott would've done, Lia thought. Miss Scott, who was always going on about how questions were like doors. The right one could take you anywhere.

She unpacked the transcripts.

Lia started with the shows closest in time to the James interview. She would treat that show as the story's epicenter and slowly extend from there. It was painfully slow at first. She didn't know what she was looking for. A story about the facility James mentioned, maybe. Its opening, or other anecdotes about its successes. She eliminated pop culture pieces, as well as sports, but everything else, every news report, every feature and profile, could have contained a clue to what happened to James, who those two men were, and what they did to him.

She awoke to the room phone ringing. It took her a moment to gather herself, to realize where she was, that she was on a different continent. She was in bed somehow, fully clothed and under the covers. Her chest and legs were wet with sweat. Her cell said it was four in the morning. Julie's bed was empty. Lia picked up the room phone and whispered hello.

No one spoke. Lia tried to think who would have this number.

"Julie?" she said. "Wiley?" Then, desperately. "Mom?"

At the mention of her mother the line clicked dead. Lia lifted the phone away from her ear and stared at the receiver, as if doing so would bring the line back to life. Then she hung up. She sat down to steady herself. The transcripts were splayed across her desk in a mess she didn't remember making, no longer carefully sorted by subject and date. She tried to recall what she read last. It was unrelated. Something about abused children. Kept in a closet? Or was she thinking about the attic? About Emile and her father? No, there was a room. There was a two-way mirror, someone watching. She closed her eyes and the face in the mirror became her own.

She shook her head, trying to separate what she'd read and what she'd dreamed. She scanned the transcripts but didn't find a description matching the image floating in her mind. Julie returned half an hour later. Lia was still at her desk, staring at nothing, at everything.

"Are you all right?" Julie asked. She smelled like sweat and alcohol.

"I'm fine."

"Still stuck on States time?" She grabbed a water bottle from the mini fridge. "Well, the sheilas were underwhelming. But there was this one bartender. Totally your type." Julie laughed and collapsed on her bed. "Oh, I forgot earlier. You got more mail." She retrieved a folded manila envelope from her bag. "How is it you're so popular here?" She peered over Lia's shoulder. "Who's it from?"

"I don't know," Lia said. She didn't recognize the return address.

"Fair enough," Julie said. She was a carefree, malleable drunk, part of what must've attracted Lia to her in the first place.

"You didn't text me," Julie said. Lia apologized, said she must've fallen asleep. "No worries," Julie said. Then, "I believe I'll pass out now, thank you."

Lia waited until Julie was sufficiently snoring before she climbed into her own bed. She grabbed Julie's flashlight and opened the envelope. At first she thought someone was playing a prank on her. Wiley maybe. It was another transcript from the radio station. A news item this time. Though really, it looked like some producer had gotten lazy and just photocopied an article from a local newspaper.

Deakin Professor's Death Remains a Mystery.

Victoria Police continue to search for answers regarding the death of a beloved Deakin University faculty member, Professor Christopher Moyer. Dr. Moyer was discovered dead in his home by authorities late last Wednesday. An autopsy revealed no signs of trauma or toxins, investigators say. Nor were there any visible signs of forced entry into Dr. Moyer's home. His colleagues remain in shock. "I just don't understand," says Dr. Tracey McNellis, head of Deakin's neuroscience department, where Dr. Moyer worked for over five years. "Everybody loved Chris. None of this makes sense." At this point, friends and family are left to wonder. Victoria Police would not comment further on the ongoing investigation, but are calling the death "suspicious."

Next to the text was a photo of the deceased, Christopher Moyer. He was an ordinary-looking man—clean-shaven, sharp chin, sharp nose, weighed down by wire-framed glasses. Lia flipped over the sheet of paper, looking for more, but it was blank. She reread the story. Who sent this? Why? She got out of bed and stood over the transcripts. The transcript was dated June 24, 2004. Just a few months ago, but long after the James interview. Lia checked the time. The transcripts for this year were at the station, waiting in her closet. The sun would be up in a couple of hours. The smart thing to do would be to get some sleep, go to class, then head into work fresh. But she grabbed her hoodie and ducked out into the night.

The station wasn't far, and she had the old bike. Lia pedaled ahead of the fading moon, her face chilled by the night air. September was the beginning of spring in Australia, and Lia sped past what she imagined were many beautiful wildflowers that she told herself she should one day make time to admire.

Once inside the station, Lia kept her head down. She shut the closet door behind her. She quickly found the file for last June, took out the transcripts, and flipped to the twenty-fourth, where her piece of the puzzle should have been. It was missing. Or, it would have been, if Lia wasn't holding it in her hand. She read through June, July, August, but found nothing more about Moyer's death. She sat at her desk and pulled out the envelope, ran her thumb over the return address.

The closet door opened, startling Lia. But it was only Wiley.

"Hey, would you mind grabbing me a mocha. You know the place down the street, next to the bottle-o?"

"Actually, I'm not working yet."

Wiley looked around, feigning confusion. "This is where you work, right? And you are here, aren't you?"

"I couldn't sleep," Lia said.

"Ah," Wiley said. "Bloke trouble, ay?"

"That's not it."

"No? Well." Wiley stood in the doorway, waiting for Lia to say something.

Lia showed him the envelope. "Do you know where this is?" She pointed to the return address.

"I know where Williamstown is. It's about a half hour away by the car you don't have. But that seems like a long way to go to get my mocha."

"I meant this specific address? Do you know it?"

Wiley squinted. "Nope," he said. "But there's this thing called the Internet—"

"I checked. It's not on—"

"It's pretty great. You can look up anything on it. People, places. Everything. You can even look up what an intern should do when a superior asks for a mocha. Whipped cream, please."

Wiley left on that high note. Lia grabbed her things and walked to the nearby coffee shop. The sun was thinking about coming up. There were no clouds, but Lia had read that the weather changed quickly in Melbourne, from sun to rain without warning. This too reminded Lia of her home, where the climate was just as unpredictable. There was a cliché her dad would always say: If you don't like the weather, wait a few minutes.

While Lia was waiting for her order, she looked up directions to Williamstown. She would have to take the bus. It would take forever, and she had class in an hour. Julie would be stirring by then, stumbling bleary-eyed to the shower, wondering where Lia was. Soon she would send Lia a text. *Wher r u?* She liked to abbreviate words that didn't need abbreviation. She thought it was funny. *Clas soo?* Lia packed her laptop. She rushed back to the station. She felt her pocket vibrate, and pictured Julie anxiously typing. *Gun leav w/o u.* The on-air light died. Lia busted in, holding two extra-large mochas. A minute later Lia was on the road, biking to the bus stop, forgetting about class, about why she came here in the first place.

Her pocket buzzed. *By by*, Julie said.

—

The bus driver left her at the last Williamstown stop, the one closest to the beach. She would have to get herself the rest of the way, the bus driver explained. He wasn't familiar with the address either, but bet that if she headed south until she reached the coast, followed the shoreline, she'd eventually run into it. Lia got off the bus and detached her bike from the front rack.

It was after nine by the time she got to the shore. The city was already awake. Cafés and shops had opened early, welcoming sandaled tourists who expected it to be warmer. Ships and boats of all sizes jostled in the nearby bay, the water swayed between turquoise and a darker, more dramatic blue, depending on the clouds and the sun. Lia breezed by all of it, her mind turning over the possibilities of what she might find. Once the mystery she'd discovered was solved, she could send Julie a text maybe. *Meet me at the beach*, she might write. *Il makit wrth ur w8.*

She followed the map on the GPS her mother had given her before Lia left for college, with a little note that cheesily read, *For when you feel lost.* The GPS guided her farther and farther west, away from the city, from the beach houses and the docks, though she still hugged the shore. Eventually the directions took her inland, into and then out of a warehouse district, and then back toward the coast, where it said she had reached her destination, though there wasn't a single building in sight, only a line of woods hugging the beach and the ocean. She shook the GPS out of frustration, before remembering what the bus driver had said. As long as she kept the ocean on her left, she'd find what she was looking for. She continued on.

A half hour later she found herself atop a small cliff. The sun stunned the beach below, and a few hundred yards away a family of five towering limestone pillars rose out of the ocean, as wave after wave crashed against them in vain. Lia looked for a way down, and when she found it, she walked her bike down a steep wooded path. When she reached the beach, she saw that hidden from view were two old buildings made of brick. Each had a roof that slanted in one direction, giving the impression that the buildings had been cut in half. Lia approached the buildings from the back, her GPS buzzing the entire time, telling her she had arrived.

A rusted-through sign read MENNINGER STATION. The first door she tried was locked, as was the second. She put her ear to a third door and thought she could make out the whirring of an air conditioner. She circled the buildings, looking for a way in. She saw a busted window screen. Lia ripped what was left of the screen from the frame, and when the window wouldn't open, she found a rock and threw it through the glass without thinking. Only after she cleared the glass from the sill with her hoodie and crawled in, when she was standing in the dark, the whirring audible but distant, did she think about what she had done. Miss Scott never said much about journalistic ethics, how far you should go when seeking answers. Once she'd casually mentioned the mother test—If you're ever unsure whether what you're doing is right or wrong, stop and ask yourself, *Would my mother approve?* But that test was almost laughable now. Who was her mother, the woman who repeatedly disappeared, and likely lied to both Lia and her father, to judge what was right or wrong?

Lia shook the thought off and pulled out the flashlight she'd stolen from Julie. She flicked it on. There were four windows on each side of what appeared to be the building's only room, which was empty save a couple of army cots forgotten against the wall. Lia ran her hands against the walls. The tile floor was cracked, but the walls were stunningly white, as if they'd been bleached clean not even a week ago.

Her phone buzzed. She pulled it out of her pocket.

U mist clas.

Lia didn't respond. She walked the walls until her hand bumped against a knob. It was attached to a door she hadn't seen at first. The door was white too, and Lia was surprised how easily it opened when she turned the knob. She entered another room, smaller than the one she'd left behind, but big enough that she couldn't see the other side with a swipe of her flashlight. The air was cooler here. Lia thought she heard the whirring again.

R u K?

She followed the whir. The closer she got, the louder the sound, until it became a roar. It was all around her, but she didn't see its source.

Ur bng stupd.

Just as she was about to turn back, her flashlight caught a handle. Not on the wall, where she'd been searching, but on the floor. There was a cellar.

"This doesn't make sense," Lia said to no one. But still she bent down and tried the handle. She put down the flashlight to pull with both hands. The door whined until she dropped it to the floor with a loud clang. Air rushed up at her. She took a step back, picked up the flashlight, and aimed it down below. She could make out the first few steps, but nothing more.

Don b stupd.

"I won't," Lia said.

She slowly put her foot on the first step. A test, like dipping a toe into the pool to check the temperature. Her entire leg tingled. It buzzed. *Don b stupd.* She took another step and watched her leg disappear into the darkness. She aimed the flashlight but moving forward was like driving through a thick fog; light didn't matter. She didn't know she was at the bottom until she took a step and awkwardly found the ground. The air was freezing, the ground cold and hard—uneven stone, she realized. She took a few steps, and after each dared herself one more, until she felt untethered, like she'd swum far beyond the breaker. She turned around. The light from the room above had disappeared. She couldn't see the stairs. She'd gone too far. Her leg shook.

Sum1's hear, Julie said. *Theyv ben lookn 4 u.*

She felt a tingle down her neck. She could only see as far as her hands, trembling before her.

She crouched on the ground, texted Julie. *Who is after me?*

Don no, haha, Julie said. *Mystry.*

Lia's heart quickened. She thought, somehow, of her house in Kansas. It didn't have a basement, and every spring during tornado season she worried. What would she do? Where would her family go when something bad happened?

She wrote another text. Not to Julie. To her mother. *I need help*, it said.

She was about to hit send when suddenly a switch clicked, and the basement was flooded with light, stunning Lia's eyes. A voice called down. "Hello? Someone there?"

Lia didn't respond. She took in the revealed surroundings, though there wasn't much to take in. Bare walls made of stone, as rough as the ground. Nothing else. What did she expect exactly? A cellar full of Dr. Moyer's belongings?

The voice belonged to a man, white-haired, maybe in his fifties.

"You shouldn't be here," the man said.

"Was it you?" Lia asked him. "Did you send me that article?"

The man sighed. "Lady, I have no idea what you're talking about. Now's let go before the ghosts get us."

—

Back on the beach, Lia sat cross-legged in the sand. She checked her phone. She'd missed a call from her mother. A voice mail waited. She'd listen to it later. The man was explaining how he lived in a caravan park nearby, that he got paid to come by every now and then and make sure no one had been messing around. Punk kids and the like.

"I owe you for that window," Lia said.

"Correct," the man said. "Or the owner, anyway."

He didn't know who that was. Some real estate jerk, he suspected. The property had a lot of value, or it would if they used it right.

"People love ghosts, you know. Been saying for years someone should open up a small hotel here, a restaurant. Take ya on a haunted tour. The whole thing's right on the ocean. They'd make a killing."

"Somebody wanted me here," Lia said. "They wanted me to find this place."

She pulled out the envelope, showed the man the transcript.

"Moyer," the man said. His jaw hung open, and he took the article in his hands. He mouthed the words to himself.

"You know him."

The man shook his head. "I didn't say that." He finished reading the transcript and stuffed it back in the envelope. He handed it to Lia. "Don't really read the paper."

"It's not the paper."

"Still."

"But you believe in ghost stories."

The man scowled at Lia. "I believe what I know."

"And what is it you know?"

"I know lots of things."

Lia pulled out her phone, pretending she wasn't interested, another Miss Scott interview technique. Especially useful when dealing with arrogant older men. "Like what?" Lia asked.

"Well, for example. I know that before any of us were born, this was a quarantine station. For incurable diseases." Lia looked up. "Yep. But what they don't say is that later, this is where they conducted their experiments."

"Experiments?"

"That's right." He looked over his shoulder, at the building Lia broke into. "You're telling me you didn't feel anything, when you were poking around in the dark?"

Lia thought of the whirring, the source of which she could never find.

"Ah," the man said. "See? Now who believes in ghosts?"

"I didn't say that."

"But you felt them," the man said, grinning widely now. "Didn't you?"

"I need to go," Lia said.

The man laughed. He winked at her and put his hand on her shoulder.

"Get off," Lia said, and pushed him away. She hopped on her bike and pedaled, the man shouting behind her. She lost some of his words, but caught his meaning. That Lia still owed him money. And if she ever showed her face here again, he'd make her pay.

When Lia was far enough away, when the man was a dot in the distance, she paused to catch her breath. Her brain was already cycling through the events of the day, the week, the facts and questions added to the unstable pile of facts and questions teetering in her head. There was a man named James. He'd been cured by strangers at a mystery facility. Now here was a facility, where mystery experiments once took place, or so said some strange older man. And she'd only found the facility because of the Moyer transcript, sent to her by a stranger, whose return address was Menninger.

Lia felt a phantom vibration in her pocket, reminding her of the missed call, of the text message to her mother she'd never sent. She opened her voice mail. She pressed play and listened to the familiar tone of her mother's troubled voice. Her mother apologized. She said she didn't know why she was calling. She just had the strangest feeling.

CHAPTER SIX
███████████ ||| Emile

"Tell me about your dreams," Emile said. "Tell me everything you remember."

It was his third month working for the Eldridge, his third month of listening. It turned out they wanted him to play scientist, not subject. His percipient was forthcoming, which meant his dreams were ordinary. Emile had noticed this about his percipients: the more unusual the dreams, the more reluctant they were to share. He would run through the rote questions in any case. It was important, he was told, to establish a baseline, so that when someone remarkable finally walked through the door, Emile could accurately measure how special they were. All this according to Max, who had left the Eldridge for college just two weeks after Emile started. "Don't weep for me, Haddock," he had said. "Come find me when you're ready."

Emile had not heard from him since. Nor had he heard from his brother, other than a postcard a month after he left. Jacob had settled just outside of Salt Lake at the small university where he would run track. He'd barely graduated high school after missing out on all of his finals because of Emile, but the university still honored his partial scholarship, and the Eldridge, good to their word, had taken care of the rest. *It's great*, he wrote. *I can't wait for you to visit.*

But then nothing. No more postcards. No letters or phone calls. Emile wrote and never heard back. The sensible thing would have been to leave the Eldridge, for Emile to act on his intuition that something was wrong. The problem was the percipients. More than once Emile packed his bags and planned to leave as soon as his lab shift was over, but couldn't bring himself to go. He felt connected to them, the longer he worked with them, despite Max's instructions to not get too close. But Emile couldn't help it. Since taking over for Max, he had yet to meet a percipient who was truly gifted, whose dreams were verifiable visions of the future, but he still felt closer to them than any of his so-called genius coworkers at the hotel. He saw himself in their faces, heard himself in their voices, and every time he sat down with them for an interview, he couldn't escape the feeling that he was on the wrong side of the table.

The man sitting before him rattled off his dream. It was the same as the night before last and the night before that. The man was wandering the halls of his old high school, at night. No one else was there. He was looking for his locker. He had forgotten something—something important. He had a big test the next day. Perhaps that was what was in the locker. His notes or a cheat sheet. When he finally found his locker, he couldn't remember the combination. He could never remember. And so he woke up, filled with dread.

The man leaned back in his chair, and Emile asked him the questions he already knew the answers to.

Have you had this dream before?

Tell me what is the same.

Tell me what is new.

If you had to choose, would you say the dream represents the past, the present, or the future?

Below the questionnaire was a blank space saved for Emile's assessment. In his estimation, was the percipient truthful and forthcoming? Were there any noticeable changes in behavior? How would you characterize the percipient's dreams? Vague or specific? Recurring or isolated? Ordinary or extraordinary?

Emile was responsible for seven percipients. He interviewed them first thing in the morning, before their dreams dissolved from their minds. As a result, he saw them at their worst, baggy-eyed and pale, dragged into the waking world. When Emile was finished, he tried to forget their faces. He left the laboratory, sped down the mountain, through town, and to the hotel. If he was lucky, he had half an hour to eat breakfast in the dining room before his shift at the hotel began. In the beginning, he ate with Max. After Max left, he ate alone, though he returned to the dining room each morning, in part hoping he would see the server who waved at him on his first day, the young woman who also worked as a valet. He'd only seen her a few times in passing, during his cleaning duties. Emile was a housekeeper, the same job his mother had worked in Lawrence, a fact that was not lost on him. He pushed his cleaning cart past the young woman, not noticing her until she spoke to him.

"You changed your mind," she said. "Or someone changed it for you."

She wasn't in any of the work uniforms. Instead, she was dressed casually in blue jeans and a beige sweater she let hang off her bare shoulder. Emile tried not to stare.

"So now you can tell me your name," he said.

"Yes. Now I can tell you my name. But I don't think that I will."

Emile smiled.

"My word is not my bond," the young woman said. "Same goes for everyone else around here. You should know that, if you're going to stay."

It was a weird thing to say, Emile thought, but everything at the Eldridge was weird.

"You know my name," Emile said.

"That's true."

"And probably a lot more."

"Also true."

"Hardly seems fair."

The young woman considered this. "How about this," she said. "You last a month and I'll tell you."

Emile stuck out his hand, which she shook, and after she walked away, as Emile pushed his cart from room to room, he pretended that the buzzing he felt in his entire body was from the elevation. He would see her two more times, once when she was working the front desk, and again when she was giving a tour of the grounds. Neither occasion afforded them a chance to talk, and upon Emile's one-month anniversary, though he actively sought her out, he could not find her anywhere in the hotel. Now, two months later, she was nowhere to be found.

—

Bimonthly, they reviewed Emile's work. Max conducted the first evaluation just before he left, and laughed when Emile complained that he had listened to over a hundred dreams at that point, none of which seemed out of the ordinary. They revealed nothing about the future, as Max once suggested, only the percipients' deepest desires, and the crippling fears that got in their way.

"It takes time, Haddock. You think you're gonna get the good stuff first? I worked here a full year before I caught even a whiff of the extraordinary. You're different, obviously, but you're still the same."

"A year," Emile said.

"I know it seems like a long time. Mostly because it is. But you're free to go at any moment. Isn't that what they tell you?"

Emile remembered the despair he felt after that first review, the feeling that not only was he alone, but that he had stayed for nothing, that he was wasting his time. He wrote to Jacob then, but he also wrote to Ginny. He wasn't sure why exactly. He could think of no one else, perhaps. Or, he had started to wonder what his life would have been like if he'd stayed in Lawrence, if he hadn't surrendered to his anger.

Max had said that everything they sent was screened by someone higher up, in case someone had an inkling to leak hotel secrets, so Emile told Ginny what he could. That he was sorry he had left so abruptly. That he really enjoyed her class and thought of her lessons daily. At the end, he asked if Austin had returned to school, and if so, how was he? But he felt a slight shame after reading that final question—as if he didn't deserve to know what happened to the friend he had left behind—so he scratched it out before handing it over to the front desk.

—

It was not a year before something interesting happened, but it was over three months. One hundred and eighteen days, to be exact. Of cleaning rooms. Of listening to his percipients drone through their ordinary dreams. *I have a big project due at work. The morning it's due I realize I haven't started it. I am walking with my childhood dog through an open field. The sun sets in front of us, and my dog, now dead, looks back at me, panting a smile.* One hundred and eighteen days of Emile nodding, working, checking his empty mailbox, then returning to his dormitory, where he wrote, read, and slept alone.

Until.

He had just finished his eighth employee assessment. This time his reviewer was Vince, who gave Emile middling marks for his performance thus far. Emile protested. He was doing everything right. He was asking the questions, filling out the forms. He was cleaning up the garbage the guests left behind.

Vince held a hand up. "You're making my point for me," he said. His lips were cracked even though it was the middle of August. "You were not brought here to think inside the box. Anyone can do what you're doing, correct? So then, why are you doing it?"

Emile knew the answer, though he would not say it out loud, not to Vince, whom he had seen little of since he agreed to stay here, and did not trust.

"We want you to use your gift. We don't want to tell you how, though of course we have some ideas you might be interested in."

Vince's words rang in Emile's ears the following morning as he sat in the interview room, waiting for the first percipient to shuffle in— Brenda, the woman he'd seen during his first visit to the facility with Max, all those months ago. According to her file, out of all the supposed percipients, Brenda (female, forties) had been there the longest, though Emile couldn't understand why. She was never forthcoming with her dreams, and if she was, they were invented.

"I can't force them to tell the truth," Emile said to Vince.

"Of course you can." Vince lifted his hand and put two fingers to his temple, like a fake gun. "Through here all things are possible."

Brenda slouched in her seat. She was still wearing her pajamas and a sleeping mask, which sat atop her nest of brown hair.

"Tell me about your dreams, Brenda. Tell me everything you remember." Brenda stared at the clipboard on the table in front of her. "If it helps, close your eyes and take a deep breath. Let the dream return to you." Brenda played along. "Good. Now tell me what you see."

"Park," Brenda said. "Sun. Clouds."

Emile sighed. "You're naming things to name things."

Brenda shrugged. Emile picked up his clipboard, though by now he had the script memorized. He was supposed to ask her if she had had this dream before. Emile looked at the two-way mirrors surrounding him. He dropped the clipboard on the table with a loud clack. Brenda blinked.

"Why are you here, Brenda?" he asked. "If you're not willing to be truthful, what are any of us doing here? Didn't you come here to be listened to?"

Brenda looked at him, annoyed. "I am telling the truth. Park and stuff. That's what I see."

"No, it isn't. That's not what you see at all." Emile stood up from the table. Brenda shifted in her chair. Emile felt the resistance welling up inside of her, the waves retreating from the shore. *Screw you*, she thought. *You're just a kid.*

"Close your eyes, Brenda. Would you do that for me?"

"Fine," she said.

"Now instead of recalling your dream, let me recall it for you. How about that?"

Brenda scoffed. "Whatever you say."

"Good. Here's what I want you to do. I'm going to give you a word. One word. And all I need from you is to listen with an open mind."

"That's it?"

"That's it, though it's not as easy as it might sound. When you're listening, don't hold your thoughts back. Just let them go. Many subjects struggle with this," Emile said, as if he had done this before. "Their thoughts bump into something they want to avoid, something troubling they'd rather not confront, and so their mind takes them somewhere else. Somewhere more comfortable. Like a park."

Brenda frowned. "That's not what I was doing."

"Of course not," Emile said. He sat back down at the table. "Are you ready?" Brenda straightened in her chair. "Good," he said again. "Here we go."

But before Emile said anything more, he took a quick peek inside her mind. He knew she was hiding something. If he could just catch a glimpse of what she didn't want him to see, a corner of a thought, a sharp edge, something to hold on to.

"I'm waiting," Brenda said. She painted over her worry with bravado. But then Emile saw it, through the thin layer of confidence. A spot she missed.

Emile sat in his chair. "Debt," he said. Clearly, pointedly. Immediately Brenda's face changed. So did her thoughts. Emile thought unlocking her mind would be like solving a puzzle; he just needed to find the missing piece. But it wasn't like that. In Kansas, in the guardians' living room, high on the wall opposite the TV, there was that cuckoo clock, a complicated and annoying contraption that stopped ticking every other week. Emile remembered Mrs. Sinnard standing on a chair to take the clock down, carefully laying it on the kitchen table, facedown, so she could remove the back with a tiny screwdriver. One time, and only one time, she waved Emile closer as she worked and showed him what was inside. She named each part she tinkered with: the pipes and weights, the pendulum and chains. All were part of an impossible machine, Mrs. Sinnard said. Such a grand design. The key was to not let it overwhelm you. Don't look at all the moving parts at the same time. Start with one. Figure out its function, and then, when you're ready, move on to the next. But never forget the parts that came before, the role they play, and how they all come together to make the bird sing.

Emile examined Brenda's thoughts part by part.

"You had a dream, years ago. When you were a young mother. By this time you already knew about your husband's gambling. You knew the path he was heading down, but you didn't know how to stop it."

"No."

"In the dream two men visit your house. It's the middle of summer. Humid, sweltering, eighty degrees before the sun rises. And yet the men are in suits. They tell you to have a seat. They tell you they have a little problem with your husband. He owes them a favor. The men are smart, even in the dream. They don't threaten you directly. They casually mention things about your house, your daughter. Things they shouldn't know. They talk about the importance of insurance policies, about a cousin of theirs who didn't have anything, and then bang, without warning, disaster struck, and everything was taken away."

"No," Brenda said again, but it was too late. The parts were already ticking.

"His debt was substantial. The men let you know that. They give you a week, a deadline you know you can't meet. When you woke up, it wasn't summer, like in the dream. It was winter, which meant you had time. You checked on your daughter, sleeping in her bed. You sat next to her, combed her hair with your hand, and you made a plan. Starting that day, you would save your money. You would pick up extra shifts and work overtime. And when that wasn't enough, you would sell everything you had. Your jewelry, your furniture, the house, everything you loved. You would hock every last bit of it if you had to, so that when the men came, you would be ready."

Brenda scratched the inside of her arms, raking her skin red just above the wrists. She refused to look at Emile. "Why would I do that? It was just a dream."

"Because this dream came true."

Brenda stopped scratching. She stared at her hands, the fingernails she'd used to bite her skin. She finally looked up at Emile, her eyes as red as the inside of her arms. "It wasn't right," she said. "My dream. It was so much worse."

In the end, it was the bank that took everything away. Emile saw different men in different suits who made different, legal threats, and forced Brenda and her husband to sign papers as their daughter looked on.

"They took everything," Brenda said. "Everything I saved, it didn't matter."

"It's not your fault," Emile said.

"Of course it is. I knew it was going to happen."

Brenda put her head on the table. Emile looked away. There was more to see, of course. After the foreclosure on Brenda's house, there was her pleading with her parents for money, them turning a blind eye, saying they warned her about him. There was her move into a trailer. The trailer had room for only one bed, which Brenda gave to her daughter, while she and her husband took turns on the couch and floor. Until, eventually, because her husband never learned to stop, even that was taken away.

Emile turned to the mirrored wall, and was surprised to see a face half-smiling back at him. It was his own. He was proud of what he had done, even if it meant forcing Brenda to relive losing her family, her house—everything. She would be better for it, he told himself, in the long run. It was no small thing, after all, to be listened to and understood.

"Why didn't you leave him?" Emile asked.

Brenda lifted her head. "I had to stay," she said.

"Because of the dream?"

"No," Brenda said. "For her. I did what I thought was best for her."

—

Emile thought about Brenda as he cleaned rooms that day. His first month at the Eldridge, he worked diligently, moving swiftly from one room to the next. Lately, though, he'd started to take his time. After he cleaned a room, he'd shut the door and lie on the bed, or sit in one of the chairs by the window, as he did now. There was no rush, it seemed. His performance evals never mentioned his cleaning duties, and so why couldn't he close his eyes for a minute?

When he woke up, he was in bed, fully clothed but under the covers. There was a girl next to him. Emile jumped up, ready to apologize, assuming the girl was a guest.

"Tell me about your dreams," she said. "Tell me everything you remember."

Emile rubbed his eyes. When he saw who it was, his neck grew hot. The valet. She laughed at him from the bed, at how startled or stupid he must've looked. Emile frowned.

"It's been four months," he said, doing his best to act upset. And a part of him genuinely was angry. That he hadn't seen her in such a long time. That she had caught him off guard, made him feel foolish.

"Congratulations," the valet said.

"You said all I had to do was last one."

The valet slid off the bed and sat in one of the chairs by the window. "Claire. There. Mystery solved."

"Emile."

"Yes, I know. You're Max's big catch." She tilted her head. "I heard the rumors, obviously. But I thought you looked like a tourist."

"A tourist?"

"One of them." She looked around the room. "I had the same job when I started here. But guests kept complaining about their things going missing." Claire leaned in and whispered. "I blamed it on the ghosts." She laughed. "Isn't that terrible? But I couldn't help myself. Even right now, I want to lock the door and open their suitcases, don't you?"

"Not really," Emile said.

"I guess you don't need to, do you. From what I saw."

"What you saw."

"Max didn't tell you? There are no secrets here." She grinned at him and again Emile felt foolish. He imagined her watching him from behind the mirrored glass.

"I don't know what you're talking about," he said. "This place is nothing but secrets."

"Such as?"

"Such as why they feel the need to spy on their employees."

Claire leaned back, crossed her ankles. "Good. What else?"

"Well, there's what we're doing here. I mean, I get what I'm doing. I'm listening. To the percipients, their dreams. We want to know if they can really see the future. Right? If that's something the mind can do."

"But you think there might be more," Claire said. Emile did. He hadn't told anyone. He hadn't had anyone to tell. But the suspicious feeling he had when he and Jacob first arrived, when they met Vince—that feeling had never gone away. His suspicion grew each morning, when he woke his percipients, each morning without another word from Jacob. If Vince, if the Eldridge, knew of Emile's gifts, why weren't they interviewing him? Why wasn't he part of some test? The longer he stayed, the more he believed that there was something Vince wasn't telling him.

"Well, what do you think?" Claire asked. "Can they?"

"Can they what?"

"Your percipients. Can they see the future?"

Emile shrugged. He hadn't thought so, not until that morning. He hadn't had a good reason to. "It's probably just a coincidence," he said. He paused, thinking of Brenda. "But they believe they can. They feel . . . responsible."

"You care about them," Claire said.

"They're people."

"They're subjects. And in my experience it works best if you wall yourself off when you're down there. Don't let anything in." Emile frowned. "I know, I know. I'm a monster. But trust me, it'll make it easier in the long run. When Vince asks you to do something you don't want to do."

She got up. Emile wasn't trying to read her thoughts, but he could tell she was growing uncomfortable, that she had difficulty staying still for a long period of time. Maybe that was why she had been so hard to find.

"You're going to have another meeting with Vince," Claire said. "He'll congratulate you on your work today. He'll tell you that in four months you've accomplished what took Max a year. Then, he'll ask you to take the next step."

"What does that mean?" Emile said.

"Do you want to stay here?"

Emile didn't answer right away. He'd stayed this long for Jacob, more than anything else. To give his brother the future he'd nearly surrendered when the two fled Lawrence. Though now, standing in the same room as Claire, his mind began to imagine a different future, a future of his own. In it he was agreeing to whatever Vince asked. He was in the basement, doing whatever they told him, thinking of who waited for him above.

Claire snapped her fingers, breaking his daydream.

"How do you know all this? What I've been doing. What I'll do next."

Claire flashed her teeth. They were all perfect, Emile noticed, except her canines, which were a little too narrow, and a little too sharp, like they might cut you if you got too close. "Isn't it obvious?" she said. "It was in my dream."

—

His meeting with Vince was short, congratulatory, and unfolded exactly as Claire said it would. Emile thought about her as Vince outlined the new experiment. He would still be listening to dreams, but the Eldridge wanted to test a new hypothesis. These percipients, Vince explained, they think they can predict the future. They've all visited the World's Fair and have the pins to prove it. And this belief is based on their dreams—things they have seen while asleep that later come true. But have you ever considered that the inverse might be true? That the percipients don't read what is already written. That, in fact, they are not the readers, but the writers, the very authors of their future?

Of course Emile hadn't considered it. The idea was absurd. He said, "You're saying that things happen because they dream them."

Vince raised his eyebrows, as if the idea wasn't remotely far-fetched. "I'm saying we should consider it. While we have them here."

Emile would be working with Brenda exclusively, since she was the percipient who showed the most promise.

That night, he walked the dark basement corridor until he reached Brenda's room. The experiment would begin then. Emile had to talk to

her before the dreams, not after. He slid open the window and saw her
sleeping, as Vince had promised. Her body was curled up and facing
the wall.

"What if she's awake?" he had asked.

"She won't be."

"You'll give her something."

Emile entered the room and shut the door behind him. He stood
over Brenda as she slept, her mouth open and brow furrowed. Even
now she looked worried, like she was waiting for the next bad thing
to happen.

He crouched down. He leaned in, then hesitated. It felt wrong,
what he was doing. Being there when Brenda was unconscious. Was
she aware of this new experiment? He hadn't thought to ask Vince, but
he should have. But he put his wall up, as Claire suggested, and did as
he was told.

He put his mouth next to Brenda's ear and began whispering the
script Vince had given him. He paused between each line, as instructed,
to allow enough time for the words to soak in.

Your husband finds fortune.

All debts are forgiven.

He takes your daughter to the beach. Together, they pick the nicest house.

It will be a surprise. This, they agree in secret.

They rent the nicest car and drive to you, to this hotel.

Brenda twitched in her sleep. Emile pulled his mouth away from
her ear. She stirred, but did not wake. He considered stopping. But it
felt good, what he was saying, the life he was inventing for Brenda.
It was a life she would die to live. And for a moment—even though
his dreams never came true, even though his gift was very different—
he wondered how his script would read, if he were the one lying in
the bed, sleeping. He thought of Jacob. Of Ginny and Austin. Of his
mother. Of Claire. Was it really that bad, what he was doing, trying to
create the perfect future? He leaned down to Brenda's ear and whispered the dream she wanted to come true.

You are waiting for them. There, on the stairs. The valet takes your
husband's keys. Your husband runs to you. Your daughter runs to you. You
are so happy you can't breathe.

———

Emile whispered into Brenda's ear each night for two weeks. Each morning, he sat with her as he always had. "Tell me about your dreams," he said. "Tell me everything you remember."

It was clear almost immediately that the experiment wasn't working. The absurdity of the hypothesis grew with every day of failure, as did the pained expression on Brenda's face. The drugs they gave her were messing her up, she complained. She felt tired all the time now. Worse, no longer did her dreams find her only at night. They hovered over her days too. "It never stops," she said. "I can always see them, the men, the house, my family, even when I'm awake."

Emile tried to reassure her. He promised the experiment was nearly complete. But he had no way of knowing if that was true, and the more he tried to comfort her, the more obvious it became that he was merely assuaging his guilt for continuing to play his part. When he wasn't working, when he wasn't cleaning rooms and had nothing better to do, he found himself waiting on the front steps, hoping that Brenda's husband would miraculously appear, daughter in tow.

"How are things in the dream world?" Claire said. She'd found Emile on the steps, watching the mountains snuff out the sun. "Don't worry," she said, when Emile didn't respond. "That wasn't a question or anything."

Emile remained quiet. He tried to remember what he had felt when he saw Claire here and talked to her for the first time, nearly five months ago. He tried to remember the buzzing that electrified him when they were in the same room just a couple of weeks ago.

"Her husband is not coming. You know that." Emile nodded. "So why are you waiting?"

"What else is there to do?" Emile asked. He sounded sadder than he intended. But he supposed he was feeling a little down. You couldn't just whisper the perfect future into existence.

The sun set for good. Finally, Claire stood up. She extended her hand. "Let's get out of here."

"And go where?"

"Into town. We'll catch a movie or something." She wiggled her fingers at him. "Come on, movies are fun. I am fun."

She smiled at him again, with sharp teeth, holding her mouth open long enough for Emile to find her tiny imperfection. He took her hand,

and when she squeezed his and pulled him up to her, he felt his entire body buzz back to life.

—

The theater was called the Southwind. Claire knew the usher, who let them in for free with a wink. Emile felt a pang of jealousy in his chest that he realized he had no right to feel, until he sat down next to Claire in the dark. The movie had already started. It was difficult for Emile to pick up what was going on. A man stood in a desert. A cowboy, perhaps, left by his posse to die. Though he wasn't wearing a cowboy hat or a gun. And the boots he was wearing were like nothing Emile had ever seen.

Claire leaned over and whispered in Emile's ear. "He's supposed to be on Mars. He's a convict, framed for a crime he didn't commit. Only in the future we sentence our criminals to Mars. It's like the future's Australia." He turned to face her. They were almost nose-to-nose. She blushed. "What," Claire said. "I like movies."

Emile paid little attention to the rest of the movie. He caught glimpses of scenes in between studying Claire, the way her foot twitched during the exciting scenes, the way her dark eyes refused to blink, as if afraid they would miss something. He took separate trips to the bathroom and the concession stand so he could brush against Claire's legs. Meanwhile, the space cowboy was slowly going insane. There was nothing around him but an ocean of desolation. Everywhere he looked, desert and rock. Predictably, he began to see things. The faithful dog he'd left behind, ears pinned down when the man said good-bye. The last woman he'd loved, now a sand-blown ghost, one that beckoned him closer and closer to the boiling sun.

When the film finally ended, Emile was disappointed. Not at the ending—the man died alone on Mars, calling his lover's name—but that his time with Claire was nearly over. He pretended to be interested in the credits so they could spend a little longer in the dark. His spirits lifted when Claire suggested they take the long way back to the hotel. They walked around until they stumbled upon a small park. Emile wasn't sure where they were exactly, nor did he care. In the center of the park was a white gazebo, but Emile and Claire chose to sit on a nearby bench, so they could see what the stars were up to.

"What does it feel like?" Claire said. "What you do. With other people's thoughts."

Emile looked away. No one had ever asked him directly before. An old man walked a small dog around the gazebo. He carried a camera with him, and whenever the dog stopped or did something the man thought noteworthy, he took a picture. Emile thought of the movie, the delirious space cowboy petting a rock and telling it to sit. Stay.

"It's okay if you don't want to talk about it. We can head back."

"No," Emile said, but he didn't know what to say next. The closest he'd come to telling anyone about his gift was back in Kansas, with Austin. He tried to recall the excitement he felt on the walk to Lost 80 that night, the night he would end up leaving everything behind. He hadn't realized how eager he had been to share what he could do with someone—someone he could trust, someone who would understand, someone who would listen. Someone who wasn't his brother. But those boys had beaten Austin before he ever got the chance.

"Emile?"

"It's . . . a feeling," Emile said. "A sensation. Like a wave washing over you, only you're still standing on the beach. You get wet without getting in the water."

Claire nodded. Her hands sat on her lap, and Emile wondered what kind of miracle it would take to make her hand move to his.

"Then things start to come into focus. Images, thoughts or whatever. Sometimes I can see them clearly, as if I'm standing there with them as their father calls them a disappointment or their wife says she's not in love anymore. Other times it's more difficult. People are good at putting up walls, dams that keep the water from rushing out."

"You can't see through them?"

"Not easily," Emile said. "Though I guess I don't want to, either." The few times he'd tried before, in high school, he'd only found things he didn't want to see. He learned that what people hid, they hid for a reason.

"Hmm," Claire said. She put her hands in her jacket, and Emile chided himself for missing his chance. Claire tilted her head back, admiring the sky. "What about me?"

"I don't know," Emile said. "I've never tried."

Claire faced him again. "Never? Why not?"

"Because. That would be cheating."

"Cheating."

"Yes," Emile said. "I wouldn't have earned it."

This time it was Claire who looked away, though she did so with a slight smile. If Emile had looked inside her mind then, if he was able to, he knew he would have liked what he saw, the chain reacation that finally made her hand move to his. He had never met anyone like her.

"What about now?" Claire asked.

Emile leaned in and closed his eyes. His skin buzzed. He breathed deep. Her hair smelled like some flower he didn't know the name of. The small dog barked in the distance. Emile shut it out, along with every thought surrounding the two of them. But he saw nothing. It was as if he had been plunged into complete darkness, one so dense even the stars could not punch through. He ran blind toward the ocean. Waves lapped around him. Not pushing him out, pulling him in, carrying him closer and closer to something that he supposed he wanted all along.

—

In the morning, Claire snuck out of Emile's dorm before the residential assistant made his rounds. Coed cohabitation wasn't frowned upon, but it wasn't smiled upon either. Emile had the day off from the lab— the experiments weren't working, Vince admitted; he needed to retool the script—but he was due to clean rooms in less than an hour. The day went by in a blur, his thoughts occupied by Claire. He wondered what she was doing, what she was thinking, and it felt good to wonder those things, and to know that there was someone out there wondering the same things about him.

And yet the day went by, taking the evening with it, and Emile saw no sign of Claire. Nor the next day, or the day after that. He told himself to be patient. Give her a week. In the meantime, he checked on Brenda, though after his night with Claire, he'd begun to feel sorrier for her than ever before. It became hard to look at her, to feel how sad she was, knowing that she had once had a daughter and a husband to share her life, knowing that she had once been so happy. Sometimes, when Emile was above ground, he pictured Brenda and the other percipients trapped below him.

A week passed. No one had seen Claire. He felt another wave, not pushing him back or taking him in, but a heavy, sinking current that threatened to pull him under. He worried she had left. Aged out like Max. Gone to college like Jacob. Disappeared like his mother. He tried to imagine what the Eldridge would be like without her.

It was another week before Vince gave him a new assignment.

"You should be happy."

"For what."

"For all you've accomplished."

"I haven't done anything."

"It may feel as if you've done little, but that's the way of the world, isn't it? Small steps before mighty leaps."

Emile sipped his coffee. They'd met in the dining room, and he watched every server who walked by, hoping for Claire.

"You seem distracted," Vince said.

"Have you seen Claire?"

Vince crossed his legs, folding his hands over his knee. "I'm sorry to say she doesn't work here anymore."

Emile nearly dropped his mug.

"People move on," Vince said. "Max. Claire. Someday you might too."

"She wouldn't just leave," Emile said.

"Check for yourself." Emile stood up, but Vince told him to sit, in a firm tone that momentarily drew the attention of the other patrons. "You still don't understand. Why would you go running off when the answer is right in front of you?" He uncrossed his legs and sat up straight, as if steadying himself for meditation. "Please, go ahead," he said. "I'm an open book."

Emile sat back down. He felt the grains of sand beneath his feet, as a wave rushed toward him. He saw the door to his dorm building. It burst open and Claire walked out, bundled up against the early morning in the beige sweater he loved, a yellow scarf around her neck. Vince was waiting for her. Claire tried to brush past, but he grabbed her by the arm. They needed to talk. There was nothing to talk about. *You went too far. I did what I was told. You were supposed to observe. He needed a reason to stay. That's why?*

A pause. A relaxing of Vince's hand.

He has no idea what he's capable of.

How do you know? Did you see it?

I don't do that anymore.

So you've said.

You don't believe me.

Everybody dreams.

Vince opened his eyes. The ocean disappeared, but Emile felt like he was drowning.

Emile grabbed the table with both hands, a piece of debris that could keep him afloat. "You must've known," Vince said. "You must've seen it."

Emile could only shake his head. He couldn't. He hadn't been able to.

"Is that so?" Vince laughed, quietly, as if enjoying some private joke. "Well, yes, she used to be a percipient. Then she stopped dreaming."

"But she stayed?"

"She made a deal. A good one, I would say. She could continue living here, the best home she'd ever known, and all she had to do was everything we ever asked."

"You sent her to me," Emile said.

"Don't get upset," Vince said. "We're all sent by someone."

Emile slammed his hand on the table. "Why would you do that?"

"I understand you're angry," Vince said. "Right now you're probably thinking you'll leave. That you'll go find your brother. But how will you explain to him that come the spring semester he has to find another way to pay for college?"

"You said—"

"Did you ever sign anything? Did we?"

Emile wanted to hit the table again. He wanted to stand up and throw the table across the room.

"I'll tell you what," Vince said. "You complete one more experiment for us, as instructed, and you can go. And your brother can remain where he is, fully funded."

"No," Emile said, more out of anger than any actual consideration. "I don't believe anything you say."

Vince smiled. "How about this? You'll start the experiment tonight, and in the morning I'll take you to the man in charge. If you don't trust me anymore, if you don't believe in the kingdom, maybe you'll believe in the king."

Emile searched Vince's mind. He saw the office Jacob had visited, where the voice had persuaded him to leave Emile behind.

The big man, Max had called him. "Who is he?" Emile asked.

Vince's mind closed the door of the man's office. "You see," Vince said, his eyes shifting. "There are still some mysteries worth sticking around for."

—

When Emile reported to the lab that night, he was electric with anger. They had gotten rid of Claire. Worse, for the moment, there was nothing he could do about it. Not without ruining his brother's life, again. Emile was trapped, just like the percipients.

In the lab, a young woman was waiting for him. She guided Emile down the hall and into the interview room, her mind quiet. Inside the room, on one of the tables, there was a small black leather case. The woman asked Emile to sit in a chair and to please roll up his sleeve. Emile hesitated, but obeyed. The sooner he did, the sooner he could talk to the big man, find out what happened to Claire. And from there, who knows.

The woman opened the case, though she kept her back to Emile, concealing its contents. Finally she turned to him, holding a small clear bottle and a rag. She dabbed the rag with the rubbing alcohol and swabbed the inside of Emile's elbow.

Emile closed his eyes. He pretended the woman was Claire.

"What is it for?"

"The instructions come after."

A pinch, followed by a burn. The woman smiled with her mouth closed, not fully like Claire.

She opened the door and led Emile down the hall to Brenda's room. The woman knocked.

A moment later the door opened, and Brenda stood before them in laboratory scrubs. Brenda did not protest when the woman entered first, or when the woman pulled out a second needle. The woman turned to Emile, who was still waiting at the threshold.

"Please, come sit down." She pulled out a chair from the small desk opposite Brenda's bed.

"What did you give us?"

"A little brain boost," the woman said. "In five minutes, Brenda will be asleep. When she is asleep, I want you to talk to her, but do not speak. Do you understand?"

Emile's mind began to swim. He was on the beach but he was alone. No one was waiting for him in the water.

"You're beginning to feel it," the woman said. "That's my cue to leave. Don't forget what I told you." Emile watched the door shut. He turned to Brenda, whose face beamed with haloed light. Golden streaks whose warmth Emile could both see and feel. He blinked his eyes but the light did not disappear.

"Brenda," he said, but he wasn't sure if his mouth had moved. He touched his lips with his fingers, the tips of which had started to tingle.

Emile felt his heart race, his skin twitch, his mind bend. He moved toward the door, but the handle had disappeared.

Don't forget what I told you, the woman said. The woman says. The woman will say.

Emile sat back down. He watched Brenda sleep, her back now turned to him, but then he also watched himself wrap his arms around Claire. No, Brenda. He wanted to confess something to her. He felt a heavy burden in his chest and became desperate to unload it.

Talk to her, the woman says. But do not speak.

He began. *Part of me is glad they're gone. Austin. Jacob. My mother.* He showed Brenda his dorm room, the bare walls and desk. He showed her the typewriter, the letters he still wrote to Jacob but never sent, because he didn't want his brother to know how much he needed him. Jacob had disappointed him, hadn't he? He had wanted to leave him. He had disappeared.

Brenda kicked. Her husband returned after his own disappearance, a string of nights spent at the casino. He didn't say a word as he stumbled into the shower. *Dad had a bad day at work*, Brenda would say to her daughter. *Mommy feels it too.* She would kiss the crown of her head. She would tell her daughter everything is going to be all right, despite the dream she had the night before.

We can't see the future, Emile said. Emile says. Emile will say.

But of course we can. We just have to listen.

—

When Emile came to, he was alone. He rubbed the injection site on his arm, which had purpled into a bruise. A moment later, the woman from the night before entered. Emile's head throbbed, and it was difficult to look directly at the woman's face, hovering over him.

"How are you feeling?" the woman said. She sat at the foot of Emile's bed and opened her black case.

"What was the point of that?" Emile asked. He was unsure what happened last night, what he had done, or how any of it furthered the experiment with Brenda.

The woman cuffed his arm and took his blood pressure. She made him open his mouth and say "ahh." When she was finished, she took a small notepad out of her case. "Now then, Emile. Tell me about your dreams."

"What?"

"Tell me everything you remember."

Emile felt a stab of panic. "What's going on here?"

The woman patted his knee. "I'm reading the script I was given. You understand."

Emile stood up. More of the room started to come into focus. There weren't any windows, not even on the door.

"I need to leave."

"You will. But not yet. The drug needs time to wear off. You should be back to normal by tomorrow."

"You're keeping me here?"

"We're asking you to stay, for your own well-being."

"Vince said—"

The woman raised an eyebrow at the mention of Vince's name, and a wave crashed over Emile's feet. He saw Vince sitting next to the woman, in one of the chapel pews, giving her orders.

"How about I come back tonight, yes? When you're feeling more like yourself."

The woman was gone, in between blinks. Emile rubbed his eyes, willing the drug to wear off.

—

It felt as if hours had passed. He jumped out of bed to try the locked door. He yelled for someone to let him out.

Sit down, a voice said, startling Emile. He looked at the ceiling. He put his ear to the door.

You're not going anywhere.

This time, he recognized the voice as his own. The words wormed deep into his mind. He couldn't claw them out no matter how hard he tried. He sat down on the bed, his heart pounding in his head.

You wanted this, the voice said. *Remember? You knew what would happen when Jacob left. You knew because you saw it. On Max's face. You might have looked the other way, but you knew. They will never let you go.*

Emile lay down, though he didn't close his eyes.

This is your life now, the voice said. *This was your life. This will always be your life.*

—

The woman did not come back that night, or the next morning. No one came that afternoon, when his worry was replaced by hunger, or that night when both were surpassed by thirst. His stomach ached as though it was caving in on itself, and still the woman did not return. Emile felt completely hollowed out, and when he pounded on the door, screaming for someone to please tell him what was going on, he could feel his words echo around his empty insides.

On the third day—or was it the fourth?—Emile sat on his knees, hunched over the toilet. His dry-heaving was interrupted by a knock. The night before—or was it that morning?—he decided that he would hit the woman if she came at him with that needle again. And if she refused to give him answers about what was going on, when he could leave, he would grab her by the throat, or beat her until she gave in, like he'd done to the boys at Lost 80.

But when the door opened, it was Vince who entered, not the woman. In his hands was a tray of what smelled like the most delicious food—mashed potatoes, maybe, warm rolls, meat slathered in gravy—all of it shielded with a metal cover, so only a tiny cloud of steam could escape. Vince began with an apology.

"For the nature of the experiment," he said. He glanced at the toilet and grimaced.

"You write the script," Emile said, his eyes fixed on the tray. His body told him to remain calm, until the tray was offered. "Anyway, I did what you said. So we're done."

"You did. Thank you. But the experiment isn't over."

"It is. I'm saying it is."

"That's your choice, of course."

"Is it? Or is that another one of the things you just say and everyone pretends is true?" Emile sat on his hands so he wouldn't be tempted to grab the tray. "No one leaves unless you want them to."

Vince stood up, displeased. "We have to finish the experiment. Sleep on it. Pray. Whatever it takes. When you're ready, call for me, and we'll break bread." He picked up the tray, stole a roll from the plate, and chewed it slowly. He left, though the smell of dinner remained, and would torture Emile well into the next day.

———

It was the pain that woke him next. It felt like his stomach, and everything attached to it, were mutinying. If Emile wasn't going to provide what they needed to survive, they would gnaw their way out. They would agree to anything Vince proposed.

Or was it the knock? At first, he wasn't sure he'd really heard it, his body was shaking so loudly. But then the door creaked open, and Emile willed himself to sit up, so that he could quickly agree to whatever Vince wanted.

"Emile?" the woman whispered. She was empty-handed.

"Yes," Emile said. He was angry now, angry that the woman had nothing in her hands. Not a tray of food, nor her black case, nothing that would bring an end to the experiment.

The woman stepped closer. "Hey," she said, "look at me."

Emile did as he was told. It was a moment before he realized what he saw, before his mind could put the woman's features, all of which he had secretly memorized while she was asleep, in their proper places. He started with her smile.

"Claire?"

She was dressed in scrubs, though they were clearly a size or three too big. He had never seen anyone so beautiful.

"They said you were gone."

"I was. I am. I brought you Jell-O."

"Jell-O?"

"We have to go. Can you stand?"

He scooped the cup of Jell-O into his mouth with his hand and let Claire put his arm around her to prop him up. "Ready?"

Emile laughed. He couldn't help it. He laughed loudly, even though he knew what this was. An escape. A rescue. He laughed because it was impossible. A dream. He had taken the needle and gotten lost in his own fantasy.

Claire wiped the Jell-O from his lips and kissed him. "Gross. Why did I get lime?"

The kiss jump-started Emile's mind, which cycled to the memory of the movie he and Claire had seen together, the man wandering Mars alone, dying the same way.

"I don't want to die on Mars," Emile said.

"Me either," Claire said, as she carried him toward the door.

"What about Brenda?"

They were in the hallway now. The long and empty corridor was before them.

"Brenda is Brenda. They'll never let her go."

She pushed him forward, and he told himself not to look as

they walked by Brenda's door. And he didn't. But he felt her as they walked by the front desk clerk, to whom Claire gave a knowing nod, and even now, as Claire carried Emile up the stairs and out the door into the bracing cold. And still, even now, as they sped down the mountain in a car Emile assumed to be stolen. All that time, the link between Emile and Brenda, which the drug had successfully forged, glowed within his mind. They must've continued giving Brenda the injections, Emile thought, turning her mind into a super antenna, a beacon buoy, blinking in the dark. How long, he wondered, would he receive her signals? How long would he feel the pull of her current?

Emile didn't ask where they were going until hours later, as they drove deep into the night. The sky was starless and the moon hidden. The car had to make its own light. In the morning they would still be driving, but when the sun rose, there would be no mountains, or real scenery of any kind, in sight. Only a flat orange landscape, and Emile would make a joke about a large rock being his new best friend.

"I don't know where I'm going," Claire said. "Except away from there. That's all that matters."

Emile looked out the window, at the nothingness blazing by. He felt surprisingly calm. Against Claire's wishes, they had stopped and grabbed some burgers and fries to go, and although he had the distinct feeling he would throw all of it up later—too much, too soon, Claire would say—at the moment he was content. He bought a Polaroid camera from a gift shop nearby and made Claire pose for a picture.

"I want to find my brother," Emile said. It was hard for him to admit, but it felt good once he finally confessed that whatever was next for him, he didn't want to face it alone. He explained that Jacob had never written him back after the first postcard all those months ago.

"He didn't write back because he never received your letters. Neither did that Ginny person." She kept her eyes on the road. "Everything you typed on your little typewriter went to the incinerator."

Emile thought of the fireplaces in the Eldridge's many lobbies. He pictured Vince reading the letters out loud to Claire, laughing, then tossing them into the fire. He tried to clear the image from his mind, as it reminded him that Claire had worked for Vince, which he didn't like to think about, even if she had no choice.

"I'm sorry," she said. "We had to. You know, hotel policy. Anyway, you can't go to your brother. They'll be looking for you there."

"So what am I supposed to do?"

"We'll drive the rest of the night, then I'm going to drop you off at the smallest town I can find."

"You're not staying."

Claire frowned. "My mother is sick. I need to make sure she's okay." She put her hand on Emile's knee, thought better of it, and returned it to the wheel. "I can check on your brother. Later."

"They'll be looking for you too," Emile said.

"I know. But I'm better at this than you."

Emile looked at her with wonder. He wanted to be upset with her. But she had come back for him when no one else had, not even Jacob.

Emile watched the sun rise in the passenger mirror, painfully, a sober reminder of the sleep they'd forgone. Eventually Claire exited the highway and found a small town they had never heard of, and if Emile wasn't going to stay there, he knew it would be someplace like it.

"You could always take a peek," she said, "if you're still curious." They were parked in front of a gas station that had yet to open. Claire shut off the engine. "Or is that still cheating?"

Emile rolled down his window. It was still early, but the air was already much warmer here than it ever was in Archer Park.

"I tried," Emile said. "That night after the movie."

Claire rolled down her own window and looked away, perhaps thinking of what Emile had said that night at the park, about how the most difficult people to read were those plagued with pain. It had been the wrong thing to say.

Claire didn't look at him, but she took his hand. That night, and for many nights after, when he was alone, lying in a strange bed in another strange town, he would think of her—even when he tried not to—in a wave of longing that also reminded him of Brenda. Of her latest dream, which Emile saw even though he was hundreds of miles away now. Her husband and daughter picked her up from the Eldridge, before they settled into a new beachfront house that Brenda knew would eventually be filled with renewed sorrow. In the dream Brenda and her daughter are sitting in the back seat, together, while her husband drives. The daughter is still young enough that she doesn't protest when Brenda pulls her into her arms. The daughter drifts off, just as a song that both Brenda and her husband love comes on the radio. When the song is finished, her husband catches Brenda crying in the rearview mirror. He asks Brenda what is wrong, and Brenda laughs, her tears salting her mouth. "Nothing is wrong," she says. "You came back. You came back."

CHAPTER SEVEN
IIII Lia

When Lia's mother was pregnant, her father didn't want to know what Lia would be.

"Have I told you this?" her mom would begin.

"Yes," Lia would say, "a thousand times."

This never stopped her.

"Your father didn't want to know, which meant I couldn't tell him about the dream I had every night until you were born. It was a simple dream, the same each time. I'm pushing a stroller in the grocery store when a man comes up to me and comments on what a beautiful baby boy I have. In the dream I am enraged, because I know better. I look at the man and tell him that my child is not a boy. She's a girl. A strong girl. And one day she'll be a strong woman. So strong the world better watch out.

"Your dad said it was acid reflux. When I woke up still angry. He took me to the doctor, who prescribed something, but the feeling never went away. Not until you were born. Not until I was proven right. Every day," her mother said, "you prove me right."

Lia did not feel strong when she returned to her dorm room after her trip to Menninger. Her legs were weak from biking to the coast, then hiking down the hill, then biking back again. She shut the blinds, lay in bed, and went over what she had discovered: the quarantine station, the purported experiments. In her head she connected them to Dr. Moyer, even though she had no evidence that he had ever been there. But how else could she explain the transcript about Moyer's death, sent to her in an envelope whose return address was Menninger? She'd looked the facility up on her phone on the bus ride back to campus, and found a fan site dedicated entirely to conspiracy theories. According to its author, the facility hadn't been used since the fifties, when the Australian government caught wind of what was going on and shut it down. But its author alleged that for years the government continued the work in secret. Admittedly, this theory was written in a large neon-green Comic Sans font, and thus was difficult for Lia to take seriously. Still, as she closed her eyes, she let herself wonder. What if James, the schizophrenic she'd read about in the DJHK transcript, had gone to Menninger? What if Moyer was the doctor who'd treated him?

And what if, she speculated, Moyer's untimely death was suspicious? What if it was actually a murder? Who would want him dead? Why?

Lia took a long nap when she returned from Williamstown, then rode to the station that evening. It was a Friday night. Julie and the rest of Lia's classmates were going out, but here she was, conducting cursory Internet searches at her unpaid internship. First, looking for stories on Menninger from legitimate news outlets. Nothing. Second, she searched for anything on Dr. Moyer. Friends, family. Nothing again. Lastly, when she could think of nothing else, she typed in "Limetown." She was about to press enter when Wiley popped his head in.

"Thank god you're still here. One of the hosts is out sick. I need you."

"Me?"

"Not on the air. Just work the phones. I can handle the rest."

She followed him to the booth, watched as he sat uncomfortably behind the mic, waiting for some sleepy jazz song to finish. It was nice being in that room again, so close to where stories were reported, where things actually happened, even if she was just watching.

As soon as the light went red, Wiley began to sweat heavily. He stumbled over and through the copy.

"Well, that did not go well," Wiley said when the program ended.

"You were just nervous."

"Nervous? You could hear me sweat."

"Well, it wasn't really your story. I'm sure it's hard to get a feel for something you haven't written. I had this teacher in high school. She always said: if you don't care, what's the point?"

"I don't know."

"But you're the producer, right?

"For now."

"So is this what you really want? To run the same sad local news stories every day?"

Wiley shrugged. "Worked for my predecessor. He's dead now, and nobody remembers his name, but he seemed happy."

"People aren't listening," Lia said. "You know that, right? Or if they are they're simply saying, ah, too bad, then moving on with their lives."

"Yeah. So."

"So, that's not right. Why should they have the luxury of not caring? The people suffering have to care. They don't get a choice." Lia could feel the heat building in her chest. Wiley didn't know anything about her, her family, about Limetown, but she was tired of questions going unanswered, of people telling her to look the other way. This feeling, she realized—contrary to her mother's wishes—had only strengthened during her time in Australia. "Plus," Lia said, "if we can get them to care, they'll keep listening."

Wiley sat there, considering what Lia said. He stretched his large hands over his large knees. "You're not wrong," he finally said.

Lia thought about the search Wiley had interrupted. The cursor she left blinking, like a pulse, next to "Limetown."

"Don't worry," she said. "I have an idea."

———

Maybe the sick host would be back on Monday, maybe she wouldn't. But Wiley wanted to be prepared, in any case. Lia wouldn't tell him about Limetown, her connection to it. Not until she proved herself. She didn't press enter when she opened her laptop back in her dorm that night, and "Limetown" sat there waiting. She erased it, and in its place she typed "Menninger" again. She typed "Dr. Moyer," knowing there would be no new results.

Julie stirred in bed behind her. "Turn off that stupid lamp." Lia apologized, but Julie said it was too late. She was awake. She sat up and stole a drink from Lia's coffee. "Where were you yesterday? I texted you."

"I know," Lia said. "It's my internship. I have a lot of work to do."

"You do understand that without school, there is no internship."

She sounded like the study abroad chaperone.

"I'm just saying, I miss you," Julie said. "You're never around anymore." She ran a finger up and down the length of Lia's arm. "Come back to us, Dorothy."

She tugged Lia's arm, trying to pull her into her bed, the soft cotton sheets Julie had brought from home.

"I'm sorry," Lia said, but she stayed at her desk.

Julie crawled back into bed. "Fine. But don't get mad if no one's there to save you when a house falls on your head."

Lia worked through the night. It felt good what she was doing, looking for answers, like she was satisfying an itch, even if she couldn't reach the area she wanted to scratch the most. She created a basic outline for a Menninger story, one she could take to Wiley and say, *Here. Isn't this better? Isn't this the type of story we should tell?* Granted, the outline she sketched was pretty thin, and part of Lia was relieved when the host showed up Monday evening.

Lia thought about her outline as she biked to her dorm that night. She let herself crawl into bed with Julie. She breathed in her hair and told herself to feel something, as if you could make yourself care for someone by closing your eyes and concentrating. But as Lia lay there, and her mind cycled back through the best parts of her day, as she thought about what exciting things the next day might bring, not once did her thoughts land on Julie. In the morning, when she was supposed to be in class, she would head back to Menninger. She would find that man again, the only source she knew, and make him point her in the right direction. She would lie if she had to, whatever it took to get the answers she needed to shape the story she wanted to tell. And there would be satisfaction in this, unraveling a mystery. There would be comfort in knowing that secrets can't be hidden forever. That actions have consequences, and that when you throw a stone into the ocean, though it may appear otherwise, the waves never disappear.

—

It was a windier day than her first trip to Menninger. Lia was nearly blown off her bike as she turned the bend to the beach. Thunderous waves crashed against the shore. The window she'd shattered was still broken, though someone had taped a thin tarp over it as a temporary fix. Lia tore the tarp down and waited. When that didn't work, she picked up a rock and shattered a different window to summon the old man. She shouted obscenities she hoped he might find offensive, a birdcall for someone of his generation, she thought, but no one showed. Eventually she hopped on her bike and went to look for him.

It was another half hour before she came across a caravan park. It was a warm enough day that several of the park's inhabitants were sitting in front of their mobile homes, sweating through sagging lawn chairs. A radio blared. Lia recognized the program. Its host was American, a loudmouth shock jock who specialized in political sensationalism. The residents took turns commenting on the gossip crackling through the static, drinking their beers and coffee and asking, *Can you believe that?*

Lia was thankful when, after ten minutes of keeping her distance, the old man emerged from one of the trailers. He spotted her right away and told the others to turn off that damn noise. They glowered at the man, but picked up their radio and took it inside.

"You've come with my money," the man said.

"I broke another window," Lia said, "and will continue to do so unless you tell me what I want to know."

The man dragged a chair to a dormant fire pit and sat down. He propped a foot up on his knee.

"The older I get, the more I realize how dumb everyone else is."

"So tell me what I don't know," Lia said. "Tell me who you are and what you know about Dr. Moyer."

"I told you, I don't know any Moyer."

"Now who's the dumb one."

The man laughed. Lia sat down across from him.

"I can't tell if it's because you're young or a Yank," the man said, "but you've got a real bitchiness about you that I don't think I care for." Lia took a deep breath, the only thing preventing her from grabbing the fire pit's poker and jabbing it in the man's eye. "Then again," he said, "people have said the same thing about me."

"What's your name?"

"Zeke."

"Zeke, my name is Lia. I'm here to do you a favor."

"Who said I needed any favors? Look around," Zeke said, and motioned to the wealth of detritus littering the caravan park. "I've got everything I need."

Zeke reached beneath him and switched on a small radio, tuned it to the same program his neighbors had been bickering over. He smiled as the host worked himself up about some issue he had with the government.

"You like this guy?"

"He's great. Not afraid to tell it like it is. Has a lot of good theories too. Some are a bit out there, but most make sense, if you think long enough."

"What about you? You have some theories of your own, right? When we spoke before, you mentioned something about experiments at Menninger."

Zeke shifted in his seat. "I was just wagging my chin."

"But you had heard of Dr. Moyer. You recognized the picture I showed you."

"I never said that." He pinched his elbows together in a way that did not match his bravado.

"Zeke, I work for a radio station. Just like that one. I can get your story out there." She scooted to the edge of her seat, closer to Zeke and the dormant fire. "Whatever it is you think happened at Menninger, do you think they, whoever they are, should be allowed to keep it secret? Does that seem right to you?"

Zeke didn't say yes or no, not immediately anyway, which Lia took as a good sign. The radio program returned from a break. The host was already yelling, getting undoubtedly red-faced about how he'd seen what was going on in the Australian Parliament before. Back home, where the elected officials somehow forgot their reason for existence, to govern for the people, not for themselves. Be careful, the blowhard warned. They want you ignorant. Your ignorance is their bliss.

Lia could see Zeke getting worked up. He scratched the side of his face, going against the grain of his gray stubble. He squinted his eyes at Lia.

"We could bring you in," Lia said. "Into the station. I could interview you. Tell the world yourself."

"No," Zeke said abruptly. "Leave me out of it."

He crossed his arms.

"Don't tell me you're afraid."

"I won't," Zeke said. "I'm not. What have I got to lose? You, on the other hand, little Yankee girl . . ."

"I can handle it."

Zeke sized Lia up, and she wondered what he saw. Probably just what he had said: a naive American girl, eighteen going on eight. But she had smashed a couple of windows, and in doing so maybe proven herself to be a rebel or a truth-teller, if there was a difference.

The man on the radio was telling his audience that they must act now.

"You think so," Zeke said.

"You'll save money on windows."

Zeke shook his head. "All right," he said. "Then come close, and I'll give you an exclusive."

———

He never met Dr. Moyer. Lia should know that right away. He never talked to him either. But he'd seen him? "Oh yeah," Zeke said. "I saw him." It was in ninety-two? Ninety-three? The caravan park was new back then. Zeke had settled in with his third and worst wife. She was always riding his ass about something—money, which they didn't have, friends, which they also didn't have, sex, which they did have but she claimed was inadequate. The older he got, the more he became aware that all he wanted in life was to be left alone. So he started going on these long walks. Just to get away. Sometimes he'd head north a bit, into the woods, get lost and halfway hope he'd have trouble finding his way out. When that grew old, he went down to the coast. He avoided the beach at first, thinking wife number three might see him there—she was something of a surfer in her time, had a nice beach bod that he was twenty years too late for. Anyway, he found a nice spot, and of course she was there, tanning. Zeke slinked away before she spotted him, walked until the sand disappeared and it was just him and a bunch of jagged rocks.

Lia knew the stretch of land he was describing. She had taken two of those rocks to break the windows.

"That's how you found Menninger," Lia said.

"I didn't get too close at first. Something about that place spooked the hell out of me."

The two unmarked vans didn't help. They arrived from a back road that snuck up behind the facility. As Zeke would discover on a subsequent walkabout, the road was gated off from the public and monitored by a single camera blinking its watchful red eye.

"What else did you see?"

Not much. He saw the same two guys take smoke breaks at the same time each morning. Though only one of them smoked. They both wore lab coats and never strayed far from the facility. Sometimes it appeared as if they were arguing, but Zeke couldn't get close enough to hear them. Other times, a woman appeared too, and Zeke noticed that her presence caused the men to pause.

"Blind mice," Zeke said.

"What?"

"Three blind mice. That's what I call them."

"Why?"

"Because I like to. Can I tell my story?"

Zeke never saw the vans leave. But one morning he left his home significantly earlier than usual. In part because he had a keen feeling something odd was going on at Menninger. In another part because the night before the wife had relegated him to the foldout couch, which was hell on his back. When he arrived at the facility, he saw that one van was missing. So he found a spot to squat in the woods and waited. It wasn't long before he heard the van whining up the back road. The nonsmoking man got out and slid open the back door, offering his hand to a woman Zeke had never seen before. The woman, who was much younger than any of the mice, looked very confused. She had brought a bag with her—of belongings, Zeke assumed—and she didn't try to run away, but it seemed she had no idea where she was or what she was doing there.

"I never saw her again," Zeke said. "But there were others. I went back each morning, camped in my spot. I saw the van return with a few other people, each as bewildered as the next. I never saw any of the patients leave."

"Patients?"

"What else could they be? They were all . . . sick-looking. And what about the mice in the lab coats?"

"But you never went inside. And you didn't talk to any of the patients?"

"The patients. No." Zeke grinned at Lia, displaying a row of crooked and browning teeth.

"You met a mouse."

"I set a trap. And man, Yankee, did you ever see such a sight in your life?"

The trap was a fire. A campfire fifty meters or so from Zeke's usual spot in the woods. Zeke built the fire upwind from the facility, and large enough that when the mice stepped out for their break, they were hit with the smell immediately.

"And it worked," Lia said.

"Oh, they came running. One of them anyway, like he'd got his damn tail cut off."

"So you did meet Dr. Moyer."

"Not Moyer. Moyer was the smoker. I met the other one."

Zeke was reluctant to describe the mouse he met. He was one of those men, Lia realized, afraid to acknowledge any positive feature in another member of their sex, worried it might impugn his masculinity. But he did say the man was average height, maybe a little taller. A little shifty. He looked uncomfortable standing before Zeke, next to the fire. Still, he didn't ask Zeke what he was doing out there, or demand that he leave. Instead, he asked if everything was all right.

"He was very polite," Zeke said. "Kinda opposite you."

Zeke told the man everything was fine with him. For his part, the man was surprisingly forthcoming. "He admitted everything," Zeke said. "Everything I suspected. It was a research facility. They were doing experiments. He said I could come in if I wanted. If that would put my mind at ease."

"Did you?"

Zeke's gaze fell to his feet. He hadn't gone inside, he was ashamed to admit. Something about the man.

"Are you sure?" the man had said. "I think you would feel better.

You don't have to spend every morning here, you know, in the woods. There's no reason for it."

Zeke shook his head, though he was curious.

"You don't trust me," the man said. "I assure you we're not hiding anything. It's just that our subjects tend to do better in isolation. It does them no good to be around others. Feeds their anxieties. Can you appreciate that?"

His eyes, which previously had wandered the woods, landed directly on Zeke.

"And I didn't like it," Zeke muttered to Lia. "It was like he was looking straight through me. Like I was nothing at all."

The man left Zeke there, frightened in the woods. But before he did he told Zeke to stop by anytime. They were neighbors, after all.

"Perhaps you'd like to bring your wife? Unless she's gone the way of the others. No, surely not. Third time's a charm, right?"

Then he smiled politely and returned to the facility.

"You never went in," Lia said.

Zeke's wide eyes found Lia. "Would you? How did he know about my wife? They must have done research on me. Go in? No, I don't think so. I wasn't going to end up in one of those vans."

Zeke returned only one other time, right after his third and final wife left him for good. More distraught than he expected, he wandered the beach for hours, drinking bottle after bottle of beer, making message-less vessels and hurling them into the ocean. Until night came and he found himself back in his hiding spot, staring at the stars, thinking in clichés about his life. Out of loneliness, he walked down to Menninger, thinking he might take the mice up on their offer. What was there to lose? But they were gone. The vans, the mice. The gate was left open, as was a door, so he went inside. But it was empty, the same as when Lia found it.

Zeke fiddled with the radio, which had lost its reception.

"I don't understand," Lia said. "Who pays you to look after the facility?"

Zeke smirked to himself. "No one. I made it up. Hoping to get some money off you."

He played with the radio until he finally found a music station. A piano played its way out. Soft, staccato chords, a catchy arpeggio layered beneath. Lia recognized the song, though she couldn't recall its name.

"What is this?"

"What is what?"

"This song. I know this song."

"Great," Zeke said. "So do you want to tell my story or what?"

Lia focused on the melody. "I'll need more to go on," she said absent-mindedly.

"But you'll tell it?"

She didn't answer. She knew she'd heard the song before. But where? A movie, perhaps. A TV show.

Zeke reminded her of her promise to leave his name out of it. He was pacing now, having become suddenly irritated, while Lia stared at the radio near his chair. "This was a bad idea," Zeke muttered to himself. "Why couldn't you keep your big mouth shut? Been around women too long. That was the problem. You ever get that feeling," he said, "like you're watching yourself make a bad decision." He stopped pacing. "Hey. Yankee girl. You hear what I'm saying?"

"Be quiet," she said, her ears straining to hear. The base of her skull hummed with the melody, measure after measure, taking her to her parents' attic. Eventually the instruments would die out—they would have to—and the players would go away, but the song itself would loop around Lia's mind for a long time to come, beyond her bike ride back to the bus station, to the radio station, where she would make some calls, tell some lies to set up an interview with Tracey McNellis, Dr. Moyer's colleague, the woman interviewed in the article about his unexplained death, all while the song, that feeling, pulled her forward. It would even follow her to bed, as she tucked herself in next to Julie, a mysterious soundtrack to her troubled dreams.

"Hey, don't you tell me to be quiet. You hear me?"

"Yes," Lia whispered, as the song finished. "I hear you."

———

Tracey McNellis still worked at Deakin. Lia felt like she was trespassing when she stepped foot back on campus. She was flunking both of her classes by now, having trampled over the attendance policy, as well as failing to complete any assignments. She moved quickly to Clyde Hall, head down in case she accidentally ran into one of her professors. Dr. McNellis was waiting for Lia in her office, on the top floor. The office was impeccable, the surrounding bookshelves dust free, each book alphabetized and shelved flush within its row. Her desk faced the window, and on it were two sets of neatly stacked student papers, a few scientific journals, and two picture frames, lined up across from each other at perfect forty-five-degree angles. In one frame was a yellow Labrador, panting in the sun.

"That's my lab partner," Dr. McNellis said, smiling at her own joke. "Penelope. I take her everywhere. Well, except my office. The one space in my life that is sans dog hair."

Lia took a seat. She couldn't help but stare at the other picture, which featured a beaming couple. A younger Dr. McNellis, with brighter hair and fewer lines around the eyes, holding hands with Dr. Moyer. Lia's parents had a similar picture—perhaps all married couples did—that once sat on her father's bedside table. Lia wondered if it was still there, in their new house.

"He was my other partner," Dr. McNellis said, interrupting Lia's stare, her strident voice softer now. "To be honest, Penelope was his idea." She adjusted the picture frame. "Now, I don't know what I'd do without her."

There was an awkward silence as she remembered something Lia could only guess at. Lia filled the silence by taking out pen and paper.

"You were married."

"Of course," Dr. McNellis said. "His name was Christopher Moyer."

Lia opened her notepad, fumbled to find her spot. "Your bio, it doesn't mention anything about him."

"Well, he's dead now," Dr. McNellis said. "Bio means life." She picked up the photo and stared for a moment. "And anyway, we agreed early on to keep our relationship as private as possible. Academia is very competitive, as I'm sure you know. Neither of us wanted to ride the other's coattails."

Dr. McNellis let herself stare at the photo a moment longer, before returning it to its proper place. She sat up straight and folded her hands in front of her, perhaps waiting for Lia's next question. On the phone, when Lia was setting up the interview, she lied and said she was working on a piece about distinguished women in Melbourne, women who were shining examples for others to admire. The plan, albeit a bad one, was to furtively question Dr. McNellis about Moyer by asking her about her work, and, ultimately, her colleague, before revealing anything about the radio station, and the story Lia wanted to tell. But seeing that picture, knowing that loss—

"I have a lecture in thirty minutes, Ms. . . . what was it again?"

Lia closed her notepad. "You can call me Lia."

"Wonderful. My male students call me Tracey, whether I want them to or not. Do they have sexism in America?" She gave Lia an encouraging smile that made Lia feel even worse.

"I'm sorry," Lia said.

"For what? You're doing great."

Lia nodded, trying to steady herself. She tried to recall something that Miss Scott had once said, about people wanting their story to be told. How they needed that, even if they didn't know it at the time. But the advice felt callous now, when confronted with someone who had experienced real loss.

"Actually," Lia said, "I'm not feeling well. I'm sorry. I'll reschedule."

And before Dr. McNellis could stop her, Lia grabbed her things and ran.

Lia went straight from Deakin to work, holed herself up in her closet. She transcribed a week's worth of shows, trying not to think about any of it. Dr. McNellis. Moyer. Her parents. Then there was school and Julie, not to mention Zeke. That weirdo had a point, didn't he? That part about knowing you were on the wrong path, but walking it anyway.

Wiley poked his head in looking for a mocha. "How's the story going?"

Lia held up a stack of transcripts. "It's not."

"Jesus Christ," Wiley said. "Do I have to hold your hand through this? No one ever held mine." He turned over an empty work bucket and sat down. "I don't know what's going on with you, and you can't imagine how much I don't care. But whatever it is, forget it. None of it matters. The story is what matters. Isn't that what you told me?"

Wiley said there might be an opportunity for her to tell her story, whatever it was, at the end of the week.

The next morning Lia biked with Julie to Deakin. Lia hadn't set up an appointment this time, and had to wait outside Dr. McNellis's office for ten minutes as some undergrad grade-grubbed about the C he received on his last exam. Dr. McNellis waved her in next.

"You're back," she said.

"I'm back. Sorry about last—"

"I looked you up, Lia. Or I tried to. You never did give me your last name. So I couldn't find anything online. On you or this Melbourne Women of Distinction Award that I'm assuming you made up. Though for what reason I can't begin to fathom."

Lia felt a small swell of shame. She managed to raise a hand and point to the framed picture of Dr. Moyer on Dr. McNellis's desk.

"You're going to have to use your words, Lia. I don't have time for charades."

"I'm here to ask about your husband," Lia said.

Lia told Dr. McNellis about the transcript she found, or rather, that someone found for her, about Dr. Moyer's death. She explained how the return address on the envelope led her to Menninger, which led her to Zeke, who had seen her husband at the facility and spoken to one of his colleagues. Lia even told Dr. McNellis her theory that the transcript she discovered about the miracle-working doctors who treated James was not only connected to Menninger, but was *about* Menninger. And that she believed Dr. Moyer was one of the mice who cured James. She had no proof of that connection, no direct evidence, but how else to explain the appearance of the Moyer article the same day as Lia found the transcript? She took note of how Dr. McNellis reacted, how her face changed, revealing what she already knew, what she didn't, and what she wanted to keep secret.

"That's quite the story," Dr. McNellis said, her forehead frozen in place, impassive, after Lia somehow got the whole speech out. "Who are you, really? An investigator or something?"

Here, Lia told a half-lie. She worked for the radio station (true); she was a reporter (not exactly); the station wanted her to find a story that no one else was telling (kind of).

It was then that Dr. McNellis scoffed. "I don't even know you."

"My name is Lia. I'm from Kansas."

"Kansas?"

"It's a state. In the US."

"I know what Kansas is," Dr. McNellis said. She lifted her brows—a question formed on her face. She stared at Lia for a moment, then swiveled in her chair to face her window. The office hummed to itself, waiting. "But I meant what I said. I don't know you."

Lia twirled her pen around her thumb. "What would you like to know?"

"I don't want to know anything." She swiveled her chair back around and waited until Lia shut her notepad before she continued. "Let me ask you something. Off the record, assuming there is a record. Do you know what it's like to lose someone? To have them vanish from your life without any explanation?"

Lia thought about her mother, who was always at risk of disappearing. Instead, she said: "I had an uncle."

"I'm not talking about some relative you barely knew. I'm talking about someone who you shared your life with, who *was* your life."

"Did your husband work at Menninger?"

"You're not listening. Every reporter I ever talked to, they never listened."

"What kind of experiments were they doing?"

Dr. McNellis slapped her desk. "Listen! There is no story here. The story you want, it doesn't exist. Do you understand?"

She stared hard at Lia, waiting for her to nod in agreement, to surrender. "Good," Dr. McNellis said. She stood from her desk to walk Lia out. "Now. Have you met my door?"

"Wait," Lia said. She panicked for words. None of her rehearsals ended this way. "I need this. They're going to kick me out."

"Out?"

Lia lowered her head. "Of school."

Dr. McNellis laughed. "Of course, you're a student. That explains it." She walked across the office and waited for Lia at the door. "Well, as I so often tell my students, because they always forget, your problems are not my problems."

Lia stared at her, and when it became clear that she wasn't going to change her mind, that Lia had failed, she gathered her things and made her way to the door.

"I'm going to tell this story," Lia said. "I know your husband worked there. I'll figure out the rest."

"I'm sure you will," Dr. McNellis said. "But if you want my advice, don't publish until you have all the facts. That's something else I tell my students." She gently pushed Lia out the door. "But they never listen to me, and somehow, I doubt you will either."

—

There was a voice mail waiting on Lia's phone when she stepped outside. She'd missed a call from her father's number, but when she pressed play it was ten seconds of dead air. The short ride back to the dorms she debated whether to return the call. She hadn't spoken to her father since leaving for Australia, not wanting to think about him, the bonfire, the way he gave up on Lia's uncle, and in some ways, her mother. But after sitting in her dorm for half an hour, staring at the missed call log, she hit call.

The phone rang once.

"Lia," a voice said. Lia pulled the phone away to make sure she had dialed the right number. "It's Mom. Sorry, I thought I'd have a better chance on your father's phone. Did you get my postcard?"

"What do you want?" Lia said.

"Everything's fine. Everything's fine. It's just that, I got an e-mail, well, then a phone call, from your study abroad chaperone. Something about you not attending class?"

"I'll make it up in the summer," Lia said. "I'm focusing on my internship."

"Oh, okay. That's good. I just wanted to make sure you were safe. It's not like you to miss class. Plus, you didn't return my call the other day."

Lia thought about hanging up. "I'm just really busy. Okay?"

"I understand," her mother said, and she went silent for a while. "But, well, can you tell me about it? Your internship? I want to prove to your father that I was right. This trip was a good idea." Her tone was calm, sincere. She sounded like her old self, the mother who gifted Lia a wooden hummingbird hairpin when Lia turned five. Because, as her mother explained, it wasn't just Lia's fifth birthday. It was the fifth anniversary of the best day of her mother's life.

"It's actually pretty great," Lia said, giving in. "I'm working on a story about this secret lab." She gave her mother a few more details, about Zeke, Menninger, and Dr. McNellis, leaving out the hole in the story, the missing link between Moyer, Menninger, and the miracle workers. When she finished summarizing, her mother remained silent on the other side. "Mom, you there?"

"That's great, Apple. That sounds really cool."

There was another long pause. "What is it, Mom?"

"Nothing. It's nothing. It's just . . ."

"What?"

"Well, who told you about this? I mean, how did this story come about?"

"Research, Mom. Okay? Investigation." She didn't like how her mother's tone had changed so quickly, from supportive to skeptical. So she wouldn't tell her about the James transcript someone had left on her desk. Or the Moyer transcript someone mailed to her dorm. "And so what if I've been skipping class?" Then, to cut a little deeper, "If I've been shirking my duties in pursuit of answers, no matter the cost?"

Her mother sighed. "Apple, if you're going to bait someone, you should make it more subtle than that."

Even so, Lia could tell the bait had worked.

"It was your idea to come here," Lia said. "I was fine back home."

"You weren't. None of us were. We were pretending."

"So? What's wrong with that?"

Somewhere in the background a door slammed loudly, and Lia heard her dad calling her mother's name. She pictured him coming home from a long day of work, having stopped by the grocery store to pick up a few things. She wondered what her father would see when they sat down for dinner each evening. Was it the doting Alison, the one who celebrated family anniversaries and answered the phone when he called? Or was it the woman her mother had become, the one who'd disappeared because of Limetown?

Her father continued calling her mother's name. "Alison. Alison."

"Mom?" Lia said, speaking softly, for some reason not wanting to give her mother away.

Her father's voice grew louder.

"Nothing," her mother said, in a weary whisper. "There's nothing wrong with pretending."

There was a knock on her mother's door. "Alison," her father said. "Are you in there? Is everything all right?"

A breath into the receiver.

"I have to go, Apple. Be smart."

———

After the phone call with her mother, Lia made up her mind: She would tell the story. Forget the missing link. She had a source who put Moyer, a renowned neuroscientist, at Menninger, a mysterious research facility. She had an interview transcript with a patient who benefited from a mysterious cure. She knew enough to deduce what was going on. She would tell the story, finish her internship, and if school no longer wanted her, she would fly back to the States and get a job at a radio station. It would be difficult without a degree, and she might have to start at the bottom again, but she would at least have the Menninger piece to point to, to show a producer what she was capable of.

The meeting with Wiley went smoothly. Lia could tell Wiley envied her in some ways. He saw something in her that he knew he would never have. He saw something in most people that he knew he would never have. It wasn't youth, or confidence; it was belief. That what you did mattered. That you, an individual, could make a difference.

—

The story would air on Friday. Lia spent the rest of the week cooped up in her closet, writing and revising. She studied the transcripts of her favorite DJHK shows, taking note of their structure and pace. By the time Friday arrived Lia still wasn't sure what she'd written was ready, but Wiley took the script and reminded her that it was public radio and no one was listening anyway.

Wiley read the script beautifully, surprising everyone—including himself. Lia admired the crispness of his pronunciation, his assured tone. He made the story feel inevitable, as if there were no missing link. When Wiley cut to commercial, Lia smiled at her reflection in the glass.

The phone began to light up shortly after. There weren't many calls—there were never many calls—but what the callers lacked in number they made up for with excitement. One person simply stated they really enjoyed the story, that it reminded them of a show they'd seen as a kid. Another listener had already heard of Menninger and shared his own theory as to what happened there. Things were going well enough that Wiley invited Lia into the booth to answer follow-up questions. Lia put her hand over her chest, trying to steady her heart as she took the first call. A man wanted to know if any of the doctors involved with the experiments still practiced. The man had a troubled brother, whom he was desperate to help. Lia apologized, saying that to her knowledge, none of the men—including the deceased Dr. Moyer—were still involved in the medical field.

"All right," Wiley said, "one final caller. This is Penelope and she has a question for Lia, is that right?"

A woman's voice came to life.

"Yes, thank you. I was curious, Lia, do you know of any facilities similar to Menninger back home?"

"Back home?"

"Yes, you're obviously from the States. Kansas, I'm guessing."

Lia reddened. She should have recognized the voice immediately.

"Where exactly? Kansas City?"

"Lawrence."

"Ah," Penelope said. "Lia from Lawrence. Well, what do you think, *are* there any secret facilities like this where you're from?"

Lia recognized that strident voice.

"Not in Kansas," Lia said. "Not that I know of anyway."

"What about that place where all those people disappeared? Limestone?"

"Limetown," Lia said, and she felt a startle in her throat, like she'd been exposed. She glanced at Wiley, who returned a puzzled look.

"That's right. Limetown. You don't know anything about that?"

"Not really."

"Not really? So you know a little? Why don't you do a story on that?"

"I'd have to do more research first. There are still a lot of questions."

"Of course," Penelope said. "You wouldn't want to speculate. Although, why not? Seems to me you're quite good at it. Jumping to conclusions with little proof." Wiley tried to break in, but Dr. McNellis talked over him. "How exactly did you connect these so-called miracle workers to Menninger?"

Lia took a deep breath. She tried to remain calm, even as she felt the story falling apart. "As the piece mentioned, I spoke to an eyewitness who was at the facility when it was still operational."

"Yes, I heard," Dr. McNellis said. "Your unnamed source. Did this source work at Menninger?"

"I can't reveal that."

"Were they a patient? A doctor?"

"I can't reveal that either."

"How convenient," Dr. McNellis said. "Fortunately, for the sake of your listeners, I can."

"No," Lia said.

Wiley tapped her on the arm. *What the hell is going on?* he mouthed.

"Your source, whom, in the name of professionalism, I won't name either, never set foot in that facility. He was a vagrant, really. And a fool if he let you drag him into this mess. He lurked outside, but he never dared go in. Isn't that right, Lia from Lawrence?"

"No," Lia said. "I mean, yes, but it's obvious that—"

"What is obvious?"

"The secret lab. The mysterious doctors who cured people when no one else could. It's the only thing that makes sense."

Lia looked at Wiley for help, but he put his hands up, not wanting to dirty them with Lia's mess.

"Someone wanted me there," Lia said. "They sent me that address. I'm not making this up."

There was a deep gulf of dead air. Lia's words replayed in her mind. She imagined the few listeners sitting there, laughing at this girl from Kansas, wherever that was, who had no idea what she was doing. She imagined Zeke picking up his radio and throwing it into the woods.

Finally, Wiley intervened.

"Well," he said, "this has taken a rather embarrassing turn. Penelope, you've been very helpful. But I'm afraid we're out of time."

"How do you know," Lia said. She held her hand up as Wiley tried to cut her off. "Penelope, how do you know my source never went inside?"

Another long pause, but the line crackled with life. Lia's mind crackled too, as she realized why Dr. McNellis called in, how she could know so much about Zeke, and how she could know for certain that Lia had never found a link between James, Moyer, and Menninger.

"I could tell the world your name, you know. I could say it right now. Because something happened there, the same way something happened to your husband. And maybe you had nothing to do with either, but you're the only person I know who's connected to both."

Dr. McNellis sighed into the receiver. In sixty seconds, as soon as they were off the air, Lia knew she would be fired. In a week, Lia would say good-bye to Julie and board a plane headed back to New Hampshire. And a month after that she would receive a call from her college advisor—her former college advisor—informing her that she'd been expelled. Too many absences. Too many mistakes.

But right now, she had a lead.

"Penelope," Lia said.

"Because I was there too. Because I was one of them."

And then the line clicked dead.

CHAPTER EIGHT
▮▮▮▮▮▮ ❚❚❚ Emile

On the six-year anniversary of his escape from the Eldridge, in the fall of 1985, Emile ducked out of the rain and into the movie theater where he worked in Eugene, Oregon. The lobby lights were still off inside. Emile shook out his umbrella and nodded to the concessionist as she dumped last night's leftover popcorn into the popper. She was a couple of years younger than Emile, and cute. She'd even asked him out once, but Emile had declined, lying to her face and to himself. "Sorry," he had said. "I'm seeing someone."

The truth was that he never heard from Claire after she rescued him, though he never stopped wondering about her. "Keep out of sight," she had said. "Keep out of mind." This, when she left Emile in Boise, Idaho, dropped him off in front of a run-down motel that boasted free television. The television, he learned upon check-in, was in the lobby, featured two channels, one of which was perpetually fuzzy. Claire paid for his room through the month, then walked him to his door, though she insisted on saying good-bye outside. She gave him a perfunctory kiss on the cheek, wrapped him in her yellow scarf, and told him it would be a while, but someday, when the time was right, she would take him back to the movies. It was painful to think about that promise, even now, years later, when he knew for certain he would never see her again. Claire, the woman who—when he was feeling particularly lonely—he would let himself think of as his first love. He often thought it would have been easier to move on, to forget her, if she wasn't his first, or even if she'd just been straight with him. *This is it. I'm leaving. I'm never coming back.* Instead, she left him to wonder.

—

Emile had a theory about motels, which came to him the night Claire left. They didn't want you there. They needed your money, yes, but that didn't mean they were happy about it. And it damn sure didn't mean they had to make you comfortable. How else to explain the lumpy, mystery-stained beds, the off-yellow wallpaper, the indifferent help up front? They wanted you in, out, and if you dared complain, they would remind you of their unreasonably low rates, and how they didn't raise an eyebrow when you paid in cash under a fake name. The more time passed, the fonder Emile grew of the motel's unromantic, cynical view of life, which presented a welcome contrast to the idealism that surrounded the Eldridge.

He shared his theory with the private investigator he hired in Boise, whenever they spoke over the phone. Larry would ask him about the new digs and didn't seem to mind when Emile described the various idiosyncrasies he encountered at each stop. He understood that Emile was lonely, and Emile understood that Larry, a widower, was lonely too.

Emile had spoken to Larry that morning, before he went to work at the theater.

"Larry."

"Mr. Haddock." He always addressed Emile this way, despite the fact that when they first met, Emile wasn't even eighteen. "How are the new digs?"

"You wouldn't believe the towels."

"Try me."

"The owners used to live on a commune."

"How does that affect the towels?"

"There aren't any."

"You're kidding."

"They want to keep things as organic as possible, which means I have to air-dry."

"Bummer."

"Yeah," Emile said. "You got any news?"

"Are you sitting down?"

"They don't believe in chairs."

"Well that's okay," Larry said. "Because I've got nothing to report."

It had been some time since Larry had an update worth sharing. Recently, out of guilt, he halved his monthly rate and expense fees, which, he admitted, consisted mostly of subpar coffee and pastries, a habit leftover from his police days. Emile took his no-news to work with him, worrying a little less about keeping his head down these days. In the beginning of their professional relationship, Larry suggested that perhaps Emile might be paranoid. Why would anyone follow a seventeen-year-old kid? Emile didn't tell him anything about his past then, only that after a year of living in the same Boise motel, it was time for him to move on. He didn't tell him that he was going to look for his brother, whom he hadn't heard from in nearly a year and a half.

"Where are you going?" Larry had asked. "How do I reach you?"

Emile answered only the second question. "I'll call you."

"That's it?" Larry said.

"That's it."

All Larry had to do was keep an eye on something for him. Check in with the woman who ran the motel, to see if a friend of Emile's ever came by. Before Larry could turn down the request, Emile gave him a month's retainer and a description of Claire.

—

Emile grabbed the booth key. He liked being a projectionist, a profession, if he could call it that, he cobbled together after it finally sunk in that Claire wasn't coming back. He'd wandered into a small theater in Boise, thinking of his first and only date with Claire, and overheard the assistant manager complaining about how they needed help. A felix culpa, Max would have called it. Emile was hired that day. He had to work his way up, from the concession stand to usher, to the box office, and finally, to the projection booth, but once he did he had a job that he could take with him wherever he went as he looked for Jacob. The money was terrible, but it was enough to afford the worst motel each town had to offer, with just enough left over to pay Larry.

His current theater, in Eugene, recently switched to semiautomatic projectors, a breeze compared to the enormous machines he'd threaded in the past. He only had to make one switch, and since it was a small theater with only two houses, he spent a lot of his time in the booth reading, writing, or flipping through the postcards he'd collected the past few years. He bought a postcard everywhere he went—Idaho, Utah, Oregon—and would give them to Jacob when he finally found him, proof of his search, that he'd never given up looking for his brother, though he no longer thought his brother could say the same.

Larry was always trying to persuade Emile to open up, arguing that he could track Claire down, instead of just waiting around, or help Emile find whomever he was looking for, if Emile would tell him the whole story. That was the problem with most of his clients, he explained. They're so afraid of making themselves look bad that they leave out details crucial to the case.

"I'll tell you, that's what you regret the most when you lose a loved one," Larry said, throwing down the widower card, "all the things left unsaid."

"We're not married, Larry."

"I know," Larry said. "This distance is killing us."

Emile threw him a bone on his and Larry's one-year anniversary, when Emile called him from a motel in Salt Lake City. He didn't have to tell Larry that he still believed he was being followed. That on more than one occasion he'd returned to his room to discover things not quite where he'd left them. Before he left Boise, Emile started leaving traps. He began taking pictures of his belongings with the Polaroid camera, so that when he returned from work he could prove he wasn't crazy. He plucked a strand of hair from his head and with a little lick strung it tightly across the top of his closet door, so that if someone opened it, the strand would snap. It was something he saw in a spy movie.

"That's not the craziest thing I've ever heard," Larry said. "Did it work?"

It did, which was one of the reasons why he had packed his things and headed to Utah.

"Why Utah?" Because that was the last-known location of his brother.

"Your brother? That's who you're looking for?"

He had taken a bus down to Salt Lake, found a room not far from the university Jacob had planned on attending when he left Emile at the Eldridge. Emile remembered Claire's warnings that they would be looking for him there, but he was bitter enough that ignoring Claire's advice felt like a small victory. He got a job working at a drive-in theater on the outskirts of town, and looked on with jealousy as college kids held hands and watched horror films from their parents' cars. During the day he walked the picturesque campus, where the same kids laughed and complained about their classes. After college they would leave this bubble and make another, with spouse in tow, and there was a slow realization building inside Emile, that as long as he was alone, as long as he couldn't find Jacob or Claire, he would be outside every bubble, looking in.

He didn't tell Larry any of this. He only said that he never saw his brother at that university. Emile befriended a lonely girl from a small town who worked in admissions. He spent a few days with her, looking inside her head and comforting the thoughts that needed comforting (*You are smart, you are pretty, you belong here*) but in the end, when he asked her to look through the university's records, she could find no record of Jacob having attended the university. There was a track team, but not one of several track members he purposely bumped into had heard of Jacob either.

What happened to Jacob? An ocean of possibilities swam across Emile's mind. Some of the explanations were simple. Jacob arrived, decided he didn't like Salt Lake, and transferred to a nearby college before classes started. Other explanations were darker, more complex. Jacob went to college, but once Emile escaped, breaking his agreement with Vince after less than six months of work, the Eldridge came after him. They took away his tuition and erased his enrollment, threatened to do more if Jacob didn't tell them where Emile was. Jacob didn't know. So, he ran.

Emile called Larry every time Emile moved.

"Where are you now?" Larry would ask. And, "How are the digs?"

After Salt Lake, there was Provo. There was Ogden. There was Portland and Corvallis. There were months in between each destination.

Sometimes a year. Sometime more. Time wasted mustering the courage to start over, to continue the search. Time wasted saving enough money so he could move on to the next bubble town, where he wandered yet another college campus, hanging on to the sliver of hope that Jacob had transferred after Emile left the Eldridge and his funding ran out. He knew he was looking for a needle, and most days the cynicism that grew every day after Claire left overwhelmed him. Still, on occasion, when the weather was particularly pleasant on a campus stroll, or after he threaded an unapologetically sappy movie at work, he let himself imagine what it would be like to see his brother again. Perhaps Emile would be walking down the street, head down, eyes on his feet, when a familiar wave washed over him, and he would look up to see his brother in a coffee shop window, deep in thought. Well, maybe not deep.

—

Emile had made his way to Eugene, Oregon, having meandered west after combing Utah, then slowly heading north. He called Larry again after his shift at the movie theater but their conversation was short. Larry had recently met a widow at church who understood what it meant to lose someone. They were going to a show that evening.

"You hate plays," Emile said.

"But I love women." Larry laughed. "Hey, I wanted to talk to you about something."

"That doesn't sound good."

"Actually, you should be happy. I've decided I'm done cashing your checks. I'll still run by the motel to check if she's been there, and you can call me whenever you want, but after all this time—"

"I get it."

"I'll give you a refund. A partial refund, I mean."

"You don't have to do that."

The doorbell rang in Larry's house.

"I've got to run. Take care of yourself, okay?"

Then, before Larry could hang up: "Larry?"

"Mr. Haddock."

"I don't know what to do."

The doorbell rang again, but Larry stayed on the line. "You want my advice?"

"Does it cost extra?"

"Go home," he said.

"Home?"

"I don't know what you're running from, but at some point you have to face your demons. You're from Texas, right?"

"Kansas."

"So go to Kansas. There's more than one way to make it all work."

The doorbell continued to ring, and Emile pictured Larry's date holding down the button until the melodious ding turned into a single drowning note.

"You should go," Emile said.

"I'll talk to you soon."

"Sure, Larry."

Emile would never speak to Larry again. He sat in his bed, looking around his room and thinking about what Larry said. He had a few hundred dollars saved. If he put in his two weeks tomorrow at the movie theater, he could probably make it most of the way. He would be lying to himself if he said he hadn't thought about it before. Returning to Lawrence. He could drive by his high school, visit Ginny's classroom and apologize for how things ended. And if she wasn't there, he could leave a note on her chalkboard. *I still have questions. I still need answers.* He could visit the guardians, and Austin, all the people he left behind. As he went to sleep that night, he wondered how he could feel homesick for a place with so many bad memories, and that had never felt like home.

—

Two weeks later he was on the road. Larry's refund was much more than Emile had expected. *He must be very happy with his new woman*, Emile thought. Instead of a bus ticket, Emile bought a used car from the owner of the motel. It had a million miles on it, but it still ran, Emile was assured, and it would give him the luxury of returning at his own pace, taking whatever detours and pit stops were necessary to steel himself for the final leg of his journey.

Which was how he ended up in Archer Park.

He didn't plan on returning, though he supposed the Eldridge had been on his mind since Larry had given him the advice about facing his demons. How else could he explain why he took the exit directing him northeast through Boulder and Estes, instead of south through Denver? He stopped at the same rest area he and Jacob had, what was now over six and a half years ago, expecting a sense of dread to catch in his chest, or some latent animal instinct to fire in his brain telling him to flee. But as he looked down at the town, at the Eldridge, all of which looked the same, he felt something different. He had escaped, after all, made his way on his own terms. He had the sudden desire to show them that what they had done hadn't broken him. He decided he was done running.

—

The lobby was exactly as he remembered it. The wood decor, the fireplace, even the elderly guests. Emile had changed, his face was a little fuller, his mind sharper, but this place had not. As he walked around the lobby, he reminded himself that there was power in that, in evolving while everyone else stayed the same. He sat for a moment by the fireplace, warming his hands and wondering if things would have been different if he had trusted his instincts when he first came to the Eldridge, if he had gone with Jacob instead of staying here. Though whenever he did think this way, he came back to the same thought. *If you left, you wouldn't have met Claire.*

He wasn't sure what made him remember it, but he walked toward the hallway he had stumbled upon the morning Jacob left. It had smelled like chlorine. Perhaps he was thinking of the motel he planned on staying in that night, in Kanorado, just over the state line, and whether or not it had a pool. His entire time working at the Eldridge, Emile never found the source of the smell. But for some reason, he could never get it out of his mind.

Through two lobbies, past two fireplaces. Down the long hallway. He inhaled the chemical smell. At the end of the hallway, there was the window and the locked door. But the door was slightly open now, held ajar by a sneaker. Inside the door he found a stairwell. The chlorine smell grew stronger as he climbed five flights of stairs. At the top, there was another door, propped open by another sneaker. Through this door shone a blinding, warm light, and for a moment it felt like the stairs he had climbed had gone so high they'd taken him to the sun.

"Don't shut the door! I forgot my key!"

Emile waited for his eyes to adjust. He listened to the lapping of the waves before realizing that he was standing at the edge of a large aquamarine pool, on the hotel roof. A swimmer made a beautiful turn, gliding underwater, resurfacing half the pool later. Emile shielded his eyes and waited for the swimmer's face to come into focus, and when it did, he was surprised to find that he wasn't surprised at all.

"As I live and breathe," the swimmer said. "Haddock."

Max pushed himself out of the pool and slapped his wet feet straight over to Emile, whom he gave a big, soaked hug.

"I just . . . I never thought. Quick: tell me what I'm thinking."

"You're happy," Emile said. "You're very happy to see me."

"Yes! That's right! Come, let's sit in the sun. You can watch me tan."

Max looked good. Standing before Emile, then sitting in a pool chair next to him, a large pair of sunglasses dwarfing his face. His hair was longer, thicker, and an impressive beard covered his chin.

"So you're back," Emile said.

"So you're back," Max said.

"How was college?"

"College was sunny, sinful, but ultimately boring. I graduated, started a master's, then stopped said master's. The professors and I, we didn't always see eye-to-eye." He put a fake gun to his head and pulled the trigger.

Emile lay back in his pool chair. He thought about his experience versus Max's, how different they must've been. Max had left, gone to college. Emile had barely escaped. The disparity gnawed at him.

"Hey," Max said, "I heard about Brenda." He turned to his side, propped himself up on his elbow. "That was messed up. Brenda and I went way back."

Emile didn't look at him. He stared at the sun until his eyes were on fire. "How is she?"

"Gone," Max said. "Long gone. Vince too, in case you were wondering. Things are different now. The big man is making sure of that."

Emile sat up. He hadn't thought about the big man. Or, not as much as he thought about Vince. But the idea of the same mysterious figure working in the shadows, the voice—name- and faceless, still directing cruelty—that such a thing was still possible—

"Who is in charge?" Emile asked. "I want to meet him." He'd clenched his fists without realizing it.

"All right." Max stuck out his hand. "Max Finlayson. Pleasure." Emile didn't understand. "Don't look so shocked, Haddock."

"You," Emile said. He stammered. "You?" He was picturing Max as the man in the office, the one who persuaded Jacob to leave, the one who ordered the experiments on Brenda, on Emile.

"Oh please," Max said. "That wasn't me. That was the big man. I may have a sizable ego, but it's not refer-to-myself-vaguely-and-in-the-third-person big."

He sat up and explained. How when he was in college, at Stanford, he was never really alone. He thought it would be a clean break. That was the deal, wasn't it? Put in your time, then be set free. But he always felt watched. First, in his dorm. Later, living off campus. In the beginning, he told himself it was just the Eldridge checking up on him, making sure he had everything he needed, as promised. But he began to notice the same cars in the parking lot no matter where he went. And how when he returned home after a long night in the lab, the air in his apartment was different. It wasn't a smell or a taste, he said, more of a feeling, like someone had broken in and rearranged the molecules.

Emile thought of the motels, the Polaroids sitting in the trunk of his car, the strands of hair across his closet doors.

"Anyway," Max said, "it gave me the creeps, you know. But what was I going to do? Drop out?" He thought about it, but by then he'd come so far. And why should he let his unverified paranoia get in the way of his dream? So he finished school, double-majored in parapsychology and neurogenetics. Took him less than three years too, a record he proudly touted to whichever woman would listen. Sadly, the dream of marrying his college sweetheart eluded him. There were one or two flings, of course, but no one willing to stick around while he made himself a genius.

"This one girl," Max said, "she actually said this to me. She said, 'Max, you're the smartest person I know, and you'll probably win the Nobel Prize someday, but I can't sit around forever and wait for that to happen.' Can you believe that?"

Max took off his sunglasses and looked at Emile, expecting someone with whom he could commiserate. "Tell me who he is," Emile said. "Tell me who's responsible for what happened to Brenda." He took a deep breath, but couldn't bring himself to say, *What happened to me.*

Max looked away. "Would that I could, Haddock. But I never met him."

He was telling the truth. Emile could see that. He dipped inside Max's mind and saw him receive a phone call one afternoon after he'd quit his master's program, when he was sitting in his dorm, wondering what he was going to do with his life. When the phone rang, Max answered, but Emile heard it too. And though it had been years since Emile heard the voice—and even then, secondhand, through Jacob's thoughts—he knew it was the same person who'd told them that their mother was dead, and that if Emile stayed at the Eldridge, he had no reason to worry.

"He said the hotel was mine if I wanted it. I would have total control over the experiments, the staff—everything. All I had to do was report back every now and then, and not scare off the talent like the former minister."

"What did you say?" Emile said, though he supposed it was obvious. It was what Max had always wanted, free rein to pursue whatever wild idea hatched inside his brain.

"I told him I'd have to think about it."

"That's it."

"Well, not quite," Max said. He put his sunglasses back on and Emile watched a full sun dance in each tinted lens. "I asked him where he was going."

"And?"

"He said he was moving on to phase two."

—

Emile agreed to have dinner with Max, though he refused his offer to stay the night. Max said he understood, but Emile wondered how much. He knew about what had happened to Brenda, so he must have known what happened to him.

As they sat down for dinner, underground, in the limestone tunnels, Emile felt claustrophobic. He felt like he was making a mistake. Worse, a mistake he'd already made. Max knocked back teacup after teacup of a cloudy drink, talking openly about his plans for the Eldridge now that he was in charge. He wasn't sure what he wanted to do here yet, he explained. Lately he had the strong impulse to create something. Really make something, you know? Something he could share with the world. It wasn't enough that he was the youngest person in the country running a top research facility. He wanted the Eldridge to be special again, but to stop hiding in the dark. After all, what was the point of making a scientific breakthrough if you couldn't brag about it to everyone you ever knew?

"Complete and total transparency," Max said. "Well, that's what we'll present to the public anyway. Some things will have to remain between you and me." He pointed to Emile's plate. "We won't show them every step of how the sausage is made. We'll just make it better."

Max stuffed a forkful of meat in his mouth. "So?"

"So."

"Come on, Haddock. Don't make me beg."

It took longer than it should have for Emile to understand. Max wanted Emile to join him. That was why he invited him down there.

"Are you out of your mind?" Emile said.

"You tell me, percipient. I mean, I'm a little tipsy—"

"Don't call me that." Emile pushed his plate out of the way. "You're drunk. Which explains why you genuinely believe I would consider staying here."

"But you've come back, haven't you?"

"Do you know what they did to me?"

"I heard the highlights. Right before I fired him, Vince tried to justify all that happened. I'll be honest, I never cared for that guy. Creeped me out." Max wiped his mouth with a napkin, covered up what remained on his plate. "Listen," he said. "I'm no mind reader. And my dreams, well, they're mostly sexual in nature. But I have my own talents. And part of me knows a part of you wants to stay here. Why? Because you're a helper, Haddock. Deep down, that's who you are. That's what you do. Brenda, the rest of the percipients. I need people like you, to keep me honest." Max leaned back in his seat, pulled out a cigarette. He flicked a lighter but couldn't get it to spark. "So. What do you think?"

"I think you're one of the smartest people I've ever met," Emile said.

"Yeah?"

"But I'd burn this place to the ground before I stayed another night."

Max closed his lighter. His cigarette hung from his mouth for a moment, before he sighed and put it back in its pack. "They'll never stop," he said. "The big man. The Eldridge. Someone will always be after you."

"Let them find me," Emile said. "I'm done running."

—

Emile drove all night. In the morning he sped through western Kansas, counting windmills to pass the time. He recalled his drive west years ago, how big the world seemed blanketed in night. Now, he saw things for what they were.

He made it to Lawrence that afternoon. He'd had plenty of time to plan where he would go first, but once he arrived, he couldn't decide. He ended up in the parking lot of his old high school. School was already out for the day, and Emile idled in his car, wondering if Ginny was still in her classroom, supervising the delinquents in detention. *Write down why you're here*, she might say. *Now turn to your fellow felon and ask them the same.*

The school was open but mostly empty. No one stopped Emile as he walked the familiar halls. Little had changed here too. A few more trophies in the trophy case, a fresh coat of paint in the cafeteria. The rest was as it was. It took Emile no time to find Ginny's classroom. The door was unlocked, but the room dark. She wasn't there. He clicked on the light and was startled, not by how much the room had changed—it too was the same—but by its smallness. Perhaps he'd spent too much time on college campuses, in their enormous, cathedral-like halls. He stood at the front of the classroom, where he'd once given a poorly received presentation on Williamsburg back when Mr. Church was still around.

He sat in his old desk, uncomfortable and cramped. On the desk to his right, which Austin once inhabited, Emile ran his fingers over the letters engraved. Names and places, initials and curse words. *RIP MR. C. LFK. Jonestown. Croatoan.* He thought of the tree he carved into at Lost 80, that night with Austin. Was the tree still around? Was Austin? He wrote a note for Ginny and left it on her desk. He told her where he would be, if she wanted to find him.

He ate and checked into the airport motel off Highway 40. It was too late to visit the guardians. He lay in bed that night, and when he couldn't sleep, he grabbed his keys and drove to Lost 80. He was disappointed to see that, unlike the high school, it had changed drastically. A large part of the woods had been cleared away; in its place, the city had built a picnic area, complete with metal tables and a small coal-fired grill. He parked across from a few other cars, leaned on by cocky teens. In high school, they were the type of boys he would have taken pleasure in punching. He kept walking when one of them said, "Hey man, what's up," and another, "You the guy with the good time?" He pressed into the woods that remained only to bump into more high schoolers, smoking, giggling. He eventually found his tree, and when he read John Donne's line—*No man is an island*—the words rang bitterly and untrue. After Jacob disappeared, after Claire disappeared, he had never felt more apart from the rest of the world. It was hard to imagine a geographical feature that better described him than an unattached landmass, alone in the ocean.

One of the leaning teens came up beside him.

"You're not him, are you?" the boy said. "The good-time guy?"

"I am not," Emile said.

The boy leaned against the tree Emile sat under. Emile wondered if he knew any other position. "You sure?"

The boy was thinking about beer, about getting a girl named Lucy into a questionable state of mind. "I'm not buying you beer."

"Nah. He buys himself beer. But sometimes he feels like sharing. I thought—"

"I don't drink," Emile said. "And if Lucy's smart—that's her name, right?—she won't either."

The boy startled. It had been a while since Emile looked inside someone's mind and used their own thoughts, the desires they thought private, against them. It felt good, to show his strength, to flex that part of his mind again, which he'd hidden for some time now, but never let atrophy.

"Whatever," the boy said. "You're not him."

"We've established that."

The boy made to turn away, but stopped. "You are weird though."

"So."

"My friend said he would be weird."

"Everyone's weird," Emile said. "You don't think it's weird to drive by someone's house, night after night."

"What?"

"To sit in your car, stare at her window."

"Shut up."

"I don't know," Emile said. "Sounds pretty weird to me."

The boy was about to storm off, and Emile would have been glad to let him, if he hadn't caught a thread of another thought. An older brother, telling the boy to stop leaning all the time. *Stand up for yourself.*

"Wait," Emile said. "Your brother . . . is his name Austin?"

"Yeah. So."

"He's still around?"

"Of course. That asshole's never leaving."

Emile stood up. "Huh," he said. He looked at the tree again, its words. They seemed different now, the letters sharper somehow, more pronounced. He was glad, he realized, happy that what he carved had lasted.

The boy tilted his head. "You know him or something?"

Emile put his palm flat against the tree. "We were friends," he said. "Back in high school."

—

The motel committed to its airport theme. Plane-shaped soap, house-keepers dressed as flight attendants. When Emile returned his suitcase was unzipped, but closed. He shook his head and took out his camera. After he captured images of his belongings, he pointed the camera at the mirror. How had he changed when he wasn't looking?

On the other side of Highway 40 was a small airport. Emile sat in a chair next to the window, fanning the photo to life. He listened to departures, to arrivals, and watched the red lights blinking in the distance.

—

In the morning his room was unaltered. He compared the room to the photos he'd taken before bed, to double-check. He took a few more pictures and headed out the door. It was Sunday, which meant the Sinnards would be at church until the afternoon. After Emile ate a late breakfast, more of a brunch, he drove out to their house, down the long dirt road. He wanted to get there early, before noon, to use the key hidden beneath the begonia pot and slip inside, so that when they entered their clean, perfect house, a ghost would be waiting.

It never occurred to him that he should have knocked, that someone would be waiting for him. But there he was, his uncle—Mr. Sinnard, his mother's brother, sitting in his chair, eyes on a tiny television.
The TV must've been a new purchase; it had taken the place of the
family Bible, which, once upon a time, lay open on a wooden book-
stand Mr. Sinnard had built himself.

"I thought you hated television," Emile said. He stood in the doorway. "Plenty of stories in the Good Book."

"Still are," Mr. Sinnard said. "What are you doing here?" In the
TV's glow Emile saw how old he'd become in the six years he'd been
gone. His hair, once thick and brown, had started to gray, to recede.
His eyes were still stoic, but the skin beneath them had begun to sag.

"You're supposed to be at church," Emile said.

"Gas leak."

"They finally got gas."

"Not anymore."

The TV program went to commercial. Mr. Sinnard grimaced.

"Where's your wife?"

"Address her properly."

"Where is she?"

"The house."

Emile took a step in, looked down the hall, into the kitchen.

"Your house," his uncle said.

"This is my house."

Mr. Sinnard frowned. His head tilted west. "She won't be long."

Emile looked in the direction his uncle had gestured, as if there
were a window Emile could see through, and not the wallpapered living room, the cuckoo clock perched on its opposite wall.

"It's just down the road, you know."

"I'll wait," Emile said.

Mr. Sinnard didn't respond. His eyes narrowed, and he pretended
to concentrate doubly hard on whatever program he was watching.
Emile hated when people did this, tried to conceal what was already
obvious.

"You don't have to pretend," Emile finally said. He shut the door
behind him. "You don't want me here. You never wanted me here."

"Wasn't my decision," his uncle said. He took his eyes off the television to gaze upward. "Through Him all things."

Emile thought of Vince. He thought of him anytime someone referenced God. "There's nothing up there."

"There's an attic. I can show you, if you'd like." He finally looked at Emile, reading his nephew's confusion. "Suppose you don't remember."

"I was told."

Mr. Sinnard scoffed.

"My brother. Jacob."

"A boy. The memory of a child." He tried to say more, but his scoff had lodged something in his throat, causing a coughing fit that lasted an uncomfortably long time and turned his entire body red.

Emile went into the kitchen to fetch him a glass of tap water. He watched his uncle drink it, his knotty Adam's apple moving up and down. When the glass was empty, he handed it to Emile without a word.

"You're welcome," Emile said.

Mr. Sinnard wiped his mouth, turned his attention back to the TV. The television was all the conversation he wanted. Emile stood there, empty glass in hand, and watched it with him. He couldn't tell if the program was a show or a movie. On the TV, a man took a boy fishing. He talked to the boy about some rule the boy had broken. The boy understood better now. They went home to their nice house, where the fish was already cooked somehow, waiting for them on the dining room table. Everything was black and white.

The television went to commercial but the show continued. Only now Emile could see color. Emile looked at his uncle, his unblinking eyes. It took a moment for him to realize what was happening, that the images he was seeing now weren't from the TV, but from his uncle's mind. Here was a cold and dark night, a house as black as the country. A knock at the door. *Open it.* A punch of frigid air, snow. A boy, her boy, shaking, covered head to toe. His face red, too cold to cry, his brother in his arms.

"You broke her heart, you know," Mr. Sinnard said. "When you left."

Mrs. Sinnard yelled at Mr. Sinnard to get a fire going, find a change of clothes. He grumbled to himself, struck out to the side of the house to collect some wood. When he returned, his wife was huddled with the boys in his chair, one big bundle of a family.

"But you didn't care about us," Emile said. "Neither of you did."

"You can care," Mr. Sinnard said, "and be careful."

Winter disappeared, rewound to a fall, decades ago. Two kids played in the dirt on a dust-blown farm, a brother and sister. Mr. Sinnard was the older of the two, but his sister was bigger and stronger. She pushed him around with ease, teased him with all the names she knew he hated. Emile willed the clips to slow down so he could get a clearer picture. But the scene shifted again, dust picked up as a car roared up to the house, enclosing the brother and sister in a thick cloud. The boy stuck out his hands to make sure he hadn't disappeared. There was a scream. Two men were dragging a woman out of the house. Emile understood it was Mr. Sinnard's mother, Emile's grandmother. Her husband was trying to calm her, telling her that her family would be waiting for her when she was in her right mind again.

Mr. Sinnard turned off the TV. That's all he would let Emile see.

"You thought I'd end up like your mother," Emile said.

He never saw his mother again, the same way Emile would never see his own.

"You know that she locked us up. She needed help."

"Your mother was trying to protect you. She didn't know how. She wasn't like your grandmother. She wasn't like you. She was like me."

"Like you."

"Normal," Mr. Sinnard said.

He went silent again, reflecting on all the things he should've done to save his sister. He thought of the car taking his mother away, the cloud receding, his father stomping back into the house, until it was only his sister and he, standing outside, holding hands.

Emile should have told him then what he learned, about his mother's death. But he couldn't make the moment right.

Outside the gravel road crunched. A car. Mrs. Sinnard.

"I'm sorry," Emile said. "That we left. Will you tell her?"

Mr. Sinnard swallowed a thought, nodded. The porch creaked, and the door opened. But by the time Mrs. Sinnard took off her jacket and set her purse down, Emile was gone.

———

Emile drove back to the motel to think, but once he was in his room, the phone wouldn't stop ringing. He supposed it could have been Ginny, reaching out after finding the note he left for her. But he was also worried it was Mrs. Sinnard, calling to chastise him for leaving her house without saying good-bye once again.

Eventually he got back in his car. He was halfway to Lost 80 before he realized where he was going. He needed a quiet space to think. Thankfully, the park was empty. Too early for the leaning teens. Emile found his tree and sat under it, and thought some more about everything Mr. Sinnard had told him, waiting for it all to make sense, for the apple to fall on his head. A lot of what Mr. Sinnard said confirmed what Jacob had learned from the big man at the Eldridge. Their mother hadn't had some irrational fear about what might happen to Emile because he was different. She'd seen it herself, with her own mother. They had taken her away because she was like Emile. But who were "they"? Mr. Sinnard hadn't said, and Emile supposed it could have been anyone. The local hospital, a sanitarium, some government agency. Perhaps it didn't matter. Perhaps the Eldridge, the big man, was right. The world is not kind to those who are different.

Emile closed his eyes and when he opened them again the sun started to set. The moon hung faded in the purple sky, unsure of itself. He returned to the parking lot, where someone was leaning on his car.

"I'm not him," Emile said.

"You are too him," a man said, deeper in tenor than the leaning teen. "You're exactly who I'm looking for. Excuse me, whom. For whom I am looking."

It was difficult to get a clear view of the man, hiding from the weak moonlight, but Emile could sense his excitement. The waves were small, but quick and continuous.

"I'm sorry to meet you like this," the man said. "I tried calling earlier in the arvo. I'm sorry, afternoon." He had an accent Emile couldn't place. "My name is Christopher Moyer. You are Mr. Haddock, correct?"

He stepped out of the shadows and offered Emile his hand, which Emile left hanging. The man was wearing a light-gray suit, complete with a thin-knotted tie choking his neck.

"You're the one following me?" Emile said. He supposed he should have been more alarmed, afraid even, but Emile was tired, and the waves that rushed at his feet felt more like invitations to swim than threats to drag him out to sea.

"Oh, no. I mean, I'm sure he has someone . . . but it's not me, no, no, no. Is that what you think? I'm a professor. Well, I will be. I'm on the market. It's very competitive, as you may know. Actually, why would you know that? Never mind." He took a handkerchief out of his back pocket, dabbed his brow. "The humidity here is unbelievable. I assumed your Oz would be like my Oz. A silly mistake."

"Oz?"

"Sorry. I'm not very good at this, I'm afraid. I'm not sure why he sent me."

Emile stepped to the driver's side, putting the car between him and this stranger, just in case. "Do you know what I'm going to ask you?"

"Oh! Of course! Who sent me? Well, he's very secretive about his name. But if I know it, and he knows I know it, and he knows you would know that I know it, the name, that is, I don't see why I can't tell you." Moyer paused, nearly out of breath. "Totem," he said. "Dr. Oskar Totem."

"Totem," Emile said. He had never heard the name before. "Do you know what I'm going to ask you now?"

"Well, I suppose it could be any number of things. Who is Oskar Totem? Why has he been following you? Not him, personally, of course. At least, I don't think so. Though I wouldn't know really. I suppose he could—"

Emile cut him off. "Stop. Please. One question at a time."

"Right," Moyer said. He paused to gather himself. "Dr. Totem is the world's leading neuroscientist, a pioneer who has set the field afire with his groundbreaking experiments, all of which aim at the same purpose: to unlock the human mind." Moyer straightened his suit jacket. "How did I do? I've been rehearsing that for some time now."

"You did great," Emile said. "Now tell me what he wants."

Moyer looked confused. "Isn't it obvious? He wants you to work with us. It's the future, you see."

"I don't care about the future," Emile said.

"That's because you haven't seen it."

"But you have."

"Well, no," Moyer said. "I suppose not. But I've heard it. Or, I've heard him talk about it." He walked around the front of the car and stood next to Emile. "You can too, if you'd like."

Moyer closed his eyes. "Here, does this help?"

"No," Emile said. "You don't have to—you can just tell me."

"It's fine. Faster this way, I imagine."

Moyer's was a busy mind. Emile waited for his thoughts to slow down, for the cogs of the clock to grind to a stop. There. Moyer, in a hospital room. He was working. No. Visiting. He turned to a man lying in the hospital bed. A brother. No, a friend. He was a classmate of Moyer's, at uni, a roommate, an undiagnosed depressive who had suffered for months. After the body was covered, wheeled away, the scene changed. Moyer warped to the hospital parking garage. A man was waiting for him there, the same way Moyer had waited for Emile. The man whispered his condolences. There must be a way, the man said, to help those suffering similar afflictions. He offered Moyer a cigarette, which he accepted. You're wary, the man said, as you should be. But think of it like this . . .

Emile's mind retreated from Moyer's. That voice. Those words. One synapse shot a dart to another, said, *Remember me.* "The voice," he said. "The big man." He had a name.

"You see now? Apparently he had been following my work, even read my dissertation. No one read my dissertation. Not even my girlfriend, and we were in the same field!" Moyer took a pack of cigarettes out of his jacket pocket. "Ciggy? Anyway, Dr. Totem made a very convincing case. I could help him, and others, like my dear friend, rest his soul."

"How?" Emile asked.

Moyer took a quick drag, as fleeting as his thoughts. "With you. We need someone who can get through to them. My friend, he was a psychotic depressive. Had delusions that the world was out to get him. Very troubling. The doctors tried a variety of treatments—drugs, psychotherapy. None of it worked. No one could reach him. We're hoping it would be different with you. That you could see—scratch that—that you could hear what we're missing. And that, maybe, you could find a way for them to hear you too."

Emile took a step back. An instinct. He felt like he had when he returned to the Eldridge, like he was making a mistake he had made before.

"Oh. You look worried. You can bring your family, if that's the problem. I understand the doctor used to have a different policy, but I told him, 'Look, sir, I have a serious girlfriend. I mean, we're serious.

About each other. Well, actually, she's serious too.' Did I mention she's a neuroscientist? Anyway, I said to him, 'We're a package deal. If you want my services, she comes too.' Hey, where are you going?'"

Emile had unlocked his car, ducked inside. The alarms that sounded during his return to the Eldridge were at full volume now.

"Mr. Haddock?" Moyer leaned in the window, put his hand to the steering wheel, as if this would stop Emile.

"Let go of the wheel."

Moyer stepped away. "You know, Dr. Totem warned me you might react this way, but I guess I didn't want to believe him." He stood there for a moment, brainstorming a way to make things right. "I know I'm forgetting something." A lightning bug buzzed around him. "Ah! Your brother! That's it! You're looking for your brother, right? We know where he is. We can help you find him. That's supposed to change your mind. Does it?"

Emile got out of the car. Years ago, right here at Lost 80, he would have grabbed Moyer by the throat and punched him until his thoughts went quiet. Even now, without realizing it, he found his hand strangling Moyer's tie, staring blankly into his terrified eyes.

"Tell me," he said.

"Do I have to?" Moyer said.

Emile tightened his grip. "Do you have to?"

"No. I mean, can't you just look?"

A moment later, after Emile saw what he asked to see—but couldn't believe—he got back in his car. "In case you change your mind," Moyer said, as he tucked a piece of paper with a telephone number beneath the windshield wiper. Emile told Moyer that he had no interest in making any deals, and that if anyone bothered him again, if they followed him to a park or messed around in his motel, he would bother them back.

CHAPTER NINE

IIII Lia

On Lia's two-week anniversary from being expelled from college, her mother got her a gift. She gave it to Lia when they got back from the airport. Lia had said nothing on the car ride to her parents' new home in Eugene. She was still angry—at Dr. McNellis, at herself, the world—and wasn't in the mood for her mother's weird celebrations. But after an early flight from the East Coast, she was too tired to put up a fight when her mother directed her to the dining room table, on which sat a beautiful maroon typewriter. Lia recognized it as the same model as Emile's, the one she found in the attic and her father tried to burn.

"What's this for?" Lia said.

Her mother pointed at the card resting on the typewriter's keys. Lia opened it up. On the inside it read, *For your next story*.

—

The late fall weather in Eugene was fitting. The interminable gray, the pestering rain. It reminded Lia of a book she vaguely remembered her mother reading to her as a child. Something about a lonely boy whose feelings reflected the weather, or was it vice versa? She spent those first few weeks in her parents' A-frame, sleeping, reading, self-loathing. The house didn't have an attic exactly, but the top room, previously designated as her father's office, was only accessible through a narrow set of stairs her parents had yet to venture up since her arrival. They left Lia alone to wallow up there, her father, she presumed, not wanting to deal with his moody daughter, while her mother refused to acknowledge that she had raised a young woman of such weak resolve.

They seemed better, Lia had to admit. This new start had shaken them free from the past. At dinner, the only time Lia shared their company, their faces were bright as they exchanged details about their respective days. Her mother relayed an anecdote about one of her students who was always late. Her father talked about how well his landscaping business was doing. "I know it's a cliché," he said, "but the grass is actually greener here. Must be all the rain."

Yet Lia remained unconvinced, by her mother in particular. She remembered their last phone call, how with just a little pressure she'd been able to make her mother reveal what Lia thought was her mother's true self. Lia studied her now, as her mother spoke, as her mother listened, looking for a twitch of the mouth or flicker in her eyes, any crack that might break her façade. It was difficult. Either because her mother had finally mastered her role, or because, and Lia thought this much less likely, she was genuinely happy. Unlikely, but not impossible, Lia supposed. Her mother was teaching again, this time as an adjunct at another community college. But what about Limetown? Emile? Lia didn't dare bring either up to her mother or father, though she did wear Emile's scarf around the house, draped over her jacket, upon which she prominently displayed his pin, her uncle who had heard the future, though no one in the present or recent past had heard from him.

In late November, exactly one month after Lia's expulsion, her mother ascended the stairs to the top room, where Lia was alternately reading John Donne and gazing out the octagonal window.

"You could be reading that for school," her mother said.

"I did," Lia said, "for Brit Lit. It was one of the classes I failed."

Her mother sighed. She once said being a parent was the best workout she ever got, but all the exercise was in patience. "This isn't you," she said. "This isn't the daughter I raised."

Lia turned from the window. "And who are you? Today, I mean. The dutiful teacher? The disappearing wife?"

"Apple."

"Don't call me that."

"Lia."

"Alison."

"I'm not here to argue with you," her mother said.

"And yet."

"I'm letting you know that you're enrolled. At my school. Classes start first week of January."

"What? What are you talking about?"

"Part time. Only six credit hours. Your tuition is free because I'm faculty."

"Mom," Lia said, "I'm not going back to school. Especially a community college."

Her mother folded her arms. "Then you have until the new year to find a job and a place to live. This isn't a shelter."

—

The campus, if Lia could call it that, consisted of a single building—a converted mall—located in the one part of Eugene without verdant trees. The walls of each classroom were faux stone, too hard to hang any decorations, so most remained blank like a jail cell. Lia was enrolled in two classes: Topics in Mathematics, a pre-req she was certain she would never use, and JOUR0165: Introduction to Mass Communication, a course she assumed would repeat everything she already knew.

"My name is Tamra Dobbs," the journalism instructor said on the first day of class. "You can call me Tamra or Ms. Dobbs. Not Professor Dobbs, not Doctor Dobbs. I'm neither. And if there's one thing I like about journalism, it's that we aim for accuracy. For facts."

Lia zipped up her hoodie a little tighter. Since her expulsion, she made a daily attempt at forgetting the failure that was her on-air debut, but it seemed the world had an infinite number of ways of reminding her. She kept her eyes down as Tamra listed other facts about herself. She was twenty-six, with a master's in journalism from Oregon. She taught not because she was good at it, but because it supplemented the meager salary she made working for the local paper.

Lastly, she was married, but didn't have any kids. And she didn't want any either. She had practically raised her little brother and wasn't interested in doing anything of the sort again. "So make sure you have your shit together," she said. "Know the syllabus. Know the assignments. And if you're going to miss class, keep your lame-ass excuses to yourself."

Perhaps the worst part of the community college, Lia realized, was that she would consistently run into her mother, whose office was just down the hall from Lia's math class. Early on her mother made a point to wait for Lia outside the classroom each day and invite her to her otherwise poorly attended office hours. She was obviously trying to keep an eye on Lia, and by week two Lia had grown weary.

"You don't have to check on me," Lia said. "I'm going to class."

Her mother forked at the salad she brought from home. She'd grown the lettuce and spinach herself in the garden she started in their backyard. A new hobby she said was good for her and the environment.

"Just making sure I'm getting my money's worth," she said.

"You said tuition was free."

"Tuition, yes. Books, no. Learn anything good today?"

"I learned no one wants to be here, including my instructors."

Her mother looked around her dreary office. "Yeah. It's not great, is it?" She chomped a baby carrot. "But I'm happy."

Lia stole a crouton. As angry as she was at her mother for enrolling her, it was, at the very least, something—a path she could pretend led somewhere.

"You're really happy?" Lia asked.

"I am."

"Dad too?"

"It took some work, some apologies on my part, but I think so."

"What about Limetown?" The question had escaped her mouth before she had a chance to stop it.

"What about it?"

"Mom," Lia said, and waited for her mother to look at her. "You don't have to pretend with me."

Her mother paused her lunch, put her fork down. "Who said I was pretending? No, I'm serious. Did you hear what I said? Lia, I'm happy. Let me be happy."

Lia opened her mouth, but this time was able to snag the question.

She said nothing. She watched her mother pick up her fork and finish the rest of her salad, leaving a few cherry tomatoes behind, which she had grown but never liked.

"I don't even know why I put these in here," she said.

—

Math was held in a renovated movie theater auditorium, big enough that Lia could sleep through class without anyone noticing. With Mass Comm she wasn't so lucky. She was one of eleven, which by the second week shrunk to nine. Tamra made Lia sit up front after catching her sleeping in the back, zipped up in her gray hoodie, an artifact of her relationship with Julie. From that point on Tamra kept an eye on Lia. She called on her whenever her hand wasn't raised. At the end of the month each student would present their first unit projects to the class, and Lia, who avoided eye contact when Tamra asked for volunteers, was assigned to go first. She had two weeks. Two weeks to figure out what specific area of mass communication she wanted to explore. To conduct firsthand interviews (recommended), collect a wealth of credible information via three scholarly sources (mandatory), and present those facts to the class in a compelling fashion.

Lia complained to her mother about the project, how it seemed high schoolish in nature, how she couldn't think of a single topic that wasn't obvious (the Internet, television) or wouldn't be done to death by her classmates. They were sitting in her mother's office again. She'd stopped stalking Lia after class, but Lia found herself lunching with her anyway.

"What about this?" her mother said. She held up an empty envelope. "I still get mail, personal mail, to the adjunct who was here before me. And when I say personal, I mean personal. Love letters. You know, the kind of stuff your dad pretends he doesn't like."

"So."

"So this adjunct has been dead three years. Isn't that, I don't know, tragic? I tried writing back, telling the poor soul that this woman is dead, but there's no return address. Just a name."

"Where are you going with this?"

"Well, where did my letters go? Where do they go if they're not delivered? I mean, something has to happen to them, right?"

"Sure, Mom."

She threw the envelope at Lia. Maybe it wasn't the worst idea. The topic did fit all of the assignment's criteria, or it would if thoroughly researched and properly presented. As Lia sat in her room that evening, brainstorming, she had no trouble imagining how her project would unfold. Though for all the well-laid plans, the outlines and word clusters, she couldn't make herself care. This wasn't Limetown or Menninger. This was the US Post Office.

That night she dreamed she was back at Deakin, in her dorm, lying next to Julie. She was sleeping in her dream. No, she was awake. There was a thud at her door, and when she opened it, she found a manila envelope tucked under the mat, the same kind that had contained the transcript about Moyer's death. She tore it open and pulled out not a transcript, not a letter, but a stack of postcards. From Utah. Colorado. Idaho. Even Kansas. They were blank, but Lia recognized the pictures from Emile's box of belongings. They were the same cards she'd found in the attic, the ones her father burned in anger and memoriam. She spread the postcards on the table, trying to make sense of them. Perhaps she could find a pattern. But she couldn't tell what was the starting point and what was the destination. What did it all lead to? In her dream, she sat at her desk and flipped over the manila envelope to look for the return address, which before, in the waking world, had led her to Menninger, to Moyer, McNellis, and a dead end. There was a different address in her dream. The words were jumbled. But when she woke up, sweating, her mouth dry, her mind had no trouble putting every letter in its proper place, until the puzzle was complete and she knew with certainty: Limetown.

"Lia," her mother said. "Apple, wake up."

Lia blinked away the dream. She had no idea of the time, but it was dark. The moon glared outside her window, a watchful eye. Her mother stood over her with a glass of water.

"Mom?"

"I heard you moaning," her mother said. "All the way downstairs. I thought you were a ghost."

——

There was mail at Limetown, a piece of trivia that always struck Lia as odd. In the Limetown Commission Summary (the official report, which was promised, had yet to be released), Lia recalled, there was that brief description of the town itself: the single-family homes, the picket fences, and, contrary to all logic, the mailboxes. They were all empty of course, and not a single piece of mail, incoming or outgoing, had ever been located, but as Lia ate breakfast the following morning, sitting across from her mother, she wondered what would happen if someone sent a letter now. If she bought a postcard from Eugene, addressed it to Emile Haddock, Limetown, Tennessee, where would it end up?

"Mom," Lia said. "Those letters you keep getting at your office. Have you tried sending them back?"

"Of course," her mother said. "But without a return address, there's not much they can do. You know, I went to the post office after our talk yesterday, and the lady said if I handed the letters to her they'd just end up in the dead letter office. She didn't explain what that was, but it doesn't sound pleasant."

"They shred them?"

"Shred them, burn them. I don't know. You should look into it, for your project."

So Lia followed her only lead and went to the post office. She carried with her feelings of doubt, misgivings leftover from her Menninger mistakes. But her mind performed its trick, the same maneuver it first used in Lawrence, practiced and repeated in Australia. Ignore the fear, the shadow looming a step behind you.

Inside the post office, at the help desk, she found a woman who looked miserable and not much older than Lia. She'd probably only worked there for a year or two, Lia imagined, which in post office time translated to an eternity.

"I have a question," Lia said, when she finally made it to the front of the line, "for the dead letter office." She hadn't spent too much time planning what she would say, only that she was a college student working on a communications assignment. She wanted to know what happened to dead letters. (Though, in the back of her mind, she told herself that if she learned something that might shed more light on Limetown in the process, so be it.)

"We're not called that anymore. You're not a philatelist, are you?"

"A what?"

"That's a no. How can I help you?"

The woman—Robyn, according to her upside-down name tag—was already looking at the customer behind Lia. Lia adjusted her plan. Robyn didn't want to answer any questions for some college kid's class project.

"I lost some mail. Or, I think I did. A friend of mine sent me something, but I never got it."

"Was it a package?"

"I don't know."

"If it was a package, it was probably auctioned off by now. Was it valuable?"

"He never said." Lia paused before the next lie. "He's dead now."

Robyn pursed her mouth, unaccustomed, Lia guessed, to dealing with any human emotion other than anger.

"I'm sorry to hear that," she said. "Here's a form."

"That's it."

"That's it. Fill it out and we'll let you know."

"How long does it take?"

"Forever. But your friend won't mind. Next."

"Hold on," Lia said. The emotional appeal wasn't working. "I'm working on a project. For school."

Robyn put her face in her hands. "Oh my god. Make it stop."

"Could I interview you sometime? It wouldn't take long."

"If I say yes, will you leave?"

"Yes."

"Then here." She handed Lia a business card, not from the post office.

"You're a DJ?"

"I follow my dreams. Can't you tell?"

Lia called Robyn the next day.

"Really," Robyn said, "the forms just go to my friend at the central branch. We used to be in a band together. He owes me a favor."

Lia wondered if all postal employees were failed artists, or if it was just everyone who lived in a college town who wasn't in college.

———

They met that night at a place called the Bourgeois Pig, a coffeehouse and bar downtown. Robyn was buying. She didn't mind, she explained. Having spent most of her adult life thus far as—in her words, a broke-ass musician—she had yet to figure out what to do with the modest amount of money a normal job provided.

"To giving up," Robyn said. "And to the dead letter office." She winked at at Lia. After class that day, Lia had gone home and changed, ignoring her mother's look of approval when Lia told her she was going out with a friend. Her mother, who so obviously wanted Lia to go along with the fantasy that this was a normal life they were leading. The whole thing made Lia want to drink.

"So," Robyn said, "are you chasing ghosts or bringing them back to life?"

Lia glanced at Robyn, unsure what to say, what to reveal. She wouldn't even fully admit to herself what she was pursuing. Was it just the project, or was there something more?

"Neither?" Lia finally said. "It's just a project I'm working on for this journalism class."

"Right on, right on. So is that your thing? Journalism?"

"It used to be, yeah."

"But not anymore?"

"I don't know," Lia said, and peered into her empty shot glass.

"Well," Robyn said. "I know all about running into the wall of reality." She raised her glass again. "But I say, fuck reality. Here's to busting through."

"To bursting through."

"You're yelling."

"What? No. It's the music. The music is yelling." Lia laughed. "I don't drink a lot."

"No kidding."

"And I don't have many friends."

"Is that right."

Lia shifted in her seat, and felt the notepad she'd brought with her in her back pocket. She was supposed to be interviewing Robyn, taking notes. Instead, she scooted closer.

"I took this test," Lia said. "It said I have a sympathy problem. Not an empathy problem, mind you. I'm very good at that. I get what people are feeling. I just don't care. How do I fix *that*?"

"You drink, Miss Fish," Robyn said.

"Miss Fish?"

"It's Haddock, right?"

Lia took the first shot.

Robyn smiled. "We're going to have so much fun."

—

Lia didn't remember calling a cab. She didn't remember the ride across town to the central branch. But here she was, standing in front of the post office, a beige brick building built in the fifties and refusing modernization ever since. Robyn kept saying they shouldn't be here, though she did so with a childish giggle. "This is wild," she said. Lia steadied herself as Robyn unlocked the back door with the key her friend had slipped her. The world was off its axis.

Inside a few auxiliary lights glowed. Robyn woke a desktop from sleep mode. "You know there are laws, right? I could get into so much trouble."

"But I filled out the form," Lia said.

Robyn clacked at the keyboard with her long fingers, and Lia knew she was still drunk when it made her sad to think that those long fingers, perfectly designed to play the piano or the guitar or any instrument, really, would spend the rest of their lives punching keys in the post office.

"I'm drunk," Lia said.

"Now what am I searching?" Robyn asked.

"Hold on," Lia said, and dug around in her pocket for the empty envelope her mother had given her. "Here we are. Max Finlayson."

"Let me see." Robyn took the envelope from Lia.

"Wait. Is this the scientist guy?"

"Who?" Lia said.

"I read this book, *Signals*. It's a novel, but it's based on this guy who I guess is a real person. He's obsessed with finding aliens. I just got to the part where the aliens contact him through a filling in his mouth. But he's never had a cavity. He thinks it's a government implant," Robyn said. "You've never heard of him?"

An alarm pulsed momentarily in Lia's brain. Two wires sparked at each other, just out of reach.

"All right," Robyn said, "let's do this before I sober up. So your mother wants an address so she can break this guy's heart?"

"Something like that," Lia said.

"Well, I can narrow it down. But there are a lot of Max Finlaysons in the US. Look: Max of Maine, Max of Mississippi, Tennessee. This thing will give a count of how many letters at a specific address ended up undeliverable, but that could mean anything. If it was the wrong address, or we couldn't find the place, say if it was up in the mountains or something. Like, look at this one. Max of Colorado. Bunch of letters died trying to make it to this guy. Same thing for this one, Max of California. I assume it's a guy. Hey, what if it's Maxine?"

"Does it say who sent the letters?"

"It does for the California ones. Deirdre Wells. That who your Max mailed?"

"No," Lia said, and double-checked the envelope. "It just says Dorothy. All right. I guess give me the top ten then. The Maxes with the max hits."

"Coming up," Robyn said. "But can you write them down? They monitor everything we print."

Lia took out her notepad, flipped to the last used page, marked with notes about Menninger, about Moyer and McNellis. She turned the page and wrote. Max of California, of Colorado, of Wyoming and Tennessee.

"You good?" Robyn said.

"Wait," Lia said. A spark crackled. The computer's cursor blinked a secret message to her. She closed her eyes and felt it in her teeth. "Can you look up international addresses? Like for Australia or someplace?"

"Nah," Robyn said. "Actually, maybe. I don't know. I've never tried." She grinned at Lia. "What are you up to, Miss Fish?"

—

Lia woke up well after noon, her head swirling with the events of the previous night. The drinks she'd downed, the bushes and dumpsters she'd peed behind. Thankfully Robyn was there, in her drunken memories, lifting her spirits, keeping her company. It felt good to think of her, to not be alone for once, when she was making questionable decisions.

When Lia sat up, she was relieved to be in her own bed, though why she was wearing Robyn's jean jacket she couldn't say.

"Was it worth it?" her mother asked. She was standing in the doorway, arms folded across her chest. "You missed class."

"It was for class."

"And how's that."

"I went to the post office, like you told me," Lia said, but didn't have the energy to explain any further. And truthfully, she wasn't sure she could if she tried. At the moment, the last thing she could remember was Robyn yelling to order pizza or she'd burn down the whole building.

"I didn't know they had a two-drink minimum," her mother said. She stepped out of the corner. "Well, let's see it then. Your 'homework.'"

Lia groaned. "Mom."

"No, come on."

"I don't know where I put it."

"Check that jacket."

Lia reached into the side pockets and pulled out a lighter. Her mother rolled her eyes. Lia searched the jacket's inside pocket, found half a pizza crust and her notepad. She handed them both to her mother and dropped her face into her pillow.

Lia heard her mother flipping through the pages. She wondered what she saw there. The Moyer and McNellis mess, yes. The manifest of Maxes, maybe. What else? Return addresses for dead letters sent to Menninger? Names of family members who could shed light on what really happened there? She felt a familiar burning in her chest, though it was quickly overruled by the nausea in her throat.

"Lia, what's this?" her mother said. Lia kept her head in the pillow. "This. This note about Emile."

Lia rolled over. "What?" She crawled off the bed and snatched the notepad from her mother's hands. There it was, her uncle's name, though she could barely recognize her own handwriting.

"Lia, this isn't what we talked about."

"Mom, I don't remember any of this."

She ran her finger over a list, eight names or so, jotted after the top ten Maxes. Emile Haddock. Helen Mueller. Warren Chambers. And more.

"Lia? What did you do?"

There was a flutter of panic in her mother's voice. Her face looked frightened and white in the room's gaunt light.

"What? I didn't do anything."

"Did you contact these people?"

"No," she said. "I mean, I don't think so." But how could she be sure? She didn't even remember how she got home. Her mother took the notepad and sat down on Lia's bed. Lia didn't understand what her mother was getting so upset about. They were just names, one of which happened to be Emile. Unless—what if they were next to his name for a reason?

Lia looked at the names again. She'd seen them before. Of course she had.

"Mom, are these—?" But she already knew the answer. Every one of them was listed on the Limetown Commission Summary. She remembered finding Emile's name with her finger, how it affirmed something in her, a sense of loss, like reading the names on a war monument. And though she understood she was supposed to feel sad, she couldn't, not in the way she felt she was supposed to, not for a man she couldn't remember.

"Mom, I really didn't mean to do this. I'm trying—"

"I know," her mother said. "It just gets stuck, doesn't it? Keeps tugging at you."

Lia nodded, though she wasn't sure what was tugging at her mother. For Lia, it was the mystery, the not knowing, but when she looked at her mother and saw the sadness lurking in her eyes, she wondered if there was something more.

Her mother closed the notepad and patted Lia's hands. "Anyway, there's no harm. I already went looking for half these people."

"Is that where you were, when you disappeared?"

"Some of the time, yes. But I never found anything. Only abandoned houses, apartments."

Lia thought of her own dead ends—of Menninger, of Dr. McNellis—and how a smarter person would have turned around and gone the other way.

"How did you make yourself stop?" she asked.

"I didn't," her mother said. "Your father did. That was his one condition. No more searching."

"But he'd asked you before."

"I guess I finally realized something, when you were away." She took Lia's hand. "Why do I need to keep searching?" she said. "I have you."

—

Lia tried to convince herself that what her mother said was true. That the mystery didn't matter as long as she had her family. But something still felt off. She watched her mother closely over the next few weeks, and sometimes, in the evening, Lia would catch her mother staring out the kitchen window, frozen over a sink full of dishes. Or, once, during the middle of math, Lia excused herself so she could sneak down the hall, past her mother's office, where she spied her mother sitting in her office chair, pen in hand, gazing directly at the blank wall.

"I think there's something wrong with her," she told Robyn one night at the Bourgeois Pig. They'd hung out a few times since the night they snuck into the post office. Most nights Lia sat quietly and listened to Robyn complain about her job. But tonight, the discussion found its way to family, and when the attention was turned to Lia, it felt good, for once, to not hold back, and to have a friend to share her worries with. "I'm worried she's depressed. Legitimately."

Robyn swirled a glass of scotch, watching the rocks melt. "I had an aunt like that," she said. "Worked the same job cutting cards at a greeting card factory since she was eighteen. Did that for thirty years straight, retired early. Can you imagine that, being done with work in your forties? She had like half her life left to do whatever she wanted. Anyway, one day my uncle comes home and there she is, sitting at the kitchen table with a bunch of paper, just cutting away. All the pages were blank, but she didn't care."

"You made that up," Lia said.

"I did not! I think about that shit all the time. It's genetic, you know. Stuff like that." She made her fingers into scissors, cut at Lia's arm.

More drinks came, and although she told herself to be careful, a part of Lia embraced the buzz that washed over her body. *Is this what the ocean feels like?* she wondered. She couldn't say. She'd never been. Not in the water, anyway. Not even in Australia. She'd seen it, but never swam.

"You've never been in the ocean?" Robyn asked. They had stopped at a pizza place that handed out slices to drunk college kids through a twenty-four-hour magical window. Lia was sitting on the hood of Robyn's car.

"Did I say that out loud?"

Robyn laughed at her. "Kind of. Something about Australia."

She grabbed Lia's arm. "Let's do it. Are you ready?"

"What?" Lia said. "Right now?"

"Why not? It's only an hour away."

"Won't it be, you know, freezing?"

"Oh, right," Robyn said. She looked up at the cold black sky, then puffed her breath out before her, testing the temperature. "Well, so we won't swim for long. Just a quick dip. It'll be better that way. You know, invigorate the spirit."

Lia tried to laugh the idea off, but Robyn wouldn't quit. "Fine," Lia said. "If it'll make you happy."

Robyn downed some coffee, sobering up for the drive. Lia reclined in the passenger seat, nodding off intermittently, so that the entire night began to feel like a dream. She woke to the sound of tires on a gravel road, as Robyn snaked through the fog. The headlights only revealed ten feet in front of them, so that even when they were close, and Robyn rolled down the windows, Lia could smell the ocean but not see it. Robyn parked the car. Outside, the rain had stopped, but the air was colder than in Eugene. Robyn remained undeterred, grabbing extra shirts she kept in the trunk for some reason.

"Oh!" she said. "Lia! I almost forgot. Your letter came." She held up an envelope that she pulled from the trunk.

Lia shivered beside the car door. "What letter?"

"Um, the one you asked for, that night at the post office?" She glanced at Lia. "I almost got fired for this. I still might."

Lia didn't know what to say.

"Jesus," Robyn said. She shook her head, threw a shirt at Lia's face. "You need to learn to hold your liquor."

Lia wrapped the shirt around herself for warmth. "Can I see it?"

"Sure," Robyn said. "After we swim."

"It's like fifty degrees. You're seriously going in there?"

"I am. And so are you, if you want to know what the letter says."

She stashed the letter in the trunk, slammed it shut, and set off toward the ocean. By the time Lia made it to the beach, Robyn had already stripped down to her underwear.

"Miss Fish," Robyn said. "Strip."

There was something overwhelming about all that water. It made her feel so small, insignificant, like the world could toss her away and it wouldn't matter one bit.

"This letter better be worth it," she said.

"Beats me," Robyn said. "He's your uncle."

"What did you just say?"

"You really don't remember?" Robyn said. "After we did all those Max searches, you started going on and on about your uncle. How you never knew him, didn't know anything about him until he disappeared. You made me do a search."

"And we found something?"

"One letter, I think. To a Claire somebody. You requested the letter be sent to my office, forged Claire's signature right in front of me. Man, any of this ring a bell?"

Lia kicked off her shoes. She pushed down her pants and peeled away her jacket and shirt. Her body turned cold immediately, but Lia didn't feel it. She felt a warmth in her chest, the pull of the ocean, the desire to know what the letter said.

"I guess that's a yes," Robyn said, but Lia wasn't listening. She was tearing down the beach, wading into the unknown.

When she first jumped in, the initial jolt was so cold she thought her blood would freeze in her veins. She heard Robyn's voice, saying she would have to go farther out if she wanted her letter. Lia's body resisted. She couldn't make it move. Then came the wave. It pushed her out before pulling her in. She felt her veins open up.

—

She shivered for hours afterward. Robyn blasted the heat, but her body wouldn't stop shaking. She held the envelope in her hands. She hadn't opened it yet, wouldn't until she was home, in her room, where she could read it without anyone peering over her shoulder. When Robyn dropped her off, she squeezed her hand. "Sorry about that," she said. "I should have stayed closer to you, in the water." Lia pulled her hand away and got out of the car.

Her dad was in the living room. Not waiting, he claimed, but awake. "Old habits," he said.

He patted the couch cushion next to him, and Lia sat down, reluctantly, the unopened letter crumpled against her chest. Above the TV ticked a cuckoo clock, a beat behind Lia's pounding heart.

"Whiskey?" her dad said.

"Scotch."

"Whatever happened to beer?"

"I grew up."

Her dad laughed. He kissed the top of her head. It felt good to be next to him, his warmth, to pretend for a moment that he was just mildly upset that his daughter had stayed out too late, drinking with her friend.

"I'm glad you're happy," Lia said.

"Of course I'm happy. I've got my Apple back."

"And Mom."

"Who?" her dad joked. "Oh yeah, her too."

He rubbed her arm, still pocked with goose bumps from the plunge into the ocean.

"So you forgave her?" Lia said. "For everything."

Her father sighed. He closed his eyes, as if he'd find the right words if he thought hard enough. "It's not a zero-sum game. I've made mistakes too. None of them are unforgivable."

But if Mom had kept going? Lia wanted to say. If she kept searching, how long would it have been before she crossed a line? Or had she already crossed it, without Lia's dad knowing, then quickly jumped back when she saw what was on the other side?

She didn't say any of these things. She didn't want to get into it, not with the dead letter resting secretly with her.

"That's all in the past," her dad said. "Tell me about your day."

"It was fine," Lia said, but didn't go into any detail. She slipped under her dad's arm, her hand holding the envelope to her chest. She crept upstairs to her room, closed the door, and sat cross-legged on her bed. She took out the envelope and laid it in front of her. She didn't believe her dad: the past wasn't a thing you could forget. *What's past is prologue*, Miss Scott would have said, and as Lia opened the envelope, slowly, so the slightest tear wouldn't make a sound, she wondered if what was inside would indeed foretell the events to come.

Inside the envelope was a short note, and a picture. She read the note first.

Claire,

Tell me about your dreams. Tell me everything you remember. No? Then let me tell you mine. I'm a kid again, in the attic. You rescue me. Flash forward. I'm a teenager in school, alone in the parking lot. You talk to me. I'm a lab rat trapped in a cage. You free me. I'm in a motel. You return to me. In the dream, everything is perfect. Outside it is where the real problems lie. I mess up. I find you. I fail you. You say the past is the past, and I say, yes, exactly, it's a foundation. Cracks and all. You say your future is here, with your family, and I say that is not the future I hear. I hear popcorn popping. I hear you whisper in my ear to be quiet: The show is starting. I hear her scratching on the sidewalk with chalk. I hear her crying in my arms, wondering why she feels different. I hear us sitting her down, explaining that different isn't bad. To be different is good, especially when you find someone to be different with.

Later, I hear even more. I hear without having to listen. Without having to ask. (Tell me.) Your thoughts. Her thoughts. They're always with me. I hear the sound of none of us ever being alone.

All this to say: there is still time. Tell me about your dreams. Tell me the future you see, and I'll tell you what I hear.

My love to the Apple,
Emile

The wave socked Lia in the chest. Before she could catch her breath, another wave struck. Apple. She was drowning. She looked for Robyn's hand to steady herself. She found the photo instead. Two people sitting on a bench. A couple. The man wearing a yellow scarf. The scarf Lia found in the attic, buried beneath books. The woman rested her head on the man's shoulder. Lia had never seen her so young. So happy. A wave pulled her under. She fought to the top. The photo was in her hand. She left her room. She was descending the stairs. She was walking down the hall. She kept her head above the water, long enough to read the caption. *Emile and Claire.* She was opening a bedroom door, creeping into her parents' bedroom. She put the photo next to her mother's sleeping face, and as a final wave pulled her under, this time for good, through the blue of the night, the black of the ocean, she wondered what would happen if she bent down to the woman lying in her mother's bed, the woman in the photo, and whispered into her ear, *Claire.*

CHAPTER TEN

IIII Emile

The drive across town gave Emile time to replay what he'd seen in Moyer's mind. The scenes that unraveled before him didn't make sense: Jacob, his brother, here, in Lawrence, all along. In one scene his brother skipped up the steps of his front porch, opened the door to a warm and happy home. All this while Emile moved from one motel to another, wandering campus after campus, calling out his brother's name, so that the last six years of his life became one long, undocumented montage of misery.

He pounded on Jacob's door. Night had arrived. The house was dark. Emile continued to knock, if only to make noise, to announce his existence. He backed off the porch and looked up at the house. Small, one floor, with an attic with a window. A starter home for a bubble family. Emile shouted Jacob's name. He picked up a rock to break a window. The neighbors came out. A neatly bearded man asked if Emile needed any help. He held a baby in his arms.

"I was looking for my brother," Emile said.

A woman stepped forward—the man's wife, the baby's mother—and smiled. "They're at the hospital."

"The hospital?" Emile said.

"Yes," the woman said. "You must be Emile. Jacob's told us all about you." Behind the woman the baby started to cry. She returned to her family, dabbed the baby's nose with her sleeve. "We better get back in." They climbed their porch, and the woman said good night. "He's going to be so happy to see you."

—

Emile sat in his car in the hospital parking lot. The conversation with Jacob's neighbor had stunned him, causing the waves of anger and resentment to recede from his mind. But now they came flooding back, this time with worry. Why was Jacob at the hospital?

Inside he gave his brother's name at the registration desk. He took an elevator to the third floor as directed, then swung left down a long hallway. He passed a pair of smiling nurses, and at the end of the hallway he pressed a button and was buzzed through a set of double doors. A doctor, killing time at the nurse's station, nodded. "Congratulations," he said.

Emile knocked on the door, and his brother opened it. After all this time, it was as simple as that.

"I don't believe it," Jacob said, and before Emile could think to ball up a fist, Jacob pulled him in close. He had grown stronger, his brother. Bigger too, Emile noticed, when Jacob finally let go. It wasn't all muscle. He was thicker in the face, the waist. It was a body that was living well. "I was hoping—" Jacob began, but didn't know how to finish the sentence. "Come in, come in. She's resting."

Emile followed him into the dark hospital room. A nurse stood over the bed.

"She's been here two weeks," Jacob said, "and they still can't figure out what's wrong. Or if it's affecting the baby. They don't think so, but if, if . . ." His voice broke off. Emile waited. "Everything was fine. Then one morning she woke up with these red dots all over her legs. I thought it was just a rash. Thank god she didn't listen." He shook his head. "They're called petechiae. Means her blood isn't clotting. And if her blood isn't clotting when the baby comes. Well."

The nurse pulled the privacy curtain around the hospital bed. "Everything looks fine," she said. Everything, it was understood, except the mysterious disease that brought the patient there in the first place. Emile didn't know what to say. His mind went to the neighbors he'd met a little while ago. The bubble family in their bubble house.

"Where were you?" he finally said.

"What?"

"Where the hell were you? I've been, for years I've been—"

"Keep your voice down," Jacob said, his focus drifting back to the curtain, at the woman resting behind it.

Emile grabbed his brother by the shoulders to make Jacob look at him.

"Take your hands off me," Jacob said.

"We had a plan," Emile said. "You were here the whole time? With your wife?"

"She's not my wife."

"And now you're having a kid? Man, look at me."

Jacob threw his arms up, knocking Emile's hands off his shoulders. "What? You think I planned this?"

"How the hell should I know?"

"I'm twenty-four, Emile. I've got no money, a shitty job."

"You have a house. A home."

"That's Alison's. And how did you—"

Alison stirred behind the curtain. Jacob's attention shifted away from Emile once more, to her. Emile could feel the worry wrapped around his brother's chest, clutching tight. It was a helpless, suffocating feeling, one that could crack his ribs.

"I tried," Jacob said. "I swear I did. You were already gone. They wouldn't tell me where."

"So you quit looking," Emile said.

Jacob sighed. "That's not—not everything is about you."

Of course it is, Emile wanted to say. *None of this would have happened without me. You left Lawrence because of me. You gave up your dream because of me. But then you thought better of it. You convinced yourself that you'd done enough, that you didn't owe me anything, not even what you promised.*

"You said you would come back," Emile said.

Alison groaned. "I can't do this right now," Jacob said. "Let's talk tomorrow."

"You're serious. After all this time."

Alison groaned again. "Listen to her."

Emile looked at the curtain. He didn't hear anything, this time. But he saw how anxious his brother was, how distracted, so he gave in. "Fine," he said. He wanted Jacob's undivided attention when Emile listed all the ways he had failed him.

"You can crash at my place if you want," Jacob said.

"I have a room."

"Oh," Jacob said. "Well, all right." Jacob thought of the Eldridge, of the last room they shared together. He could not imagine what Emile had been through since. "Hey Emile," Jacob said. "It's good to see you." Then he disappeared behind the curtain.

—

They kept a key under a pot, like the Sinnards, except this pot featured nothing but dirt and dead leaves collected from nearby oak trees. Exhausted, Emile collapsed onto the couch. When he woke, it was morning. Jacob still hadn't come home, giving Emile the freedom to wander the house and snoop. There wasn't much to it. Hardwood floors, sparse walls, a few cacti. There were no pictures on the walls or above the small fireplace mantel. Emile wondered how long his brother had lived here, with Alison. Last night, even in the darkness, the house looked so cozy, with its quaint white porch and large, front-facing window. But now that he saw it up close, it seemed cold, almost perfunctory.

Jacob returned from the hospital a few hours later, pale and tired. He went straight to the kitchen and made himself a peanut butter and jelly sandwich that he wolfed down in three bites. Emile waited for him on the porch. Jacob handed him a beer that Emile refused. Jacob opened one, put the other at his feet.

"Alison's awake," Jacob said, "if you'd like to meet her."

"How'd you meet?" Emile asked.

"Fate. That's the way I tell it, anyway." He drank half his beer in one tilt, before looking at Emile with his bloodshot eyes. "Would you like to see it?"

"No," Emile said. "I want you to tell me. Tell me what was so great that you gave up looking for me."

"It wasn't like that."

"Tell me."

Jacob finished his beer, opened the other. "You probably thought college was a dream," he said. "That I lived on some beautiful campus, made friends with my roommate, met Alison at a dorm party. But it wasn't like that. It wasn't anything, actually, because I never made it. I mean, I went where they sent me, but I didn't last. Not even a month."

"Why not?"

"I just had this feeling. Everything reminded me of them, you know? Of Vince and Max, and their boss." *Oskar Totem*, Emile thought. *I know his name now*. "If I stayed in school, I would always be in debt to them. That's all I could think about. I felt like I traded you in for a future I didn't even want anymore."

He paused to finish the rest of his beer. He had come home, he said, or the closest thing to it, not because he wanted to, not because he liked it here, but because here, in Lawrence, was where it made the most sense to wait. Here was where Emile would someday return when things went wrong.

"It's hard—I can't explain what I felt. I wish you would just look," he said. "You might not want to know that I felt guilty. I know I never should have left you at that place. I told myself I was doing the right thing, the safer thing, and I probably was, but that doesn't mean it's what I should've done."

The neighbors popped out of the house, their screen door screeching, slamming shut. The wife pushed the baby in a stroller. They waved from their front yard.

Jacob waved back. He lowered his voice. "They followed me, you know. To college."

Emile nodded. He felt a twinge of sympathy for Jacob then, but he didn't tell his brother that they had followed him too. He didn't tell him about the motel rooms, the photos he took every morning before he left, or how his things were often not in the same place he left them when he came back.

The neighbors stopped in front of Jacob's house. "Beautiful, isn't it?" the wife said. She looked up and admired the clear blue sky. "Such a perfect light."

"Yes," the husband said. "A wonderful day for a reunion."

They paused long enough to make Emile wonder, before setting off down the street. Jacob and Emile sat in silence while the neighbors circled the block. When they returned, they asked Jacob how Alison was feeling, and to holler if he needed anything. Emile watched them go inside their house. He waited for a hand to pull back a window curtain.

"I want you to meet her," Jacob said.

Emile finally turned to his brother. He snuck a look inside Jacob's thoughts, to see what Jacob felt when he spoke of Alison. He didn't see a particular image, not a moment or a scene. It was just a feeling. A buzzing. Of excitement, of hope, but also that worry again, that it was too good to be true. It was a feeling Emile hadn't felt since his night with Claire.

"What do you think?" Jacob asked.

Emile stood up and walked off the porch. He didn't want to see his brother happy.

—

Emile went back to his motel and called the number Moyer had given him. They would meet that night, at Lost 80, and Emile would hear him out. Until then, he had the day to kill, a whole heap of time to think about what his brother had said, the excuses and explanations he'd given. Maybe he would go to the Sinnards, ask them if they knew their other non-son was in town, that he had been for years.

He got in his car and drove. The wind picked up, turning the gravel road into a cloud of dirt and rock. He was a mile or two past his turn before he realized he'd missed it. But he got an idea and drove farther north, away from the city, until he saw a sign advertising apples for sale at Beckett farm. His car crawled down the dirt road and parked at a safe distance from the house. The house looked worse off than when Emile last saw it, blurry in Austin's thoughts. The paint was chipped, and a chunk of gutter dangled off the roof. Emile got out of the car. A dog busted out the screen door and met him with a loud bark. Emile stopped.

"Don't listen to him," Austin said, emerging from the house. "He doesn't know what he's talking about." It took him a moment to recognize Emile.

"What's his name?" Emile asked. He could feel Austin's shock, like plunging into freezing cold water.

"His name is Stick."

Emile let the dog sniff his hand, crouched down and pet its head. "Stick. Do you like sticks, sir?"

"He doesn't like sticks," Austin said. "It's what he does. Came up to me one day while I was out with the cattle. Tried to shoo him off, but he wouldn't listen. Been stuck with him ever since." Emile stood up, and the dog retreated to Austin's side. "What are you doing here?"

"I don't know," Emile said. "I heard you were still around."

Austin spit brown into the dirt, and Emile recognized the color, the wad inside Austin's lip.

Austin looked east straight into the sun. "I've got a lot of work to do."

"I could help," Emile said, without thinking. "Or at least keep you company."

Austin sized Emile up. They had been about the same height in high school, but Emile was taller now. "Not up to me," Austin said. He lowered his truck's gate and, without prompting, Stick jumped up and onto the bed. "Ask him."

Neither of them spoke as they rode a mile or two around what come summer would be a field of corn. Now it was just acres of dirt, still empty from the harvest. They stopped when they reached a barbed wire fence, and Emile and Stick followed Austin as he secured loose posts. The fence stretched as far as Emile could see, which, in Kansas, was practically forever.

"You didn't know what you were getting yourself into," Austin said, an hour in.

"Guess not."

"Well, feel free to say your piece and move on. I don't want to waste anyone's time."

"My piece?"

Austin stopped mid-hammer. His thoughts snapped to the night Emile found him in the woods, a night, over the years, Emile had gotten pretty good at not thinking about.

"I was trying to help."

"You think you helped?" Austin threw the hammer down, where it stuck in the mud. "I was in the hospital for three weeks. No one came to see me." Emile saw him lying in a hospital bed, his entire body, it seemed, bruised or broken. "Everyone knew. The school, the whole damn town. My parents wouldn't even look at me. And where were you?" He picked up the hammer and pounded a nail into oblivion. "Nah, man, you didn't help shit. You just left."

"I'm sorry," Emile said. And he truly was. Though as Emile followed him to the next post, he wasn't just thinking of Austin. He was thinking of Jacob, how, like Emile, he had also just tried to help. In that way, Austin's anger reminded him of his own.

Emile followed him the rest of the day out of guilt, offering his company as penance, though Austin didn't speak to him again. When they were done, he drove Emile back to the house, and went inside without a word, Stick trailing closely behind.

Emile did not go to Lost 80 as he had promised Moyer. He spent that night at the airport motel, watching planes leave and land. The departures were much louder than the arrivals, he noticed. His mind stayed on Austin and his brother. Austin had never forgiven him. *Could he forgive his brother?* The question kept Emile up long after darkness fell. When his phone rang, after midnight, he answered just so he could hear a voice that wasn't his own.

"Mr. Haddock," Moyer said. "Apologies for the late call." He cleared his throat. "But I need an answer. Dr. Totem has become quite insistent."

"I don't even know what you're talking about," Emile said, still lost in his own thoughts.

"The project. He wants to know if you plan on playing a part in this groundbreaking venture of his."

"A part?"

"Not a part. I don't know why I said that. You are the venture. Did I mention you would work in Australia? My homeland!" He began to sing. "*We've golden soil and wealth for toil; our home is girt by sea.*" He paused. "I never knew what a 'girt' was. You still there?"

"I'm still here."

"Did my singing persuade you?"

"It did not."

"Was it the girt? I can sing a different verse."

"It's not the girt," Emile said. "It's your boss."

"I don't like the sound of that."

Moyer chuckled on the other side of the line, misunderstanding the moment. He must've not known about what had happened at the Eldridge, or the vow Emile had made when he returned to the hotel. He must've not known that the only reason Emile would even consider hearing Moyer out was so that he could learn more about

Oskar Totem. So that one day, if Emile still desired, he could meet him and enact any one of the vengeful thoughts buzzing around his brain.

"And what of your brother?" Moyer asked. "The daddy-to-be."

"How do you know about that?"

"Dr. Totem takes pride in always knowing these kinds of details. I think he's a little envious of you. You know so much, so easily."

"Then he doesn't know me at all."

"Maybe," Moyer said. "Who knows better than you who knows yourself the best? I mean—you understand." Moyer held the phone away from his ear and sneezed. "Anyway, he did want me to convey one more thing. Keep in mind, these are his words, not mine."

"What is it?"

"Well, he suggests—no—he *believes* that there is no future for you here. Your brother, yes. You, no. He couldn't believe you'd want to stay after you talked with your brother and, you know, met the mother of his child. That must have been quite the introduction."

Emile went quiet. He didn't like the idea of Moyer, Totem, who-ever, knowing more than he did. "Actually, I didn't get the chance."

"Oh," Moyer said.

"Who is she?"

"What? Oh. No. I couldn't possibly spoil that for you. But shall I ring you tomorrow? Or how about this: I'll wait at Lost 80. I like it there. It's sort of romantic, in a seedy, American way."

Through the receiver, Emile heard Moyer take a long drag.

"Tell me," Emile said.

But Moyer refused. "I'm sorry," he said. "I really am."

—

Emile sped to the hospital only to be denied. "It's the middle of the night," the nurse on duty said. "Visiting hours are ov"—he pushed past her and tried the locked door. "Sir," she said. "I can't buzz you in." Emile kicked the door. The nurse threatened to call security. Emile ran down the hall, down the hospital stairs, and out the emergency exit. He would drive to his brother's house, drag him out of bed, and back to the hospital if he had to. But as he was running out, Jacob was running in, and the two nearly collided. "You're here," Jacob said. "Good." He rushed upstairs, down a different hall and into the maternity ward, where a different nurse was waiting with an open hand that she put on Jacob's shoulder.

Alison had gone into labor. The nurse guided him through a set of doors, and no one protested when Emile followed. A doctor met them in Intensive Care. He explained that Alison's platelet count was low and they would have to take precautions, though neither Emile nor Jacob was really listening to him. Jacob looked past the doctor and into Alison's room. Emile listened to his brother, his racing thoughts.

"Can we see her?" Jacob asked.

The doctor looked at Emile.

"He's my brother. I need him here."

"I understand, but—"

"Good," Jacob said, and pushed past the doctor and into Alison's room. Another nurse stood sentry bedside. "Allie," Jacob said, and in that moment, even before the nurse moved, Emile knew. How had he missed it? The way his brother felt. That buzzing feeling, electric but fleeting, as if he had a thing so good, so far beyond what he deserved, that he wouldn't blame the world for taking it away. How did Emile not recognize that which he had experienced himself, if only briefly?

"Allie, this is my brother. Emile."

"Hi." Claire didn't feign surprise when she saw Emile's face. She had known. She must have known the whole time. Which made everything so much worse.

The nurse finished taking Claire's vitals, said she would be back in a few minutes to check on everybody. "Honey," Claire said. "I forgot to ask her. Will you get me some ice chips? There's a machine down the hall."

"Of course," Jacob said. "Emile, you watch her for me, okay?"

Jacob left, and for the first time in six years, Claire and Emile were alone together. What he wouldn't give to read her mind, to make sense of it all. But he'd never been able to before. Instead, he had to rely on what she said, which, he realized, he could never trust again.

"I know, I know," Claire said. "Perfect timing, by the way." She tried to sit up, but something seized inside her. She groaned as a contraction tore through her body. "Emile. Help." She needed to stand, she explained, to walk through the pain. Emile pulled her up, close to him. "The window."

He walked her over and pulled back the curtain, revealing the construction site for a new, better maternity ward.

"God," Claire said, in between clenched breaths, "what a terrible view."

Emile held her as she waited for the contraction to pass.

"This isn't fun anymore," Claire said, and Emile helped her back to the hospital bed. He looked at his hands, holding this body, supporting it. "I messed up," Claire said. She reclined and closed her eyes for a long minute. Emile took the opportunity to study her face, to note how it had changed with time and pregnancy. "Hey. Are you still there?"

"Yes," Emile said.

"You're upset. You want to yell at me, but you can't. Because I could die. That makes you even madder."

Another contraction ripped through her.

"Shit," she said. Her face scrunched with pain. "I'll tell you what, I'll make you another deal. If I live, you can kill me. How about that?"

"Don't act like this is a joke," Emile said. "That's not fair."

Claire opened one eye, taking a peek to see if the pain was gone. "Listen. Your brother will be back soon. Do you really want to break his heart right now?"

Emile heard Jacob's voice echo down the hallway. He was talking to one of the nurses, explaining that he had to go down a floor because the maternity wing's ice machine wasn't working. "How long have you been lying to him?" Emile asked.

"It doesn't matter."

"Of course it matters. I waited for you."

"It's not that simple."

"It could've been."

"Jesus," Claire said. She pushed herself up so she could look at Emile fully. "We spent a few nights together a million years ago. And look at me now. Look at my legs." She pulled up her hospital gown, revealing a smattering of bloody dots, a red legion crawling up her calves. "You see this? They don't know what it is. No one knows—"

Emile saw the fear in her face. "You'll be fine," he said. "You always end up okay."

It was the wrong and right thing to say. "You don't know that," Claire said. "No one knows that." She put her hands on her stomach, her fingers spread wide like a safety net. "I haven't felt her kick in days.

The doctors say it's normal, but I don't know. God. Ever since I found out, everything is a worry."

"Her?"

Claire looked down at her body, then at Emile. "Can I ask you something?" she asked. "Can you hear her?"

"That's not how it works," Emile said.

"Have you ever tried?"

He had not.

"Try," Claire said.

She spoke in a way that made him momentarily forget why he was there, why he needed to be angry. Emile closed his eyes. He willed the world to disappear. Jacob's voice was outside the room now, talking to the doctor. *Were there any updates?* There were no updates. There was nothing positive coming out of the doctor's mouth.

Emile pushed it all away, the sounds of their voices, the anonymous beeping of some tedious machine. He kept his eyes shut, closed as hard as he could. He held his breath and dove deep beneath the ocean. Deeper still, until an immense pressure built in his chest, squeezing him tighter and tighter until he couldn't breathe.

"Well?" Claire said. "Anything?"

He opened his eyes. He'd heard nothing. From Claire, from what was inside her. All he saw was worry, the fear in her face, which had not been immune to time, but had not surrendered its beauty either.

—

If he was a good brother, he would've stayed at the hospital. He would've stood by Jacob's side. Instead he left. He drove out to Lost 80 and this time he was the guy with the beer. He took a six-pack past the leaning teens and sat under his tree. He drank can after can until all that remained were six rings of plastic that he wore on his wrists like handcuffs. Moyer found him sometime later. He spread a handkerchief on the ground and sat down in the dirt next to Emile.

He lit a cigarette. "How was the family reunion?"

"I didn't stay."

"That's a shame," Moyer said. He leaned against the tree. He sighed. "I miss Tracey," he said, and there was a long moment in which neither of them spoke. If it were summer, crickets and frogs would have chimed in, out of politeness.

"I don't know what to do," Emile finally said, if only to get the repeating thought out of his head.

"Me either," Moyer said. "Part of me wants to give up, you know. Tell Dr. Totem you're a boat without a buoy."

"An anchor?"

"No. You've got a million things tying you down, good and bad, even if you won't admit it. Your problem, mate, is you don't know where you want to go. You're floating in the middle, clueless which way is the shore."

Emile frowned. "You're much more eloquent when you're sad."

Moyer ashed into one of Emile's empties. "There are things I can tell you, you know, things that Dr. Totem doesn't want me to share, but that might help you make up your mind."

Emile turned to Moyer, whose face remained hidden in the dark. "Why would you do that?"

Moyer tapped out another cigarette. In a few hours the sun would begin to rise, and if Emile stayed with Moyer long enough, he might finally see his face in the light of day.

"I told you," Moyer said. "I miss Tracey. With or without you, I want to go home."

—

Here was what Moyer knew: the Eldridge never lost track of Claire, despite her detours, her snaking around the country. Where did she go? Eventually, to her mother. She had not lied to Emile. Her mother lived in an assisted living center in Claire's hometown. This, in southeastern California, on the edge of the Mojave Desert. Emile never made it that far west in his search for Jacob, but he pictured the stark nothingness of Mars in the movie he and Claire had watched together.

They were the ones who met her at the door. They told her that her mother had gotten worse, her depression—that's what they called her gift—more severe. She pushed past them and into the facility, where she found her mother sitting alone in her room, staring out the window at the desert and reciting her dreams. They covered the exits, and when Claire came out—pale, shaken—they reminded her that she had not fulfilled the terms of their deal. That it was contingent upon Claire staying. They would pay for her mother's care if and only if Claire saw the experiments through. "I don't know where he is," she said. "We do," they said. "He's in Boise, waiting for you. But it's not where he is that's the issue; it's where we want him to be. We need him back, before it's too late." "So grab him," she said. "Lock him up." "We tried that," they said. "That was a mistake. Shortsighted. What we want is longevity. We want him to feel like he's home."

"A deal's a deal," they said, and they leaned in when they said this, to drive their point home. "He won't come alone," she said. "He needs more than me." They looked at her skeptically, but eventually understood. Home meant Jacob. "It'll take time," she said. "And even then, he'll need some convincing."

Emile expected the story to end there, for Moyer to say, "See, look how devious she is." But he continued.

They told her where Jacob was, how he'd tried college but ended up back where he started. She'd never been to Kansas, never been east of Archer Park. She found Jacob washing dishes in a restaurant downtown. After his shift, she followed him to an unfurnished basement he rented from an old man whose favorite pastime was yelling at the television. All these things she reported to them. What she did not tell them then (though she would later, after her mother died, when she screamed into the phone, standing in the apartment she shared with Jacob, who at her request had run out to buy some mint chocolate chip ice cream, a specific craving she could not explain, that they had nothing on her anymore. They had nothing because she had nothing. Though that would change a week later, after the doctor congratulated her. And when they talked to her next, they said, *See, there's always something that can be taken away*.), what she knew right away when she saw Jacob that first night, slinking from job to home to job again, was that what they wanted from her was impossible. Here was a man who had given up on doing anything great with his life. Who'd once, in the naivety of youth, dreamed far into the future, but now settled for a quiet existence. More importantly, here was someone who lost a mother he couldn't admit he longed for, and failed a brother he couldn't admit he'd wronged. He would never persuade Emile, or anyone else he loved, to do anything they didn't want to do or go anywhere they didn't want to go. That was the man she ended up choosing, a man whose love wasn't predicated on getting anything in return. A man who would always be there, no matter where she went or what impulses she followed.

"Does that help?" Moyer asked. He'd finished his cigarette and sat on his hands, fighting the urge to light another.

"She chose him," Emile said, in disbelief.

Moyer stood up, brushed the leaves and dirt off his linen pants. "In your brother's defense, he doesn't know anything about her. He thinks her mother left her that house when she died. That she's just a biology major, a late bloomer at the local uni. Can you believe that?"

Emile couldn't. He couldn't believe any of it.

"Anyway, the rest you'll have to get from them. Or her, I suppose, unless you're in the business of exposing secrets and ruining lives. It's your decision, ultimately, but please make it quick. Women like Tracey, they won't wait around forever."

—

Emile returned to the hospital. He needed to talk to Claire alone.

He felt a leap of panic when a different nurse—how many were there?—refused to buzz him in. "I'm sorry," she said, "but we don't have anyone by that name."

"I was just here," he said. "Claire was just here." It took him a moment to realize what he'd said, what he'd called her. He was lucky Jacob wasn't around.

The room was dark, quiet. Jacob slept in a chair, swaddled by a hospital blanket. Claire was awake, though she looked exhausted, her face pale and eyes resigned. She breathed deeply. "It was just a virus," she said. "Some mono variation. That's what was causing my blood to not clot. They figured it out right before the real labor began. Thankfully giving birth is a long, excruciating process. Gave time for the drugs to work."

Emile looked around the room. He told himself not to worry, to remember why he came here. But he saw no sign of a baby, other than an empty crib pushed against the wall.

"She's getting shots," Claire said, "or sleeping. I don't know. I forget what they said. I may or may not have accepted every painkiller ever invented."

"But you're okay."

"I'm great."

"And she's okay?"

Claire smiled. "She's perfect." Jacob stirred in his chair. "Come here," Claire said.

He sat on her bed, but wouldn't look at her. She reached for his hand, her fingers landing on his only for a moment before there was a knock at the door. The nurse came in, cradling a bundle to her chest. She gave the bundle to Claire.

"She should be ready to eat," the nurse said before leaving.

Emile turned and faced the wall while the baby fed. He didn't know what to do. He wanted so badly to be angry. All this time, he had been waiting for Claire, looking for Jacob, and they had found each other instead. And now they had a baby—a family. The time he spent with Claire felt insignificant, by comparison. Maybe what he thought he felt, what he'd carried with him all these years, wasn't what he thought it was. How would he know? He was so young.

"Would you like to hold her?" Claire said.

Emile shook his head no, but his hands reached for the bundle. He held the little heater to his chest. She had already fallen back asleep, her tiny eyelids twitching with dreams.

"What do you think?" Claire said. "Me or him?"

"What?"

"Who does she look like? I can't tell."

Emile studied the bundle's face. *You,* he wanted to say. *She is you. Maybe not every feature, maybe she has Jacob's nose, but everything she adds up to, the sum of her parts, is you.*

A few minutes later the nurse returned and took the baby from Emile. He rubbed his arms where he'd held her. Already they grew cold.

"Do you have a name?" the nurse asked.

Claire looked out the window at the terrible view and smiled.

"Lia," she said. "After my mother."

CHAPTER ELEVEN
IIII Lia

The morning after Lia read the dead letter from Emile to her mother, she waited downstairs in the living room. She left the photo of her mother and Emile taped to her mother's bathroom mirror, where she would be sure to see it. When her mother finally came downstairs, she was already fully dressed. She walked straight up to Lia, tossed the photo in her lap, and said, "Wait until your father's gone."

After her father left for work they sat out on the screened porch. The sky was its usual gray, the weather chilly enough for a sweater. Lia zipped up her gray hoodie and wrapped herself in Emile's scarf, which had suddenly taken on a different meaning.

"What would you like to know?" her mother said.

Lia looked into her mother's dark eyes and wondered whom she was talking to. Alison, or Claire. "Everything," she said. "Tell me everything."

—

Alison was elusive, apologetic, and when Lia's questions nudged the story down an undesirable path, Claire took the wheel. Alison was from a small California town just outside the Kelso Dunes in the

Mojave Desert. Her father left when Alison was little, six or seven; her mother was diagnosed with psychotic depression shortly after. That's when Claire was born. In the beginning, out of necessity.

In high school, when Alison's grades began to drop, she was called into the counselor's office. By this time, she would only answer to Claire. She sat crooked in a chair, one leg hanging over the armrest, listening to the counselor go on and on. "What you're going through is normal," the counselor said. "It's a phase, this name change of yours. It's an expression of your flexible self. But know this. What you call yourself doesn't really matter. There is no running away. No name will change who you are, or who you will eventually come to be."

"Do you ever dream, Lia?" Lia's mother asked her. "No. About the future."

Her mother explained that her dreams started when she was Lia's age. Younger actually. She saw little things at first, bursts of minutiae: a pair of shoes strung on a power line, which she walked under the next day; a dead skunk in the middle of the road that she found a week later. Gradually the dreams grew longer, more vivid, and the things she saw in them more significant. "I remember this one time—it was two nights before a classmate broke her arm in a car accident. I saw the color of the cast. I saw my signature and what I wrote below: *Told you so.*" Her mother blew on her mug of coffee. "I prayed they would go away." When they didn't, she broke down and told her mother, expecting skepticism. Instead, she put her hand on her shoulder, told her the best thing to do was embrace it. Dreaming is seeing, she said.

Her mother told her not to tell anyone. She said they wouldn't understand. "I ignored her," she said. "I told my counselor, who didn't laugh but didn't take me seriously either." She saw a doctor, who recommended a clinic downtown. The next day she skipped school and drove to the city. She met with a nice physician who asked if she had considered checking herself in. She signed a form that she didn't read and was shown a room. That first week they asked questions to tease out the real problem, some underlying psychological disorder they could prescribe a drug for. But the drugs just made her groggy, so that she dreamed even more, only now through a fog. She saw partial pictures, enough of the mystery to make a person go mad. A week later she tried to leave, reminding them that she was a voluntary patient. She didn't have to be there. But everyone simply smiled and said they would look into it. Meanwhile, her dreams became worse, more distorted. She saw things that couldn't possibly be real. From a cloud she looked down upon a town. She saw people singing and dancing, as small as ants. She saw them grow tired. She saw them grow thirsty. They gathered in a field and they drank, the big helping the little. Afterward, the ants lay down, all thirsts quenched, all desires satisfied.

Then, a man came to the clinic. A specialist, the other doctors called him. He was much younger than they were. He sat in her room and said, "I can help you. Would you like that?" He called her Claire when no one else would. "Well then, Claire," he said, "tell me about your dreams. Tell me everything you remember."

He asked her to check into another facility, close to a hotel he owned in Colorado.

—

Lia drove for twelve hours straight, stopping only for gas. Her mother told her where to go, though Lia spent most of the drive wondering what the hell she was doing.

Well after midnight, when it made no sense to go any farther, she pulled into a rest stop. She wrapped herself in the blanket her mother had given her, locked her doors, and slept. When she woke, her toes and fingers burned from the cold. She cranked the defroster and watched as the ice receded from the windshield, giving way to mountains.

This was where the man took her mother. His name was Oskar Totem, her mother had explained.

Lia knew that name.

"Of course," Claire said. "He was at Limetown."

But first, Oskar Totem was at the Eldridge, overseeing things, digging in his nails. As young as he was at the time, he somehow owned the hotel in the town below, and the facility nearby where Claire had stayed. He would visit Claire in her room and ask how she was feeling. Her fretful dreams had waned as of late. No longer did she see any ants.

More time passed, and as the dreams decreased, so did Totem's visits. Every day became every other day; every week became every other week. "I'm better," Claire insisted, one afternoon. Totem dismissed her. "These dreams of yours—why don't we wait a little bit longer, to see if they come true? That way we know for sure you're cured."

It was his way of making her stay without force. But a few months later, when the dreams had completely stopped, she was let go. An orderly released her one morning, put some forms in front of her (she read them this time, skimming through the language that demanded nondisclosure) and showed her the door. She left the Eldridge in a daze. Outside the sun was brighter than it had any right to be.

Before she left town, she used a pay phone to call her mother. A stranger answered the phone. Some man who claimed to be a cousin. He'd taken over the property last month when Alison was away and her mother fell ill again. *Ill?* Troubled, he explained. Alison raced back to the Eldridge, demanded to see Totem. She found him outside, roaming the grounds.

"My mother," she said. "They have her in some run-down county hospital. I can't afford— she needs help."

"But there's no reason for you to stay," Totem said. "You're better. Isn't that what you said?"

Alison stopped walking. "I can't make myself dream."

"You can't?"

"You fixed me," Alison said. "Didn't you?" Totem didn't respond. He wasn't very tall, about the same height as Alison. "You never wanted me to stop dreaming. You never wanted to help me."

"No," Totem finally said. "Not in the way you imagine. I wanted to understand you. Your . . . telos."

"I don't know what that is."

"Telos is your purpose. Why you're here on Earth. Everyone has one."

Alison fell to her knees. "She needs me," she said.

Totem stood over her, his face eclipsing the sun. "So stay," he said. "Help me, and we'll help her."

And so Alison became Claire again, carrying out Totem's wishes for several years, waiting for her mother to get better. Waiting and waiting, until Emile arrived, with Lia's father.

——

Lia headed down the mountain in her mother's car. She kept the radio off and in her mind replayed her mother's words.

"The dreams," Lia asked. "Did they ever come back?"

"Yes," her mother said. "But Totem never knew that."

"What were they about?" Lia thought she saw a quick tremor in her mother's face. Another question formed immediately, in the absence of an answer. "Mom, did you dream about Limetown?"

Her mother looked out the screened porch.

Lia said what her mother couldn't. "You knew what was going to happen."

Her mother covered her mouth with a trembling hand. Lia crawled out of her chair and kneeled by her mother's side. "What is it?" she said. "What did you see?"

—

She still didn't understand it. Most of her dreams came in snippets, her mother explained. Flashes. It was only when she was awake that she could splice the images together, build the bigger picture. But this dream was different. It came to her fully formed, and whereas in the other dreams she had always felt like she was intruding on the future, here, she felt invited. She wasn't spying. She was shown.

A young girl wakes with a scream. It is the middle of the night. She covers her mouth, worried she'll wake her parents. But her parents are already up. She can hear them yelling in the living room. She jumps when a door slams, and slides out of bed to the window, watches her father huff out of the house. Streetlights guide him into the dark. The girl crawls back into bed and waits. This is not the first fight. This is not new. In a moment her mother will creak open the door and sneak into the girl's room. She'll slip into the girl's bed, though there is little room. She thinks the girl is asleep. She thinks the girl can't hear her when she whispers, "We have to get out of here."

The mother is sad. This is new. The girl likes to think of the world in this way, what is new and what is not. It makes the world easier to understand. In the morning the mother makes the girl breakfast. She holds the girl's hand as they stroll down a peaceful street, waving to neighbors, but not saying much. This is new. In the beginning there were barbecues, late-night drinks while the girl turned sleepless in her bed that was and wasn't exactly like her old bed, the bed in her old home. Now there are no more barbecues or late-night drinks. Everyone keeps their distance, as if they're scared of one another. The girl saw a movie like this once. She doesn't like movies. She prefers books. But the theater is the only place her mother will take her. "I like it there," her mother once said, when the girl asked why they couldn't go someplace else. "It's quiet." The girl has theories of her own. One is that her mother likes the theater because it is on the opposite side of town from where the girl's father works. That big bubble built into the mountain. Maybe Daddy likes the distance too.

They are the only ones in the theater. The girl has seen the movie many times before. It is an old story. Much older than the girl, perhaps even older than the mother, though maybe not as old as the father, who is old enough that, before, in their old town, when the three went out, people would stare. As the movie plays, the girl mouths the lines before they appear on-screen. This is the only way to stave off boredom, to stay awake. She doesn't even like the movie. The bright orange hurts her eyes. And she doesn't like that there aren't any girls in it. Just a sad man in a sad place, wishing he wasn't sad. She closes her eyes sometimes, when the man finally takes off his helmet and calls out for his wife.

On the walk home the town is still. The girl cannot tell if this is new. It is difficult to keep track sometimes. A letter is missing from the movie theater marquee. The sun is lower than before. The moon is a sideways frown. A few people have gathered in the town square. They were not there before; the girl is sure of it. They are gathered around something—a big piece of wood, sticking out of the ground. It is as tall as her father.

The mother pulls the girl by the wrist, tells her to come along.

That night her father doesn't come home. This isn't new. That night the mother does not come to the girl. The girl waits and waits, watching the cracked door, but there are no footsteps in the hall. She doesn't mean to, but she falls asleep.

She is woken by an earthquake. No, someone is shaking her bed. But when she reaches out to tell her mother to stop, no one is there. The girl tiptoes out of her room and down the hall; the entire house smells of smoke. Her mother is in her bedroom. She has taken off her day hair and wears what God gave her. She looks beautiful, but the girl knows she is not happy. She is wrestling with something. She is deciding on the right thing to do.

The mother opens her arms and calls the girl to her. She asks the girl how she would like it if the two of them went back to their old home. Right now. The girl doesn't answer. She knows the mother has made up her mind. "What about Dad?" the girl asks, and her mother squeezes her tighter. "Your father will find a way," she says. "If it's important to him, he'll find his way home."

They make the mistake of going out the front door. Several neighbors are outside too. At first the girl thinks they are waiting for her and her mother, that they know they plan to leave. But the neighbors barely glance in their direction. They're looking down the street, toward the town square, at a large orange glow blooming into the night. The smell of smoke is undeniable, and the neighbors, they walk toward the fire without speaking.

The girl's mother pulls her the opposite direction. The girl protests. She wants to see the fire. The mother picks the girl up, even though she is too big for this, and carries her six houses before stopping. The mother is not tired, but she puts the girl down. She crouches to the ground. She holds her face. This is and isn't new. The girl has seen her mother like this before, though never when the mother was alone. But then the mother stops, and when she pulls her hands away they are wet. Her face is stricken with fear and something else the girl can't recognize. Something she has never seen before. Something new.

The mother stands up. She takes the girl by the hand and pulls her back the other way, toward the fire. They are running now. The mother is fast, but the girl is faster. The girl breaks free from her mother's hand. She can feel the heat rush her face. She wades into a crowd of people. She doesn't hear her mother anymore. She pushes through the people. When she finally sees the fire, it is not what she expected. Already it has started to die down. It takes the girl a moment to realize what she is looking at in the flames. A blackened figure slumped against a post. Is it new? She turns to look at the faces of the townspeople, on which she sees rage and despair, pain and pride, familiar expressions she has seen on her mother and father. She finds a man whose head hangs low, and it's only when she looks at this man that she understands that what has happened is nothing new. It is her mother when she realizes her father isn't coming home for the evening. It is her father crawling out of his car in the middle of the night, sighing to himself before taking on the front porch steps. And lately, it is what she feels when she sees the neighbors, their tired, old faces. It is the feeling of extraordinary guilt, the knowledge that they have done something terrible they can never take back.

"Sylvia," the girl's mother says. She has finally caught up. She grabs the girl by the shoulders and turns her away from the fire. "Don't look, honey. Don't look." But the girl can still smell it.

"Is it him?" the girl asks.

But the mother doesn't answer. She picks up the girl and carries her away from the fire, from the blackened figure, away from the people, away from the town and away from what happens next. This was the Panic at Limetown.

—

Lia's mother didn't know who burned. But she had found Sylvia's name in the Limetown Commission Summary, and the name of the girl's mother. Their last names didn't match any of the men listed. Perhaps they weren't really married, the girl's mother and the man she called her father in the dream. Anyway, the who didn't matter, Lia's mother had argued, as much as the why.

"Mom," Lia said, "it was just a dream." It was her turn to console, to pretend.

"No," her mother said. "It was a warning."

"You couldn't have known—"

"Of course I knew. And still I didn't save him."

"Who? The man?"

"Your uncle. Emile. He came to me. Before the dream, but I already knew something bad would happen if Totem was involved."

"Emile." Lia rolled off her knees.

Her mother closed her eyes. "I don't know. God, I don't know. Every night I go to sleep with this dread. Wishing that the dream will show me more, but fearing I'll see his face in the fire."

Lia watched her mother for a moment. She knew there was still so much that Alison wouldn't allow Claire to share.

"Let's say the dream was real," Lia said. "If it was a warning or whatever. Why do you still have it? What's happened has happened."

Her mother rubbed her arms. She pulled a blanket from a basket and wrapped herself in in it. "Well," she said.

"I'm listening," Lia said.

Her mother took Lia's hand. Alison, Claire. This woman of mystery, of power, whose dark eyes and dazzling smile, though changed by motherhood and time, had never truly faded in the years since the photograph was taken.

"Maybe the dream isn't a warning," she said. "Maybe it's a calling. I couldn't stop what happened. And we can't change the past, but you can reveal it." The dream was now a scene from a movie burnt out of existence, her mother explained, erased from prying eyes. But that doesn't mean it didn't happen. "Doesn't that story, your uncle's story, deserve to be told? Aren't you the one to tell it?"

Lia shook her head. She'd never told her mother the whole story about what happened at her internship, but she knew that her story-telling days were over.

"Lia. If not you, then who? What was it all for?"

"What was what for?" Lia asked.

"Everything!" her mother said, with a sudden burst. "The letter! The transcript! The boxes in the attic! All those clues, Lia. All those . . . nudges."

"What do you mean?" Lia said. "I found those. I did."

Her mother looked at Lia like she was a co-conspirator, not her daughter. "Oh, Apple. You wanted to, yes. I know you wanted to."

"No," Lia said. "That's not—" But already her mind was rewinding to everything she'd found since her mother first disappeared, searching for Emile. All the clues that fell into Lia's lap. The boxes in the attic. Emile's books, his pin and scarf. And when she returned to the States, what her mother called a "fresh start," there was the dead letter envelope from Max Finlayson to Dorothy. All of this was her mother's doing. All of this was her mother's plan, to continue her search for Emile without having to search for Emile herself, without her father knowing. Lia suddenly remembered what her mother said to her when Lia first got to Oregon, when she asked her mother why she finally gave up looking for Emile. *Why do I need to keep searching?* her mother had said. *I have you.*

"Wait," Lia said. "The transcript. What does that have to do with Emile?" But she knew the answer to that too.

"Everything," Claire said.

Lia understood then that Emile must have been one of the mice, Moyer and McNellis the others. "That was you? But how—" She tried to stand up, but she felt the weight of everything she'd discovered crashing down on her, crushing everything she thought she under-stood. She backed into the corner of the porch, suddenly afraid of what her mother might say next.

"Apple."

"Stop," Lia said, backing against the corner post. "This whole time. I thought I was going crazy."

Her mother bristled. "You're not crazy, honey. It's just— you're a part of this. You always have been."

Lia ducked away from her mother. She grabbed the blanket and ran out the screen door, down the porch steps, and into the rain. "Apple. What are you doing? You're going to get all wet."

"You used me?" Lia said.

"It's more complicated than that. Come on, Apple. You'll catch a cold."

"You used me," Lia repeated, this time as a statement. "Why? Why not just find all the answers yourself?"

"I told you. Your father. I couldn't leave him again. I couldn't—"

"Bullshit," Lia said. "You don't care about him. You don't care about either of us." And as she said that her mind flashed to the photo. Of her mother with Emile, the happiest Lia could remember seeing her. "That photo. Are you in love with him or something? Is that what all this is about?"

"No. Lia. It's not that simple."

"Stop saying that," Lia said. The rain picked up, soaking through the blanket. But Lia barely felt it. "Does Dad know? About any of this?"

"Lia," her mother said.

"He doesn't, does he? About you. Claire."

Her mother didn't answer, or if she did, Lia couldn't hear her over the rain, which pounded the roof of the porch like a million tiny hammers. "This is insane!" Lia shouted. "You're insane!"

Her mother shook her head. She frowned out the side of her mouth. It was the same face she made when Lia, then in fifth grade, confessed that a girl was bullying her at school, sitting behind her in class and kicking her feet beneath the desk, where the teacher couldn't see. "You need to fight back," her mother had said. "Does she wear sandals? Next time that girl puts her feet under your desk, jab her with your pencil. If she doesn't stop, jab harder. Break skin." Lia could still remember the look on her mother's face once the frown disappeared, how excited she became giving her advice, and how proud she was that Lia had come to her and not her father. And though the advice frightened Lia at the time, as she grew older, when she thought of her mother in that moment, Lia also thought of her with awe.

"Apple," her mother said. "Come out of the rain."

Lia looked down the street, her heart still pounding. There was no one else outside. There was nowhere to go. The rain was coming down hard. The dark sky showed no sign of letting up, and Lia began to feel like she did the night before, after her swim in the ocean. Wet to the bone, unable to shiver away the cold. She sneezed. Her mother held out her hand in the rain, said a ghost was passing through.

—

"You're a lot like him, you know," her mother said, once they were back inside. Lia had gone upstairs to change into dry clothes. Her mother followed her to her room.

"Well, he is my dad." She toweled her short hair dry in an instant, surveyed herself in the mirror.

Her mother stood behind her, head tilted. "Not him. Emile. He was quiet too, kept to himself. He didn't always get along with others, but he wanted to see the best in people. I think you do too."

Lia unraveled the yellow scarf from her neck. It was what she wanted to hear all along, she supposed. That she wasn't alone. That there was someone out there like her, who understood her, who could explain the pull she always felt in her chest. But now, she didn't feel relieved, as she thought she would. Now, when she thought of Emile, she pictured him with her mother, in the photo. Lia was nowhere in the frame.

"You didn't sleep with him, did you?" Lia said. "He's not my father or something."

"Your father is your father," her mother said.

"Then why?" Lia asked. It was the same question she'd asked when all of this started, when her mother returned from her first disappearance. Her mother hadn't told her the truth then, and Lia wondered if she would now.

"Because it's our fault," her mother said. "The reason Emile is the way he is. We abandoned him when he needed us most. The only difference between me and your father is that I can admit it. I take responsibility for it." Her mother sat on Lia's bed, beckoned Lia to do the same. Lia refused, still feeling the need to keep a safe distance. "He wanted me to go with him, to Limetown. He wouldn't tell me what they were doing there, not unless I went. But I couldn't," her mother said. "Whatever you think of me, I couldn't do that to your father." Her mother stood up, since Lia wouldn't sit down. "But you could—" she said. "You can—"

"Can what? What am I supposed to do? Find Emile? You tried that and look where it got you."

Her words were more hurtful than she intended them, but she also thought that her mother deserved them. Either way, her mother didn't flinch.

"No," she said. "I need you to find Max," she said. "Tell him where I am. Give him my number. I'll handle the rest."

"Max? Finlayson?"

"If there's one person who made it out, it would be Max."

Her mother patted Lia's shoulder, then left the room, leaving Lia standing there, with so many questions. A moment later she returned with a dry blanket, fresh out of the dryer. She wrapped it around Lia, and for the first time since she swam in the ocean, Lia felt warm.

"It's up to you, Apple," her mother said. She rearranged the tangle of Lia's hair. "Whatever you decide. But everyone has a role to play. I finally figured out mine, and I've done my best to show you yours." She rubbed Lia's arms, kissed her on the cheek. "Now, maybe I have to let you find the rest out for yourself."

—

Lia huddled in the hotel lobby with all the other tourists. She was the youngest one there and the only one who'd come alone, though it soon became clear they were all there for the same reason. They'd all heard the rumors about the ghosts, about the owner and his mysterious death, but at some point, the group agreed, you had to seek the truth for yourself.

She skipped the tour. Her mother didn't tell her much about her time at the Eldridge or the facility nearby, only that this was where she met Emile, and that the two of them both worked there with Max Finlayson. A part of her still struggled to believe everything her mother had said, but she muted that part in favor of another. It wasn't the burning she'd experienced before, the sharp thrill that came from seeking answers. It was a dull knot in her chest that came from actually having them. From knowing that her family was directly connected to Limetown, and that there was a reason she felt drawn to the story from the beginning.

At the end of the tour Lia booked a night in the most haunted room. The room was on the top floor and at night was supposedly visited by the hotel founder's spurned lover. That night, as she sat in her hotel bed, waiting for a ghost that would never show, she tried not to think about what would happen next. She had no plan beyond this. Find Max, her mother had said. But how? There wasn't anything special about Lia. She'd never had any dreams, not that she could remember anyway. She was smart, yes, but the world was full of smart people, and the majority of them never bombed on a radio station, flunked out of school, made friends only to use, then lose them. How could she find Max when no one else could, not even her mother, who'd nearly thrown away her entire life looking for Limetown survivors?

Still, in the morning, she made herself go down to the front desk, where she charmed the receptionist into showing her a list of past employees. This was the only idea she had. The records dated back just a few years, however, when the hotel came under new management, after the previous proprietor suddenly sold the property.

"Where did he go?" Lia asked.

"No one knows," the receptionist said. The receptionist's name was Lance, and his hotel uniform was two sizes too big for his thin frame. "It's a mystery," he said, and leaned in a little too closely to Lia's face. "There are rumors, but nothing verified."

"Rumors. Of course."

"Yep. He nearly ran this place into the ground."

"What do you mean?"

"I mean the feds shut the hotel down. The paper said it was because of health code violations, but a buddy of mine says he heard the dude was conducting secret experiments. Like, he snuck into guests' rooms at night, pretending to be a ghost, and tried to brainwash them." Lance waved at a passing patron, before returning his attention to Lia. "Bet they didn't tell you any of this on your spooky little tour." Lance stood up straight, beaming. "You know, there's something else I probably shouldn't tell you," he said. "I think you're pretty. There, I said it. You remind me of this girl I dated in high school."

"Do you remember their name?"

"Sure," Lance said. "Jennifer Wade."

"Not the girl," Lia said. "The owner."

"Oh. Well, of course I remember. You don't forget a name like that." Lance leaned on the counter. His work jacket arched up around his neck like he was wearing football shoulder pads. "I'll tell you if you meet me for a drink later. Or maybe you like movies? There's this cool theater downtown that—"

"Forget it," Lia said, and she started to walk away.

"Wait!" Lance said. He ran around the counter. "It was Max. Max Finlayson."

Lia's mind snapped back to Eugene, to her mother. To Robyn and the post office. She couldn't believe her luck. "Seriously?"

"Yeah," Lance said. "You know, from *Signals*? Underrated book, actually. Have you read it? I've got a copy back in my room, if you'd— hey, where are you going?"

"I've gotta go," Lia said, already walking away. "I'm sorry."

She ran up the stairs as Lance called after her.

"What about the movie?"

—

She returned to her room and pulled out her notepad. If Max wasn't at the hotel anymore, then where was he? She found the page with the list of Maxes she'd made that night at the post office with Robyn. Max of California, of Colorado, Tennessee. There were so many. The Eldridge Max, the Max her mother wanted her to find, could have been any one of them. Where would she start? She flipped through her notes looking for an answer, but found nothing. She took out her phone. She would call her mother. This was her idea. But her phone was dead. She had forgotten to charge it last night after she checked in. She dug in her bag for her charger. It was at the bottom, next to the dead letter envelope her mother had given her. Lia read the envelope again. Dorothy. What if she found Dorothy? What if Dorothy could point her in the right direction? Lia got online, went to the Limetown Commission Summary. She found Max Finlayson, a column away from Emile. She quickly scanned the list for Dorothy, but there was nothing. Only a Dave and a Drew, a Darian and a Deirdre.

Her phone buzzed to life, and Lia waited for it to load, to see all the missed calls and messages. Her father would be worried, her mother curious. She would text her mother back. *I found something.* But the only message she'd missed was a text from Robyn. *I got fired. You're buying.* Lia deleted the text. Her mind was too busy; she didn't have time to care. She tried calling her mother, but she didn't answer. She texted her—*Who is Dorothy?*—but there was no reply. She threw her phone across the room, out of frustration, a feeling of futility. She crawled into bed and pulled the covers over her head. Her mind cycled through the past twenty-four hours, through everything she learned, all the answers she'd gleaned and been given, until she drifted off. She dreamed her mother's dream, or a poor facsimile altered by the day's events. Dave, Drew, Darian, and Deirdre, along with the others, stood in a line that began at the town square and ended at Sylvia's house. At the front of the line, standing beneath the burning stake, was Lance, in his ill-fitting jacket, holding the census from the Limetown Commission Summary. He read the names of the citizens alphabetically, and watched as each man, woman, and child climbed atop the fire, eager to burn.

Lia stood at the end of the line. The man in front of her stepped forward, but just before he got to the fire he turned around. He smiled at Lia, a yellow scarf tied tightly around his neck. "I'm still here, Apple," he said, though his mouth did not move.

Lia reached out her hand to pull him back, but the man was already ascending the post, submitting his bones to the flame.

CHAPTER TWELVE
IIII Emile

What Emile came to hate was the smoke. For all its pluses, the remote location, the ocean view, there was no central ventilation at Menninger. So when Moyer smoked inside, during interviews, the smell lingered in the air for hours. It was a reflex, of course. Emile understood that. Moyer was stressed. If it weren't written inside his mind, Emile would've read it on his face, which had turned yellow and gaunt, despite the facility's proximity to the beach. It didn't help that they only left the facility at night. Sometimes Moyer would suggest a walk with Tracey, holding her hand if she allowed. Emile would walk behind them, but keep his distance, as their thoughts stretched out of his range.

Tonight, Moyer was working late—punching up a report on Emile's latest patient—and Emile and Tracey walked alone.

"Chris told me what happened," Tracey said. They'd climbed a small hill, sprinkled with a receding line of trees. In the distance a campfire flickered with the wind. "Well, he told me a little. There was a woman. Correct? You loved her?"

The fire grew taller, and the shadow of a man appeared, a tiny ant alone at the bottom of an anthill.

"That's none of your business," Emile said. He turned to head back but found Tracey blocking his way. She was a formidable person. Small in stature, but brilliant and persistent. Emile liked to think that in another life the two of them could have been friends.

"You'll have to decide sooner or later, you know," Tracey said, refusing to let the subject go. The two started their descent, winding their way down the hill toward the ocean. When they were just outside the facility, she stood in front of Emile, blocking the way again. "What do you think? That you can hide here forever?"

Emile grinded his teeth. He wasn't hiding. And he wasn't going to stay forever, only long enough to finally meet Oskar Totem, who had caused him so much misery. Totem had yet to visit Menninger, but Moyer assured Emile that he would arrive any day. Emile had thought about that moment for a long time now. What he would say. What he would do. He imagined that no matter what happened, it would end with a promise that Emile would extract from Totem by any means necessary. Emile would make it clear: This was it. He didn't want to hear any more offers. And wherever Emile chose to go after this, he better not be followed. The question was how would he get Totem to agree. What would it take? Would it take a physical threat, Emile standing tall in front of him, the way he stood up to the bullies back in high school? Perhaps Emile would have to get inside Totem's mind, pull the clock apart and leave the pieces scattered in the sand. With Totem on his knees, Emile could say, *This is for the Eldridge, and everything after*. He had taken this job so he could deliver the blow in person.

Emile didn't say any of this to Tracey. He hadn't traveled across the world to explain himself. He changed the subject.

"Does he know?" Emile said.

"Who?"

"Your husband."

"What's there to know?" Her eyes narrowed, and Emile saw the parts of her mind move a little faster.

"That you're leaving, with or without him."

Tracey clenched her fists. "You promised you wouldn't do that," she said, but she didn't deny anything. She had imagined it, going inland, leaving this life of secrets for a more boring one, working at an underfunded university somewhere.

"You're worried he'll stay," Emile said. "That he won't go with you."

"I'm not, actually. He'll go wherever I go. He's very loyal, as I'm sure you can tell." A light blinked on behind them, Moyer readying one of the observation rooms. "We better get back inside," Tracey said. She turned to go inside, but stopped, her hand on the doorknob. "He feels very loyal to you too, you know. After all the persuading it took to get you here. He feels like he has to protect you."

In the window behind Tracey, Moyer's silhouette skittered about, working in a fever.

"Protect me from what?" Emile asked.

Tracey opened the door. "I guess whatever's next."

—

Emile tried not to think of the patients as percipients. Menninger was not the Eldridge. Late at night, when he couldn't sleep, he listed the differences. The different continents, the different scenery. The different missions. *His* mission. He knew what he was doing here. He was helping people. The results were visible, empirical. Patients arrived in a troubled state and left healed, or, if not healed, at the very least, understood. Every day Emile visited them in their rooms. He listened to what they had to say, what they thought, and in doing so was able to hear them in a way no one else could. He learned that his patients existed on a different wavelength from the rest of world; light moved at different frequencies, creating different images. With practice, Emile could make his wavelength match their own. More than once, while Moyer wrote his reports, he asked Emile how he was able to accomplish this. But Emile did not know how to explain it in anything more precise than a metaphor. He could only say that in matching wavelengths, he could see what they saw and then tell them what was real and what was not, if that was required. But he never forced anyone to do anything.

Though perhaps the biggest difference between the Eldridge and Menninger was Emile himself. He was in his thirties now, his face a little baggier, his body softer. But if he was being honest with himself, as honest as Tracey liked to be with him, neither time nor gravity was the impetus of his biggest change. It was what he'd done back in the States, four years ago now, in Lawrence. "Home," he caught himself calling it, because what other name fit? Home was living in Claire's house those first years after the baby was born. In the beginning, he stayed to punish them, didn't he, wandering the rooms like one of the Eldridge ghosts, a constant reminder of how they had betrayed him. To leave, he convinced himself, would be letting them off the hook. He stayed because they deserved worse.

The problem was that the reminder worked both ways. Claire and Jacob did their best to hide their affection, but it was a small house, especially with the newborn. Every other day, it seemed, he stumbled upon some precious family moment, like when he came downstairs for a glass of water and saw Claire and Jacob cheering the baby on as she successfully rolled from her back to her stomach for the first time. Emile could spend an entire day outside, walking the river trail, as he did one afternoon, only to return to the house and find Jacob helping Claire with the dishes, their hands submerged in the sink, finding each other underwater.

He packed his bag the following morning. The sun hadn't dragged itself out of bed. It wasn't the first time he'd planned to leave. The problem was he didn't know where he would go. He could phone Moyer, he supposed, though it had been months since they last spoke. But if he became desperate enough, he could make the call. There was a certain appeal in that, in knowing he had a place to go if he wanted, where people were waiting for him.

As he walked across his room—an attic Jacob had converted into the world's smallest loft, the floor creaked. Or was that someone on the stairs?

"Emile?" Claire said.

He turned to hide his bag. "Oh," she said.

"What is it?"

"It's nothing. Jacob got called into work. I'm going to be late for class."

"You need a babysitter."

"I'll find someone. It's—so . . . you're leaving?"

She looked tired. After taking the spring semester off, Claire jumped back into school, enrolling in extra summer classes to make up for lost time. Really, she had explained, it was a lost life. Emile had overheard her discussing it with Jacob one night. The goal was to finish school as quickly as possible, land a good job with a solid salary and benefits for the whole family. No more paying the pediatrician in cash.

Emile put his bag down. "How many classes?"

"Four," Claire said. "Back to back. The last is a lab."

They had talked like this before, about their day-to-day lives. Emile never said much, but he did ask courtesy questions—*How was the baby doing? Did she sleep?*—and in this way they sketched an existence.

"I'll watch her."

"Yeah?"

"What's one more day."

He had never been alone with the baby before. After Claire left that morning, when it was just Emile, and Lia, staring wide-eyed at him from the floor, the house was strangely quiet. This lasted for exactly thirty seconds, at which point Lia began to cry, as if she needed to let the whole world know that the man in front of her was in no way qualified to take care of another human being.

Emile did everything he'd seen Claire do to get her to stop. He picked Lia up and bounced her in his arms. He swaddled. He cradled. He made disingenuous funny faces. None of it worked. He carried her around the house, making laps—kitchen, living room, hallway, bedroom; bedroom, hallway, living room, kitchen—and the only time the crying waned was when they walked by the living room window. It was the only window in the house with its curtains drawn open, and for whatever reason, the filtered daylight appeased Lia. Emile stopped. He bounced her in that spot for over an hour, until his arms deadened, and he had to drag a rocking chair over so he could camp out in front of the window. They spent the rest of the morning like that: Lia, finally calm; Emile, statue still, too afraid to move.

She eventually fell asleep. Emile was thankful, but bored. He stared out the window, his one-channel color television, which gave him a clear view of the neighbor's house, their own window, the curtains of which were pulled shut. He glanced at the clock in the kitchen. Not even noon. He played with Lia's hands, wrapped her tiny fingers around his thumb. They were a tiny version of her mother's. Emile tried to imagine what Lia would be like when she grew up. He took each feature and stretched it into adulthood, then gave her Claire's intelligence, her craftiness. Of course, it was possible she would inherit the worst of her parents. Claire's duplicity, her indifference; Jacob's cowardice. Lia could end up the sum of her parents' most awful parts, and Emile thought it would be exactly what they deserved.

He turned back to the window to see that the curtains of the neighbor's window had been drawn open, giving Emile a clear view into their home. A moment later, the neighbor wife appeared in the neighbor window. She sat down at a bedroom vanity. She pouted her lips to apply a shocking shade of red lipstick, only to frown at her reflection, wipe her mouth clean, and start the entire process over. Emile felt as though he shouldn't watch, but there was nothing else for him to do. If he moved, he might wake Lia. When the wife was done making faces, done pulling on her ears and scrunching her nose, she sang into her brush, swaying back and forth to a private tune. Was this what she did all day?

Eventually the performance ended, and the wife disappeared from the window. When she returned twenty minutes later, her hair was pulled back into a loose bun and her face was more modestly made up. She had a glass of water in her hand and she used it to swallow a pill. Afterward, she stared at herself in the vanity mirror, then calmly picked up a nail file and traced it across her throat.

Emile jumped out of his seat.

"Hey!" he shouted, involuntarily. Lia woke up. She began to cry, skipping the whimpering and going straight to a scream. Emile pleaded with her to be quiet. He offered her the pacifier, and when she finally accepted it, when Emile could look back up, the wife was staring at him. The nail file had not drawn blood; it didn't even leave a mark. Emile felt his face redden.

The woman waved at him, then closed the curtain.

—

When Claire got home a few hours later, Emile told her about the neighbor.

"Who, Sue? Susie Q?"

"I guess."

"That's odd. She's always seemed pretty boring to me. Robert too. Couple of real normals."

Emile tried to shake the thought off. He didn't tell Claire that he'd spent the rest of the afternoon peeking through windows, first in the living room, then in the kitchen. He even went outside and thought about sneaking up to the neighbor's house to see if he could see anything. And he would have, if he weren't watching Lia. But there was something off about Sue. He kept picturing the placid way she'd looked at him after he saw her put the nail file to her throat. She reminded him of the woman at the Eldridge, the one who'd given him the shot during his final experiment with Brenda.

"We could have them over for dinner," Claire said. "That way you could get a better read on them." Emile shook his head. "Well, what do you care? Your bag's packed, right?"

But he didn't leave. He volunteered to watch Lia the following day. Claire didn't push it; she and Jacob needed the help.

"I think she likes you," Claire said.

A wide-awake Lia stared at her uncle. Emile had forgotten she was there.

"She just likes to be held," he said.

———

The following morning, Emile returned with Lia to the window. He knocked on the glass when he saw Sue sit at the vanity and take out the nail file. "Hey," he said. "Hey!" Lia stirred in his arms. With one arm, Emile raised the window.

Sue finally heard him. She came to her window and lifted it open. "Hello neighbor," she said.

"What are you doing?"

Sue looked at the nail file, back at the vanity. She smiled sheepishly. "Oh, you caught me," she said. She shook her head in fake shame. "But I just love Patsy Cline. I have all her records. Robert doesn't care for them, so I have to do all my singing while he's at work."

"I saw you," Emile said. "Yesterday."

Sue's smile did not falter, though something flickered in her eyes. A small alarm, maybe. "Did you like it? If you didn't like it, maybe you shouldn't be watching."

Her mind washed to a memory. It was nighttime. She stood before a door, turned its engraved brass knob. Steam wafted out. It was a bathroom. Robert, her husband, stood in front of the mirror, shaving with a straight razor. His face was covered with cuts, small nicks along his cheeks, across his throat. He did nothing to stop the bleeding. He wiped the steam off the mirror, and when he saw Sue's shocked face, he said, "If you don't like it, maybe you shouldn't be watching." Sue shut the door, her hand lingering just long enough.

"Where are you from?" Emile asked.

Sue tilted her head at the subject change. "Omaha."

"And your husband?"

"He's from Virginia. Like Patsy Cline."

"Why did you come here?" Sue looked at him with that placid expression, and Emile recalled the night he met her and Robert, when he first returned to Lawrence. How calm they had seemed, even though it was late at night and he was yelling at Jacob's house with a rock in his hand.

"What do you mean? To the window?"

A car door slammed. Sue's thoughts shifted to her husband, coming home from work. "I better go," she said. "It was nice seeing you, Emile."

She shut the window. Emile did not see her the rest of the week.

—

The doorknob. The initials, at first obscured by Sue's hand, but when she took her palm away, there they were. *SE*. Shalor Eldridge.

Emile tried explaining it to Claire, catching her in the kitchen that night. She was making dinner, peeling potatoes and dumping them in a pot. She wore an apron and, standing over the sink, looked so domestic, something Emile could have never imagined when they first met.

"You know I don't like calling people paranoid," she said. "Especially people who have a right to be paranoid." She took out another pot and filled it with water. "So they went to the Eldridge? It's not that long a drive, as I'm sure you remember."

"Did I tell you I went back there? Do you know who's in char—?"

Claire held her hand up, cutting him off. "Emile. Stop. It's probably just a coincidence."

She didn't want to talk about it. She wanted, what, to pretend that that part of her life never happened? Emile stepped behind her. Outside the kitchen window, Jacob was overseeing the grill. Emile watched his brother, to see if he would turn around.

"Emile," she said.

Emile took a breath. Her hair still smelled the same, the same flower he didn't know the name of. Eucalyptus, maybe. He'd once read that it meant well-hidden.

"You don't have to pretend with me."

Claire turned around and faced Emile. It was the closest they'd been since she left him. She put her hand to his chest. "Please. He'll see." She pushed him away, gently, a small reminder that she had chosen his brother. That she would continue to choose him.

Emile retreated. He stayed in the attic through dinner. His bag remained packed, watching him from the corner. He was kidding himself, wasn't he, by staying here. His feelings would never change. The bitterness, the jealousy. Why did he have such a tough time letting go? He lay there in the attic, as Claire and Jacob dined happily below, clacking their dishes, cleaning their plates. Afterward, they would settle down to bathe Lia and read stories to her, before tucking her, then each other, into bed.

He should leave. Make a promise he had no intention of keeping and dare Claire to call him on it. He knew she was counting on him to watch Lia again tomorrow. Maybe when she came to wake him, he'd be gone, his bed in the attic neatly made, a note resting on his pillow. *Wait here*, it could say. *I'll be right back.*

All this he imagined.

Instead she came to him in the middle of the night. He was nearly asleep when she appeared, in between blinks. She lay next to him. The floral smell from before was even stronger. Her hair was wet. She had just gotten out of the shower, even though it was after midnight. He had loved her once, he was sure of it, but now his feelings were more complicated: he loved the life she had given his brother, and, for whatever reason, could not get over the fact that it could have been him.

"This is my life now," Claire said. "This is how it turned out."

"You act like it's over."

Claire rolled on her back. She stared at the ceiling as if it were made of stars. "Part of it needs to be."

"I know what I saw," Emile said. "Sue's been there. At the Eldridge."

"So what?" Claire said. "If you think they're spies or something, then do something about it. You don't need me."

"But I want you," Emile said, before he could stop the words from escaping his mouth. There was a long silence, long enough that Emile turned to Claire to make sure she was still there, that she hadn't left him and gone back to Jacob.

A loud cry erupted beneath them. Lia, waking for a night feeding. "I'm sorry," Claire said. "She needs me."

—

That Sunday Claire invited Robert and Sue Gilmore out to the lake. Robert was out of town, with the baby; Sue readily accepted; Emile politely declined. He had other plans. The Gilmores left both the front and back doors locked, but not the bedroom window. Emile pushed it open by the frame, careful not to leave any fingerprints on the spotless pane, and pulled himself inside. The bedroom was as expected—a couple of dressers, his and hers, a neatly made bed, above which hung a framed cliché about love—*I carry your heart with me. I carry it in my heart.* Poetry that Emile might've appreciated once upon a time. Emile sat at the vanity and opened its drawers. He found the brush Sue sang into, and the nail file. The only thing missing were her pills.

The hallway was lined with framed family photos of older relatives who lived in a more serious time. Their stern gazes followed Emile down the hall and into another bedroom Robert must have used as his office. Emile spent a good amount of time here, opening desk drawers, sifting through papers and folders, all of which revealed Robert to be a boring college professor, guilty of no crime other than recycling the same assignments year after year. There were no postcards from Archer Park, no Eldridge souvenirs.

The room across from the office was some sort of art studio, presumably Sue's, filled with unfinished sketches and paintings, jointed models and mannequins. Emile checked the living room, the kitchen, before realizing he had yet to find a single baby toy. He went back down the hall, turning on the light to make sure he didn't miss a closed door. He glanced at the family photos, and here he noticed a strange thing. Robert and Sue were in none of them. Nor their baby. He returned to the art studio and turned on the light. Most of Sue's work was quite good: a couple of watercolors, a few acrylics. In the corner behind an easel, Emile found a stack of what must have been dozens of charcoal portraits. He flipped through them, face after face, all of them strangers. Each face belonged to an adult, save one. Emile pulled the sheet out of the stack and held it up to the blue daylight. The face belonged to baby Lia, her eyes closed.

He took the portrait with him back to Claire's house, wondering why it existed. He should've looked more closely at the others. He'd flipped through them too quickly, but perhaps there were other faces he would've recognized. Claire, Jacob. Moyer, Brenda, Vince. He spent the rest of the day debating whether or not he should tell Claire about the portrait. Maybe he was making too big a deal of it. Maybe Claire had commissioned it. If he hadn't looked inside Sue's thoughts that day at the window, if he hadn't seen her at the Eldridge with her husband, would he have thought anything of it?

Finally, in the early evening, they returned. Emile climbed down the stairs, the portrait rolled up in his hand. He went into the living room, where Claire sat in the rocking chair, feeding Lia.

"Look who it is," a voice said. He had not seen the other figure in the room. Sue, sitting on the couch. "Mister I'm-too-good-for-a-good-time." She grinned at him. "What do you have there?"

Emile put the portrait behind his back.

"Emile," Claire said. "What is it?"

"It's nothing." He should have turned and retreated to the attic. Instead, he said: "Actually, it's a drawing I've been working on."

"I didn't know you were an artist," Claire said.

"I picked up a thing or two when I lived in Colorado."

Claire arched an eyebrow, but Emile watched Sue, hoping that naming the state would trigger a memory.

"Oh my god," Sue said. "Robert *loves* Colorado. That's where we met, you know. He drags me back there every chance he gets."

"Emile too," Claire said. "Won't stop talking about it, in fact."

Emile bristled. Claire knew what he was up to.

"Have you ever visited Archer Park?" Claire asked Sue.

"We have! They've got this spooky hotel, I forget what it's called. We stayed there a couple of nights. Robert's idea." She leaned forward and cupped half her mouth. "Don't tell Robert," she whispered, "but I hated it. All that wood and wood paneling—seemed a bit *dated* to me."

"That's too bad," Claire said. She shot a quick grin at Emile, as if to say *I told you so*, then excused herself to change Lia. "Don't stop gossiping on my account. I'm sure you two have plenty to talk about."

After she disappeared down the hall, there was an uncomfortable silence. Alone with Sue, Emile felt unsure of himself, of his theory that Sue was somehow connected to the Eldridge just because she went there once with her husband. The longer he stood there, the more absurd he felt for breaking into their house and stealing her artwork.

"Can I see?" Sue finally said. "Your drawing."

"It's not finished."

Sue stood. "That's okay." She crossed the living room. "I have something of an eye myself, you know." Emile kept the portrait behind him. "C'mon," Sue said. "Please?" She put a hand on his chest, felt his jumping heart. "Or perhaps you'd like me to sing?"

Emile froze as Sue slid the portrait from his hand. "Wait," he said, but it was too late. She unfurled the portrait.

"Oh my. This is very nice. Very . . . familiar. Wouldn't you agree?"

"I'm sorry. I didn't mean—"

Sue held out the portrait, admiring her work. "There is something special about her, isn't there? I mean, look at that face." She handed Emile the picture and wandered over to the rocking chair, stood in front of the window. "Maybe the two of you can come over sometime and pose for me."

"Actually," Emile said. "I might be leaving."

"Oh no," Sue said. "But you seem happy here."

"Yes. Well."

Sue stared out the window at her own house. "You know, before we started a family, Robert and I made a point to see the world. We thought if we could see everything—Europe and the like—we wouldn't have any regrets once we settled down and had kids. But I can tell you, we didn't find anything out there. Nothing better than what we ended up having here."

"What about now?" Emile said. "Your boy . . ." He didn't know his name. He had yet to hear her think about him.

"Brad," Sue said. "Our Bad Bradley." Her mind did not go to him. Instead, she thought of her studio, her unfinished paintings and portraits. "He's great. Truly the best thing that's ever happened to me. Maybe he and Lia can be friends someday." Sue checked her watch. "Anyway, I should go."

Emile walked her to the door. "Stop," Emile said. He ran back into the living room and returned with the portrait. "I'm sorry. For, you know." He tried to hand her the portrait but she refused. She touched him gently on the elbow.

"For what," she said. "I wanted you to see."

—

At Menninger, there was a patient who made up stories he believed to be real. He appeared as they all appeared, at the tail end of the night, right before dawn, brought to Menninger with his family's consent. He said his name was James and that he didn't understand why he was there. "Did I tell you about my mother and father?" he would say. "They're trying to kill me."

"You're not doing him any favors by waiting," Moyer said to Emile. "You know what you can do, so why don't you just do it?"

They were sitting at Emile's desk, in the facility basement, surrounded by thrumming machinery. Emile liked it down there. The white noise helped him think. "I need to see all the moving parts first," Emile said, "before I figure out how they fit." He didn't tell Moyer that part of him liked to hear the stories, the amazing things the mind could imagine. He had spent so much of his adult life paranoid, looking over his shoulder, that it felt good to hear that he was not the only one.

"You're wasting time," Moyer said. "Just do your thing and let's get out of here." He'd become increasingly short as of late, an irritating side effect of his deteriorating relationship with Tracey. He spent all his words and energy on persuading her to stay just a little longer, so that by the time he got to work, he wanted Emile to fix the patients as quickly as possible. But as he often reminded Moyer, Emile wasn't going anywhere until he talked to Totem, face-to-face.

"Have you spoken to him?"

"Absolutely. He's very excited about your progress. He has great things in store for you. Though of course he never shares what those things are exactly." Moyer sighed, dropped his head on Emile's desk. "She's going to leave me. I just know it." He sat there like that for a long moment, until a thought suddenly occurred to him. Emile could see the light go off in Moyer's head.

"I can't," Emile said. "I promised you. I promised Tracey."

"Please," Moyer said. "I need to know how much time I have left. A day? A week?" He dropped to one knee. "Surely you know by now, begging is not beneath me."

"I am aware," Emile said. He tried not to laugh, as Moyer clasped his hands together, dropped his other knee. "Fine. But I'll need something from you."

"Deal."

"I haven't even— just bring Totem to me. Now. Do whatever it takes. Tell him his most valuable employee is losing interest. That the business of helping others isn't everything he thought it would be."

Moyer looked up at him. "Is that true?" he asked.

"Does it matter?" Emile said. Though it was true. As much as he enjoyed the work, the fact was that no matter how many people he helped, there would always be more. He could cure a patient every day but by dawn the following morning the van would return with another, and when he went to bed the next night, he would always be alone.

"I suppose not," Moyer said. He rubbed his hands together like he was starting a fire. "Okay. Now. Shall I fetch Tracey? Maybe I should create an excuse of some sort. Say there is something wrong with a patient."

"That's not necessary."

"But how will you . . . you know?"

Emile extended his hand. He had a strong desire to embrace Moyer, this honest man, naive enough to believe Emile had ever stopped listening.

—

Emile hadn't left the night Sue came over and let him keep the portrait he stole from her house. In the morning, he found Claire at the kitchen table, drinking coffee, going over her biology lab notes, waiting. She handed him Lia, smiled, but didn't say a word.

Jacob came into the kitchen a few minutes later in his work clothes—faded jeans, faded T-shirt. He was normally the first one out the door, but there'd been a storm earlier that morning, delaying the landscaping job he'd been assigned to. He filled his thermos with coffee and leaned against the counter, eyeing Emile, who sat there, bouncing Lia on his knee.

"Why are you doing this?" Jacob said.

"She likes it," Emile said, pretending he didn't know what his brother meant.

"You haven't forgiven me. You don't want to be here."

"So."

"So why are you here? Why do you talk only to Alison? Why do you volunteer to watch Lia?"

"You can't afford day care," Emile said. "You need me."

"That's it?" Jacob was upset, but his mind was eerily calm, like the breath before you throw a punch.

"I don't know what to tell you," Emile said. "Your family likes me."

In all their years growing up together, not once had Jacob and Emile come close to fighting each other. But as Jacob put his coffee down and stood over Emile, Emile wondered if that was about to change.

"Is there something going on here that I should know about?"

"Relax," Emile said. He readjusted Lia on his hip.

"Give her to me," Jacob said, and he took Lia from Emile's hands.

"What are you doing? You have to work."

"Listen," Jacob said. "You're my brother, and I love you. I'm sorry about all that crap before. And you can stay here as long as you want. But understand something: This is my family. This will always be my family. I won't let anyone come between us. Got it?"

"Hey, I'm not—"

"Emile. Tell me you understand."

"I understand," Emile said, and he grabbed his keys and left the house.

—

He couldn't bring himself to leave, but he needed something to occupy his time, to get him out of the house. He got a job at Aspera Hall, a small, independent movie theater downtown. He worked there most evenings, after handing Lia off to Claire once she returned from class or lab. He saw little of Jacob after their confrontation, save an awkward nod made in passing if they came across each other in the kitchen—two polite midwestern ships passing in the night.

A year passed like this. Two. Emile noticed this about time, the older he got. How it had a way of hiding behind jobs and routines, until he started to think about his life in chunks—a workweek, a pay period, a quarter and a season. Until one day he looked up from the kitchen table and realized the calendar expired months ago. A week later someone at work asked him how old he was, and there was a pause that wasn't there before. He had to do the math.

He saw Sue less and less, though this required some effort. He avoided the window and picked up a shift at work if Claire and Jacob had the neighbors over. Things became easier as Lia got older, as she learned to crawl, walk, fly, Emile's arms lifting her to the sky. The two of them started taking trips. To the park. Lost 80. They sat under his tree and watched the leaves fall and crumble. They picnicked in the spring and summer, and Emile discovered different ways to make Lia smile. He disappeared behind his hands and reappeared like magic. He put his thinking face on and let Lia take an apple from the picnic basket and drop it on his head, making her own little Newtonian discovery. She squeezed his heart every day, most of the time with simple things—her tiny hand holding his as they walked from the door to the curb; or, later, how she swayed on his shoulders when he carried her by the street musician on Massachusetts Street, who only knew one song, which he played on what must have been the world's smallest piano.

She was a serious child, not prone to fits of laughter. She had a certain, what, gravitas, an absurd word for someone so young, but Emile couldn't think of any term that would better describe her. All of which made him so unexpectedly happy. So happy that when he couldn't read her mind, he convinced himself that it was okay to not stop and ask why. And when she had a bad dream once during naptime, when she woke herself up screaming in his arms, he did not say, "Tell me about your dream. Tell me everything you remember."

Instead, he said, "It'll be okay."

"I don't like them," Lia said. "I don't want to think them."

All of a sudden, it seemed, she was nearly four. They were cloud-watching on a blanket at Lost 80. It was a random warm day in the fall. Emile lay down and put his hands behind his head, and Lia copied him. She'd had a bad dream the night before and hadn't said much all morning. When Emile asked her if anything was wrong, she said she was fine.

Emile rolled on his side so he was facing Lia. He wanted to make her feel better. "Apple, can I tell you something secret? Something only a few people in the entire world know?"

Lia turned her head.

"But you have to promise not to tell anyone."

Lia nodded.

"Here it goes," Emile said. "I can read minds, Apple. Me. Your uncle Emile. Can you believe that?"

He paused for Lia's reaction. Her brows hardened, her mouth defaulted to a frown.

"I can tell what people are thinking, even if they don't say it out loud."

"Mee-eel," Lia said.

"It's true. Ask your mom." Lia's little eyes narrowed. Emile could see her start to believe. "So when you say you're fine, I can tell if you're just pretending." He wondered if it was true, if one day he'd able to hear her, or if his head and his heart would always feel overwhelmed, the way they were when he saw, listened, or spoke to her mother.

"Nuh-uh."

Lia looked away.

"Is it your dreams?" Emile said. He had to ask this time, if only to see if they were still bothering her.

"It's not dreams," Lia finally said. Her face changed, grew older somehow in that single moment. "I don't know what it is."

"Hey, it's okay," Emile said, and ran a hand through her hair. She had been bald as a baby, but this last year she had finally grown soft dark locks, which Claire put up with handmade pins she bought downtown. "I was the same way, you know. When I was little. I always had this feeling. This feeling that . . ." He realized he still didn't know how to explain it. "Anyway. Maybe you're just like me." Emile took a few strands of her hair between her fingers. "This pin is really neat."

Lia put a hand to her hair, as if suddenly remembering it was there. "It's a humbird. Mom got it." She pulled the pin out and looked at it.

"Do you think it would look good on me?"

"Your hair is too short," Lia said.

"I know. But it gets hot up there, in my room."

"Do you miss your hair?"

"No, not really. It's easier this way."

"To know minds?"

Emile laughed. "Yes. To know minds."

Lia's tone remained serious. "Can I do that?"

"Do what?"

"What you do."

"I don't know," Emile said. "I don't think so." He could tell immediately it was the wrong thing to say. "You don't want to. Trust me, Apple." He sat up. "Besides, you'd have to lose all your hair. Where would you put your pins? This humbird needs a nest to live in, doesn't she?"

Lia thought about it. She didn't have an answer she liked, so she stayed solemn. She would stay this way the rest of the picnic and the drive home. He carried her to her bedroom and tucked her in for a nap she refused to take. She still seemed angry with him.

"Hey, maybe I can teach you," Emile said. He took the pin out of her hair. "What I do. You know, someday, when you're older."

He waited for Lia to smile, but she never did.

—

They threw a big barbecue for Lia's fourth birthday. It was November, but Jacob, the griller, didn't care. Claire invited a few classmates from graduate school, and Jacob bribed his work buddies with the promise of free beer. The Gilmores came too. Emile avoided Sue and the rest of the crowd and played with Lia instead, chasing her around the backyard. But when it was time for presents and cake, she forgot about him. Jacob and Claire hovered over her chair, clicking pictures, helping her smash cake in her face. Emile retreated inside. He sat in the kitchen and stared out the window, at Lia and Claire, the family he wasn't exactly a part of. Sue found him there.

"You cut your hair again," Sue said. "It's so short."

Emile kept his eyes on Lia, opening presents outside. She seemed disappointed by every one of them.

"You love her," Sue said. "It's so obvious." She ran her hand over Emile's buzzed head, with, then against the grain. "She loves you too, you know."

"You think so," Emile said. He let his gaze drift to Claire.

Sue moved her hands to his shoulders, dug around for knots.

"Why don't you pose for me?" Sue asked. "Tonight. Why don't you meet me in the chair and let's see what we see."

"I don't know," Emile said. "Maybe." He stood up to return to the party. "I better get back. She'll be looking for me."

A smile wormed across Sue's face. She swayed past Emile as she made her way to the back door. "It's never the one we want, is it?"

—

That night, after the party died, Claire and Jacob decided to go out. Robert too. Spur of the moment, they said. Just a drink or two. When was the last time? And would Emile mind watching Lia? She'll never know they were gone.

After they left, the house was too quiet. Emile checked on Lia, balled up tightly in her big-girl bed. He watched her sleep, her mouth open wide, the way he remembered Claire sleeping their one night together.

He went to the kitchen and busied himself with the dishes. He washed sticky plates, silverware, a cake server, kitchen shears, and set them to dry next to the sink. When he was finished, he went to the living room. He looked out the window. A warm glow in the chilled night.

Sue was there, as promised, her back to the vanity. She was already facing Emile, a large sketchpad standing at attention to her left. Emile sat.

She kept the pad hidden from him. Her hand moved quickly at first, darting across the paper with long, violent slashes. She slowed down for the details, switching to a finer point to fill everything in. She glanced up on occasion, and when she did Emile tried to glimpse the drawing through her thoughts. But it was difficult. She had a strange mind tonight. Too many waves racing toward the beach. Images and sounds crashing into each other. He heard questions without answers. *How is he? Is he lonely? How long will you keep him there?*

Sue pointed at Emile. Or, not at him, but near him. Behind him. She mouthed Lia's name. Emile turned around.

"Apple, you're supposed to be in bed."

"I had another dream," Lia said.

"Okay. That's okay."

"It was dark. Someone, someone grabbed me."

"I'm sorry," Emile said. He turned back to Sue, his mind trying to make sense of her competing waves. "Go back to bed, okay?"

"I can't," Lia said, nearly crying. "I don't want to go. I miss you too much." She leaned against Emile and he put an arm around her. "I miss Mommy. I miss Daddy."

Emile kissed her head. He took her in his arms and pulled her up on his lap. She hid her face in his neck. Emile held up his hand to tell Sue to stop, but she kept drawing. He turned his back but could still hear her thoughts. They poured out of her now. *I need to see him. He needs to see me. You can't keep him forever.* Emile felt his stomach fall. Something was wrong here. He opened the window with one arm.

"Who are you?" he said, but Sue wouldn't look up.

"I'm your apple," Lia said.

"Lia, quiet," Emile said, more firmly than he intended. Sue's thoughts whirred around him. He saw the Eldridge hotel room again. Robert frowning in the chair, upset about something.

Suddenly, Sue stopped drawing. She smiled at Emile then disappeared from the frame, and the window went dark. Emile waited, but she didn't return. He had to get over there. He had to know what was going on. Before Robert returned. He told himself it would only take a minute. He put Lia in her bed and told her to shut her eyes. She obliged, but as soon as Emile shut the door, she started crying.

"Meel, Meel! I don't want to miss you!"

But he had to know. He ran over to Sue's. The front door was unlocked; inside, the living room was lit lowly with lamps. Emile announced himself. He made his way down the hall, past the sneering portraits, hissing at him that he shouldn't be there. The studio was empty.

The light was still off in the bedroom but he could see Sue's shadow, sitting at the foot of her bed. From somewhere unseen a scratchy record warbled a country song.

"Robert was right," Sue said, when the song was over. "I have to be myself. Only then will I be well."

Sue laughed. The record player found the next track, a slow, waltzing melody. "Here," Sue said, extending her hand. "Shall we?" Emile pulled her up to him, closer to the waves. Sue found his other hand and made him sway. "The word's out about you," she said. She bit her lip and ran a finger through Emile's hair, her eyes fixed on his. "We're all just waiting, aren't we?"

"For what."

"For you. To decide."

Sue rested her head on Emile's chest. "Listen," he stammered, barely louder than his pounding heart.

Emile pushed her from his chest, but held her by the shoulders. "Your husband. He works for Oskar Totem."

"Who?"

"He sent you here. To watch me."

Sue's face soured. "I don't know who that is."

"You're always watching me."

"I'm not sure—"

"Your son. You have a son. But where is he? Where's his stuff?"

"Emile."

"Tell me. Please, just tell me."

Sue's eyes widened. The waves receded, in a rush. *I'm not well*, Sue thought. She continued to think, over and over. *I'm not well. I'm not well.*

Emile released her. It was possible, he supposed, for him to make a mistake. But after the Eldridge, after all these years being followed, he knew what Totem was capable of. "I'm sorry," he said. "It's just—"

"Oh my god," Sue said. "Lia."

"I know. I thought that—"

"No. Look."

She spun Emile around to face the window. On the other side, in the other window, stood little Lia. Her face was dark, her mouth open in a perfect, horrific circle. Emile jumped to the window, and when he lifted it open he unmuted the scream. A screech he had never heard before. He shouted her name but it was lost in Lia's wail. Behind him Sue kept repeating herself. *Oh my god, oh my god.*

He could not get over there fast enough. But there he was, in the living room, Lia still screaming, still facing the window, the kitchen shears at her feet. When he said her name and she turned around, her chin was dripping. Blood. It started at the crown of her head. Emile ran to her, scooped her up, and carried her to the bathroom. He put her in the bathtub. He turned on the shower and held her screaming face to the cold water. The blood kept coming. He didn't know what to do. Large chunks of hair were missing. He could see it now, the jagged lines where she cut herself.

"Apple, what did you do?"

He turned the water off. He pulled her soaking body from the tub and wrapped her head in towels, carried her to the kitchen, where he would call 911. How long would that take? How long could she continue to bleed?

"Oh my god," someone said. Not Sue. Emile turned and saw Claire. "It's fine," Emile said. "She's fine."

Claire took Lia from Emile's arms. She didn't say a word until she was at the front door. "Grab your keys," she said. "Drive."

———

There was plenty of time to argue afterward. After Emile raced Claire and Lia to the hospital, after Claire ran Lia into the emergency room, after she pushed ahead of the other patients, who said they didn't mind, but thought differently. *What kind of parents . . .* Luckily, they didn't have to wait long. "I remember you," the nurse said to Lia, as she cleaned her up. "We met when you were just a baby. Do you remember that?"

Lia shook her head. She had stopped crying on the drive to the hospital, and sat in a strong silence as the nurse flushed and sterilized the wounds.

"I like your haircut," the nurse said. "Did you do that yourself?" Lia nodded. "It's so short. Were you trying to look like your daddy?" The nurse glanced at Emile. Lia shook her head again. "Then who?"

Lia raised her tiny hand and pointed a finger at Emile.

———

"What does that mean?" Claire said. "She wants to be like you." They talked quietly on the drive home, Lia sleeping in the rearview mirror. She needed fifteen stitches, eight across one plate of her head, seven across another. Emile explained that he was just trying to help. He told her about the tree, about the clouds, Lia's dreams.

"Her dreams?"

"They're just nightmares," Emile assured her.

"How do you know? Can you—?"

"No," Emile said. "In that way, she's like you."

He glanced at Claire when he said this, but she'd turned away. Outside, streetlights glowed. They were almost home.

Claire said, "This isn't fair."

Emile parked on the side of the street in front of the house and cut the engine. "I know you don't want to hear this now," he said. "But your neighbors—"

"Stop, Emile. She's just depressed. Robert told Jacob all about it.

They're still at the bar. She won't take her pills or something. The doctors don't know what to do. Robert's been staying in a hotel, with their boy."

"No. I heard—"

"Just stop, okay?"

Emile looked out at the street. All the bubble homes with their locked doors. The families hiding inside, thinking they were safe.

"I can't believe you live here."

"Me either," Claire said.

"So," Emile said, "you're just going to pretend that nothing is happening?" Claire wouldn't answer him. He felt a burning at the back of his throat. "You know, the old you, she would've hated this. She would've called Alison a tourist and laughed at her behind her back."

Claire shrugged. "This isn't about me."

"Of course it is," Emile said. "It's always about you. It will always be about you."

Claire breathed on the window and wiped the fog away. "Not if you leave."

"Leave?" Emile said, as if he didn't understand. But he knew exactly what she meant. She wanted him gone, because as long as Emile was there, living with them in their home, the family that Claire had created with Jacob could never be what she wanted it to be. A safe place, somewhere she could settle into.

She spoke calmly now, and Emile realized she had given this a lot of thought, maybe even rehearsed what she would say to him when the time finally came. "You're not happy here, Emile. You'll never be happy here. You've convinced yourself this is the life you want, but you don't want me. You want what you've made me to be, in your mind."

Emile searched his thoughts, trying to grasp at a day, an hour, a moment, anything he could, anything that he could hold up to Claire and say, *You're wrong. This. This makes me happy.* He found it in the rearview mirror before he found it in his mind. Sleeping heavily, her mouth slacked open. He thought of the tree, the clouds, her dreams. Her small hand in his. He tried to imagine leaving her. Saying goodbye. Would she understand? Or would she run around the house the next morning, searching for her uncle, calling his name?

Claire opened the passenger door and went around to grab Lia from the back seat, who was so big now, nearly too heavy to carry.

"Aren't you coming in?"

Emile started the car. He lowered the window to say good-bye.

"Emile," Claire said. "You don't have to leave right now. What about your stuff?"

Emile looked at Claire. He looked at Lia. Part of him understood, had always understood. What it meant for him to be there. How it would end if he stayed. There was no escape from the coming tide. There was only walking into the unknown, head on.

He reached a hand out the window, grabbed Lia's foot one last time. She was asleep, but he tried to talk to her anyway, to send her a message. That if she continued to feel the way she did, like something was wrong, like she was drowning inside, she should come find him. When she was older. When she was ready. And he would help her. Because he'd felt it too. He hoped she could hear him.

"But you need to be careful," he said.

"I am," Claire said, thinking Emile was talking to her.

CHAPTER THIRTEEN

IIII Lia

Lia spent the next few days at the Eldridge draining her checking account and looking for leads to Max Finlayson's whereabouts. She found nothing. Only second- and thirdhand stories about what he was like. Young and brash, they said, always with an eye on the horizon. But no one knew where he was presently. Or if he *was* presently. If he existed in the here and now, or if like the man in her mother's dream, he'd gone up in smoke.

She headed north to find Max of Wyoming, the next Max on her list, and when she found no Max living at that address, she drove east to Max of Nebraska, another dead end. She was on her way to Max number four when her father finally called. Lia hadn't spoken to him since leaving for Archer Park, but she had sent a text to her mother requesting some funds after her savings dipped to zero in Colorado. Her mother didn't message her back, though the following morning, when Lia went to the ATM, cash spit out into her hand and the balance wasn't printed in red.

She let the call go to voice mail. What was there to say? *Yes, Dad, I dropped out of school. No, Dad, I don't know where I'm going. And even if I did, I couldn't tell you where or why.* What would it do to him if he found out what she and her mother were up to?

The voice mail was short:

Lia, there's something wrong with your mother. I . . . I don't know what to do. Call me when you get this.

Lia didn't call him back. She told herself it was because she was driving, and her father would have wanted her to be safe as she sped down the highway, cutting through the corner of Kansas on her way to Max of Missouri, next on the list. *Yes, there is something wrong with my mother*, she thought. *She has been lying to you, to me, for my entire life.* Lia tossed the phone facedown on the passenger seat, refusing to look at it until her next stop. It was dark. Soon she would need to find somewhere to stop for the night. Her headlights flashed across a sign for Kansas City. She was north of the river, about an hour away. She didn't have the money for a hotel. While her head mulled over a few different options, her hands steered the wheel toward the next exit; some part of her mind knew what to do. It was only a little out of the way. And it would be nice to stay somewhere familiar for a change.

The cheapest motel was off Highway 40, across from a tiny airstrip. Growing up, Lia had driven by the motel countless times, and always thought it looked pretty shady. The shifty clientele smoking in the gravel lot, the neon sign that failed to light up all its letters, like a wide smile missing a prominent tooth. The price was right though, even if her room was airport themed, complete with a ceiling fan shaped like a propeller. She slept well that night, and in the morning she was pleasantly surprised when she found no bug bites welting her body.

She would drive into town. She deserved a day to revisit her past, even if her mother had proven that most of it was not as she remembered. All the places, the memories that made up her life—none of it was as she'd previously understood. She drove by her elementary school, where her mother had dropped her off on her first day, telling Lia to be strong and brave. Nearby was her childhood home, the house she didn't remember, but was told she took her first steps in, said her first word—*Mama*. Here she gave herself a haircut when her mother wasn't looking, a bloody affair that ended in a trip to the emergency room and two long scars that cowlicked her skull to this day. Here she thought she fell in love with the boy next door, who died without knowing how she thought she felt, which ended up being nothing at all.

She got out of the car and sat on the hood. She stared at the house, the small porch, the dark window in the attic, like a sleeping eye. She wondered how much of it was true, the history she was told but couldn't remember. What was fact and what was otherwise, a fiction invented by her mother to disguise a hidden life? She might never know.

But here was her former neighbor, tiptoeing out of the house in her paint-stained dress shirt to snag the paper. She froze when she saw Lia. "You," she said. She crossed the street. "I know you."

"Hi, Mrs. Gilmore," Lia said. "How are you?"

"I was doing yoga," she said. She put her hands together and offered Lia half a bow. "I always do yoga before I read the paper. Helps get my head right. Then I read the news and it gets all scrambled again." She laughed a strange laugh. "My goodness. Lia Haddock. You must be, what, a freshman in college by now?"

"I'm just passing through," Lia said. "You know, visiting old places." She looked across the street. "I used to live here, huh?"

Mrs. Gilmore smiled. "You were a funny little thing. Always giving your parents fits."

"Yeah. I don't really remember."

"Well, you were young. God, so was I." She laughed at a memory. "How are they? Your mom and dad."

"They're good," Lia said. She thought of the call from her dad she missed last night. "I'll tell them hello."

"Oh, good. That's wonderful." She turned to head inside before freezing in the street. "Say, how's that uncle of yours doing?"

"My uncle?"

Mrs. Gilmore slapped her knee with the paper. "Emile! Gosh, you used to give him so much trouble too. Do you remember—" She started to laugh. "The time . . . the scissors . . . your hair." Her laugh grew uncomfortably loud. "I thought your mother was going to kill him." She put a hand to her chest, as if to make herself stop.

"I thought I did that to myself," Lia said.

"You did," Mrs. Gilmore said. "But you did it *for* him, after he cut his hair short. You always wanted to be like him."

"I did?"

"Of course," Mrs. Gilmore said. "You two were peas in a pod. Didn't your parents tell you any of this?"

"No," Lia said. "They didn't tell me anything." She slid off the hood. "So you knew my uncle well?"

"Oh, yes," Mrs. Gilmore said. "I was a very big fan. He was so . . . special."

"Special." Lia didn't like Mrs. Gilmore's use of the word, its vagueness, or the way she said it. As if Lia should know exactly what she meant.

"Well, yes. You understand."

"No," Lia said again. "Actually I don't." She realized none of this was Mrs. Gilmore's fault, but no one else was here for Lia to be mad at. "He left when I was little," she said. "And my parents won't talk about him." She stared at Mrs. Gilmore, until Mrs. Gilmore looked down at her paper.

"I'm sure they have their reasons."

"Do they?" Lia asked, and that familiar burning feeling welled up inside her. "He's gone, you know. My uncle. Emile. He disappeared at Limetown. You know about Limetown? He was one of them. The citizens. My mom went looking for him but she stopped when my dad found out and now here I am, and no one really knows what happened to any of *them*." A car roared by, as fast as Lia felt she was talking. "You know what—never mind. I'm sorry. This is—I should go."

But Mrs. Gilmore wasn't fazed. She waited for the sound of the car's obnoxious engine to die down the block. When everything was quiet again, she said, "Lia. Little Lia. Why don't you come inside?"

———

Lia pretended that she hadn't been in Mrs. Gilmore's house before. Mrs. Gilmore brought out some green tea, which Lia didn't like, but drank politely as the two sat in the living room and chatted. They talked about small things at first, the weather (it was so cold), school (*going fine*, Lia lied), all a prelude to the only subject really worth discussing—Emile.

"So they never told you what he was really like," Mrs. Gilmore said.

Lia shook her head over her tea.

"I was troubled too, or so they kept saying. But there's something I could take." She poured herself another cup of tea. "Do you know Patsy Cline? That's my medicine."

"Not really."

"Well, I paint too, and that's good enough most days. But your uncle, he didn't have anything. He had no one, except your mother."

"I know about that."

"You know he loved her."

Lia nodded. She hadn't thought about it in such a simple way, but of course it was true.

"Good," Mrs. Gilmore said. "That's good." She sipped her tea and cleared her throat. She stood up. "Would you like to see something strange?" She left the living room before Lia could answer, disappearing down the hall. Lia was unsure whether she was supposed to follow. It felt weird to sit there alone, in this odd woman's house. But she was an odd woman who knew Emile. So Lia went down the hall and into the master bedroom, where Mrs. Gilmore stood in front of the bedroom window, which looked directly at Lia's old house.

"Can I tell you a secret?" Mrs. Gilmore asked. "My husband. Sorry, my ex-husband—he wasn't very good to me. He had one of those jobs where he pretended to be one thing but really was another. He pretended so much that he forgot what was real and what wasn't. When someone pretends that much, you start to wonder."

Mrs. Gilmore moved to the bed, but Lia stayed at the window, waiting for someone to appear in her old house. "What did your husband do?"

"He pretended to be a professor. But really he worked for the government. That's all he would tell me."

Lia turned from the window. She didn't know why Mrs. Gilmore was telling her this. What this had to do with Emile. She opened her mouth to ask those questions, but others came out. "Where is he now? Was he at Limetown?"

"Limetown?"

Lia's pocket buzzed. She pulled her phone out and stared at the screen. It was her dad again.

"Take it," Mrs. Gilmore said. "I'll make more tea."

Lia let her phone ring as long as possible before answering. Her father was shouting, over the wind, it sounded like, which roared around him.

"Lia? Are you there? Say something."

"I'm here," Lia said.

"Did you hear? Your mother! Honey, they found her in somebody's cellar. A restaurant or something. I'm on my way now."

"Is she okay?"

"What? Where are you?"

"What restaurant?"

"She broke in. The manager found her when they opened. I don't know. I don't know what to do. Hold on. I can't hear you."

The wind beat his phone and there was a long pause as her father tried to find a quieter spot. Lia returned to the window. She stared at her old house and waited for her father's voice to come back. She heard a door slam—she imagined he was in his car. "She's not well, honey. Do you understand me? They called the police. She refused to leave. Kept saying something about a dream. About a clock ticking away. She had to find you. That's what she kept saying. 'I have to find Lia.'"

"I'm fine, Dad. I'm in Lawrence."

Lia kept looking out the window, into her old house. She wished she could remember what happened there.

"Lawrence? Lia." Her father sighed into the phone. "Well, I could really use your help, honey. Your mother could too. Can you come back? What are you doing there?"

Lia heard a creak behind her. Mrs. Gilmore stood in the doorway, eavesdropping with a cup of tea.

"I've gotta go, Dad."

"Lia."

"I'm sorry."

She ended the call. Mrs. Gilmore cleared her throat, and when Lia turned to her, she handed Lia the tea. "I didn't mean to interrupt. Do you need to go?"

Lia sipped the tea. It tasted different somehow, more bitter. She turned back to the window to hide her grimace.

"No," Lia said. "It was nothing."

———

She didn't stay much longer. Mrs. Gilmore didn't know much more about Emile, only that he left suddenly after the haircut incident. She never saw him again. After tea, she made things weird again by putting on country music, insisting that Lia check out her art studio. It got weirder when Lia saw what she had been working on—the subject of all her pieces. Brad. Her dead son. Weirder still when Lia realized the paintings and drawings weren't of the Brad Lia knew, the Brad of the past. They were scenes from Brad's future, the one he never got to live. Here was Brad as a college senior, smiling proudly in his cap and gown. There he was on his wedding day, exchanging vows with a faceless bride.

"I've only made it to his thirties," Mrs. Gilmore said. "He still has such a long way to go." She set the paintings down. "I could do one of you, if you'd like. Your future, free of charge."

She had declined. Lia left Lawrence that afternoon. She did not go by her old high school to see Miss Scott, nor did she run by the Sinnards. She felt the pull of those people and places, but what would be the point? They all belonged to a previous life, one that was no more real than the one Brad lived in Mrs. Gilmore's sad paintings. And if her dad was right, if there was something wrong with her mother, the best way to help wasn't by dwelling in her childhood haunts or even by reversing course to Oregon. It was by finding Max, finding Emile, and putting every mystery to bed.

Her dad texted constant updates as she drove. Lia titled the texts with the cities she was near or passing through at the time.

SEDALIA, MISSOURI
Home now, got a date in court.
When are you coming home Lia?
she keeps asking

Dad

LEBANON PT. 1
Bad night last night
Had the dream again
Really thinks its real
Don't know how to tell her
When she's awake its worse

LEBANON PT. 2
Wakes up saying
Get out Lia now
She says she yells
but you never do

There was no Max in Missouri. The house at the address she had listed had been bulldozed months ago. No one knew why. She checked it off the list. Kept eastward. She knew where she was going. She had been making her way there all along.

MOUNTAIN GROVE TO MOUNTAIN VIEW
Why won't you answer me?
Are you scared?

JONESBORO, ARKANSAS
It's ok to not know what to do.
Its not ok to run away. Though I guess
you are your mothers daughter.
When problems knock
you two are never around.

MEMPHIS
Sorry
(drinking)

JACKSON
Shouldn't have said that
(drunk)

FRANKLIN, TENNESSEE
Had the court-ordered psych eval.
They asked about her dreams but she wouldn't talk.
Told her to tell them so they can understand.
She kept quiet stared out the window, while this asshole
decided her mind, wrote it out on paper

We'll hear back in a week or 2.
Will you be here when we do?
Will you answer the phone
when they take her away?

SPARTA (WHITE COUNTY, TN)
The same dream, the same reply
when I wake her she blinks

the fear, the panic
Is it happening? she says
Is it happening?

Then, for a few days, the texts stopped. Lia expected to feel guilty when she didn't hear from him, but what she found was relief, a weight off her chest, and the farther she drove the lighter she felt. It was the same way she felt the last week of high school, like everything she could remember doing in her life had led her here, to this moment, and that whatever was about to happen, she deserved.

Sparta was surrounded by rolling hills, and driving into town Lia saw signs for waterfalls and caves, creeks and rivers. But the town itself was small and flat. It reminded her of Kansas, of the towns she'd driven through without even realizing it, until she passed a sign thanking her for visiting and asking her to please come back again. She popped into a diner, keeping an eye out for the locals she'd seen on the news. The husband who thought Limetown was an elaborate magic trick, the wife who blamed the government. A tall woman eyed her suspiciously. The entire town had a thrum to it, even now, a little over a year since the Panic, a lingering sense that things were still a little bit off. It made sense, Lia supposed. Every other day people like her must show up, nosing around, asking if the rumors were true. *Is it really real? Have you seen it? Do you know how to get there? Have you been? Or do you stay away out of fear?*

Unlike the rest of the world, no one here could move on.

She encountered multiple eye rolls when she asked her questions. But she had come this far, scratched off a lot of Maxes on her way— all dead ends. Plus, how many other nosy outsiders had relatives who were actual citizens of Limetown?

A lot, it turned out. Lia learned she wasn't the first relative to come searching for their lost loved one. Some came by hoping for an update, an answered prayer. But no one knew anything, or nothing more than what was reported by the Limetown Commission's superficial summary. Lia supposed she shouldn't have been surprised. Most mysteries only grow murkier with time.

After the diner closed, she walked to a bar a block over, slid in with the fake she recovered when she moved back in with her parents. It was a seedy place, low-lit and empty save a couple of blue-jeaned hulks hunched over their beers at the bar. She thought of Robyn. It would have been nice to have her here, sharing cheap drinks, making fun of the townies. As Lia hid in a booth in the back, a part of her wanted to text her, apologize. But she wasn't sure she would have forgiven her, and she wouldn't have blamed her.

A few patrons trickled in. She recognized one of them from the diner, the tall woman, flanked by two friends. All three were in their late twenties. Lia tried not to stare but the alternative was looking at her phone, where another message from her dad might suddenly appear. The tall woman caught her looking and eventually came over, a dark well in each hand.

"Do you have cash?" the woman asked. "I prefer cash."

Lia sat up straight. "I didn't order anything," she said, and felt foolish immediately after. She still didn't know how to talk to women in these situations. Or if this was a situation.

The woman set one of her drinks down, wiped her hand on her jeans, and extended it to Lia. "I saw you snooping around earlier, back at the Ladybird. Asking about Limetown. So if you have cash, we can get started."

Lia relaxed, remembering why she'd come to Sparta in the first place. "Started with what."

"You want to see it, right? You want to go inside."

Lia nodded. She tried to act calm, to hide the excitement sparking inside her.

"So what's stopping you?"

"I heard the road was closed to the public."

The woman laughed. She turned back to her friends but they had disappeared. She looked confused for a moment, then shrugged and sat down next to Lia. Lia could smell the alcohol burning off her breath.

"One hundred bucks," the woman said.

"What?"

"I can take you. They closed a road, but they didn't close the road they don't know about."

"I don't have—"

"Fifty. Final offer."

"Listen," Lia said.

"Max."

"Max?"

"Yeah. Don't tell me your name. Safer that way."

"Max," Lia repeated. The name made her pause.

"Short for Maxine." She finished one of the wells. "So are we doing this or what?"

Lia sat there for a moment. Max of Tennessee. She wasn't the Max Lia was looking for, but maybe she was the Max she needed. She recalled the original plan. Find Max Finlayson, report back to her mother. But she felt her mind pushing it away in favor of another.

Lia snapped out of her fog. "You want to take me to Limetown."

"Why not?"

"You're drunk."

Max laughed. "I'm drunk *now*," she said. "Thirty minutes. That's all I need."

"Are you sure?" Lia asked. After all this time, all this searching, she couldn't believe it was this easy. Her mother confessed that she had come here, during one of her disappearances. But she never said she'd been inside.

"Twenty."

Lia didn't say anything, but in her mind she was already on the road, driving toward the answers she and her mother needed. She was walking the streets of Limetown, comparing everything she saw to her mother's dream.

"Fine. Fifteen," Max said. She folded her arms and put her head down on the table. "But now you're putting us both in danger."

—

It was after midnight when they stepped out of the bar. It turned out that Max needed more than thirty minutes to sober up. Also, she needed a shower. So she told Lia to meet her outside the Ladybird in a couple of hours. Lia said she could drive, but Max laughed and said no, she couldn't. Lia was from Kansas, which was cute, but Kansas country wasn't Tennessee country. It wasn't flat and empty. It was hilly and overgrown. Plus, it would be good to wait until later in the night, Max explained. The darker the better.

Lia went back to her car to grab a few things. The night turned cold, so she threw on the yellow scarf. She restocked the old Polaroid camera she'd found in the attic and wished she had invested in a newer camera. Two hours later Max still hadn't shown. Lia regretted giving her half of the fifty up front. Another hour passed and she thought she would never see Max again. But then, just after three in the morning, she appeared, staggering down the middle of the street.

"Where the hell were you?" Lia said. Her toes were nearly numb from waiting.

"Sorry, sorry. I got lost."

"You live here." Lia rubbed her arms for warmth.

"That's the embarrassing part. Hey, look at you, all wrapped in yellow." She reached out for Lia's scarf. Lia slapped her hand away. "So are we ready? Ready, ready, for the mystery tour."

"You're not driving," Lia said.

"Probably a good idea. But check this out. I wrote it all down." She gave Lia a crumpled napkin, on which there appeared to be detailed and surprisingly legible directions. "It should only take us a couple of hours. I'll sleep the first leg—it's easy—wake up right as rain and help navigate the rest."

"When did you do this?"

"Right when I sobered up. Right before I started drinking again." Lia put the napkin in her pocket and pushed Max away from her car. "Hey," Max said.

Lia reached in her pocket for her keys, and when she did she felt her phone buzz. It was her dad again. It would be just after one in the morning his time, and Lia wondered if he was up late again, alone.

THE LADYBIRD
Jesus Christ Lia
your mom just told me
where she thinks your going
Are you serious?

I don't know what is going on
with you or why you won't listen
but your wasting your time

Answer me

I told him not to go back
But he didn't listen
No one listens

Answer me

Help your mother
Don't be your mother

The messages stopped. Lia waited for a follow-up apology (*sorry, beer*), but it never came.

Max cleared her throat loudly. "Sooooo, are we going or what?"

Lia flipped her phone shut. Her father's disapproving voice buzzed in her ear. *Your wasting your time.*

"Text from an ex?" Max asked.

Don't be your mother. She could almost see his face, the way his eyebrows pinched when he was upset and disappointed. And she didn't know what angered her more—the assumption he knew more about Limetown than she did, when he didn't, or the accusation that she was just like her mother, which she wasn't. She hadn't deceived her family for years. She hadn't disappeared on them. She didn't want any of this. Whereas Lia's number-two strength was empathy, she had no idea what her mother's would be. Duplicity, maybe. After manipulation.

Lia got in the car and started the engine. Max stumbled to the passenger door and tried the handle, but Lia kept it locked.

"Hey," Max said. "Hell-ooo?"

Lia stared ahead, not acknowledging her. *Answer me.* Max stepped to the driver's window to get Lia's attention. "What's going on? Hey!" She slapped the hood and Lia flicked on the headlights, blinding Max with the brights. "What the hell?"

Lia put the car in drive and nudged it forward, jostling Max enough that she almost fell backward.

"Are you crazy?" Max said.

Lia rolled down the window. "Get out of my way," she said, and gave the engine a rev to show that she was serious.

Max scowled, stepped to the curb.

"What about my money?" Lia threw the rest of the fifty out the window. "Man, what is your problem?"

No one listens.

"You'll never find it," Max said. "Not without someone to show you the way."

Lia didn't answer her. She took her foot off the break and peeled into the street, leaving Max of Tennessee in the rearview mirror.

—

Max was right. The first half of the drive wasn't bad. The directions had Lia take a state highway in lieu of the interstate, and after a couple of hours (longer than she thought, but still) Lia got off the winding highway and onto a county road, the sign for which she missed multiple times—it was poorly marked. The paved county road devolved to gravel, the gravel to dirt. The dirt road ended unceremoniously in a cul-de-sac of trees. The directions told her to keep going. She got out of the car and set out into the forest. The directions explicitly stated to not use a flashlight unless you wanted to get caught, spoiling the secret path and ruining everything for everybody. *A mile or so*, the directions read. *Straight shot. Use the moon, your phone if you must.* Lia pulled out her phone. She hadn't looked at it since she roared out of town. There was no reception, but a text from her dad, one she must've missed before entering this dead zone, was waiting.

THE FOREST
Forgot to mention
your mother
wont come down
from the attic. Not until
she knows your safe

She held her phone in front of her, lighting up very little. She pushed forward, and ten minutes later, like magic, the forest opened before her. After all of it, every question she'd asked, everything she'd done, here she was. Her racing heart flung itself against her ribs. The moon poked its head out from a cloud, casting blue light on a fence. *You'll arrive on the west side*, the directions said. *The fence runs a semi-circle around the town, where it meets up with the mountain. Get in and get out. They don't come around like they used to, but they still come around.*

The directions didn't specify who "they" were.

Lia approached the fence. She stuck a foot in and climbed over. As soon as her feet hit the ground an alarm sounded. She should have known. It couldn't be this easy. But the alarm stopped, then sounded again, interjecting at measured intervals. She felt for her phone. Reception had returned.

LIMETOWN, PART ONE
Fine

One last thing

When I was your age
I left him behind.
The reasons why:
It was good for him
he was better off—
none of it true. But
I convinced him
and myself.

Don't make my mistake

Whatever happens to
your mother
you'll always regret

if you're not here.

Lia put her phone away. She crept out from the fence. It was a long distance between that fence and another, and in between the two, she had never felt more exposed, walking where she was easy to see if anyone was watching. Her heartbeat slowed when her hand touched the second fence's pickets. White, what a cliché. She followed the fence around to the front of the house it guarded, and when she saw what the house was, what it really was, her heart caught in her throat. In her mother's dream, Sylvia and her mother lived with a man in a house. But Claire did not describe the house in the dream, so Lia's mind did what she imagined most minds did when they read a book or heard a story set in an unfamiliar place—it filled in the gaps with images from her own life. She had already done this, subconsciously, with the rest of the dream family; Sylvia was a friend she remembered from elementary school; the mother and father, that friend's parents. And the house, the house was Lia's childhood house, the house that stood next to the Gilmores'.

What Lia saw now, what she had to remind herself was real, didn't make sense. The small porch, the dark window in the attic. It was her house, the house she lived in as a child.

Lia braced herself against the fence. She took a moment to let her mind accept that what she was looking at wasn't a dream. Or, it was, and it wasn't. There was a word for this, a term she learned in Miss Scott's class. What was it? She could only remember parts of the definition. Something about the semblance of reality, the appearance of being real.

Lia stepped back from the fence, and from her periphery, a slow realization: the shadows to the left and to the right, they were the same. Every house on this street was her childhood home.

She told herself to go inside. She grabbed a rock but the door was open. No locks, no police tape. The house was dark, empty. But it was her house. The open living and dining room, the secluded kitchen. The layout gave life to vague memories. Here was Lia, running around the dining room table and into the kitchen, seeking sanctuary, chased by some unknown menace. She found her mother's legs, standing in the kitchen, her mother's face smiling down at her. In the living room she sat in someone's lap, in a chair by the window. She was describing a bad dream. In the present, Lia looked out the window and saw the window of the neighboring house. She saw her reflection in the neighboring window and waved, startled when it waved back. She left herself and found the attic stairs. At the top the room was as she now remembered it. The low, slanted ceiling, the oval window, the house's eye. She tried to picture the rest. The cot in the corner where Emile slept, a stack of books bedside. She lay down on the floor, to see the ceiling as Emile would have seen it. She closed her eyes—for how long?

A light splashed across the ceiling, through the window.

Lia rolled off her imaginary bed. She army-crawled to the wall, pulled herself up to see what was out there. Her chest stopped. Someone was outside, standing in her front yard. They flicked a flashlight off and on a few times, running it over the windows, blinding Lia when it swept the attic. She dropped to the floor and held her breath, waiting to hear the front door open.

Nothing.

Lia waited a few minutes to be safe, then snuck another peek out the window. They were gone. Had they come inside? She watched the attic door, waiting for a shadow to emerge from below. When nothing happened, she went back downstairs, unable to shake the sense that she was being watched.

She snuck down the street, careful to stay in the shadows. Some logical part of her understood that she probably should leave, but she had come this far, and who knew when, if ever, she'd be back. She tried not to think about each empty home, all their ghosts watching her from the windows. But the citizen names she'd memorized kept rolling through her mind like movie credits. This house could have belonged to Kenneth Wendall, this one to Warren Chambers. There was Deirdre watering her flowers, stopping to chat with her neighbor, Frank Banner. Lia saw all these people like holograms projected in her mind, transparent and ephemeral.

She was thankful when she turned a corner and ran into the downtown area. Jesus, it was an actual town. To her right there was a corner pharmacy, across the street a little coffee shop, and a pizza place with a charming awning and outside dining. It wasn't Lawrence, but it could have been. It could have been any American town, or how America liked to imagine its small towns, gilded against its dark past, its injustices and atrocities. There were ghosts here too. Smiling at Lia from every window. The barbershop. The department store. The box office at the movie theater.

The movie theater.

Her mother was right. It was all here, everything she described from her dream. She could almost see Sylvia and her mother, coming here for the quiet, watching the same movie on repeat. Lia looked up at the marquee. A few letters were missing. NOW P AYING – DE TH O M RS. It was like someone was playing a game of hangman, but had the stool kicked out from beneath their legs before anyone could guess correctly. Lia thought about going inside, sitting where Sylvia had sat, but she pressed on. There was too much to see, though all the while she wandered, she had a singular destination in mind, a pin on the map pulling her forward like a magnet. She stuck to the sidewalk and let her fingers graze shop windows as she drifted by, an unknown tune humming in her head. She was strangely calm. She couldn't explain why she felt this way, filled with purpose, not anxiety. But she did. She did, and when she came to the end of the street, she hopped off the sidewalk and onto the brick road, her destination now finally before her.

She understood she should have been scared, now more than ever. A man had died here. And the stake, the wooden post, was exactly where her mother said it would be, still burnt blacker than the night sky. She reached out and touched the post, her fingers blackened with ash that a year of rain couldn't wash away. Beyond the post, beyond the town square was another street, and she knew somehow that at the end of that street was the research facility, and in there perhaps an answer to the question no one—not the Limetown Commission, not the conspiracy theorists, nor the families the citizens left behind—had figured out.

What happened here?

She began to head in that direction, when the light returned. It was down the street, far off but getting closer. Her skin told her to hide, but the rest of her watched as the light grew larger, a silent train racing down the tracks, directly toward her. She took a step back. But the train was steady and fast. It hit her before she knew what was happening. Her hands stung from the fall before she realized she was on the ground.

"Careful," the light said. "Are you all right?"

Lia held her hand up, trying to see. "I'm fine."

The light clicked itself off. It was still too dark to see its face.

Lia stood up, brushed her hands off. "I'm Lia. Lia Haddock."

The light tilted its head. "Are you supposed to be here, Lia?"

Lia shrugged, acted like she belonged there. "Are you?"

The light didn't say anything. It turned to the side and Lia caught a glimpse of its silhouette. A man, forties or fifties maybe, around her father's age. He had a thick beard, so it was difficult to tell. The man looked around. "There's something off, isn't there? This place. It's like an amusement park. Trying to be real, but not quite right."

"I know," Lia said. "There's a word for it." She still couldn't remember what it was.

"Verisimilitude," the man said. "The surreal passing as real."

Yes. That was it. Lia felt a small relief. She thought of Miss Scott, what she would do if she were here. "I'm a reporter," she said. "That's why I'm here."

A lie, but one that she hadn't even thought about telling since Menninger. She reminded herself that this was different. That she was exactly where she was supposed to be.

Lia took out her phone, as if that would prove something.

"Oh, is this an interview?"

"Are you someone worth interviewing?"

There was a playfulness in the man's voice, and he scratched his beard in consideration, or maybe just to buy time. "Were you headed somewhere? Before I found you?" Lia pointed her phone behind the man, down the street to the research facility. "I could walk with you," the man said, "if you'd like. I was just there."

"You were?"

"Oh, yes. I like it there. Far away from the maddening crowd."

Lia felt her hair raise, her skin lift itself away from the bone. She put her phone away, and when the light disappeared, she tried not to feel afraid.

"Can you tell me your name first?" Lia asked. "It can be off the record."

The man clicked on the flashlight, waved it around the ground in circles. He pointed it at Lia's face, for what seemed a very long time. She could feel him studying her, looking for what, she didn't know. Something to help him make up his mind, perhaps. The light clicked off, and by the time Lia blinked away the blindness, the man was already a ways down the street, walking toward the research facility. Lia ran to catch up with him, and when she did, he told her his name.

"Austin," he said.

———

The research facility was farther away than Lia imagined. There was another block of shops, and after that, on what was the east side of Limetown, more residences. Slowly, her fear returned to her.

"If you're afraid," Austin said, "that's good. So am I."

"But you've been here before."

"I have."

"Did Max take you?"

Austin stopped. "Max?"

"Maxine . . . I don't know her last name. She lives in Sparta."

"I came here myself," the man said, and resumed walking. From somewhere unseen, an owl called out the hour.

"Should we, you know, hurry?" Lia said. One block of houses ended, but another began.

"What do you know about this place?" Austin asked. "Just what the news told you?"

"No," Lia said. "I know someone who lived here. Or, I used to."

Austin stopped at an intersection. He looked both ways, despite the streets being dark and deserted.

"Ah," Austin said. "So did I." He crossed the street quickly. Lia trailed closely behind.

"A relative?"

"A friend."

"What was their name?"

"It doesn't matter," Austin said. "He's gone now."

Austin paused again. He looked around, and Lia followed his eyes. All the houses were behind them. The shops too, as well as the moon. Lia couldn't see the facility, but she convinced herself that if she relaxed her eyes, she could make out the base of the mountain in the wall of black in front of her, darker than the hues of blue the night normally kept for itself.

"Do you know what happened to him?" Lia said.

"I know he's not here."

"Then why are you here?" Lia asked. The wall of black in front of her began to feel like another dead end.

"To help." Lia felt his hand take hers. He unballed her fist and put the flashlight in her palm. "You're going to need this."

Without thinking, she aimed the light at Austin's face, only catching a brief glimpse of his beard and eyes before he covered himself with his hands. "Lia, please."

She lowered the flashlight to his hiking boots. "Sorry."

"We're close, if you'll lead the way."

Lia nodded. She stepped forward and pushed the flashlight into the dark, but the dark pushed back. She was reminded of her brief stint in the ocean, back in Oregon with Robyn. How Robyn had dared her to go under with her. She threw her arms up and let herself sink, deeper, deeper still, and when she finally opened her eyes there was nothing.

Nothing above her, nothing below. She waved her arms and legs but they barely made a ripple. She pushed herself to what she thought was the surface, but how could she be sure? Even afterward, when her head emerged, gasping for air, her eyes drinking in the night, she still wasn't certain she'd made it back.

She ignored the dread and pushed farther.

"We're almost there," Austin said.

But she didn't feel like she was almost there. She felt like—

She kicked something. It rattled.

"Watch yourself," Austin said. He took her hand and helped her wash the flashlight over another chain-link fence, a sign that read TELOS RESEARCH FACILITY. "Eureka," Austin said. He stepped in front of Lia, unlocked the gate, though the fence itself only came up to Lia's chest and was easily climbable. Austin said it was just to keep the kids out.

"I always forget," Lia said, "there were kids."

Austin held the gate open. "Shall we?"

The research facility had a glass door like any other office building. The door was unlocked, the glass intact. No brave vandal had made it this far, or maybe they had but were struck with reverence upon arrival, as Lia was. Inside there was a check-in desk, complete with an empty clipboard and bank pen still dangling from its chain. Lia tried to imagine some secretary type, smiling at the citizens, keeping their secrets. Past the desk was a long linoleum hall. At the end of the hall there was an out-of-order elevator, a side door that opened to a stairwell.

"It's all so ordinary," Lia said.

Austin took a deep breath. "I think that was the idea." Then, "Come on. There's more."

They descended five levels. Lia counted. She was careful to take note where they had been, where they were going. Five floors down, beneath the surface. She wondered aloud why the town kept its facility so far underground.

"There was a belief," Austin said. "More of a superstition really. That minds work better down here. Pretty foolish, I know."

Lia thought of Menninger, of the thrumming she heard before she descended into the cellar.

"What were they doing here?" she asked. "Do you know?"

"Just a little farther," Austin said. "You'll see."

They emerged into another hallway. Down that hallway and to the left, down that left and to the right. Austin was leading now, the flashlight in Lia's hand now more of a spotlight.

"How many times have you been here?"

"More than enough," Austin said.

"Why?"

"Why what?"

"Why do you come here? Do you think they'll return? Like, your friend."

Austin stopped. They had come to a set of double doors. "This is as far as I'll take you."

He stepped to the side, and Lia shone the light on the doors, but all she saw was the light's reflection. "What's in there?" she said.

"Nothing," he said. "Not anymore."

"Not anymore? Do you know what they were doing here? Were these experiments? On people?" Austin didn't answer. Lia held her phone up, as if she was ready to record. "Why won't you—"

"You have a message," Austin said. He squinted at the phone, and Lia could see his face change in the phone's limited light. Lia expected another text from her father. But it was her mom.

THE RESEARCH FACILITY
Apple, the dream

There's someone after you
you think you're safe.

You're not.

Just because you can't see it
doesn't mean the clock
stopped ticking

Lia put the phone to her mouth. Her hand began to shake.

"Is there a problem?" Austin asked.

"Who are you?"

"I told you—" And she saw his hand reach out for her, his hand floating in the darkness, yellow and detached.

"Don't," Lia said.

She pushed him aside and opened the double doors, shut them quickly behind her. She didn't need to lock them. The handles didn't shake, the doors didn't rattle. Austin didn't move.

"Lia," he said, calmly on the other side. "I know what you're thinking. I know what you want. I can help you."

"You don't know anything about me," she said.

There was a long pause. "That message," Austin finally said. "It was from your mother."

Lia didn't answer. So he had seen *Mom* on the screen. That didn't mean anything.

Austin continued. "There's something different about her, isn't there?"

"No," Lia said.

"That's why you're here. That's why everyone came here."

"No."

"But you need to go home, Lia. She needs someone there, someone who will listen to her."

"Stop," Lia said. "You don't know her. And you don't know anything about me."

Her phone buzzed again, startling Lia so much she nearly dropped it. She wrapped her hand around the screen and slid to the floor, afraid what the text would tell her. She flipped her phone over and over in her hand, but didn't bring it back to life.

"My friend," Austin eventually said, "he had problems too. No one understood him, no one except me. And there was a time, there's always a time when you have a choice. Whether or not to do the right thing. It should be easy. It seems so simple, from a distance." He exhaled. "I should have stayed. I should have been there."

Austin stopped talking. Lia looked at her phone. Just one line. From her mom.

I love you.

"You know," Austin said. "I once had a teacher who said that if your mother says she loves you, you should check it out."

Lia had heard that cliché before, from Miss Scott, during a lecture about the importance of fact-checking. What she meant was that you shouldn't trust anyone. Lia stood up and aimed the flashlight down the hall, where Austin wouldn't go.

"I'm going to go now, Lia. When you're done looking for whatever it is you came here for, I suggest you do the same. It won't be safe for long."

"Wait," Lia said.

"I'm sorry we won't get to finish our interview. They'll be here soon."

"Wait," Lia said again. "Who—"

There was a click. It took Lia a second to realize what had just happened. She tried the door.

"Hey! What are you doing?"

"I'm sorry. I really am."

"You can't—Hey! Let me out!"

She pounded on the door.

A jolt of fear zapped Lia's brain. She stopped screaming. She froze. She thought of her mother's dream. Sylvia's mother pulling her away from the Panic. She put her hand to the door's glass, cool against her palm. She couldn't see Austin's face, only the whites of his wide eyes.

"They're coming," he said. "Run."

CHAPTER FOURTEEN
▰▰▰III Emile

James liked his stories. Here was the last one:

You're waiting for a man you think can help you. But the man is not who you think he is. You want him to be a friend but he's your enemy. You call him brother when you should know better. Or maybe it's your mother. Maybe she's in on it too. What do they do to the water when you're not looking? What poison do they drop in the well? Still, you wait for this man. You go out to the well and you wait. To catch him poison-fisted. You grab his wrist. *Aha*, you say. But when the man opens his hand his palm is empty. You know what you saw, though, what you tasted. It's still there, at the back of your throat. The medicine they make you swallow. Perhaps they put it there while you're asleep. You release the man. Your head starts to swim. Your brain feels water-logged. No. You know what you saw. You know who he is. You push him out of the way and peer down the well. Expecting what? You can't quite see, so you lean over. Farther. Farther still. You hear the man behind you. *You're right*, he says. *You were right all along*. And then you feel it. The man's hand on your back. Not patting. Pushing.

—

"Took you long enough," Tracey said. She and Emile were sitting in Emile's office, the fan humming around them. James was better now. Tracey typed up how Emile had gotten through to him, by listening, by matching wavelengths. With James, there were waves upon waves. A swift-moving tide. Emile had to learn their patterns, which ones pulled and which ones pushed, which ones lifted and which ones dragged. Only then could he get James to listen, to understand. That his last story was just that, a narrative his mind made up. After Emile showed him a fiction, he could show him a fact, and show James the difference. That way, long after he left here, James could spot the rogue waves that threatened to pull him under, and stay far, far away.

"You know there are machines that can measure this kind of stuff," Tracey said. "We could throw some electrodes on you, read your brain waves, and see when they're synced. Might go quicker."

"No," Emile said. "No machines." He knew what it would do to James to be hooked up to something like that. He would feel like a lab rat, as Emile had at the Eldridge. "It just takes time."

"What does?" Tracey asked.

Emile stood up. He patted Tracey on the shoulder on his way out. "To get someone to listen."

He walked down to the beach. It was late, a few hours before dawn. The limestone family was still hidden in the dark. He figured he'd find Moyer there, sitting on the sand, staring at the ocean, a small part of him wishing a rogue wave would suck him in and get it over with. He'd been melodramatic about Tracey as of late, noting the irony that here they were helping patients become well enough to reintegrate into society, only to end up alone themselves.

Emile watched the water churn until he heard a familiar pattern. That quick pace, those thoughts that couldn't wait to rush out.

"Emile!" Moyer said. "You did it! I'll admit, I had my doubts. But I should've known. It's finally happening."

"It's just another patient," Emile replied.

Moyer turned. Emile felt a realization in him, a blip of joy. "You haven't heard."

———

After Emile talked to Moyer, he saw James to the van, where James hugged him. He saw the calm in James's mind, the peaceful sea. But beneath its surface, in the dark of the water, where the sun couldn't reach, an undercurrent of worry. What would happen if he lost control again? If he couldn't separate the fact from the fiction?

"We'll be in touch," Emile said, knowing it wasn't true. Tracey would drive James back to his family and that would be the end of it. Before dawn, the van would return, and in James's place another addled soul.

"It's not enough," a voice said. "Is it? You think it would be. Saving these people's lives. And make no bones about it, son, that is what you're doing here."

Oskar Totem had arrived earlier that evening, somehow without Emile knowing. Perhaps because Emile expected a more outlandish entrance—a private helicopter, a plane that skimmed the ocean. Instead, Totem drove an ordinary car up to the gate. He had to tell Tracey his name three different times before she let him in.

"Should we take a walk, Emile? Before another patient arrives?"

It was the moment Emile had been waiting for. He led the way, tracing the path he and Tracey had traversed many times before. After years of feeling like a puppet, here was his chance to sever the ties with the man tugging the strings. And now that Totem was so close . . . Emile prepared to dive into Totem's mind, to break him the way the Eldridge had broken Brenda, the way it had nearly broken Emile. To needle at his sanity.

At the top of the hill, Emile paused, steeling himself. In the near distance the lonely man built another bonfire.

"Is he too close for your liking?" Totem asked.

"He's fine," Emile said. He didn't reveal that he had once talked to the man, invited him to the facility, before dipping into his mind deep enough to scare him away. "He's just a little lonely."

"Ah," Totem said. Emile stole a glance at him. He was and wasn't what Emile expected. The thin, premature silver hair fit, but the face was less stern than Emile had imagined. Emile thought he would be taller. But that voice, the one he'd heard filtered through Moyer's and Jacob's minds, and in Claire's memory, was exactly what he remembered.

"I know you've been waiting for me," Totem said. "The good doctor has relayed all your messages. And I would apologize—I really would, I'm not above it—but that's not what you want to hear."

In the valley below them the man's bonfire grew. When Emile closed his eyes, he felt the heat on his face.

"The reality is you don't want me to say I'm sorry. You want me to stick to my guns, as it were, proudly proclaim that I'm a pioneer, a genius, and geniuses never dwell on mistakes, do they?"

"I wouldn't know," Emile said.

"You want an enemy. But the truth is you're not angry with me. Though you may think you are."

Far above them, a plane blinked its red dot among the southern hemisphere's strange constellations.

"If you knew how I truly felt about you," Emile said, "you never would have come."

Totem laughed uncomfortably. The plane hummed its way out of view. "You know," he finally said, "I have this reputation—I don't know what you've heard—but I have this reputation that tends to follow me wherever I go. This idea that I don't get along well with others.

"But the thing is, I have no problem with people. They are a necessity, after all, if we want to live in a civilization. And we *must* live in a civilization, Emile, despite what you or that man in the distance there might desire. How does the quote go? 'A man with no need for others is either a beast or a god.' Are you familiar with Aristotle?"

"I didn't finish high school," Emile said.

"But you understand his point. We need each other. To survive. To progress. Otherwise we're just, well, animals." Totem clapped his hands. "So. Why am I telling you this?"

"You want to create a new civilization," Emile said. He saw it all, there in Totem's head. "You want to use me to change the world."

He faced Totem. He wanted to see his expression when he realized Emile already knew every word to his speech.

"You don't want to play god. You tell yourself you're too humble. You were raised with religion. You don't believe like you used to, but there will always be a bit of the supernatural seeded into your DNA. So you don't want to play god; you want to help Him."

"Yes."

"God set us on this path, gave each of us a purpose. Telos, you call it, thinking the Greek gives your idea more importance, more credibility. You don't want to change our purpose, alter what God assigned us. You want to help us achieve our purpose sooner. You're confident that not only are our best days ahead of us, they're right in front of our faces."

"That's it."

"And here you circle back to what you said before. The idea that you don't work well with others. They misunderstand you. It's not that you dislike them as people. As human beings. It's that you have no time for those who refuse to acknowledge their purpose. Why we're here. When you see an ordinary person middling about their life, you want to shake them, wake them from their dream. You see yourself as a liberator."

"You forgot the best part," Totem said. "How everyone has a role to play."

"I didn't forget," Emile said. "It's just so trite I didn't want to say it out loud."

Finally, Emile felt it. A swell of anger.

"You're disappointed?" Totem said.

Emile looked Totem in the eyes, or the best he could in the purple darkness. "I was disappointed the moment I heard you, even before you opened your mouth," Emile answered. He stared at Totem until Totem blinked, then Emile started down the hill.

—

It was true. Emile had wanted more. More from the man who broke Brenda, who persuaded Jacob to leave him, Claire to spy on and use him. Who had convinced Emile someone was out to get him, to the point that he sabotaged his last chance at happiness. Emile had spent all this time building up Totem in his mind, the voice, the big man, this bogus bogeyman, but once he met him, once he stepped inside his thoughts, he knew it had been a waste. Totem was a man. A visionary, fine, but still a man, filled with greed and weakness like anyone else. He took pleasure in helping others not because it brought him joy to see a life saved, but because of the way the saved looked at him when they realized they were better. The awe and marvel of it all. There was power in that. There was ascension. And none of that mattered to Emile.

Totem found Emile at the beach half an hour later. It was still dark.

"You know what I want to do," Totem said. "What I want to build for you."

Emile nodded. Yes, he had seen it. The town. The people. Though it was mostly hazy in Totem's mind. The houses were sterile blocks, the people faceless. Everything else remained gray, save a large shadow at the edge of Totem's imagination.

"What you saw is only an outline," Totem said. "It can be whatever you like, Emile. It could be the place of your dreams."

"My dreams," Emile said.

"Yes," Totem said, not realizing his mistake. "It could be the home you never had."

"You ruined my life," Emile said. His mind was yelling, but he kept his voice calm. "You promised me. You promised all of us."

"And I kept my promises," Totem said, "to those who kept theirs. Your brother left school of his own volition. You, *you* could have had any life you chose—if you'd stayed. If you'd had a little more . . . faith. In the experiment."

"You locked me up."

"I trusted the wrong people. At the Eldridge, I placed all my emphasis on devotion and vision. Left out the humanity."

Emile grinded his teeth. To this day, he could still call up Vince's smile, as he looked down at Emile in that grim cell.

"Another reason why I need you," Totem said. "I've been all over the world, handpicking the brightest scientists. Lining up the richest investors, the R. B. Villards of the world. But are they good people? Are they well suited to build a town from scratch? It's difficult to say. One of my failings is that unlike the philosopher, I struggle to see the utility of morals. But," Totem said, "you could select anyone you see fit. Friend, family member. Anyone your heart desires."

Emile shook his head. He told himself his mind was already made up, that he'd have to be insane to work with Oskar Totem again. He had waited and plotted and waited so he could confront him in person, look into his eyes and say "no" to the next big thing he was planning.

But then, without his permission, his mind thought about what the perfect place would look like. Emile sat in the sand. He took a fistful and let it fall through his hand like an hourglass.

"You know," Totem said, "Plato wrote an entire book about how to construct the perfect city. Everything it would need to survive and flourish."

Emile wasn't listening. He was aware of Totem's voice the way you might be cognizant of a housefly. Instead, he conjured up the moments he found perfect. He saw Lost 80 and Austin, himself at sixteen. He saw his brother, when it was just the two of them versus the guardians, against the world. He remembered the pizza place they ate at in Archer Park before they went to the Eldridge, before everything changed. He remembered the feeling of possibility, that his future was his to write, not something foretold in anyone's dream.

He saw the movie theater. He saw Claire. He felt her hand in his, afterward, in the park, their fingers woven together in the dark.

Then he saw Lia. The house in Lawrence. He saw her take his hand under his tree at Lost 80, the way he had once held her mother's.

"Emile," Totem said. "Are you listening?"

Emile snapped back to reality. "I'm always listening."

"Then you know that I can't let you say no. You know there are people depending on me. People I have made promises to."

"Always more promises."

A wave reached Emile's bare feet. The water was ice cold. Emile shivered. He saw them now. Dark meeting places, menacing, shadowy faces.

"Tell me what it will take," Totem said.

Emile let himself consider the question. His mind kept swirling to the same answer. Totem shifted his weight from foot to foot. Emile heard his mind churning, trying to find another way to reach Emile, weighing various advantages until—

"Don't," Emile said.

"You saw it."

"I'm telling you."

"You did, didn't you?"

"No," Emile said, but of course he did. Totem wanted him to see. Claire. She was outside a house, a different house, one that Emile didn't recognize. She was loading a bag into the back of her car. A girl watched from the front porch. Emile didn't recognize her at first. Lia was older now. Seven or eight, he couldn't say. But she had the same serious face, only now it looked even more like her mother's.

She wanted to know where Claire was going.

Claire told her nowhere.

Claire shut the trunk. She looked around, her face scrunched with worry. No one on the sidewalk, no neighbors maintaining their yards or walking their pets with their kids. She thought her way was clear. She did not see the man in the car parked catty-corner across the street, watching the scene unfold in his side mirror.

Lia stayed put. She didn't believe what her mother was saying, and neither did the observer.

"I need to visit someone. That's all. I'll be back."

"Who?"

"Emile."

Lia tilted her head. "Who's that?"

"Your uncle," Claire said. "You don't remember him."

"I do too."

"No," Claire said. "You don't."

"When will you come back?" Lia said.

"I don't know."

"Does someone have to watch me?"

"Your dad will be home any minute. The neighbors can watch you until then."

Claire set Lia down on the porch. Lia stood tall at the top of the steps. "I don't need them," she said. "I don't need anyone."

Claire smiled. "How will you get to school?"

"I'll walk. Or I won't go."

"Who will make you dinner?"

"I'll have cereal."

"Again?" Claire asked. She brushed Lia's hair behind her ear. The scars they called cowlicks wouldn't let the hair stay in place. "What about bedtime? Who will tuck you in and say 'Sweet dreams'?"

"I don't have dreams anymore," Lia said, matter-of-factly.

"None?"

"None," Lia answered. She looked her mother in the eye. Claire's face weakened. She looked back at the car, packed with her bags, then down their still quiet street. She climbed the steps and sat down, beckoned Lia to do the same.

"Do you want to know something?" Claire said. "About my dreams? They're about you now. Your future. I see the places you'll go and the people you'll meet."

"Are they scary?"

"Some are," Claire said. "But there's nothing I've seen that you can't handle."

"Because I'm strong."

"Because you're strong."

Lia's face remained solemn.

"I need to go now, Apple. Will you be all right?"

"I'm strong."

Claire kissed Lia on the head and made her way to the car. The observer watched her get in, start the engine, back out, and drive away. When she was gone, Lia stayed on the porch, unsure perhaps whether she was supposed to go inside or stay out and wait for someone to come get her.

"What happened?" Emile asked. "Where did she go?"

"It's just as she said. Looking for you. Obviously she wasn't successful."

Maybe she drove to Colorado, searched the Eldridge once more, but found nothing and turned around. Maybe she went to the Idaho motel where she left him.

"What did she want from me?"

"I have no idea."

"You followed her though," Emile said. "You must've seen something."

"Why would we do that? We knew where you were."

Here. At Menninger, a world away, where Claire would never find him.

Totem stepped in front of Emile, blocking the ocean. "Maybe she's worried, son. You heard her. Her dreams have returned. Maybe she's scared that she'll end up like her mother. That she won't be there for Lia."

Emile tried to dismiss the thought. He knew what Totem was trying to do. "That won't happen."

"She doesn't know that. And neither do you." Totem put his hands on his hips. "God Almighty, think about your work here. What would happen to your patients, to people like James, if you weren't here to help them? What if you're the only one who can help her?"

Totem placed a hand on Emile's shoulder. He had the sick vision of himself as a father figure.

"I can't," Emile said. "Even if I wanted to."

He pushed Totem aside and stepped closer to the ocean. The nearer he got, the higher the waves climbed. Past his shins, teasing his knees. A part of him wanted to keep walking.

"You can't hear her," Totem said. "Is that it?"

He'd crept up behind Emile, his thoughts and footsteps muted by the ocean. Emile didn't say anything. He was trying to tune it all out, the water, the past. But he still heard Totem's next words, in between the waves.

"But what if you could?"

———

Emile stumbled from the beach in a fog. He needed to talk to someone, someone who could confirm that Oskar Totem's ideas were absurd. He needed Moyer. Or Tracey. Really, he needed them both. But he found only the former, sitting glumly in the latter's room.

"How could you not tell me?" Moyer asked. His eyes were puffy and stung red. "I thought I had more time."

"What are you talking about?"

"She's gone, you Yankee imbecile. Can't you see that?"

Emile quickly surveyed Tracey's room, its neatly made army cot, its bare stone walls. The room looked no different from when she was there, which, Emile now realized, probably was the most obvious sign. She never wanted to be there. She was always ready to go.

"I'm sorry," Emile said. He sat on the bed and waited for Moyer's anger to wane. It didn't, so he changed the subject. "I spoke with Totem."

"Great."

"He wants to build a city. He wants everyone in it to be like me."

Moyer shuddered at the thought.

"You knew that too."

"He told me all about it," Moyer said. "Vaguely, anyway. He wants to knock down the past to make room for the future. Blah blah blah."

Emile pressed his palms against his knees. "I don't know how it would work exactly. Some sort of new technology, a chip or something. He tried to explain the science."

Moyer's mind moved from disgust to disbelief. "You can't seriously be considering it."

Emile didn't answer him. He knew what he was supposed to say, but didn't.

"My, my," Moyer said.

"You work for him. For years you—"

"No," Moyer said. "Not anymore. Not if it's cost me Tracey."

He stood up and paced around the room, stopped in front of the doorway. The light from the hall shrunk his shadow to that of a small child. "How has he helped you, Mr. Haddock? Have you asked yourself that? What has he brought you that didn't end in misery and pain?"

Emile stared at his empty hands. He thought about his plan. To break Totem, for what he did to him. To break free. But another part of him whispered *That was years ago*. He was a different person now. He didn't say what he hated to admit, that without Totem he never would have met Claire.

"You know how he sees us," Moyer said. "We're mice. That's all. Mice in a lab, here to help him achieve some greater design. He talks about purpose, eh? That's our purpose. That's our role to play."

Moyer reached into his breast pocket, retrieved a folded sheet of paper. It was a note from Tracey, which Moyer had already committed to memory, the phrases looping into a mantra.

"You see this," he said. "This right here is my last chance."

"I know it's crazy," Emile said. "But it wouldn't be for me. I think you understand that."

Moyer dabbed his nose with a handkerchief. He blew into it and laughed. "Two fools," he said. "Two absolute fools."

Emile let himself laugh. When the moment passed, he asked Moyer what he would do next.

Moyer tapped his pocket. "I'm going to do exactly what this note tells me to do. And, I'm going to stay as far away from you and Oskar Totem as humanly possible."

"He's not going to like that," Emile replied.

"No. I suppose he won't." Moyer lit a cigarette he'd hidden behind his ear. In his mind he said *So what if Totem is upset*. The old man could bugger off, for all he cared, though he still wouldn't say any of these things out loud.

"Is this it?" Moyer said. "I can't talk you out of it?"

"I don't see how."

Moyer shook Emile's hand. He clapped him on the shoulder. "Oh, I nearly forgot. Tracey left you a note too. It was on your bed and now it's in my back pocket." He gave a second folded sheet of paper to Emile. Moyer's mouth twisted in mock-shame. "I was curious."

Emile put the note in his pocket. He wouldn't open it yet. He would wait until he was on a plane, over the ocean somewhere, on his way to taking the next step. Eventually, he would drift off to sleep. Perhaps he would dream.

When he woke, he would take out the note.

And maybe he would smile because Tracey started the letter off by calling him a dolt. And maybe the smile wouldn't fade when he read the rest, line by line, and saw that his note was no different from Moyer's. Maybe Tracey, in her wisdom, saw that Moyer and Emile suffered from similar afflictions.

Stop wasting time.

Follow the future you can't live without.

She's waiting for you.

Moyer walked Emile to the van. "Fare thee well, Mr. Haddock. May we both find what we're looking for."

And then Emile was on a plane, over the ocean, on his way.

—

The house was as he remembered it. It was always as he remembered it. Even in the dark, he could trace its watchful eye. He saw its ghosts. Here was Jacob, sitting on the porch after a long day working a job that was only a job to him, nothing more. Claire joined him outside, Lia in her arms. She set Lia down to play in the front yard before sitting on the porch next to Jacob. He draped an arm over her shoulder. Together they watched their serious daughter engage fireflies in a very important conversation.

But they weren't there anymore. They were in their new house, the home they had made without him. He found their address in the phone book, where anyone could see it. They weren't trying to hide.

Emile waited, until it was late enough that Jacob would have gone to bed. A light remained on in the kitchen, and Emile pictured Claire inside, reading for class, studying. He knocked lightly on the door and receded into the empty street, ready to run away, if his brother opened the door. But it was Claire who answered. He watched her face carefully as he emerged from the shadows, the range of her expressions. Alarm to recognition, familiarity to worry. She left the porch light off, as if she knew better.

"Emile, my god," Claire said. She closed the storm door behind her and went to him. "What are you doing here?"

He wasn't prepared to answer. He thought he was. After some time, he managed to speak. He didn't use the word he should have, but he said everything else. "There's an opportunity here," he told her. "For a new life. For all of us to get closer."

Claire stared at him, confused. Emile was confused too. The voice was his, but the thoughts belonged to someone else.

"Don't you want something better than this?" The words weren't right. "It doesn't have a name," he said. "Not yet. But it could be anything we want it to be." He told her what he'd envisioned. The houses. The movie theater. The downtown.

"Sounds like a nice little bubble," Claire said. "You hate bubbles."

"You're not listening," Emile said. "I decide everything. What it looks like, who lives there. Do you understand? I've already talked to Max. He says—"

"Max? Finlayson?"

"Yes."

"That's the first person you pick?"

"No," Emile said. "Not the first."

Claire looked away. "Max will only cause trouble." She searched his face, to see how it had changed. Emile did the same. Her face had aged too, a few more lines around her dark eyes, but Emile saw her as he'd always seen her. As he would always see her. "This is absurd," she said. "Every time I see you . . ." She didn't finish the thought. She turned toward the house, where Jacob slept. Emile could feel him inside now, the steady whir of his mind. "What about your brother?"

"What about him."

"He's her father."

"He wouldn't be happy there," Emile said. "This is a place for those of us who are special."

Claire's face registered a small shock, a flinch that shifted to disappointment. She took a step back and pulled her sweater tighter around her, as if she suddenly remembered the cold.

"He worries about you," she said.

"He's good at worrying."

"You should talk to him."

"And say what? Thanks for stealing my life?"

He backed away. His eyes began to burn.

"Emile."

"Why not?" he asked. His voice rose to the attic but he didn't care. "Don't I deserve it? Doesn't it make as much sense as anything else?"

Claire stepped off the porch. She touched Emile's shoulder. It wasn't what he wanted.

"I know about your dreams," he said. "Totem told me."

"Totem?" She released him. "That's who—"

"He can help you. We can help you."

Inside the house another light came on. Jacob called for Alison.

"Go," Claire said.

"Your dreams—"

"Now."

"—like your mother."

"I know!" Claire hissed. "Okay? I know exactly what's in store for me."

"Then come with me. I can protect you."

"I can't."

"Why not?"

"Because it's not about you!" Claire shouted, loud enough to catch Jacob's attention inside. "It's not about me or you or Jacob. It's about her. She may have a role to play someday, but for as long as I can, I want to keep her out of it."

Jacob was at the door, looking out into the dark, but Emile no longer cared if he was seen. "From me, you mean."

"I don't know what you think Totem can do, but he can't help you. He only cares about himself."

Emile stepped closer to the door. He waited for his brother to see him. He wanted it. To see the shock and fear, the jealousy. And it was there, wide-eyed and wonderful, but only for a moment. Something else leaped into Jacob's chest. A warmth. "What are you doing?" Lia asked, looking up at her father. When Jacob didn't answer, she followed his gaze out the storm door window, toward Emile. Emile felt the tears on his cheeks before he realized he was crying. He wiped his eyes so he could see more clearly.

"Who is that?" Lia said.

And it would have been easy then for Jacob to say nothing. To pull Lia from the door and say that he was no one. But he didn't. He took Lia's hand and pressed it to the storm door glass, so that Emile could do the same. Emile heard the wave rushing across his brother's mind. "That's your uncle, Lia. That's my brother, Emile."

And then they were gone. Jacob gave Emile a half-smile and sent Lia back to bed. The light went dark and the door closed, but Emile kept his hand on the glass, desperate to hold on to what was already gone.

—

Lia would find him eventually, when she was ready. And when that time came he liked to imagine the breadcrumbs would be waiting. Claire would see to it. He saw Lia picking them up and following them into the forest. The note he wrote, the belongings he left behind. Because there was no escaping. That much was certain. When the world is set to change, you can try to hide, but no matter where you go, it's still under your feet. Build a new town, full of everything you love. Pull the chair closer to the fire. Don't make them in your image. Make them in your mind. Make them hear what you hear, feel what you feel. Who will refuse you then? Who will turn down your hand when they're drowning in the ocean, overcome by the towering, suffocating, relentless waves?

And if it all burns to the ground, let it. You'll run. You're good at running. Pretending you don't need anyone else. They'll try to catch you, but you'll hear them coming. You always hear them coming. You won't fight your gift. You'll surrender to it. You'll hear more now, so much more than before, so clearly. You'll feel the waves beneath the waves.

When she wants answers, when her mother has pointed her this way, out of regret and guilt, you will show her. You will walk her through town. Take her to the facility. Lead her down the stairs the way they led you. Keep the glow in front, so she doesn't see the fear that will come flooding back. The way it will come back to you when you first arrive, when they give you a tour and you know immediately that you've made a mistake. Because even though the facility and shops are different, and every inch is by your design, the heart of the place beats the same. The walls will thrum with the echoes of the past. High school. The hotel. Menninger. Will they see you sweat? Will they feel your pulse quicken? They will try to comfort you, these people you know. (You chose them, remember?) They will remind you that you are special; that you are the man everyone is here for. *Don't worry*, they will say. *You can stop all of this at any time.* But will it be true? Maybe in the beginning, before the breakthrough. Before the tech and the control and the Reverend and the pig and Max and Deirdre and Oskar and the fire and the girl and—

No.

You will show her the room where they will experiment on you. Where they'll shave your head, wire your skull. You'll think of her then. How could you not?

Lines will race up and down a sheet of paper as with a lie detector. *The peaks are your emotions*, they will tell you. *The valleys your resistance. How fascinating*, they will say. *They look like waves.*

You will not run your hand over your scalp.

You will not reach out to hers, searching for the scars from when she tried to be like you.

You will not go in the room with her.

They will be on their way.

You will tell her that.

You will not tell her who. You will tell her it's not safe. That she needs to run. There's a back way out. Find it. Find the woods, find your car. Find your way home. Find your mother. Tell her you know that her mother isn't well. Ignore her when she asks how you know that. You've done the math, but don't show your work. You'll tell her it will only get worse. That her mother will need her. And that the best thing she can do is be there for her mother, the way you couldn't be there for yours, the way no one will be there for you. Forget about this place, you'll tell her. Push it out of your mind and live your life. She'll say she can't and you'll know she's telling the truth. But you will tell her to try, for as long as she can. No one knows you've been here. No one knows your uncle. No one knows what you can do.

What will happen if I stay? she'll say. *What will happen if someone finds out?*

You will tell her they can't. They must not. You will not tell her why. You will not tell her about Moyer. Why he will die. Your friend. That it will be because of you. That he'll go looking and they'll kill him because he'll know where to look. Poor Tracey. You will not tell her that they've been strangely patient since then, perhaps not wanting to stick their necks out too far until the world has forgotten. Until this place becomes a Roanoke or a Jonestown, a weird mystery, fun to whisper, easy to forget. But they will not wait forever. It is only a matter of time until someone more ruthless will take charge. Someone who will see her as bait, maybe. And that's why you'll be there. That's why you'll watch her.

They will enter the facility.

You will shut the door. You might tell her that you'll never see her again. That's okay to say. But you will not tell her that you love her. That you'll always love her. That one of the best things you ever did in your life was leave her and her mother. That the only thing better than leaving was staying away.

They will be a floor above you.

She will be afraid. She will want to know why you're doing this. She'll put her hand to the glass and the past will burst out of its coffin. You'll see her at her home, her new home, at the door, leaning against her father, and you'll want to tell her. What you should have said back then. That when you saw her standing there, your biggest worry was that you wouldn't be able to read her. That she would be like her mother or, worse, like you. But when she looked at you, you felt the wave immediately. It was small, coasted just below her consciousness. She probably wasn't even aware of it. And you wouldn't have felt it before, when you were weaker. But you felt it then, didn't you? The thought, the memory. The two of you lying down at the park, staring at the clouds and talking dreams. You like to think it's one of the best memories of her short life. That your time together mattered. Matters. Will matter. You'll feel that flicker of recognition, even now, staring at her, but it will fade away, and you know it will not come back. Not unless you tell her. So tell her. Remember.

But you will not tell her.

You will kick the past back into its grave.

You will lock the door.

You will tell her to run.

You will take the danger with you.

ACKNOWLEDGMENTS

COTE

Thank you to my agent, Claudia Ballard, the dream maker. To Eve Attermann, the matchmaker. To Emily Graff—editor, inspirer, beacon of positivity. To Tracey Lien, for answering all my Australia questions. Thanks to Zack Akers and Skip Bronkie, for inviting me into the wonderful world they created. And to Nicole, the most generous and supportive person I know.

ZACK

Thank you to everyone who came together to make this book happen: Eve Attermann for her foresight in teaming us up with Cote Smith, Cote for being a genius who makes our story infinitely better, and Emily Graff for her wisdom in guiding this novel to what it is now. To my brothers, Nathan and Nicholas, who helped shape my taste early in life, and who continue to make me feel like my brain isn't a complete anomaly. To Dad, who taught me how to be a compassionate and thoughtful man in this world, and who has done more to evangelize *Limetown* to people who hate computers than anyone else. To my wife and my rock, Bethany Reis, who—among countless other systems of support—literally paid the bills while I chased this crazy idea and never, ever questioned why. To the rest of my family (including the Reis family) and friends, whose love is the best source of renewable energy and gets me through.

Finally, to Mom, who is directly responsible for anything good about me, including daydreaming and never being afraid to fail.

SKIP

Thank you to Eve Attermann, the entire WME team, and Dean Bahat, who all believed in us well before we did. Thank you to Emily Graff and everybody at Simon & Schuster. It is a privilege to have worked with you, to be published by you. Thank you to my family, Mom, Dad, Anne, David & Eva, and all of my dear friends who listened to the rambling mystery of Limetown long before it was real. While too many to name, thank you to everyone who has touched *Limetown,* in any form, over the years. This story is richer because of you. To Cote. It's hackneyed, but very true: our friendship has been the greatest outcome of this *Limetown* hullabaloo. Finally, to Tracey. Every day I try to make you proud.

ABOUT THE AUTHORS

ZACK AKERS is the cocreator (with Skip Bronkie) of the podcast *Limetown* and the Two-Up podcast channel. He graduated from Tisch School of the Arts in 2008 with a degree in Film & Television and became a documentary producer with Flagstaff Films whose work has appeared on HBO, ESPN, CBS, and NBC.

SKIP BRONKIE was raised on a farm outside of Buffalo, New York. He graduated from Tisch School of the Arts in 2008 with a degree in Film & Television and worked as a creative director at Facebook and Pinterest. He went on to cofound Two-Up with Zack Akers, producing *Limetown* and *36 Questions*. He lives in Brooklyn and can be found in Prospect Park any given day.

COTE SMITH grew up in Leavenworth, Kansas, and on various army bases around the country. He earned his MFA from the University of Kansas, and his stories have been featured in *One Story*, *Crazyhorse*, and *Third Coast*, among other publications. His first novel, *Hurt People*, was a finalist for the 2017 PEN/Robert W. Bingham Prize for Debut Fiction.